Jurica Pavičić was born 1965 in Split, where he still lives. He is a Croatian novelist, screenwriter, short story writer and journalist. Author of nine novels and two short story collections, he is known for his unorthodox thrillers and crime novels which mix social analysis with deep insights into morally complex situations and human destinies. His novels have won several Croatian literary awards. *Red Water* was awarded the Ksaver Šandor Gjalski Prize for best Croatian novel in 2018, and the Fric Prize for best Croatian fiction in 2019. In France, it won the Great Prize of Detective Literature 2021, the Prix Mystère de la critique 2022, Prix Le Point du polar européen 2021, and the Prix Transfuge, for the best foreign crime novel 2021.

RED WATER

Jurica Pavičić

Translated by Matt Robinson

BITTER LEMON PRESS
LONDON

BITTER LEMON PRESS

First published in the United Kingdom in 2025 by
Bitter Lemon Press, 47 Wilmington Square, London WC1X OET
www.bitterlemonpress.com

First published in Croatian as *Crvena Voda* by Profil Knjiga, Zagreb, 2017

This edition by arrangement with Agullo Editions, France

Bitter Lemon Press gratefully acknowledges the financial
assistance of the Arts Council of England.

This book was published with the financial support of the Ministry
of Culture and Media of the Republic of Croatia.

© Jurica Pavičić i Prol Knjiga, 2017

English translation © Matt Robinson, 2025

A CIP record for this book is available from the British Library

PB ISBN 978–1–916725–157
eBook USC ISBN 978–1–916725–164
eBook ROW ISBN 978–1–916725–171

Typeset by Tetragon, London
Printed and bound by the CPI Group (UK) Ltd, Croydon, CRO 4YY

Supported using public funding by
ARTS COUNCIL
ENGLAND
LOTTERY FUNDED

Contents

PART FOUR: RED WATER

PART ONE

SILVA DISAPPEARS

1
VESNA

First of all, Vesna remembers the weather.

It was a warm September day, a beautiful day, as if the sky was mocking them in advance. All afternoon, a welcome sea breeze had taken the edge off the Indian summer and as dusk fell a pleasant evening chill stole into the streets, the kitchens and bedrooms, heralding autumn.

Vesna remembers the place, too.

She remembers the house at the top end of Misto in the street behind the church, the house in which she spent most of her life. Closing her eyes, Vesna can see clearly the arrangement of the rooms and everything inside them: the entrance from the small porch at the top of the stone steps; the glassed-off veranda; the living room; the kitchen and its terracotta floor tiles. In the living room stands a table and opposite the table a sofa of worn-out fabric. In the hallway is a metal coat stand, and next to the coat stand a door, the door to Silva's room, on which Silva has written *Keep out*.

Vesna remembers what the living room looked like that day: in the corner, a Yugoslav-made Ei Niš television; on the armchair, a pile of washing waiting to be ironed; on the wall, a calendar of Canadian landscapes; and above the kitchen door, an oleograph of Jesus. The Jesus in the picture has watery, sleepy eyes, a bowed head and a wavy beard. His forefinger is raised, as if warning them of what is to come.

That's what their old house looked like that day – 23 September 1989.

A Saturday. And like every Saturday, they eat dinner together, all four of them around the table, Jakov at the head, Vesna opposite, and their children, twins Silva and Mate, on the side facing the terrace.

That's how the scene begins, the scene Vesna remembers: all four of them at home, seated around the table, dinner in front of them, the dinner she has cooked – runner beans with garlic, fried whitebait and bread. Just like any other evening.

The news is on the television in the corner of the room, dramatic news from exciting times: demonstrations in China; uprisings in Eastern Europe; talk of a new constitution in Slovenia; and calls for reform of the Yugoslav federation.

Everywhere, people speak of politics with a new, restive fervour. But she and Jakov aren't interested in politics. They firmly believe that if they stay as far as possible away from trouble, trouble will stay away from them.

Vesna remembers everything: the smells, the tastes, the scene. She remembers the tender whitebait melting in her mouth and the beans she garnished, as always, with chopped garlic. She remembers Jakov, as always, eating modestly, taking his time. She remembers Silva greedily devouring the fish, fighting with the bones and spitting them onto the plate. She remembers Mate too, of course. She remembers him eating carefully and calmly, arranging the fish spines at the edge of the plate, lining them up like corpses. Mate always ate slowly, methodically, cutting the food into small pieces as if feeding tiny, invisible Lilliputians.

Four silhouettes, four bodies hunched over the table, tucking into fish and spitting bones. That's how Vesna remembers that evening, the evening normal life ended.

In September 1989, Vesna and Jakov Vela have been married almost eighteen years. They became husband and wife in the autumn of 1971, on a Saturday three weeks before Christmas in a civil ceremony presided over by the Misto registrar. The reception was held in a hotel restaurant and they spent their first night in a room upstairs. Out of season, the room was cold and damp.

After the wedding, she and Jakov moved into a house in Misto, at the top end of the street behind the Church of the Holy Spirit. They shared the house with Aunt Zlata, Vesna's unmarried aunt, who would be their housemate for the next seven years.

Quiet and unseen, Zlata lived with them until one afternoon in 1978, when they found her motionless on the kitchen floor, struck down by a stroke. The funeral was quiet and proper, and a week later they emptied her room off the hallway. Zlata's room became Silva's. That Saturday in 1989, Silva is still the occupant of the room off the hallway, the room where she keeps her clothes, her knick-knacks and adolescent secrets. On the door, she has hung a sign in English telling the grown-ups to stay away.

Vesna and Jakov moved into the old house, Aunt Zlata's house, in the autumn of 1971, the day after their wedding. One morning, about a month later, Vesna felt sick and threw up in the kitchen sink before breakfast. The following week, the local doctor informed her that she was pregnant. Not long after that, a gynaecologist in Split broke the good news: she was carrying twins.

To look at Mate and Silva, one could see similarities: in the eyebrows and the profile of the nose, in the same fine forehead and smile lines, lines that suggested stubbornness. But if Mate and Silva were physically alike, in character they could not have been more different. Mate was a sedate and responsible boy, conscientious and cautious, the kind you could rely on and who Vesna knew would support her and Jakov in their old age. Silva was different. Silva was a brigand, Aunt Zlata once said. Silva would go far, Jakov once said, because she always knew how to get her own way.

In September 1989, Mate and Silva are almost eighteen. Mate is in his final year of studies at the shipbuilding school. He plans to enrol in the university shipbuilding faculty the following summer, after graduating. Silva is nearing the end of her economics and administration courses; when quizzed by her parents about her future, she becomes evasive and carefully changes the subject. Both schools are in Split. When he started, Mate was working afternoons in Misto unloading the fishermen's catch. Not wanting to lose his afternoon earnings, he continued to live in Misto and travelled to and from school. For that reason, Mate wakes at six every day and takes the commuter bus along the coastal road thirty-five minutes to Split. Not Silva. Silva lives in the girls' student dorm on Ćirilometodska in Split. She visits Misto every Saturday, including that Saturday, the last weekend of the summer.

In September 1989, Jakov is forty-two years old. He is already beginning to lose his hair, but he is thin at this point and particularly proud that his stomach is still flat. Jakov is a bookkeeper in a factory making plastic goods. The factory is located in a metal and glass building above the main road, a building that today is little more than a ruin. The factory produces plastic balls, boat fenders and inflatable dinghies. Jakov works in the salary department. He works patiently and conscientiously, with care but without ambition.

After work, after finishing dinner, Jakov likes to relax on the sofa and read the newspaper. Then he goes down to the ground-floor *konoba*, where previous generations kept wine and tools for working the land but which is now home to Jakov's foremost passion: amateur radio. Jakov could spend all day long connecting, soldering and sticking, assembling appliances covered with little lights which to Vesna seem to hold some secret magic. When it gets dark, Jakov sits there in the *konoba*, twiddling dials and talking for hours in English to people he will never see. Vesna sometimes listens as her husband converses with strangers on the other side of the world. She will never understand the point of it, but never would she say that to Jakov. Vesna knows every man needs a hare-brained passion.

In 1989, Vesna is thirty-eight years old. For the past fourteen years she has worked as a geography teacher at the primary school in Misto. Monday to Friday, Vesna teaches the local kids about gulf currents, oil-exporting countries and the river basins of Yugoslavia. Misto is small, so Vesna often runs into her pupils in the street. They say hello in the shop and their parents nod at her in approval when they spot her in church on Sundays.

When she started the job, Vesna believed she liked school and liked children. Fourteen years on, she is not so sure. She is increasingly aware of the stifled irritation she feels when entering the classroom, the way the pranks the children play drive her to outbursts of rage completely out of proportion to the offence. After fourteen years, Vesna has the growing feeling that children are not inherently good.

Vesna will turn forty at the end of the following year. Sometimes, she thinks about that ugly digit, four, about the weight she has put on, how she is suffocating under the monotony of work and a marriage that is peaceful, happy, but boring.

Very rarely, during these moments, does it occur to Vesna that she is at a point in life when she could still do a lot with herself. She could change job or change address. She could lose weight, learn Chinese or change her hairstyle. But such misapprehensions quickly pass. Vesna doesn't really want change, and she knows that neither does Jakov. They have good lives. Monday to Friday, they do their boring, dependable jobs. In the afternoons they read on the terrace – she a book, he the newspaper – and in the summer they go to the beach. Saturdays, they head down to the shallow marina and buy fish from a fisherman. Sundays, in the yard, they light a fire and cook fish, sausages or chops on the grill. Jakov enjoys barbecuing, his forehead red, sweat beading above his eyebrows. He always overcooks the meat and ruins the fish, but it makes him happy, so Vesna lets him play.

In the early evening calm, she and Jakov sit together on the sofa, a bottle of cheap wine on the coffee table in front of them. Around ten, when Vesna's eyes are starting to close, Jakov turns off the television and takes her to bed. Back then, in the summer of 1989, they still have sex. Not often, but slowly, skilfully, as if each other's body were a familiar, well-tuned appliance they are adept at handling.

In September 1989, Vesna is happy.

She remembers it all. She remembers the four people sitting at the kitchen table beneath a drowsy Jesus and a calendar of Canadian landscapes. Dusk is falling over Misto and from the small square in front of the marina can be heard the soundcheck for the fishermen's fair. She remembers the four shadows at dinner, pouring wine, talking. Jakov stands, takes his plate to the kitchen sink and puts the wine away in the cabinet. Silva rises from the table and lazily, coyly, withdraws to her room.

Vesna remembers what follows like a film she'll play back a thousand times. She remembers rinsing the plates in the sink, Mate shaking the tablecloth and sweeping up the crumbs from the floor, Jakov sitting at the table buried in that day's crossword puzzle. Silva goes to her room. When she returns, she's dressed to go out. Vesna remembers exactly what she's wearing, as if Silva is still standing before her: a floral dress that's too short, red All Star high-tops, and a loose shoulder bag. She has a red jacket tucked under her arm, knowing that nights by the sea can get chilly during an Indian summer.

That's that moment: Silva standing at the door in her floral dress and All Star high-tops, standing there as if waiting for a round of applause. Then she says: "I'm off."

"Who with?" asks Jakov. "Brane?"

"No, not Brane," Silva replies. "Not today. He's not here. He's in Rijeka, for the maritime enrolment. He's back tomorrow."

"So where are you going?" Silva's father asks her.

"To the fair in the cove," she replies. "Don't wait up, I'll be late."

"Take care," Jakov tells her. He tells his daughter to take care, and to this day Vesna still wonders why.

Silva fixes her shoulder strap, lifts her bag and quickly, casually, says: "See you."

She steps out the door, quickly, silently, like a gentle breeze.

Silva leaves and Jakov pays not the slightest attention. As his daughter leaves, he is still doing the crossword and does not lift his head. As her daughter leaves, Vesna is busy drying plates with a kitchen towel. To this day she does not know whether she looked up at Silva as she walked out. She's almost certain she didn't say goodbye, because at that moment she could not have known. Now she knows. That moment, when Silva said "See you", flicking her dress as she headed out the door, was the last time they would ever see her.

2
MATE (1989)

Mate woke up with a hangover, the ceiling above him swaying and a dull pain pulsating between his temples and his forehead.

He opened his eyes, but the strong morning light made the pain even worse and he quickly closed them. He lay there, eyes closed, trying to sleep a little more, hoping it would drive away the headache. But it was too late for that. The sounds and the light had woken him for good, so he stayed there, prostrate, eyes closed, listening to the noises of the world around him.

At about seven he heard his father's footsteps in the hallway, then the sound of the shower, and again footsteps. He heard his parents talking quietly in the kitchen. The smell of Turkish coffee wafted to his room. He found the smell comforting.

He lay there like that, eavesdropping with his eyes closed. He heard the pounding of feet on the steps outside and then his father opening the *konoba*. From the *konoba*, he soon heard the sounds of work. Like every Sunday morning, his father was gluing and soldering something.

At 8.15, the bells of the Church of the Holy Spirit rang for morning Mass. Mate again heard footsteps on the porch steps. He heard Vesna leaving for Mass, and Vesna returning from

Mass. He heard his mother coughing in the hall, hanging the washing out to dry and – finally – opening the door to Silva's room, with the intention of waking her.

And then again he heard his mother's footsteps on the stairs, descending to the yard. She opened the door to the workshop.

Shortly before ten o'clock, Mate heard from the yard the sentence with which the turmoil would begin. Vesna entered the workshop and uttered the words that Mate heard loud and clear. "Silva's not here," she said. "She's not in her room."

It was 9.50 in the morning on Sunday, 24 September 1989.

That morning, they weren't worried. Mate would later think that terrible, but he knew it was true. They weren't worried – not his mother, nor his father, nor Mate.

So Silva wasn't home. She must have slept over somewhere or gone out early. She'd be back. Nothing bad could have happened. Misto wasn't some American metropolis. There were no kidnappers in Misto, no muggers or serial killers. Nothing ever happened to anyone in Misto.

When Mate got up, when he'd showered and washed his face, his mother casually asked whether he knew where his sister was. Mate told her what he knew. That she had been at the fishermen's fair, like him. There had been a band, followed by DJ Robi. Silva had danced. That was the last time he saw her, when she was dancing, about eleven o'clock.

That's what Mate told his mother. But that wasn't everything. He didn't tell her that he and his mates had left the fair at eleven because they had two bottles of Stock 84 and some good weed. He didn't tell her that he'd spent the rest of the night on the beach in Travna cove, trying to seduce a girl from Novi Sad in Serbia who spoke with a seductive, drawn-out dialect. He didn't tell his mum that besides smoking a few joints he had drunk almost a litre of Italian brandy and that his head was killing him.

He didn't tell her either that at eleven, when he'd left the fair, he'd seen Silva dancing with Adrijan Lekaj, the son of the Albanian baker. Nor that Silva had requested "Red Red Wine" not once but twice from DJ Robi, and that as he left she was entwining herself in Adrijan's embrace to UB40's slow reggae rhythm. Silva wouldn't have told their parents about Mate's transgressions, so nor would he tell on her.

His mother heard him out, gave a reproving nod of her head, then returned to the kitchen and began peeling potatoes.

"She must be at Brane's. She'll be back," said Jakov. He went back down to the workshop, completely calm and unconcerned.

Jakov happily devoted the next hour and fifty minutes to his passion for amateur radio. Vesna placed the potatoes and chicken in a roasting tray, sat down at the kitchen table and began reading the Sunday papers. Mate surreptitiously popped a painkiller for his head and once more withdrew to his room – now darkened – to wait for the pain to ease. By the time he woke, the headache had gone. He looked at the clock: 1.15.

At 1.30 he entered the kitchen. The table had been set for lunch: plates, salad and a bottle of white wine, and from the oven the smell of roast chicken. But no Silva. Mate would remember that moment. For the first time he was ever so slightly worried.

At 2.15 there was still no sign of Silva. Vesna leaned against the fridge, a look of exasperated disapproval on her face. Mate's father stood at the kitchen table, next to the glasses and plates, and looked at the clock on the wall on which the big hand was approaching the number four. Finally, at 2.20

on 24 September 1989, he said: "Mate, go and have a look around. Find out where she is."

Mate didn't know it then, but his life's search had just begun.

At 2.20, Mate pulled on his shoes, left the house and set off to look for his sister. He walked the short street to the square in front of the church then turned sharply downhill, passing the van of the local cooperative parked behind Lekaj's bakery. When he reached the marina, he set off along the shoreline all the way to where the concrete waterfront finished and the houses thinned out.

He continued walking the coastal path, between drystone walls and the pitted grey limestone along the shore. The path went from concrete to gravel to trodden earth, taking him all the way to the headland and the tiny Stella Maris chapel. There he caught sight of the place he was trying to reach. Far from the village, isolated behind the headland, was the home of the Rokov family.

That summer, 1989, Silva had been going out with the Rokovs' son, Brane. They had got together just before the summer, at the end of May or beginning of June. One evening, after a party of wine and weed, Brane and Silva had disappeared somewhere by themselves. When they returned, they were arm in arm and Brane was glowing with happiness.

"Me and your sister are together," Brane told him the next day. Mate was too stunned to reply.

He had known for a while that Brane liked Silva. All the guys in Misto liked Silva. He remembered everyone going together in the first year of school to prise mussels from the rocks in Travna cove. Fifteen of them, tourists and locals, went in three small plastic boats. Early evening, when they'd finished plundering mussels, they'd tied up the *pasaras* and lit a fire on the beach. Some lads from Zagreb started playing guitars and a bottle of bad local wine was passed around the fire. At one point, Mate noticed Brane looking at Silva. It was as if he was devouring her with his eyes. But that evening Silva was all over one of the Zagreb guitarists. She let herself be cuddled up to and by ten o'clock they were kissing, his hand wandering far down her waist. Mate felt uncomfortable and wanted to look away, but the only other thing to look at was Brane. Brane stood by the fire, sullen and stern, a look of complete despair on his face.

Silva had gone back to school in Split in the September and Brane seemed to cool down. His patience had paid off, however. The following May, Brane and Silva finally got together and their relationship lasted in spite of Silva's absence. From Monday to Friday, Silva was in Split, living her life. She spent weekends in Misto, when she and Brane would be together. Brane would come knocking for her and they'd go out to one of the two and a half cafes Misto had to offer. It seemed like Brane wanted them to spend as much time as possible together, preferably just the two of them. But Silva had other plans. Silva would steer them into company, drinking and laughing, and to wherever Mate might be. Mate had the impression Brane wanted something else. But it had become plain early on that Silva was the leader in the relationship and Brane an unswerving follower.

After a short walk, Mate reached the Stella Maris chapel. Before him lay the headland, the point where the land protruded farthest into the channel. It was exposed to the south; grey, bare, salt-whipped rock stretched high up the cliff. The headland had once been spoken of as dangerous for sailors, hence the shrine to the guiding spirit of those at sea. The chapel was small, no bigger than a doghouse or an outdoor grill. It sat hunched on the peak of the headland, above the exposed limestone, pitted and grey. It had a gable roof and a small metal cross on the ridge that had been eaten away by rust. Beneath the ridge, in uneven letters, was carved the name *STELLA MARIS*. A plaster statue of the Virgin Mary stood inside, locked behind bars. It looked to Mate as if the Virgin Mary was a prisoner in her own small, private jail.

Mate continued along the path between the cliffs and the high drystone wall. On one side of the path was bare, grey rock washed by waves that were whipped up by southerly winds. On the other side, behind the wall, was a vast stretch of untended land covered with carob, brambles and olive trees left to grow wild. The locals had named it after Brane's family: Rokov's Land. He walked across Rokov's Land until he reached Brane's home.

The Rokov house stood alone on the coastal plateau. In front of it was a dry dock – a sloping concrete slipway that finished in the sea, with rails running down the middle. Brane's father, Tonko, had inherited the slipway and the boat repair business. He worked with plastic. He applied filler to plastic boats, patched them, reinforced them with webbing and treated trapped moisture. It was a noisy, dirty, toxic job. He could only do it in a place like that, as far as possible from other people or houses.

As he neared the house, Mate heard the buzzing of a sander. He approached and called out. The sander went quiet. Tonko popped his head out from behind one of the boats. His beard and hair were white from plastic dust, like a badly disguised Santa Claus. He spotted Mate and motioned to him with his head to go into the house.

The Rokov house was no ordinary house. When he was a boy, Mate had thought of it as a kind of castle, a big castle ringed by a wall that enclosed the courtyard inside. To enter the courtyard, one passed through arched doors beneath a pediment on which were scratched the words ROCCO ROCCOV AND HIS CHILDREN and the year 1812. The sign was carved in the old dialect in an unskilled, uneven hand, as if by someone who barely knew how to write.

But if it looked like a castle from the outside, inside was a very different matter. Mate was used to Vesna's insistence on order, a fastidiousness that sometimes grated. So every time he went to the Rokov house, he was amazed at the all-encompassing, indescribable mess. Scattered around the courtyard were wooden planks, blocks and logs, scrap metal and machine parts. On the concrete terrace in front of the *konoba* he saw several outboard motors without cowlings. There were open cans of filler and rolls of white, woolly material Tonko used to repair plastic. The pickled foods prepared by Brane's mother only added to the air of a witch's grotto. Uršula Rokov pickled shallots, capers, onions, olives and sea fennel, filling jars that sat around on the floor, on the steps and on the porch, green, brown and dark blue.

Mate entered the courtyard, listening for Brane's voice or Silva's, looking for either of them. But there was no one in the courtyard. Finally, unsure what else to do, he called out Brane's name.

A slender, dark-haired woman in her forties stepped onto the porch. It was Uršula, Brane's mother. Seeing Mate, she smiled kindly. "Brane's asleep," she said. "He came back this morning from Rijeka. He went to enrol in the maritime faculty. Is it urgent?"

"Might be," replied Mate. "We don't know where Silva is."

"She's not with Brane," said Uršula. "He got back this morning and went straight to bed. Hold on, I'll wake him."

Uršula went into the house and a feeling of shame washed over Mate. Brane wasn't in Misto last night. He was travelling on a night bus. And his girlfriend, Mate's sister, was knocking back brandy and Coke and wrapping herself in Adrijan's embrace to the sound of "Red Red Wine". He had come to ask Brane where Silva was, when in fact Mate was the one with the dark secret.

"He'll be out in a sec," Uršula said, stepping back out onto the porch. "He's washing his face." But she didn't come down to the courtyard or call Mate up. She just watched him from above with her light grey-blue eyes.

Uršula was still an attractive woman. According to Mate's father, Uršula had been the prettiest girl in Misto twenty years before. Jakov would say this in front of Vesna, but Mate never had the feeling that it made Vesna jealous. Uršula's beauty was admired in the same way people admire a Greek vase or archaeological artefact, ruined long ago and now beyond repair. *Who'd have thought she'd end up out there in the sticks,* Vesna would say. *Everyone thought she'd go far,* she would add, *but look where she is – on Rokov's Land, with Tonko, in a filthy house covered in plastic dust.*

That was how Mate's mother and father spoke of Uršula. Waiting in the courtyard for Brane to rouse himself, Mate saw the scene in front of him through their eyes: disarray, rust and filth; a decaying house, tiles falling from its roof. And in the midst of it all Uršula, who despite the years still stood proud, walked tall, her grey-blue eyes hinting at past beauty.

There they stood, Uršula at the top of the steps, Mate at the bottom. They heard the dull thud of footsteps and the sound of running water in the bathroom, and Brane finally emerged onto the porch, still wet from washing, his hair barely combed. When he saw who it was, he went red with discomfort. As Silva's brother, Mate knew that Brane always liked to leave a good impression on him.

"I'm looking for Silva," said Mate. "Do you know where she is?"

"No," Brane replied. "I came back from Rijeka this morning. I was going to call her after I'd got some sleep."

"When did you last talk to her?"

"Day before yesterday."

"Do you know where she might have gone last night?"

"Nowhere. She said she was going to stay home last night."

But she didn't, thought Mate.

"Nothing bad's happened, has it?" asked Brane.

"Doubt it," replied Mate. He said goodbye and left.

Mate set off on the path home. At the Stella Maris chapel, he turned and looked back. Uršula was standing at the door, watching him go.

Heading towards the centre of Misto, Mate came to the church, but it was locked. He went to the cafes instead. It was a warm Sunday and all the locals were sitting out: sailors on leave, students on vacation and the local riff-raff in their Ray-Ban sunglasses. Employed or unemployed, everyone was there, lounging in the heat like lizards, holding forth on politics, slurping espressos. Only *she* wasn't there. Silva wasn't anywhere to be seen.

Finally, Mate headed to the only place left – Adrijan's father's bakery. It was afternoon, and the bakery was shut. He entered the yard and found old Lekaj dozing beneath a fig tree after working all night. Mate greeted him from the gate and old Lekaj mumbled drowsily in reply. Mate went on in, but as soon as he saw Adrijan, he knew Silva wasn't with him any more.

Adrijan was sprawled on the sofa in a pair of Adidas shorts, naked from the waist up, watching Italian soccer on the television. He looked at Mate with surprise.

Mate asked him where Silva was and an awkward look came over Adrijan's face.

He didn't know where she was. True, he said, they'd been together last night. They danced until eleven, when Silva suggested they go somewhere alone. Those were his exact words – "go somewhere alone" – and it was obvious he felt uncomfortable. Yeah, he said, they'd been together till about one o'clock. They'd been at Cape Cross, by the big cross on the mound above the old water cistern, a dark, hidden spot they both knew had been used by generations of Misto residents for clandestine sex. Mate remembered feeling a wave of shame sweep over him, as if he had never really known his sister.

"When did you split up?" Mate asked, trying to remain calm and businesslike.

"About half past twelve, maybe one," Adrijan replied. "Silva said she had to go, that she was in a hurry."

"A hurry to get home?"

"She said she had to get up early, that she was travelling somewhere."

"Travelling somewhere? Where?" asked Mate.

"Don't know," replied Adrijan. "Reckon you and your parents should know that."

Mate suddenly had a bad feeling. The sound was turned down on the television but the commentator could still just about be heard; Fiorentina were attacking Inter, or Inter were attacking Lazio. For the first time, Mate had that leaden feeling in the pit of his stomach, a feeling of dread at what might be to come.

He hurried out of Lekaj's house, past the church and up the street. Bursting into the house, he found his parents at the kitchen table, waiting for him. Mate said nothing. He went into Silva's room and opened her desk drawer.

It was empty. No purse, no phone book, no passport.

He knew Silva had a secret hiding place. He knew that was where she kept her savings. He squeezed his hand under the closet and pulled a wooden box from the false bottom of the drawer. It was the box where Silva kept her secrets. He opened it.

The box was empty. No money or anything else.

Mate returned to the kitchen and sat down at the table. Then he spoke the words. He spoke them as calmly as possible, so as not to trigger even greater panic. He told his parents they should call the police.

The police officers came that afternoon, three of them. Two were in uniform and were obviously junior. The third was in civvies and clearly the boss. He was in his late twenties and carrying a few extra pounds. He introduced himself as Gorki Šain. Mate had never heard of anyone called Gorki.

Although the two uniformed officers walked around the yard and looked in Silva's room, they showed little real interest, as if they found the task unimportant, irritating. Meanwhile, Inspector Šain sat down at the kitchen table and opened a large notebook with a vinyl cover. He listened to what they had to say, taking notes, and asked some general questions. Then he asked to see Silva's secret drawer.

Inspector Šain looked at the drawer and then at Silva's room. He looked around with a kind of indifferent nonchalance, as if it was all the stuff of teenage cliché. He returned to the kitchen and sat down at the table to write something down. Closing his notebook, he stood up and headed for the door. He told them not to worry. *When teenagers disappear,* he said, *in eighty per cent of cases they come back of their own accord. They turn up within twenty-four hours without a word of warning, just the way they left.*

Those were his words. He wrote his name and number on a small piece of paper and handed it to Jakov. He told him to call the next day if Silva still wasn't back.

When the police officers had left, Vesna sat down at the table and sank her head into her hands. Jakov went out onto the balcony, as if the balcony were a crow's nest from which he'd be able to spot his daughter. He showed no sign of anxiety. But Mate knew him too well. He knew a nervous restlessness was eating him up inside.

Lunch was still on the table, untouched. In the roasting tray rested a now cold roast chicken, surrounded by cold potatoes swimming in congealed fat. The kitchen still smelled of chicken skin and grease. Suddenly, Mate could hardly bear to look at it.

Mate stood up. He put the bottle of white wine back in the fridge. He threw away the salad and the potatoes. He took the chicken, sliced it into pieces with a knife and put the pieces on a plate. He put the meat in the fridge and then, finally, took a wire sponge and scoured the roasting tray.

When he had finished, he sat at the table across from his mother. Vesna had not moved, seemingly impervious to anything happening around her. He waited, as if expecting some kind of reaction from her. When it didn't come, he picked up the unused plates and placed them in the kitchen cabinet.

The next morning, Silva was still not back.

At exactly eight o'clock, Jakov called the police and told them there was still no sign of her. By midday, the house and the streets were full of police. The same day, Silva was officially declared missing.

Police officers crawled all over Misto. They searched the drystone terraces and olive groves above the old part of the village. They trawled the harbour floor and the dark rock at the water's edge. One patrol went behind Cape Cross to investigate the area around the barracks and the old naval tunnels. Another climbed up the cape to search around the water cistern and the stone cross.

Mate and his parents stayed at home and waited. Jakov mooched around the yard like a tormented spirit. Vesna lay on the sofa, numbed by sedatives, her eyes bloodshot.

Around mid-afternoon, Inspector Šain came round and sat them at the table. He explained what they had found out – that numerous witnesses had seen Silva at the fishermen's fair; that she had spent the whole evening dancing and had requested "Red Red Wine" by UB40 three times in a row; and that she had slow-danced with Adrijan Lekaj. At least four people had seen them leave together at about eleven o'clock. Lekaj said they were together until one o'clock. At some point, she'd told him she was leaving, that she had to go home because she was travelling early the next morning. They parted at the old water cistern below the stone cross. Silva had said goodbye and headed downhill to the first houses. That was the last time Lekaj had seen her. He had also been the last person to see her.

"We checked him out," Inspector Šain said, as if trying to soothe their doubts. They'd checked his prints and under his fingernails and subjected him to a lie-detector test. He seemed to be telling the truth. "Have a think," the inspector told Jakov. "Where could Silva have been going in such in a hurry?"

"Nowhere," Jakov replied. "She didn't go anywhere. She was supposed to go back to the dorm on Monday, to school, in Split."

"Are you sure?"

"We're sure," Mate's mother said.

"Are you? Because that's not the way it looks to us."

Nor me, Mate thought. He sat there, not speaking, but composed enough to know how it must look to the inspector. Like a premeditated escape. Silva had taken her money and her passport. She must have planned the whole thing.

A police officer entered and asked Inspector Šain to go outside. The inspector followed him into the yard. They spoke to each other quietly, heading to the top of the garden and a drainpipe behind a cactus. Stooping, the officer inserted a long stick into the pipe, rummaging around for something. The officer put his arm deep inside and pulled out a plastic bag. Gorki and the officer studied the bag. Returning to the house, Inspector Šain entered the kitchen holding the bag, his face tense and dark. He tossed the bag onto the table. "I'd like to hear what you know about this," he said.

The inspector opened the bag and took something out. It was a small brown bundle wrapped meticulously with adhesive tape. Mate knew immediately what was inside and his head began to pulsate with terror.

Inspector Šain cut through the tape and a brown powder spilled from the small bundle onto the table. Mate's mother and father both seemed to know what it was. There was a mixture of rage and shame on Vesna's face; she looked at the bundle as if an ugly, poisonous insect were on the table in front of her.

"Heroin," said the inspector. "But I think you already knew that. Tell me, is it hers? And what do you know about it?"

Mate's father said nothing. Vesna said nothing, but looked at Mate. She looked at him, scowling, full of accusatory rage. A look that said: *You must have known something.*

Mate dropped his gaze. He looked at the table and at the bundle from which a dry powder was slowly spilling.

After dusk, the police left. "There's no point searching in the dark," Inspector Šain said, and at nine o'clock he ordered the officers to their cars. Ten minutes later, peace was restored. Street lights blinked in the cove, television screens flickered behind window shutters. The streets were empty. But Mate knew: behind all those shutters, slats and porches, his sister was the only topic of conversation. While the television droned in the background, while they ate dinner, made tea or cleaned the dishes, the neighbours were talking about Silva's disappearance.

The three of them were left alone in the house. Mate's mother was beside herself, lying on the sofa in a foetal position, moaning intermittently. At some point, Mate's father motioned with his head and the two of them took Vesna in their arms and carried her to the bedroom. They placed her on the bed, and she curled up once more.

Mate's father returned to the balcony, where he had again spent the day. He stood leaning with his elbows on the rail and stared into the darkness, as if convinced he'd find Silva if he looked hard enough. Mate approached him and Jakov placed his palm on his son's hand.

"Don't be mad at her," Jakov told him.

"Mad at who?"

"You know," replied Jakov. "It's not easy for any of us."

Neither of them said anything for a while.

Then Jakov started up again. "What they found in the drainpipe. Did you know about it?" he asked.

"No."

"You didn't know she kept drugs?"

"I knew she had weed. She used it, a lot of it."

"This wasn't weed."

"No, Dad, it wasn't. This is much worse."

"Why didn't you tell us?"

"Would you have done in my position?"

"No."

"There you go then."

They fell silent again, but remained standing there, as if soothed by the evening air.

Then Mate felt the cold. "I'm going," he said.

"Sure. I'll stay a bit more," Jakov replied, and continued to stare into the darkness, not moving.

Mate entered the house, which still smelled of roast chicken. Before going to bed, he peered through the door to his mother's room. Vesna still lay curled up. But she wasn't moaning any more. The sedatives were working.

He went to his room. He didn't undress. He just lay down on the bed and stared at the ceiling, wide awake. His body needed rest, but he knew neither he nor his parents would fall asleep that night.

Silva's disappearance became news over the following week.

The media then was not what it is now. There were no satellite uplink trucks or packs of journalists with microphones hanging around in front of the house. But Silva's photograph was in all the newspapers and an appeal went out during the evening news on state television. Within a week, everyone knew that Silva had vanished.

During the first week, the police combed Misto and the surrounding area. With dogs, they searched the mound where Silva and Adrijan had been that night. They searched Rokov's Land, the mountainsides and the Prosika canyon, a narrow mountain passage where bandits had once lain in wait for Turkish caravans. Inspector Šain and his officers went house to house, questioning people one by one. Where were they that night? Did they see or hear anything? Everything he found out, Inspector Šain wrote down in that vinyl notebook Mate had seen the first evening.

After seven days, the police withdrew from Misto. On the seventh evening after Silva's disappearance, Inspector Šain told them there was nothing else the police could do in Misto – they had searched everywhere, questioned every witness. He said he believed Silva had indeed left, just as she had informed Adrijan. Either she had been taken away or she had run away, and he would try to find out where.

They spent the following days in a state of uncertain anticipation. Inspector Šain would get in touch every second or third day, usually in the evening, usually by phone. He would update them on the police search of bus and train stations, motels and border crossings. They had questioned bus drivers, ticket sellers, train conductors and border officers. They had taken cassettes from CCTV cameras, but there were lots of them and it was slow work. Inspector Šain's updates grew shorter and emptier as the days passed.

On the fifth day, Mate's father slipped into Silva's room and began digging among her things. He came out holding the best picture of Silva he could find. The photo seemed new. It showed Silva looking straight at the camera, bold and brazen, a lock of hair falling across one eye. They had no idea who had taken the photo or when. Suddenly, it looked like Silva's life was full of secrets and this was just one of them.

That morning, Jakov stuck Silva's picture on an A4 sheet of paper. Beneath it, in neat, bureaucratic handwriting, he wrote her name and a description of her, her height, the colour of her clothes and a contact telephone number. Then, in letters that screamed, he wrote: MISSING PERSON.

Jakov made 800 copies in the printer's shop near the post office. The next morning, Mate suggested they go together to distribute them.

Every day they got in the car and spent hours wandering the roads. They pinned and taped up the posters at bus stops, post offices, shops, travel agencies and public buildings. At first they kept to the main coastal road and the area around it. Then they began to widen the circle. By the end of the second week they had gone inland to Vrgorac and Imotski, and into Hercegovina. Over the following ten days they took the coastal road north to Zadar and Rijeka, then south into the Neretva valley towards Sarajevo in Bosnia. They plastered posters across Imotski, the port of Kardeljevo, to Lištica on the road to Mostar, and Duvno. One morning, Jakov sat in the car alone and headed for Bosnia. He came back late in the evening and said he had left posters along roads from the Kupres plain to Jajce and Banja Luka.

In return, Mate took Split. Over the course of a long weekend, he covered Split with 300 photocopied posters. He wandered between socialist high-rises, visited shopping centres and warehouses, hotel receptions and schoolyards, discovering parts of the city he never knew before: endless newly built neighbourhoods, DIY stores, rows of tyre fitters and brick-built workshops on the rough edges of the city. By the time he'd finished, Silva's picture hung in the entrance to every school, at every tourist information point, in the guard booth of the shipyard, the port and the cement factory.

By the end of the following week, Jakov had made another 300 copies. One day he left early and was away for the night. When he returned, he told them he'd been plastering posters across Ljubljana and Zagreb.

For a few days, they neither saw nor heard from the police. Then one afternoon Inspector Šain called. He had nothing concrete to report, but said cryptically that "new circumstances" and "new developments" meant he would have to question them again, one by one, in Split. Mate thought it all sounded ominous.

His father went first. He returned in the evening, quiet and looking even more sullen than before. Saying nothing to Mate about what had happened, Jakov withdrew with Mate's mother to their bedroom, where they spoke quietly for hours. When she emerged, Vesna's eyes were bloodshot.

Mate could see something was up, but he didn't have the courage to ask what. The next day, his father readied to return to Split; when Mate suggested they go together, Jakov abruptly turned him down. He was gone the whole day, and when he came back his mood was worse than ever.

They ate dinner in silence. Afterwards, Mate tossed the remains of the boiled cabbage in the trash, washed the dishes and dried the glasses. And then his father asked him to sit at the table.

"Does the surname Cvitković mean anything to you?" Jakov asked. Had Mate ever heard of anyone who went by the name Cvitko? Had Silva ever mentioned anyone with that name? Had he ever seen that person in Silva's company?

"No," Mate replied, telling the truth. But Mate could tell his father didn't believe him.

"If you hear anything, please, tell me," said Jakov. He paused, then added: "Tell me first. Me. No one else. Got it? You tell me, and I'll tell Mum and the police."

Two days later, Inspector Šain summoned Mate to the police station. That week, Mate had morning classes at school; he went to the central police station on Sukoišanska after lessons had finished. Inspector Šain had scheduled him for two o'clock, but Mate was already at the guard booth at 1.15. He hung around in front for a while until the uniformed officer in the booth noticed him. He approached Mate and asked him who he was there to see. "Either go in or take a walk and come back later," the officer told him.

Mate left his ID at the booth and climbed the stairs. The central police station consisted of a row of straight, identical corridors with light wood floors. Along the length of the corridors were rows of identical rooms with fanlight windows above light plywood doors. Mate was disappointed. The police station had the air of a banal, bureaucratic office.

He wandered the building for a long time, reading the names on the doors. At the end of one corridor, he found a door on which was written GORKI ŠAIN. He knocked. He heard Inspector Šain's voice calling him to enter. He went in.

Two officers were inside: Inspector Šain and another man Mate did not recognize, a bigger, older man who introduced himself as Tenžer. They were sitting in an office full of papers, with plywood cupboards. An Olympia typewriter sat on the desk in front of them. On the wall above Inspector Šain's head was an oversized portrait of Yugoslavia's late leader, Tito, in profile. Mate recalled such portraits from his school classroom. Wherever you stood, you had the feeling Tito was watching you.

Inspector Šain and Tenžer questioned him carefully, for a long time. Mate expected to be asked about the evening of the disappearance and the people in Misto. Surprisingly, the officers weren't at all interested in that. For two hours, they didn't mention Misto. All they cared about was Silva's life in Split. They asked if he ever visited her in the student dorm. Did he know her room-mates and friends in the city? They were interested in whether he usually went home straight after school, or whether he sometimes stayed in the city for a while. They got him to list the people he knew Silva hung out with in Split. They asked him a series of specific questions concerning Silva's life in the city. Did Silva's room-mates do drugs? What was her attendance like? Did he know where Silva had been on a certain Tuesday? Or where she had been on a particular Wednesday? Mate surprised himself with how little he knew. Silva's life in Split, he realized, was a secret to him too.

Finally, Inspector Šain mentioned a name and asked if it meant anything to him. It was the same name: Cvitko. Mario Cvitković. Waiting for his answer, Inspector Šain regarded him suspiciously, as if watching for the slightest sign of a lie.

Mate shook his head. "No," he said. He had never heard Silva mention any Cvitko. "Who is he?" Mate asked, but Inspector Šain didn't reply. The other officer, Tenžer, nodded darkly and said it didn't matter.

At five o'clock Mate left the station, genuinely scared. He didn't feel like going home. He walked the city for a while, taking in its streets and houses, its familiar places. He had the feeling they had taken on a whole new meaning. A place he had known so well now hid a threat.

When he got home that evening, his father looked at him with an unsettling curiosity. Jakov made him a toasted sandwich and poured him a glass of milk. He asked how it had gone with the police. Mate told him briefly.

Mate bit into the sandwich, then asked his father: "Who's this Cvitković the police are asking about?"

His father didn't reply. He rose silently and began to rinse the dinner plates in the sink. He had his back to Mate, and Mate had the feeling it was so he wouldn't have to lie to him to his face.

"Do you know this Cvitković?" Mate asked again.

"No," his father replied. "I don't know him." He turned off the tap and left the room.

3
JAKOV

After he left the police interrogation, Jakov went to Silva's student dorm. He went without a plan. The day felt heavy, the sky was dark with October clouds, and from the southeast the *šilok* had begun to blow, bringing damp, close, hot air to Split. On the ground floor of the police station, a mass of people waited at counters for passports and driving licences. The wind had electrified them. They were sticky with sweat, short-tempered, hateful of themselves and everyone else.

At first Jakov intended to get in the car and head back to Misto. Then he changed his mind. He slipped the car keys into his pocket and set off on foot for the city centre.

Until that morning, Jakov had thought they led a normal life – a normal family with normal, petty problems. He believed his daughter to be headstrong, capricious and uninhibited; how often had he wished her mild-tempered, meeker and less rebellious. But he'd thought they were minor, adolescent issues. Since her disappearance, he had come to realize he was wrong. Silva's problems were bigger. If he hadn't understood before, he certainly did then.

Jakov had spent three hours in the interrogation room. For those three hours, two officers – Šain and Tenžer – had questioned him about every detail of Silva's life: her social circle, phone calls, nightlife. They didn't ask him about Misto or about that night. They asked him about her life in Split and who she had been in contact with. They asked him about the parcel they had found in the drainpipe, the parcel that had sat there under his nose for God knows how long, and about which he had no idea all that time.

"Did anyone from Split drop by to see her?" Inspector Šain asked. "Did she go to see anyone? Did you notice whether she had more money than usual? Did you notice anyone loitering around the drainpipe?"

The questions kept coming and Jakov didn't have the answers.

At one point Tenžer glared at him angrily. "This isn't a fucking joke," he told him. "Do you know what was in your drainpipe? There was a year's salary in that parcel. That's serious stuff. That's not something that just falls into a girl's lap."

That's something lives are lost over, Jakov thought. He thought it, but didn't say it.

At some point the officers mentioned that name: Cvitković. Cvitko. They asked if he knew him, had heard of him. Had Silva been to the cafe – The Butterfly – where he hung out? In the Manuš district. Jakov knew only vaguely where Manuš was. He had never heard of any Butterfly cafe.

Finally they showed him a picture of Cvitko. Looking back at him was a man with a shaved head and an earring. He had the air of an affable rogue. Jakov shrugged and passed the picture back despairingly to the officers. He'd never seen him in his life, not in Misto nor in Split.

He was broken by the time he left the police station. He headed for where the car was parked, but realized on the way that he couldn't simply go home. Instead he turned towards the city centre and into a narrow street that curved between the student canteen and the theatre. He passed the Franciscan monastery and a department store. Finally, he found himself in front of the building he was looking for – the girls' student dorm.

Jakov had been inside only once, three years before, the day Silva had moved in. When they visited Silva in Split they never met there, always somewhere else, in the school hall or the cafe, and Jakov always found it unusual, bordering on suspicious.

He hesitated and then entered. Jakov had an overwhelming urge to go to her room, to see and touch Silva's things, to feel them under his fingers.

Climbing to the second floor, he stopped before a white-painted door. From inside, pop music could be heard playing low on a transistor radio. It didn't sound like a place of poignancy or mourning.

He entered. In the room were four beds. One was unmade and empty, and on two others were sprawled two teenage girls. One was blonde, her face scarred by acne, the other brunette, with braces on her teeth. From Silva's stories he knew they were called Mirna and Nina, but he didn't know which one was Mirna and which Nina.

Silva's bed was in the corner by the window. The bed was a mess and her things were still all over the place.

When he entered, Silva's room-mates looked at him with hostility. "You a journalist?" asked the blonde, her tone one of undisguised insolence.

Jakov stopped for a second before replying. "Yes," he said. "I'm a journalist." No sooner had he said it than Jakov was shocked by his lie, as if he had leaped into ice-cold water.

"Your colleagues have already been," said the blonde.

"But you won't find anything here," added the brunette. "The police already took everything. Everything that was suspicious."

"Suspicious?"

The girls laughed conspiratorially and then, as if realizing how inappropriate it was, fell silent and grew serious. "They took her things. The things they needed for the investigation. That's what we meant."

Jakov approached his daughter's bed. There weren't many of Silva's things left – some pyjamas, underwear and an orange alarm clock. But looking at those few items, he felt a sharp pain he hadn't expected. He looked at Silva's clothes, her pens, her hairbrush, and he felt the realization of her absence all over again. He noticed there were no family photos anywhere. If the police hadn't taken them, that meant she hadn't had any in her room. That explained why the girls hadn't recognized him.

They looked at him suspiciously.

This isn't a good idea, he thought. It wasn't smart to come here.

Jakov went out into the corridor. Stopping briefly, he leaned on the cold wall and took a few deep breaths, allowing the weakness to pass. Then the brunette followed him out. Mirna, he recalled. Silva had said Mirna wore braces on her teeth. The girl approached and spoke to him under her breath, as if they were conspirators in a plot. "I didn't wanna say anything in front of her," she said. "But this had to happen."

"What had to happen?"

"What happened to her. It had to happen. No one's gonna tell the truth here. And the truth is that she had it coming."

Jakov looked at her, stunned. "Had what coming?"

"That. Everything. Whatever happened, she deserved it, the bitch. She got half the girls in the dorm hooked on smack. It must have been her dealers who killed her."

"Her dealers?"

"Them. That Cvitko. He used to come here to see her. What a guy."

Jakov stood in the corridor and listened to her. He listened to a girl with braces as she trashed his daughter. Right then, he wanted to throw her onto the linoleum floor and lay into her with his fists and his feet until he reached hard, raw bone.

"But please," she said, "don't write that. Don't say that I told you, you hear me?"

He nodded, and the girl looked relieved. She motioned to leave and Jakov watched as she waved goodbye and disappeared back into the room.

Jakov left the building. The south-easterly wind had picked up. A wave of heavy, suffocating rancidity almost knocked him to the ground.

The next day, Jakov resolved to find Cvitko. On the way to Split, on the coastal road, he noticed his hands trembling as they gripped the wheel. He became aware of a new and unfamiliar feeling: fear.

He arrived in Split just as the city was taking its morning coffee. He parked on Manđerova and walked around Manuš looking for a cafe called The Butterfly. It didn't take long to find it. The cafe was located near a garage and consisted of a small, dark interior and a terrace with a cover of plastic and glass. The cafe looked ordinary, no different to dozens of others.

Sitting down on the bench opposite The Butterfly, Jakov opened a newspaper, pretending to read it. He was prepared to wait for hours if necessary, but the man he was looking for was already there.

He recognized him immediately. Cvitković was sitting at a table by the door, in a green Adidas tracksuit. He looked like any other local lout, an unshaven dropout with the beginnings of a beer belly. He looked at ease, relaxed, like a man without any serious problems in life, swigging from a bottle and reading the write-up on Hajduk Split's away win at Spartak Subotica in Serbia. He took a gulp of beer and started talking to the server. Jakov couldn't make out exactly what they were saying, but it was obvious it was about soccer.

Jakov sat in wait for almost half an hour. Finally, Cvitko finished his beer, left some money on the table and stood up. It was only then that Jakov saw how tall he was. Despite signs of gaining weight, Silva's dealer was a well-proportioned and athletic man.

Cvitko pulled on his sunglasses, stuffed his rolled-up newspaper under his arm and left in the direction of the city centre. Jakov followed.

After a while, Cvitko turned into a side street in the direction of Veli Varoš. He walked through a labyrinth of abandoned, ruined hovels, once home to small farmers who lived in the city but had rights to cultivate land outside it. He turned into a secluded courtyard; Jakov stopped and peered inside.

The courtyard was in fact the empty cavern of a building that had long ago fallen into ruin. Rubble and burned timber lay on the ground and the remains of ceramic tiles stuck out from the wall of the adjacent house. It wasn't immediately clear to Jakov what Cvitko was doing there. Then he understood. The man in the green tracksuit set his newspaper and sunglasses on the ground. Then he turned to face the wall, unzipped his trousers and started to piss. It went on for ages, and he was obviously savouring the moment. When he finished, Cvitko left the courtyard and continued zigzagging through the maze of pedestrian streets towards the south, then the west. Jakov followed. At one point, the man in the tracksuit stopped at the window of an optician. Not wanting Cvitko to notice him, Jakov continued down the street and hid around the corner. When the man set off again, Jakov set off too.

Cvitko turned onto Lenjingradska and headed north. He walked for a few minutes and then turned east into a narrow street that led to the Church of the Holy Cross. Jakov followed.

When he reached the church, the man in the tracksuit cut through the churchyard. He again headed west until he came out near the old gasworks. He headed south. Jakov followed, increasingly aware how pointless it all was. Silva's dealer was walking in a circle, his route empty and aimless. He made a figure of eight within a hundred metres, and Jakov did the same.

They were back at the same rubble-strewn courtyard where they had already been. When he turned the corner, Jakov lost sight of Cvitko. He thought briefly that he had lost him. But there he was, standing tall at the same spot where he'd pissed against the wall. He looked at his watch, clearly waiting for someone.

And someone arrived. A skinny girl with long hair entered the courtyard carrying a limp backpack and dressed in a coat that was far too warm for early autumn. She nodded at Cvitko, and he nodded to her.

Jakov looked at the girl. In contrast to the heavy coat, she wore light linen tennis shoes without socks. She looked abandoned. She was roughly Silva's age, but her face had a disconcerting maturity about it.

When the girl arrived, Cvitko glanced around and called her into the nearest doorway. They didn't stay long. When they emerged, the girl hurried away.

Jakov waited for Cvitko to go too. He thought for a second, then decided to follow the girl instead. He quickly caught up with her in the street below the Church of the Holy Cross. The girl was walking towards the city centre. She crossed Prokurative Square, cast a cursory glance at the cinema billboard and continued in the direction of the fish market, which by that time of day was already empty. She entered the Roman city-palace built for the emperor Diocletian and continued east along the main pedestrian street. At the adult education centre she turned the corner and came out in a square between houses. The skinny girl leaned against a wall and lit a cigarette. Jakov hid in a doorway waiting for her to set off again. But she didn't. For a long time she stood there doing nothing. Jakov began to think it had been a mistake to follow her.

Then a lad, slightly older, approached the girl. He wore a Spitfire jacket and an earring in one ear. He said something, and the girl nodded. He gave her some money and she gave him a packet wrapped in cellophane. Jakov didn't know much about drugs, but he knew enough to know what that was called: smack. She had sold him smack. The girl was dealing, and obviously for Cvitko.

Jakov stayed there, standing in the doorway and watching the scene in silent consternation. A girl, probably no older than Silva, perhaps a friend, was dealing drugs in broad daylight on a square in the city centre. She had three or four more customers over the next hour. They'd hand her the money and she'd give them the goods from her backpack.

At about four, Jakov considered calling off his surveillance and leaving. But then another buyer turned up, a thin, stooped kid with shaggy hair. He looked a little scared. He approached the girl, but timidly, as if he didn't know her or didn't trust her. He mumbled something and she nodded.

He took out the money and offered it to her. She gave him a package. And then the skinny kid asked her a question. He asked it loud enough that Jakov could hear: "Where's Silva?"

The girl replied, but too quietly for Jakov to make out what she said. Nevertheless, it was clear to him what he had just witnessed. The buyer knew Silva. He was surprised not to see her. He had expected her to be there. He had expected to buy from her.

Jakov waited for the buyer to leave. He left the doorway and headed in the direction of his car. He passed the Museum of the Revolution and the main post office and came out on the square by the theatre. It was at the theatre that he felt his heart beating irregularly, felt that he was suffocating.

He stopped by a wall and swallowed a pill, without water. He walked around the city for a while, aimlessly, until the tablet started to work. Then he got in his car and sat behind the wheel. He remained there, calmly, for half an hour, until he felt his blood pressure come down. Only then did he set off back to Misto.

Jakov didn't go straight home. He left the car in front of the house and set off on foot to the village centre and then the other side of the cove. He took the path behind the last houses, the path that ran along the wall of the cistern and up the hill. Within ten minutes he was at Cape Cross, at the spot where his daughter was last seen.

The cross stood at the top of a round hill above the village. It had been raised by the Brotherhood of St Spyridon at the time of the phylloxera as a pledge to God, who had sent them the plague and mercifully destroyed the vineyards. The cross was the peasants' pledge, and it looked like one – plain, without decoration, made of four rough limestone slabs. It stood on a platform of steps, and on those steps, in the summer months, would sit the more adventurous tourists, taking in the vista. The steps afforded a view of Misto and the bay, the first row of islands and the sharp, serrated ravines of the nearest mountains.

Jakov sat down on the platform and looked out towards Misto. The sun had just set in the west, the aureole darkening to crimson as it slipped behind the Prosika ridge. There wasn't a hint of wind. The surface of the sea was as flat as a tabletop, and the houses and harbour were barely visible through the early evening mist. Beneath Jakov's feet stretched the old municipal cistern. Before the water system had been built, the locals had cemented the steep slope of the hill to catch and contain rainwater for the summer during the wet months. Then, in the 1960s, Misto was connected to the water system and no one ever needed the cistern again. Moss and mould grew over the cement slope and marjoram and fennel sprouted from the cracks.

When he was younger, Jakov would go to the cross for the same reason as Silva had done that night. Couples would go there for the seclusion, to touch, nip and lick in the dark, far from prying eyes. Jakov had last gone there with Vesna, a few months before their wedding. They had laid his coat on the ground, had sex and waited, locked in each other's arms, for dawn and the sun to rise. Jakov remembered how terribly cold he had felt without a coat on before dawn.

Now he was looking at that same spot, twenty years later. But he didn't think about that distant morning, about shivering at dawn in just a T-shirt, with Vesna's arm around his shoulders. He thought about Silva, who had been in that very same place on the night of 23 September; Silva, who had led Adrijan to that dark, hidden spot, or had been led by him. And something had happened, there or somewhere else.

He stood up and looked around. He looked in the bushes under the cross and spotted a discarded condom wrapper. A sharp, unsettling shiver shot through him. Then he saw another discarded wrapper, and another. He saw used and discarded condoms, one after another. Jakov couldn't tell how long they had been there. There were too many to count. The bushes under the cross had patiently archived the traces of decades of fornication.

Looking around, Jakov tried to imagine the spot where Silva and Adrijan had lain. He searched for where the ground looked soft and trampled, without stones or brambles. He spotted a place that seemed to fit. He felt the ground with his fingers, as if the grass and earth might have preserved Silva's warmth. He poked around in the surrounding bushes with a stick. Then something caught his attention. In a clump of Spanish broom he spied an off-white object, plastic and cylindrical. He picked it up. It was a syringe, the leftovers of an injection.

He studied the cylinder and tried to determine how old it might be. It was smeared with earth, dirty and battered. It seemed to Jakov that it must have been there for some time. He wished that were the case. But he couldn't be sure. When it came to Silva, he was no longer sure of anything.

Meanwhile, the sun had gone down behind Prosika and small boats began emerging from the harbour. The locals went out trolling for fish at dusk. *Pasaras* and *gajetas* slipped through water smooth and dark like ink, and the quiet, intermittent rattle of diesel boats could be heard from the cove. At 7.30, the bell of St Spyridon rang for evening Mass. By way of defiant reply, the sound of a trumpet came from the Communist army barracks as the flag was lowered. Night after night, church and army battled it out for the soul of Misto. Another day was coming to an end, another ordinary day. So ordinary, Jakov thought, that it stung.

He stood up. He still held the ugly, dirty syringe in his hand. Unsure what to do with it, he slipped it into his pocket. Jakov set off on the steep goat trail, then the wider dirt path that led past the cistern. He soon reached the first houses.

If Adrijan was telling the truth, Jakov was at the exact spot where Silva had last been seen. She had taken that same path, trodden the same furrows over the same sea-beaten stones pressed into bare earth. Then she had missed a turn and vanished as if in a puff of smoke.

Jakov still had the remains of the syringe in his pocket. He wondered what to do with it. Finally, he came to the first fork, where a trash can stood. He looked around. There was no one there. He wrapped the syringe in a tissue and threw it away.

He walked down to the village centre and headed for the old part. Darkness had fallen, and as he walked between the houses he saw windows illuminated by the light from television screens. He could hear the evening news. There were demonstrations among Albanians in Kosovo, in the south of Yugoslavia.

When he got home, Jakov quietly took off his shoes and coat in the hall. He opened the living room door a crack and saw Mate poring over his homework. Mate looked at him quizzically.

He entered the bedroom and Vesna rushed in after him. She had clearly been nervously waiting for him. "Did you find him?" she asked. "Did you talk to him?"

Jakov fell silent, as if unsure what to say. "I found him," he eventually said.

"And? What did you find out?"

Jakov hesitated, as if weighing up the best response. And then he decided. He decided on the least painful course. "Nothing," he said. "I didn't find out anything. He's never heard of Silva. And he didn't recognize her from the photo either."

"I knew it," said Vesna. "I knew it. I know my Silva. Someone planted that stuff on her." Closing the bedroom door, Vesna said it again, only quieter, so as not to be overheard.

"Someone set her up," she said. "And that someone is *here*. In Misto."

4
MATE (1989)

By the beginning of November, the days were shorter and the Dalmatian autumn had finally descended on Misto.

The beach bars had already closed at the end of September, followed by the only pizzeria and two out of the three cafes. In the first week of October, the bus service was cut back and the tourist office closed its doors. In the second week, the sky darkened and a sapping, unrelenting rain fell for days on end, drenching everything. The rain, heavy and monotonous, inundated Cape Cross and the Stella Maris chapel, Prosika and Rokov's Land, the harbour and the barracks, the mountain and the channel. Dry land turned to soggy mud, and in the craggy hollow of the quarry sinkholes and pools of water appeared where during the summer it had been lifelessly dry. The rain fell and fell, and Mate's father, watching from the balcony, said one day: "Whatever traces there might have been, the rain has swept them away."

There was still no sign of Silva. Weeks passed, and the police were in touch less and less. Inspector Šain would call every five or six days, but the little information he had for them became increasingly vague. It was as if the police had run out of ideas.

Mate still took the bus to school every morning and back in the afternoon, back to a home he found harder and harder to bear. His father generally wasn't around. He'd sit in his car early in the morning with a bundle of posters and wander around God knows where, conducting his own little investigation that Mate struggled to understand. Sometimes he'd see him in Split, hurrying sullen-faced along the street, immersed in something he no longer shared with them. Mate had the impression Jakov was simply wandering around so as not to go home. He could understand that. For the last few weeks he had also felt better anywhere but home.

His mother, on the other hand, was there constantly. In the first few days, Mate's father told her it would be good if someone was always in the house, "to wait by the phone". It seemed Vesna had taken that literally. She hardly left the house at all, except on the rare occasion when she would go to church. After a brief attempt to return to work, she was again on sick leave. She didn't even go to the shops. She spent entire days lying on the sofa staring at the ceiling, numb, unmoving, the radio always on at her side. The news told of political parties being founded and preparations made for the first ever multiparty elections. In Hungary, protesters had declared a new constitution, and in East Germany, Communist first secretary Honecker had resigned. The world was changing, but right then neither Vesna nor Mate could care less.

Their home was gradually changing too. Vesna didn't cook any more; clothes weren't washed; the dust wasn't wiped. Every day, Mate would do the bare minimum, like boil their underwear. Taking money from the cookie tin, he would go to the shop and buy something simple to prepare – frankfurters, tinned tomato sauce or canned peas. He'd make lunch and wash the dishes. He tried at least to keep the kitchen tidy. But he lost the battle with the rest of the house. Layers of dust piled up, brambles took over the yard and the stack of ironing grew higher and higher. The house itself seemed to be asleep and completely still. It was as if nothing had moved on since that Sunday in September. Everything was resting, motionless, in anticipation: Silva's tidy bed, the television that was never turned on, the pages of the calendar that were never turned, Jakov's radio gear, his electronics, dismantled and forgotten. Everything was hibernating, as if sleeping through the winter, waiting for some magic kiss that would bring the house back to life.

Sometimes, though not often, Mate would sneak into his sister's room. He'd slip inside when Vesna wasn't paying attention, and she hardly paid attention to anything any more. He would open the door on which was written *Keep out* and step inside, without turning on the light. He'd sit on the bed, taking in any sounds or smells. The room still smelled of Silva, that sharp, dark scent that Mate remembered she called patchouli. The smell had penetrated her pillows, her clothes, pyjamas, even the curtains.

He would stand there in the half-dark and look at his sister's things. As in every child's room, the stages of growth were reflected on its walls: in the corners, out of the way, were the picture books, the garish scrapbooks, the Garfield stickers on the bed's wooden headboard; posters and music cassettes, the ephemera of adolescence, had gradually taken over the central space. Then, at some point, it was as if Silva had lost interest in that too. With surprise, Mate realized there had come a time when Silva had stopped listening to music and having ordinary, teenage conversations. It had happened overnight, and he hadn't even noticed.

Mate sat there in her room and again, for the umpteenth time, looked at Silva's things – children's books, her school atlas, old paints, her globe with its gold meridian. He looked at her cassettes, the music she listened to: Sade, UB40, Dire Straits, Grace Jones and Yugoslav band Idoli. He looked at all the music Silva had left behind, all the clothes, all those unnecessary things she hadn't taken with her.

He looked and thought back. He thought back to the summers when they would swim beneath the Stella Maris chapel, roam the fractured rock, prise off limpets with stones and store them in buckets filled with seawater. He remembered collecting bottle tops in front of Agata's store and getting a Coke for every handful. He remembered Silva playing soccer, the only girl among all the guys on the basketball court near the entrance to the barracks. She wasn't bad at soccer. She was nimble and quick and the ball would stick to her right foot.

Silva had always been there, from uterus to nursery, from the placenta to the Monday morning bus to school. There wasn't a single recollection or scrap of his life that Silva wasn't part of. He thought it was also true the other way around. But it wasn't. Silva had her other life, a parallel life, a life Mate wasn't part of. He felt betrayed. But such thoughts served no purpose, and Mate would drive them away. He stood up, straightened out Silva's bed and left her room. He closed the door bearing the words *Keep out* and went to check on Vesna.

Adrijan Lekaj was arrested on the morning of 23 October, before dawn.

Mate remembered it well. Since Silva's disappearance he had struggled to sleep and always woke early. He woke up tired that morning too. He stood at the window and looked out at Misto, at the grey, damp morning. Everything was still asleep: the houses, the church tower, the harbour and the boats in the marina. Half an hour would pass before he'd hear the familiar sounds: the workers' bus, the newspaper delivery van, the St Spyridon bell, the wake-up siren at the barracks.

But that morning he heard other sounds. He heard the sound of cars, lots of them, heading down the coastal road in the direction of Misto. Then he heard voices coming from the square in front of the church. Then a brief siren and something that sounded like a walkie-talkie.

Police, he thought. He didn't wake his mother. Or his father, who had come home late. He rushed out of the house in the direction of the square.

He saw a police van in front of Lekaj's bakery and around it several police officers holding rifles. The doors of the bakery were shut, but shouting could be heard from inside the house.

The residents began to gather. Mate spotted the parish priest, Father Dražen, not in his clerical robes but an ordinary shirt. He spotted a few of the factory workers. He saw Brane too, standing to one side and staring at the scene unfolding.

Then Adrijan was brought out, struggling in the grip of three officers. Adrijan's father, the old baker Lekaj, came to the door. He stood in the doorway with a face like he wished the ground would open up and swallow him. Adrijan cried out as they bundled him into the van, begging to be released because he hadn't done anything.

At that point, Mate caught sight of Gorki Šain, standing in silence in civilian clothes next to the van, as if overseeing the performance. Mate approached and asked what was happening. Inspector Šain ignored him, as if ignoring a child.

The police officers climbed into their cars and drove off through the crowd. Mate ran home and woke his parents. He told them that Adrijan had been arrested.

Jakov called Inspector Šain's number, but there was no answer. He kept calling, in vain. In the end, he decided to drive to Split and wait outside his office until he found out what was going on. Mate and his mother stayed at home, at the kitchen table, waiting anxiously. At one point Mate asked Vesna whether she'd like him to make her a cup of tea, but when he saw the look of outrage on her face he dropped the idea.

They waited for hours. It was early afternoon before Jakov returned. As soon as he saw him, Mate knew the news wasn't good.

"They got an anonymous tip-off," Jakov said.

It had arrived in the evening, from a payphone. An unidentified person had called, speaking through a cloth, their voice obscured. From the accent, it sounded like someone local. They said that Adrijan Lekaj had struck Silva with a piece of wood and killed her. The caller said they would find the wood in Lekaj's *konoba*. He was very precise about where.

Vesna screwed up her face in horror. Mate stood there stunned. Up until then, the idea that Silva might be dead had been a theoretical possibility, but at no point had Mate actually believed it.

"And did they find the wood?" asked Vesna.

"Yes," said Jakov.

It was right where they had been told it would be, beneath a stainless steel barrel, behind some old brooms. The piece of wood fitted the description. There were nails sticking out, which potentially made it a lethal weapon, and it had whitewash marks on it, some drops of boat paint, and traces of blood. They still didn't know what blood type.

As he listened to his father, a cold, bitter mass formed in Mate's stomach. He tried to imagine Silva's face, bloodied and mangled. He imagined Adrijan in a murderous rage. But in front of him he saw another Adrijan – in shorts, pathetic, watching Italian soccer.

"And what did he say?" Mate asked his father. "What did Adrijan say?"

"Nothing useful," Jakov replied. "He denies everything. He doesn't know anything about anything. He claims he's never seen the piece of wood before and doesn't know how it got there. He still claims he left Silva alive at one o'clock."

"So what now?" asked Vesna.

"Nothing. He's still there, at the police station. They're interrogating him."

"What does Šain say?" Vesna asked insistently.

"I spoke to Tenžer, not Šain. He said they'll break him. If he's done anything at all, they'll break him. They won't let him go till he confesses. That's what he said."

Jakov sat down impotently at the table. But Mate wasn't going to wait. He pulled on his shoes and left the house, heading downhill along St Spyridon Street.

He couldn't get the pictures out of his head: the wood with Silva's blood on it; Silva lying in some sinkhole or pit, covered in branches, slowly rotting until she dissolved into some unrecognizable mass, while her family sat there despairing.

Mate reached the square in front of the church. Lekaj's bakery was shut. In front of it was the baker's van. All four tyres had been slashed and letters sprayed the length of one side, big blue letters that read: MURDERER.

Adrijan was released after three days. He appeared unexpectedly, without warning, just the way he was taken away. Those who witnessed his arrival said Adrijan simply climbed off the bus, without reception or escort. He limped home, entered his father's house and lay down on the sofa. He took off his T-shirt, and underneath – they said – could be seen the marks from the blows.

Unfortunately, it was Vesna who heard the news first. Worse still, she heard it from a pupil in school. At Jakov's urging, Vesna had gone back to work. That morning, tanked up on pills, she had barely got up in time for morning lessons. She made it through the first two hours, and then, during the third, just as she was explaining the Cordillera relief to her students, one of them informed her that he had seen Adrijan that morning, a free man. Vesna ended the lesson and hurried home. The expression on her face said: *What are you going to do about it?*

A heavy, bleak rain had been falling since the morning. Lekaj's bakery had been shut all day and the window shutters closed. Adrijan had stolen into the house and not left since. The one man who knew what had happened to Silva was there, in the next street, behind closed shutters. He was within reach, yet they couldn't do a thing.

Mate remembers that unbearable afternoon. Jakov sat at the kitchen table looking straight ahead, at a loss to offer any kind of solution. Vesna's eyes bore into him, full of loathing. She expected something, though it was hard to say what: a blood feud, retribution, abduction, a tortured confession... Whatever she expected, Mate's father didn't do it, because he didn't do anything at all. He sat there staring at the kitchen wall, at the painted Jesus with tired eyes, as if waiting for Him to perform some biblical miracle. For the first time in his life, Mate didn't feel sorry for Jakov. No longer was he a grown-up, mature, protective father. Mate saw a new father before him, little more than a helpless child.

Gorki Šain came round that evening, alone and unannounced. Turning down an offer of coffee, he sat down at the table and said immediately that the police had had no choice but to release Adrijan.

They didn't have anything on him, he said. He passed the lie-detector test without a hitch. His fingerprints weren't on the wood. His fingerprints weren't even in the *konoba*.

"Whose blood was it?" asked Vesna.

The blood type was O positive, like Silva's. But that's the most common type – two thirds of people are O positive."

"And the anonymous tip-off? Where did that come from?" asked Vesna.

"We know that it came from Misto. Only that, nothing else."

"Someone knows," said Vesna. "Someone saw. Someone from Misto. And now they're not talking."

"Maybe. Maybe not. People do all sorts of stupid stuff over the phone."

"And the wood?" Mate interrupted, grown-up, obstinate. "The wood didn't get there by phone."

"True. We can't explain the wood."

"So what now?"

"Nothing. We keep at it."

"And him?" said Vesna. "The murderer? He's a free man?"

"*If* he's the killer," said Šain. "Yes, he's free for now."

Šain got up and moved towards the door. In the hallway, he turned back, as if about to apologize. "It's not over yet," he said. "We'll keep at it." He pulled on his jacket and shook hands with all of them, Mate too.

As the inspector was about to leave, Vesna asked the question all three of them wanted to know the answer to. "And what do you think?" she said. "What do you think about it?"

"About what?" replied Šain.

"You know what. What do you think? Was it him? Is she alive? Or did he kill her?"

"I don't know."

"I know you don't know. But what do you think? What does your – what is it – your intuition tell you?"

Mate remembers that moment. The inspector stood in the doorway, hesitating, as if weighing up his words. "I don't know," he said. "Intuition doesn't tell me anything."

"I think you know," replied Vesna. "You know but you can't say."

"I don't. Really I don't."

"You know. I know you know." And Vesna closed the door, without a word of goodbye.

That evening, Mate took a decision. If his father wasn't going to do anything, he would.

First, he waited for his parents to go to bed. Then, at about one o'clock, he put on his trainers and a dark hoodie. He slipped out and went down the slope behind Lekaj's house.

He came to the cooperative van parked on a dry patch of grass by the road. The van had been bought by the olive cooperative years ago, when olives from Misto were taken to the oil mill in the city. Then the oil mill had gone under and the cooperative had fallen apart. With no owner, the van had sat there, forgotten, at the side of the road. Children climbed on it, and anything of any value – wheel rims, wipers, windows – was stolen.

Since he had left custody, Adrijan had not dared leave the house during the day. But Mate knew that late at night, when the village was still, he came out to catch some fresh air. He would emerge through the delivery doors at the side where his father brought in flour. He did it every night, and Mate knew he'd do it again.

For a long time, Mate crouched behind the van. The night was quiet and still. The evening had been windy, but the north-easterly *bura* had subsided around midnight. There was the distant, muffled sound of a television, and the odd truck passing along the coastal road. Lekaj's house was in darkness. Then, suddenly, a light came on above the delivery doors and Adrijan appeared, cloaked in a windcheater. He stood on the empty road, directly beneath the street light like a moth drawn to the filament. Mate noticed that he had lost weight. He took a drag on a cigarette, seeming to enjoy it.

Mate hesitated only briefly. Then he leaped from his hiding place. Knocking Adrijan to the ground, Mate laid into him with his feet. Adrijan curled up, covering his head with his arms and his stomach with his knees, as if waiting for it all to pass. He didn't call for help. He didn't make a sound.

As he kicked him, Mate saw again the pictures that had been in his head for days: blood on wood; Silva's body, covered in branches, rotting in the damp. He pictured her, and he kicked and kicked and kicked. "Where is she?" he hissed. "Where did you hide her? Say where she is."

But Adrijan didn't respond. He just lay there silently, shrivelled up, folded in on himself and waiting for the blows to pass. Every time Mate struck him he would let out only a short yelp of pain.

Lights started to come on; voices could be heard. After a few minutes, Mate heard the sound of someone coming down the street. He moved away quickly, looking back only when he was far enough away. Adrijan lay on the ground like a lifeless rag, blood coming from his eye sockets and mouth.

Mate wandered around for a good hour, waiting for his heart to stop racing. He got home after three o'clock. He got into bed and stared at the ceiling for the rest of the night. He had no idea what might happen next, whether the police would come for him.

Nothing happened. Adrijan didn't report the attack. He didn't go to the police or tell anyone what happened.

But he started to go out. The next morning he appeared on the square, brazen, as if everything was fine, as if it was any normal, quiet Sunday morning. His injuries were plain to see. His lips were scabbed and swollen, one eye purple, sockets battered. He was limping. Adrijan was showing off his wounds, like a trophy, as if he were the victim.

That morning, Mate saw him. He had walked down into Misto and seen Adrijan standing in front of his father's bakery. Their eyes met. Adrijan's were full of hatred and contempt. Mate picked up his pace towards the cove. In the marina there was the smell of burning and signs of a fire. He spotted a plastic boat that had obviously gone up in flames in the night. It was a small white *pasara* with a cabin and outboard motor. The plastic was shrivelled and black from the flames.

Mate knew who it belonged to. But there was something he didn't know – which righteous local had set fire to it. Whoever it was, one thing was certain. Literally everyone would think it was him.

5

JAKOV (1989–1990)

Misto readied for New Year 1990 as it did every year. In the run-up, local kids armed themselves with pyrotechnic delights. They set garbage containers alight with flares and lobbed firecrackers at passers-by and cats; the village reverberated with explosions like a war zone.

The villagers crowded into Midnight Mass like never before. Father Dražen spoke of a great hope on the horizon and the need to take responsibility for the enslaved homeland. For New Year's Eve, like every year, the municipality laid on fireworks. But it was a poor display, as if the state and those who led it no longer had the energy even for that.

More than three months had passed since Silva's disappearance. The police were still looking, but the information grew thinner and offered less and less hope. Jakov called Šain from time to time, but it was obvious the inspector had nothing new to tell him. "We're searching," he would say. "We've searched everywhere, but we'll keep searching." Jakov wondered what this "searching" actually looked like.

Jakov was searching too. He no longer plastered posters all over Hercegovina and Dalmatia, seeing little sense in it any more. Instead, he wandered the village looking for where the body might be. He wandered about the heath and in the bushes. He roamed the hillside all the way to Prosika. He spent days searching the canyon, the old caravan route to Bosnia. He wandered gorges where bandits had lurked long ago. He staggered around like a tormented soul, searching for what he wished never to find, for the mound of a shallow grave, for a body concealed by branches, tossed into a sinkhole or dry riverbed. He searched for his dead daughter, all the time happy not to find her.

Four days after Adrijan's release, his father came to their door asking to talk. He knocked, and it was Vesna who opened the door. Lekaj tried to convince her that Adrijan hadn't done anything, but they both knew the old baker could not claim that with complete certainty. Vesna sent him packing. Jakov was upstairs in the kitchen the entire time. He listened through the door to the voices and the curses, but he didn't go down, he didn't intervene. As he eavesdropped on Vesna, he noticed Mate. His son was looking at him, and in that look Jakov thought he saw condemnation. As if Mate saw in him a pathetic coward.

The next day, old Lekaj reopened the bakery. The first few days it stayed empty; no one bought his bread. But people need bread, and the nearest alternative was miles away. Lekaj's customers soon came back. Buying his bread, they would look at the floor – both he and his customers. They would count the change, grab the warm loaf and hurry out without saying goodbye.

And the whole time Adrijan didn't leave the house. Old Lekaj told the locals he wasn't there, that he had packed him off to relatives in Kosovo. But everyone knew that was a lie. Adrijan was there, in the baker's house, hidden away and silent behind four walls, as if already in prison. Whatever he had seen, whatever he knew, he kept to himself, leaving everyone else in an unbearable state of uncertainty.

At the beginning of December, Jakov went back to his office. But not to work, since even with the best will in the world he was incapable of being productive. He would sit there at the south-facing window from seven till three, staring at columns of numbers on pieces of paper and realizing in horror that they made no sense. Not even with the greatest mental effort could he understand what was in front of him.

With the start of the year, the political crisis deepened. On every corner the talk was of a military coup that never came. On New Year's Day, trying to tackle runaway inflation, the government devalued the currency and knocked three zeros off the dinar. At the end of January, Croatian and Slovenian Communists walked out of the Party congress in Belgrade. It was as if the state no longer existed.

In the meantime, this political chaos spilled over into the factory. Wages were late for the first time ever. The company for which they made boat fenders went under. In early January the workers threatened to go on strike and the director, trying to placate them, promised cuts in the factory management. Jakov knew there was only one reason why he wasn't fired: his daughter. They didn't fire him because he wore a flak jacket made of sympathy.

The first multiparty elections were held in February. In a matter of weeks, a new type of person appeared in Misto: tall men who spoke in deep, honeyed tones and dressed in smart white shirts. They would sit in the front row at Mass and afterwards hold forth in the Lantern cafe, sleeves rolled up. They would talk politics with resoluteness, full of confident authority, until late in the night; before closing, the proprietor would bring them a tray of prosciutto and cheese on the house.

Pay was late again at the factory. The director had begun to despair. No longer could he simply call the committee to solve the problem. The country was descending into chaos.

And then came that Wednesday. Jakov remembers it well. It was Ash Wednesday. The day before – Shrove Tuesday – Misto had prepared a fancy dress parade, but the parade was spoiled by heavy rain. On the Wednesday, Jakov was sitting in his office, not doing the work for which he was anyway not being paid. Through the window he could see the sea. A strong east wind was blowing. Heavy, menacing clouds had gathered above the first row of islands and as the wind strengthened it created a white-crested grid of colliding swells. The first drops of rain had started to hit the windowpane, fat and heavy. A muffled banging came from somewhere on the factory premises as the wind slammed the metal doors shut.

At about 10.30, the telephone rang. It was Šain. "I think we have a development," he said. "A good one. It seems Silva is alive."

"Where is she?" asked Jakov.

"We don't know, but she was seen the next morning buying a bus ticket. Silva really did go away."

"Which means…?"

"That she's alive," Šain repeated. "That's what it means. That she's alive."

Jakov met Elda Zuvan the following morning.

When he called her, she sounded friendly and immediately agreed to meet. Elda worked in the Split branch of Belgrade's Yugobank. She suggested they meet during her break, in the public garden along the Workers' Promenade directly below her office. Jakov took Mate with him. They arrived at the agreed spot ten minutes early, but Elda was already there.

She proposed that they sit in a nearby cafe where they could talk in peace.

Elda was younger than Jakov had imagined, with short hair, bleached and styled. Hazelnut eyes suggested that she originally had dark hair beneath the peroxide. She had a youthful air about her but was dressed conservatively given that she worked in a bank: blue skirt and jacket, white shirt.

Sitting in the cafe, Jakov noticed the way Mate studied the woman with them, like a man observing a woman dressed to the nines.

Having ordered a coffee, Elda pulled from her pocket a crumpled, rolled-up piece of paper. She flattened it out. It was a missing poster with Silva's picture on it, one of the posters Jakov had plastered all over the city. From the crumpled paper, from behind a few strands of restless hair, Silva looked at them. Silva, whose photograph had been taken by a stranger and who had gone away without a word.

"I'm sorry you didn't hear all of this earlier," said Elda. "It's just the way it turned out."

She proceeded to tell them once more what Šain had already said in brief: that she had returned to Croatia the previous week after six months abroad; that she had seen the poster on a lamp post in her neighbourhood; and that she remembered seeing a girl who looked exactly the same in a queue for bus tickets.

That day, Elda had been standing in line at the international counter of the bus station in Split. She had bought a ticket, and the girl was behind her.

"I'm sorry I didn't get in touch earlier," Elda said.

She had been travelling, having earned a six-month Spanish language scholarship in Salamanca. She had wanted to make the most of the trip, so she had bought an Interrail pass and travelled across Spain and Portugal. Her film had been developed, and she took the photographs out of an envelope and showed them to Jakov and Mate.

Elda was in all the pictures, generally alone: Elda in Barcelona; in Avila; in Lisbon; in front of the aqueduct in Segovia; in Plaza Mayor in Salamanca; outside Santiago de Compostela Cathedral. In every photograph, Elda was smiling happily, looking even younger with her hair slightly longer.

"I was completely cut off," she said. "I didn't follow the news here. When I came back, I saw her face everywhere. Then I remembered. If only I'd remembered earlier, I'd have spared you so much suffering."

As Elda put away the photographs, Mate began asking questions, as if he were the older, more composed of the two men. Jakov was surprised to find it didn't bother him any more, that he had grown used to it.

"Where precisely did you see her?" Mate asked.

"At the counter."

"The international counter?"

"Yes. That's the counter only for international tickets."

"Exactly when was it?"

"That morning. That Saturday."

"Sunday," Mate corrected her.

"Yes, Sunday. I remember it was the weekend."

"What time was it?"

"About nine, maybe a bit before ten. I bought a ticket to Trieste, and in Trieste I got the train to Milan. And she bought a ticket."

"You don't know where to?"

"No," said Elda. "I was in front of her in the queue."

"Are you sure it was her?" Jakov asked.

"I'm sure," Elda replied. "We talked. I remembered her. She told me her name, Silva. She wasn't someone you'd forget – beautiful, striking. In front of us there was a group of Danes with big backpacks who were constantly arguing with the woman at the counter. They were really annoying. We were complaining to each other about them."

"Then what happened?" asked Mate.

"Nothing. I bought my ticket. It was her turn. We said goodbye, I wished her a good time. That was the last time I saw her."

"She didn't say where she was travelling?"

"No."

"You don't know what type of ticket she asked for?"

"No. I left straight away, I was in a hurry."

"Did she seem worried to you?" asked Jakov.

"No. She didn't."

"Was anyone with her?"

"No. I'm sure about that. She was alone."

Jakov looked at her. He looked at that girl with short hair and thought how no one had changed his life so much in such a short space of time. But still he wanted to find out more. He knew now that Silva was alive, but nothing else.

The bank clerk seemed to discern a slight disappointment in Jakov's face. "I wish I could have been more help," she told him as they said goodbye.

You don't know how much you've helped us, Jakov thought. Like no one ever before.

Jakov and Mate left the cafe and drove towards the bus station. Looking for a place to park in the ferry terminal, he felt his chest expand with new-found hope. For weeks he had imagined Silva dead, imagined that unknown, unavoidable day when he would find her decayed body in some sinkhole, cave or olive grove. After meeting Elda, he knew it wouldn't come to that. He knew Silva was somewhere. He didn't know where or why, or the reason for her silence. But he knew she was alive.

Arriving at the bus station, he and Mate headed to the international counter and asked for whoever was on duty that Sunday. A woman came out, but told them what she had already told the police, that she didn't remember the girl or her destination. She didn't even remember the Danes with the backpacks. "You know how busy it gets here in peak season," she said.

They studied the bus timetable, looking for an international service leaving at around nine o'clock. There weren't any. Jakov realized they were looking at the winter timetable. They asked the woman to find them a summer timetable. Rifling through drawers, she handed them one.

Jakov took it and his eyes travelled down the columns of place names and numbers. Number nine read: Stuttgart 9.05; Trieste 9.20; Frankfurt 9.35; Graz 9.50. He put the piece of paper down without speaking.

They didn't go straight back to the car, but left the bus station and walked along the seafront of the ferry port. The port was half-empty; boats rocked on the waves of the southerly *šilok*; a few lorries rolled onto rain-soaked ferries carrying cement, bricks, milk and flour to the islands. They watched as the stevedore pulled the rope from the bollard and the ferry, almost empty in winter, set off for one or other of the islands. They watched as the ferry manoeuvred to turn and exit the port.

Finally, Mate spoke. "She could have gone anywhere," he said. "Trieste, Frankfurt, Austria. Anywhere."

Jakov didn't reply. He just watched as the ferry completed its turn and passed through the mouth of the port into the channel.

The following Sunday, Vesna asked him to go to Mass with her. He went, for the first time in a decade.

Jakov remembers that morning. Since Silva's disappearance, Vesna had hardly slept but would spend the morning in bed anyway and get up late. That morning, however, she rose early and had breakfast waiting for him, or at least something that resembled breakfast – rancid-smelling margarine spread on day-old bread. She poured him a cup of milk, looked at him and announced her wish: that they pray in thanks that Silva was alive.

At nine o'clock they went together down to St Spyridon. Since Silva's disappearance, Jakov had avoided going out in Misto, avoided the neighbours and their looks of frightened curiosity. Outside the church, they encountered exactly what he had been steering clear of – a throng of neighbours, relations and acquaintances who averted their gaze, as if he and Vesna radiated misfortune. They entered the church and Jakov was relieved to see Vesna take a seat in the back row.

Father Dražen dedicated Mass to Jesus casting out the merchants and money changers. He stood at the lectern and spoke about a Messiah who knew to raise his voice and his hand when it was time to defeat ungodliness. Father Dražen spoke the local tongue, but from the pulpit he used an overly proper, affected Štokavian, as if in his white dalmatic he became a speaking vending machine. While Father Dražen spoke about days of hope for the Croatian homeland, Jakov tried to pray for Silva's return. He tried, but it wasn't easy. Jakov wasn't one for prayers. It was like squeezing water from something already wrung dry.

His gaze wandered. He looked at the plastic Stations of the Cross that the former parish priest had bought in Italy. He looked at the altar of St Spyridon and, beneath it, the olive growers' silver votive offering. He looked at the silver tablets in the shape of hands, legs and eyes that the locals had brought as offerings for convalescence. Had Silva disappeared fifty years ago, they would have done the same. They would have paid a silversmith for Silva's likeness in silver, the silversmith would have cast and hallmarked it, and they would have laid it at the altar of St Spyridon's, Our Lady of Rosary or St Anthony's. The world was simpler back then. One bitter medicine for all misfortune.

Finally, Jakov's gaze fell on the shrine of St Wilgefortis. Like any other shrine, there was a painting, and in the painting a crucifix. But this shrine was different. On the crucifix was a woman, and, stranger still, the woman had a beard.

Jakov remembered well the day the previous parish priest, who had since died, had explained that strange painting to him. It had been the late fifties. Jakov must have been ten years old, an altar boy and still going to church. The priest was a dried-up older man with gnarled hands like olive branches. Father Fulgencio was his name, a name Jakov had never heard before or since.

Father Fulgencio had told him that a heathen prince had wanted to marry St Wilgefortis for her beauty. Not wishing to yield to the sinful pagan, St Wilgefortis prayed to God for a beard to grow on her beautiful face. When the beard grew, someone – Jakov didn't remember who – had her crucified. Jakov had forgotten the details of the story. He understood from it that sometimes there is no greater misfortune than that which comes from having a pretty face.

Father Dražen finished the Apostles' Creed and invoked the Sacred Heart. As the parishioners repeated his words, Jakov opened and closed his mouth disinterestedly. Finally, the priest invited them to go in peace.

When Mass ended, Vesna said she wanted to stay for a bit in the church. She wanted to pray in peace and light a candle. Jakov left her there, slipped free of the crowd and walked down the street towards the cove and the harbour.

A proper, cold north-easterly *bura* had blown the evening before. The air was dry and crystalline; the first row of islands, the naval tunnels and Cape Cross were so clear it was as if you could reach out and touch them. The wind had blown trash everywhere, depositing the remains of newspapers and plastic bags on oleander and tamarisk, on bus stops and the basketball court. On a clear, blustery day, Misto was almost beautiful. Such days, Jakov would sit on a bench and look into the blue beyond, at the sea, the hillsides, at the crests of the waves. He sat down that morning too. For the first time in many months he felt something close to peace. He watched the plastic *pasaras* rocking on the swell and tried to push from his head the heavy, dark spectre that refused to budge.

Then he saw him, Brane Rokov, standing there, looking at him. Brane said hello, inordinately polite as usual. Jakov invited him to sit down.

For the first few days, Brane had called and come round constantly. Like some grieving lover, he had shared in their heartache, in the pain and the police updates. It was as if Silva had not been cheating on him that night, as if she hadn't been hiding from him a parallel life of lies. There was a sense of old-fashioned loyalty to it, as if Brane yearned to become the model son-in-law and saw an opportunity to prove himself. But as time passed and the flow of information dried up, they saw Brane less and less. And then there he was, quieter and more fragile than ever, a shadow of himself, hollowed-out and timid. There were bags under his eyes and he looked like he might collapse.

They sat there in silence for a while, until Brane summoned the courage to speak. "Is it true?" he asked. "That someone saw her the next day?"

"It's true," said Jakov. "In Split. At the bus station."

"So you think she went somewhere?"

"We know she went. But we don't know where."

Brane nodded silently, as if trying to process what he had just been told. He picked a dry leaf from the ground and turned it over and over in his hand until it crumbled. Then he spoke again. "So what now? What happens now?" he asked.

"Nothing. We'll look for her."

"Where?"

"Everywhere. Italy, Germany, Bosnia."

"For how long?"

"For as long as it takes to find her," replied Jakov. "Or until she gets in touch."

"And if she doesn't get in touch? If you don't find her?"

"Then we'll keep looking," said Jakov. "Mate and I will look for as long as it takes."

There was no reply from Brane. He sat there on the bench staring at the ground, lost in thought, motionless, silent. Then his torso, his shoulders and his back began to tremble, barely noticeably at first, then more and more, until he was shaking.

Then Brane sobbed. He wept with muffled groans, his face crumpled in despair. Jakov placed his hand on Brane's shoulder to comfort him. But Brane didn't stop. He cried in silence, his body convulsing. When it passed, he opened his eyes and stood up. "I'm going," he said. "I have to go home."

Brane left along the seafront. Jakov watched him for a long time, walking to Rokov's Land and beyond, to the chapel of Stella Maris, where he disappeared from view.

In April 1990, the bank froze the account of the factory where Jakov worked. The workers were due to be paid on Monday, 9 April, but that morning the head of the salary department walked onto the factory floor and told them there was no money and it wasn't clear when there would be. For the people of Misto, it was as if the sun hadn't risen.

Next morning, the bankruptcy judge arrived. He went around the offices and the factory floor, checked the raw material reserves in the warehouse and changed the locks on the gate. He summoned the workers and told them that from then onwards there was no need for them to come to work. They would stay at home and get the legal minimum wage until the factory was sold. Jakov learned a new word that morning. They were being "furloughed". He had already been furloughed in life. Now he was furloughed at work.

The election campaign began that month and political fever swept the country; in Misto, rallies were held in front of the church and people marched carrying candles and flags. Rade, the owner of the Lantern cafe, became the chief candidate.

Meanwhile, the search for Silva was going nowhere. She had slowly disappeared from the pages of the papers and the television news. The few remaining posters bearing her face still flapped from lamp posts and tree trunks, wet, ragged and forgotten, but the police had lost interest as soon as it became clear Silva had left of her own free will. Seven months had passed. Silva had slowly become what they called a cold case.

Jakov and Vesna could not accept it. In March, they had hired a private detective. They didn't have much luck. The detective was a former police officer but a complete beginner in his new line of work. His clientele consisted mainly of businesspeople and doctors who paid him to stalk their unfaithful wives. He worked for a day rate and expenses. He travelled a lot and dedicated considerable time to the case, but after a month without results, they ran out of money and called him off.

They took up the search themselves. In February, they had paid for Mate to take his driving test and borrowed 5,000 Deutschmarks from Vesna's cousin for fuel and sandwiches. On weekdays, when Jakov was at work, Mate would do the driving, while Jakov would take the strain at the weekend. They would get in the car and set off in the direction of one of Silva's possible destinations. They went around Bosnia once more, driving from Knin to Kupres, Imotski and Foča, leaving posters at the roadside. They went to Belgrade, Sarajevo and Zagreb.

When Jakov was furloughed from the factory, it came as a relief. He borrowed another 3,000 Marks and was in the car every day. He drove to Klagenfurt and Graz and twice to Trieste, descending from Basovizza near the border along Via Fabio Severo to the centre. He would drive slowly, studying through the window the physiognomy of the women on the walkways, searching for hair, a profile, a back that might resemble Silva's. He stopped at hotel receptions and police counters. He drove in circles around the rail station and the Silos, the old Austro-Hungarian granary, then along the seafront Riva Tre Novembre and Riva Nazario Sauro, before turning into Via Schiaparelli and Via Belpoggio, where he knew African prostitutes plied their trade. As he drove, he noticed traces of his previous visits – posters bearing a Yugoslav phone number stuck to tree trunks and bus stops, drained of colour, rain-soaked and shrivelled. Posters that called for help, the faraway cry of some unknown people searching for some vanished Slava.

During his second trip to Trieste, Jakov thought for a second that he'd found her. It was a sunny day in early April and a furious *bura* was blowing from the Julian Alps, the last, late edition of three north-easterly winds that traditionally appear in March and hail the start of spring. That morning, he had visited some more hotels, as well as stores around Ponte Rosso where he knew Jugoslavi liked to shop. Then he went to the central hospital and showed the staff Silva's picture. When he'd finished, he drove around the neighbourhood by the hospital, along Via della Ginnastica and Via Scipio Slataper. It was then, outside a shop, that he saw the outline of a person who looked familiar.

As Jakov was driving along Via Ginnastica, he passed a shop where a delivery van was parked outside. It was a fish seller, and on the van was written PRODOTTI ITTICI and a phone number. Men in overalls were unloading crates of skate, sole and mullet on ice. Then behind the van he spotted a girl. She was wearing a yellow plastic raincoat. Something about her reminded him of Silva – part of a shoulder, her back, a lock of hair. He didn't see her face. But even then he knew it might be her.

He tried to stop right there but couldn't because of the traffic. He looked around for a parking space but there weren't any. Hurriedly, he pulled into a narrow side street but another car followed, beeping when he tried to stop.

Right then, a space opened up at the back entrance to a Chinese restaurant. He just about managed to squeeze his Opel Ascona into the narrow gap beneath the restaurant's ventilation shaft. He jumped out of the car and ran back to Via Ginnastica. He turned the corner and was relieved to see the girl in the yellow raincoat walking down the street, slowly, with a bag of fish in her hand.

Jakov hurried after her. He got to within fifteen feet of her, six feet, three feet. He touched her shoulder. The girl turned around, and all was gone. She didn't look a bit like Silva. She had the same hairstyle, similar build and shoulders, but her face was completely different, elongated and unattractive. The girl in the raincoat looked genuinely scared. "*Scusa? Che cosa vuole?*" she asked him.

Pulling his hand away, he apologized in his passable English. He watched her walk away. Now she didn't look like Silva even from the back. The more he looked the more he realized they weren't similar at all.

He went back to his car and headed out of the city, up Via Fabio Severo, past the university to the east exit. Before reaching Basovizza he stopped at a viewing point. He leaned on the fence and took in the city below, the port cranes, the Silos and derricks. He looked at the city, full of strangers he knew nothing about.

Jakov stood at the viewing point looking down on the anthill that was Trieste, then got back in the car and turned the ignition key.

The last day of April was Silva and Mate's birthday. On 30 April 1990, Silva turned eighteen. Wherever she might be, whatever she might be doing, Silva became an adult.

Jakov woke that morning knowing it would be a difficult day. And it was.

Parents celebrate the birthdays of children who are alive; they bake cakes with candles and play party games. The parents of dead children go to the cemetery; they buy chrysanthemums and lay them on the grave.

Silva was neither dead nor alive. Silva had disappeared. And you can't bake a cake for the disappeared or go to their grave. You can't celebrate with the disappeared, you can't mourn them, you can't talk to them or make plans. Had Silva not disappeared, they would have spent the day talking about her future studies, about her driving test, about her room in the student dorm. Instead, they had only a picture of her, given pride of place on the wall above the dining table. Vesna had chosen a prominent position as a constant reminder that the family was incomplete, that the job wasn't finished, that there was an enduring hole that had not been filled. She didn't place the picture on a side table or the cabinet. Were the picture on a table, a candle could have been lit before it for the soul of the dead, in oil and water. Silva's picture was on the wall, because Silva was alive, and candles are not lit beneath pictures of the living.

Jakov locked himself away in the bathroom that morning, shaving slowly and carefully, putting off as long as possible the moment he'd have to open the door. Eventually he went down to the kitchen and found Vesna reading the classifieds. The classifieds had become their most important newspaper supplement: lost and found notices, apartment rentals, job ads, even horoscopes, anything that might contain a clue as to Silva's whereabouts.

In seven months, Vesna had changed physically. She was thin, having lost the extra pounds she'd been carrying; her hair was grey at the roots and her skin colourless, rough and dry. She had become closed off, impenetrable, hard. When she looked at him, her gaze was sullen and loaded with condemnation; the harder Jakov tried, the more she seemed to judge him.

He and Vesna argued properly for the first time in early April, the day after his last trip to Trieste. That morning, Mate had left in the car to place posters along the coastal road north of Zadar. Jakov said that Mate should leave the search to him, that he should focus on school because he was close to graduating and the boatbuilding entry exam was coming up. Vesna did not respond immediately. When she did, she told Jakov it wasn't the right time for Mate to be studying. "We need Mate right now," she said. "He can't leave for Zagreb and leave us in this alone. Another six months, maybe a year, till we find her. He should stay for that long, and then he can go to study."

Jakov was taken aback. Mate's future should not be sacrificed because of Silva, he said.

Vesna replied: "Everything must be sacrificed when one of us is in trouble." The way she said it, Jakov knew it was her final word.

That evening, Jakov sat on the balcony and for a long time he looked out at Misto, mostly because he didn't want to lie down next to Vesna. Right then, he despised her.

Shortly after midnight, Mate returned from Zadar. He sat down next to Jakov. "Mum and I talked," he said. We talked about *that*, he said. And it was all right. One day he'd be able to study. But right then it was more important that he was there with them. Once he finished school, he'd get work delivering frozen fish. It was a good job, he said. A lot of driving. He'd be able to search along the way. Jakov didn't reply, but in his mind he saw the poison spreading, contaminating them one by one.

It was the same the morning of Silva's birthday. In the kitchen, the scene was as expected: the wet-eyed Jesus above the door, Silva's picture on the wall, an unfamiliar, ugly woman with greying hair reading ads in the newspaper from landlords, pimps and fortune tellers, a woman who looks at him reprovingly as soon as he enters the room, her expression saying *And what are you going to do about it today?* or *Do you plan to waste yet another day?*

"I'm going to Split," Jakov said, heading off the attack. "I'll go to the police. I'll ask to see Šain. He hasn't been in touch." He drank his cold coffee, took his blood pressure medication and set off in the car. On the way to Split he listened to the election news on the radio. After the first round, the Communists were heading for a heavy loss.

Jakov arrived at the police station just before ten o'clock. Immediately, he was struck by the state of ferment he found inside. As usual, police officers and officials were hanging around in the corridors, but while some faces were morose and anxious, others were trembling with exhilaration. He knocked on the door of Šain's office. Šain called him in and straight away Jakov noticed something new – Tito's picture had gone.

"It bothered some people," Šain said. "I think those times have passed." He continued, as if justifying himself. "You know, it's a family thing. My granddad was a Partisan, one of the first. Albino Šain. You've probably heard of him. There's a school in Omiš named after him, and they made a bronze Partisan statue in Bisko based on him. You'll remember it for sure if you've been there. The thin, long-faced one. That was him."

Jakov sat down in his usual spot. He looked at the man he'd put his trust in, whom he'd bet everything he had on. But Gorki Šain no longer looked like someone you'd bet on. He looked like someone whose world was falling apart.

"Tell me," said Jakov. "Is there any new information? Will there be any?"

Šain didn't reply immediately. He shifted in his chair and looked at the mountain of papers on his smooth desk. Then he spoke. "Look," he said. "We've exhausted all our resources. There's nothing more we can do." He exhaled uncomfortably. "We know now that she left of her own free will. That's clear after Elda Zuvan's statement. All other possibilities are off the table. We don't have anything on Adrijan Lekaj. We couldn't link the wood in the bakery to the disappearance, and the witness who made the anonymous call never got in touch again. We've looked everywhere and we don't have a body, motive or method. What Zuvan told us fits with what we suspected. Your daughter ran away, probably because she got into trouble over drugs."

"Maybe," said Jakov. "But she has to be found. We can't find her ourselves. We're falling apart."

"I don't think you quite understand," Šain responded. "All this time we were able to treat this as a case of a child who'd run away. She was seventeen and she ran away from her legal guardians. Today, that's not the case. She's an adult. She has the right to go, to run away from you. She has the right to live where she wants and the right not to contact you if she wants."

"And what if someone's holding her by force?"

"Honestly, do you see any reason to believe that's the case?"

Jakov fell silent. He knew the answer to that question, just like Šain did. "So that's it?" he asked.

"That's it for now. But if she ever gets in touch, if you get any indication, any sign where she might be, we're here to help you with logistics."

Jakov stood up. He turned towards the door without offering Šain his hand. He didn't feel like shaking the hand of a man who had left him high and dry. Šain got up and saw him to the door.

As Jakov left, Šain placed his hand on his arm. "She'll get in touch," he said. "Sooner or later. Believe me. At some point, the reason why she hasn't will disappear."

Jakov said nothing. He didn't need a police officer to salve his wounds with a statement of abstract faith. He had enough of that from his relatives, neighbours, priests. He needed someone, at least one other person, who would search for Silva. Right then, he was alone.

Before returning home he went back to the bus station. He parked in the ferry port and walked to the place where Silva had last been seen, 220 days previously.

It was a warm April day. The next day was 1 May, which meant a long weekend for the Austrians and Germans. The port was full of tourists. Towels hung from small wooden cruisers swaying in the quay. A gaggle of young backpackers were besieging the international counter, young people flitting around Europe from one end to the other, from Scotland to Greece, Denmark to Italy, Italy to Scotland. His daughter had to be somewhere among them. Somewhere in that labyrinth, in that human wasps' nest.

He sat for a while on a bench, watching the boats and the buses as they departed, tin boxes crowded with strangers leaving for Germany, Serbia, Italy and Bosnia. Green, white and purple coaches boarded ferries for the islands or took on passengers heading for the West. The whole world was churning around.

Jakov sat there and watched, but a single thought would not leave his mind, a thought he stubbornly rotated, round and round, as if trying to transport it telepathically to the four corners: Silva, where are you? Silva, talk to us. Silva, where are you? Tell us where you are.

But there was no answer. Instead came only silence.

PART TWO

DIVERGING PATHS

6
VESNA (1991)

For her sixth lesson that day, Vesna had the top form. She was supposed to teach them the topography of Croatia, but from the very start things didn't go to plan. At the beginning of the class, Vesna returned to the children the tests she had marked. Thirteen out of thirty had got the lowest possible grade, but it seemed to come as a surprise to them. Little Bakić in the second row stared vacantly at her paper, her eyes welling up. In the back row, Nikša demonstratively tore up his paper. Vesna felt hated. She felt the hatred in the air like a charged cloud.

She tried to teach. She stood in front of the relief map and pointed with a wooden stick at the bulging plastic mountains, reciting the words she knew by heart. But it wasn't working that day. She couldn't get through to the bitter horde in front of her. Vesna stood on one side, and on the other were thirty faces radiating rebellious contempt.

The bell rang at 1.05. Vesna wasn't sure who was happier – her or the children. The pupils stampeded down the stairs, while Vesna, class register under her arm, headed for the staffroom.

Vesna walked in on the lunchtime news. Those days, you couldn't get away from the news. It gushed forth from everywhere. She found the school adviser and two teachers standing in front of the television, pictures of tanks, refugees and camouflaged soldiers flicking across the screen. The reporter was delivering the daily update in a dramatic baritone.

The news was terrible and getting worse by the day. Three times that morning air raid sirens had rung out over Osijek and Đakovo in the east. On the coast, in Šibenik, there was fighting on the bridge at the entrance to the city. There was no mention any more of Drniš in the Dalmatian hinterland, not in the morning news or the lunchtime bulletin. By that time, everyone knew what that meant – that Drniš had fallen – but the television didn't want to tell them.

Instead, it showed footage from Šibenik: tanks at one end of the bridge, next to the old motel, cannons firing on the city. There was chaos on the streets, burned houses, roof tiles smashed on the ground. A television camera operator, like some peeping Tom, ferreted through a hole blown in a wall. The pictures showed the ruins of a concert hall, chairs scattered, lights smashed, a piano crushed by the collapsed roof. Glass everywhere. So much glass.

"Jesus Christ," groaned one of the teachers. "This is horrific."

Hearing her despair, Vesna felt a brief but intense surge of rage. It was that same feeling of revolt that had gripped her for weeks now, waning in intensity only now and again. For weeks, Vesna had felt that others' cries for help only made her angry. That general outpouring of emotion made her angry, that collective self-pity, that chorus of complaints from people whose family members were all present and correct.

Vesna didn't like that new feeling. She didn't like the way she felt. But she knew she couldn't help it.

Not wanting her colleagues to notice, let alone draw her into conversation about the war, Vesna quietly placed the class register on the shelf, removed her shirt jacket and pulled on her coat. She left the room without a word, walked along the hallway and went out into the schoolyard, where some riotous pupils were locked in a bag fight. She headed home. Passing through Misto, through open windows she could hear the multiplied din of the television news. Everyone was listening, and the voice of the reporter could be heard on every corner – from homes, from cafes and shops.

Walking home, Vesna observed the changes Misto had undergone in a matter of months: tape on the windows of the school and the council building to prevent glass shattering; white fibre sacks full of sand in front of public buildings and basement windows; the thrum of generators outside the few shops and cafes still open, noisy metal boxes on which everything depended, since the electricity had gone off in Dalmatia weeks earlier.

Vesna passed the Partisan monument, chipped by hammers and sprayed with the letter 'U' for Ustaša, the fascists who had run the puppet Independent State of Croatia during the Second World War. Only a few cars drove past, their headlights covered with black tape so as not to break the blackout. None of the cars had licence plates.

She walked along the fence of the naval base, once a sprawling, mysterious and forbidden city and now an empty wasteland. The Yugoslav army had evacuated ten days earlier. Trucks had pulled up in front of the base and the sailors had loaded up everything they could – weapons, kitchen appliances, beds. The convoy had left, apparently for Bosnia. For forty years, Misto had lived shoulder to shoulder with the base, mutually dependent, breathing the same air. Suddenly, that secret city was no more. The sailors' barracks stood bare, defiled and plundered, waiting for someone to deign to step inside. No one dared. It was rumoured that the base was mined.

While passing along the fence to the basketball court, something grabbed Vesna's attention. A grey-green truck was parked in the middle of the court and uniformed soldiers were unloading bundles of something onto the ground. They were taking their orders from Rade, the owner of the Lantern. And while the soldiers unloaded the truck, a group of around a dozen civilians stood and watched, mostly older men. Vesna spotted Adrijan's father among them.

Vesna approached. Only then did she see the whole picture. Behind the truck stood two rows of new recruits, roughly thirty of them. Vesna recognized every one of them. They were all her former students, in their late teens or early twenties, all dressed in the same uniforms and wearing the same expression, all equally terrified.

Her gaze passed from one face to the next. And then she saw him, in the back row, in the middle: Adrijan Lekaj, the only person who knew what had happened that night but who refused to say. There he was, standing in line, as if nothing had ever happened. Standing there, like the rest, as if in expectation of his name being carved on some future memorial plaque.

Vesna watched him. And at some point, Adrijan noticed her too. He returned her gaze, defiantly.

When the soldiers had finished unloading the truck, the owner of the Lantern shook hands with a tall man in uniform. Vesna had never seen the man before, but he looked to be in charge. The tall man ordered the new recruits to take the equipment. One by one, they stepped forward and picked up the grey-green bundles containing travel bags, sleeping bags, winter overcoats and helmets. Vesna didn't see any weapons. They would probably get them elsewhere.

Once the equipment had been divided up, the man in charge called the recruits to attention and ordered them into the truck. As they began to step up, a moan came from among the parents as a father or mother finally succumbed to fear. Vesna was gripped by that same feeling, that furious resistance to the despair of others, a resistance that in no time at all became anger.

That's how she felt then, watching the recruits climbing into the truck. She watched the petrified faces of the would-be heroes and their anxious parents. Old Lekaj was among them, though he looked surprisingly composed. Vesna watched, but could feel no sympathy whatsoever.

When the last soldier was on board, the driver closed the tailgate and pulled down the tarpaulin. He sat in the cabin and turned on the engine. They headed for the front – perhaps Zadar, or Dubrovnik. Maybe Bosnia. Vesna didn't know. She didn't care.

The truck reached the coastal road, turned in the direction of Split and disappeared around the first bend. Vesna continued her walk home.

Fuck them, she thought, as she turned into the street behind the church. Fuck them all.

At home, Vesna changed her clothes and quietly set to work. First, she unloaded the dishwasher and tidied the kitchen. Then she put a pan of beef soup on to cook, checking with a fork whether the carrots were cooked. She vacuumed, first her and Jakov's bedroom, then Mate's room and, finally, Silva's. She still tidied Silva's room once a week, changing the pillowcases and sheets.

Over those two years, Vesna had come to realize that keeping busy helped her, that she found comfort in routine. Her day was composed of routine: putting on the coffee in the morning; taking the butter and honey from the fridge; emptying the machine and hanging the washing out to dry; making lunch; doing the dishes; making dinner; doing the dishes again.

Those were ordinary days. On ordinary days, Vesna found enough to occupy her mind; the day passed and things felt practically tolerable. *That* day was not an ordinary day. Other families have birthdays and wedding anniversaries. In Vesna's family, besides all those days, there was *that* day. That's what she and Jakov called it. *That day*, 23 September, the day Silva disappeared.

As *that* day approached, a noxious, invisible mass would form in Vesna's stomach. She would react with mild panic at every voice, every sound, every bang or telephone call. "Stress syndrome", her doctor called it. Vesna called it "sorrow". It would last a week, maybe two. Then *that* day would arrive. That day, Silva's day, that day around which their lives revolved, like a perverted inversion of a birthday.

When the beef and carrots were cooked, Vesna turned off the heat. She wiped down the stove with a scouring pad, took the bowls and stepped outside to throw out the trash. She saw Jakov in the yard, sitting on the bench in front of the *konoba* engrossed in something Vesna couldn't quite make out, some small device he was picking at with a screwdriver, determined not to look up at her.

Vesna knew Jakov would have liked her to leave him in peace. To not talk about it. To pretend it was any other day, not *that* day. To pretend everything was fine, even if it wasn't. Jakov would have liked that, but Vesna didn't want to give him that luxury.

"You ready?" Vesna asked him. No reply. "You ready?" she said again, and Jakov grudgingly stood up, his arms and legs like some foreign ballast. He went into the house, put on his shoes and took the car keys. Leaving the house, he stood in front of her, as if surrendering reluctantly. "Get the car out," Vesna told him. "We need to get there before they finish work."

Saying nothing, Jakov did as instructed, driving the car out of the garage into the yard. Vesna wiped her hands and looked at her watch. If there were no hiccups, they'd be at the police station in Split by 2.30.

Two years had passed since Silva's disappearance, two years in which everyone had given up on ever finding her. The police, the state, the newspapers, even Jakov. Mate was the only one still looking.

By that point, Mate had spent fourteen months driving a freezer truck for a fish wholesaler. He was constantly on the road, driving fresh fish packed in ice to Slovenia and Italy, driving country roads the war hadn't reached, crossing to the island of Pag by the bridge north of Zadar and from Pag by ferry to free territory on the mainland. He bypassed areas of military action, checkpoints and roadblocks, sirens and curfews, driving hake, red mullet, sea bream and bass to restaurants in Carinthia and Kranjska in Slovenia and Friuli-Venezia Giulia in Italy. He took fish caught in a war zone to places at peace.

And Vesna knew that as he drove, Mate searched for Silva. Like a dog with a bone, he visited motels and train stations, stopped at obscure filling stations and hunting inns. Over those two years, Vesna had come to realize Mate would not rest until he found his sister. The thought brought Vesna a deep and comforting feeling of peace.

She would have liked Jakov to do something too, for him to get in his car like Mate or pick up the phone, drive around, call the police, at least ask someone something. But Jakov didn't do anything. He behaved as if Silva had gone away for the summer, as if she had popped to the shop on the corner and left a note saying *I'll be right back.*

Jakov barely left home. Since the factory had shut its doors for good, he no longer went to work, didn't go into the village or talk to anyone. He didn't even talk to Vesna. Before, Jakov had been the kind of man who constantly kept up with events, who turned on the evening news at 7.30 sharp, who understood the Middle East crisis, who could name the presidents of Syria, Romania or Iraq. Two years after Silva's disappearance, when everyone was glued to the news, Jakov wasn't. Hearing the intro, he would turn it off and leave the room.

Since the factory had closed, Jakov had cemented the garden paths, repainted the *konoba* and planted a row of lemon trees. He spent his days fixing the car, the water pump, the electric grill, the garden fence, the drill. Vesna watched him day after day, bent over and silent, absorbed in DIY, sweat dripping from his brow onto tools, gears and wires.

Jakov did everything except what he should have been doing. And when Vesna criticized him for not doing anything to find Silva, Jakov would come up with compelling excuses: there was a war on, the roads were blocked, part of the country was occupied, the phone lines were down, and to travel abroad you needed permission from the crisis headquarters.

In silence they drove to Split, arriving fast because the road was empty. They entered a city that, like Misto, had been transformed, a city where sandbags were piled at the entrances to buildings, where cars drove around without licence plates and armed people walked the streets. And everywhere there was the rumbling chorus of generators, dozens, perhaps hundreds of them.

They parked in front of the interior ministry secretariat, the building they had been to so many times. It too had been changed by the war. It was surrounded by a parapet of sandbags, and men armed with Kalashnikovs guarded the entrance. Uniformed people were loading some kind of metal cones into trucks.

Vesna and Jakov passed by the guards, who did not deign even to look at them. They approached the guard booth and Jakov tapped on the glass. The window slid open.

"We're here to see Mr Šain," said Vesna. "If he's free."

The guard looked at them contemptuously and replied: "Don't know if he's free. But I know this Mr Šain of yours doesn't work here any more."

They entered the building and Vesna took in the changes. Hanging on the walls, instead of portraits of Tito, were crucifixes and Catholic calendars containing pictures of the Pope. Men in camouflage uniform walked the corridors, armed with rifles. Vesna recognized some of their faces. But no one paid her and Jakov any attention. The atmosphere was one of nervous haste.

Climbing to the second floor, they stopped before what had once been the door to Šain's office. It bore a different name and rank: TOMISLAV ČOVIĆ, SENIOR POLICE INSPECTOR.

That was the man who had taken over from Šain. He had taken over Šain's office and all his cases, including Silva's.

"Knock," said Vesna, and Jakov knocked hesitantly on the door. From inside they heard a voice calling them to enter.

Vesna expected a senior police inspector to be older, but the man they encountered was young. He had dark hair, was clean-shaven and smelled of cologne. He didn't look even thirty.

They introduced themselves and explained why they were there. Panic flashed across the face of the young police officer and Vesna realized he had no idea who they were. He had no idea what was going on.

Vesna broke the silence. She explained that they were still looking for their daughter, that the investigation was still open, that Šain had constantly been in touch but that for six months they hadn't heard from anyone. "We'd like to know," she said, "if anything is being done."

The officer listened in silence before he stood up and began rifling through files in a box. Finally, he pulled a file from the bundle and opened it on his desk. Vesna spotted Silva's picture on the top.

Čović gave the file a cursory read, pretending to recall its contents. Vesna knew he was bluffing. As the senior inspector leafed through the file, she eyed him carefully, breathing in his offensive aftershave before finally losing patience. "Where's Gorki Šain?" she asked. "Why is he not in charge of the case?"

"He doesn't work here any more," Čović replied, adding sarcastically: "He didn't like the ambience."

"It's been two years," Vesna said testily. "There's been no progress. No one's dealing with our case. Not even you. This is a disgrace."

Čović closed the file and fixed Vesna with a look of suspicion. "Right," he said. "Do you see what's going on around here?"

"Yes," Vesna replied.

"I don't think you do," Čović told her. In a clipped, caustic tone, he began to explain how the police were no longer police but soldiers, how mortars were being loaded into a transport truck on the street outside and that men were dying at the front. Last night, he said, two police officers had come under attack in nearby Otišić. One had got a bullet in the head, the other had lost an arm. "Do you really think we have time to deal with some girl who's run away from home?"

His bitter monologue over, Čović pushed the file to the edge of his desk. That was when Vesna realized. It was all over.

The file would end up in a pile along with hundreds of others, and no one would ever open it again – not Čović or anyone else. Nothing could be gained from their presence.

They left and walked outside. Near the building, they again saw trucks. This time she paid attention to what was in them. They actually were full of mortar tubes, jutting out dumbly, threateningly. From a nearby cafe, a radio blasted out stirring patriotic songs.

Getting in the car, they headed back to Misto, driving slowly behind a military convoy. Every few miles, they were stopped by military police and asked for their papers. They didn't talk on the way, but just before reaching Misto, almost home, Jakov took one hand from the wheel and placed it on hers. It was the first time he had touched her for months. "Don't be surprised," he said. "You can see what's going on around here."

"I can see, but what good does that do me? Who's going to help us?"

"We have to wait," said Jakov. "She'll get in touch. Sooner or later. She'll call, if she wants to."

"What if she can't?"

"Why wouldn't she be able to?"

"Then why doesn't she?"

After a hesitation that felt to Vesna like an eternity, Jakov said what he thought. What Vesna already knew he thought.

"Why doesn't Silva call?" Jakov said. "Because Silva doesn't care."

Vesna pulled her hand away angrily. "Shame on you," she said. "Shame on you. What kind of a father are you?"

They drove the rest of the way without talking. Jakov turned on the radio to break the silence, just as an air raid was announced.

7
ADRIJAN (1995)

The artillery hadn't stopped. All night, Croatian cannons thundered from the direction of the Malovan and Rilić mountains. Adrijan listened. He knew what that meant. The next day, after so much waiting, they would go on the attack.

At four in the morning, the commander woke them and gave them the order to move out. Dawn found them advancing on Kupres in Bosnia. After four years of static warfare, they had broken deep into what until recently had been the enemy rearguard.

For four years the two sides had fought a war without either advancing. Now the Serb army was collapsing before their eyes. The enemy was no more. It had fled in small, scattered groups, offering no resistance. The Sixth Regiment of the Croatian Army broke through to the seemingly endless mountain plateau of northern Bosnia. And Adrijan went with it, into the heart of Bosnia.

They walked all day, advancing constantly. Sporadic shooting could be heard in the distance, but Adrijan and his company had not fired a shot. They simply walked through a vast and magnificent nothingness. Mountain plains covered in yellow grass stretched out in front of them as if without end. In the dry yellow they saw black patches like typhus spots, where the grass had been burned away by falling grenades or mortar rounds.

The Sixth Regiment moved forward beneath a vast sky, Adrijan with it, walking for hours through empty landscapes part scorched, part abandoned. Adrijan took a swig from his water bottle to fight back the heat, though even in August it was never hot at that altitude, just uncomfortably warm. He put the bottle away and took in the scene. Up in the mountains, he could see the rusted remains of the pre-war cable car, ski lift and hotel. By the road, a small shepherd village had been razed, obviously intentionally. Adrijan saw a tiny Orthodox cemetery surrounded by a metal fence. Further on, he noticed a Muslim *türbe* and a handful of tombstones sticking out from the grass like exclamation marks. There were graves everywhere, of all kinds. And bodies too. But the living were gone. They were either fleeing before the Croatian forces or approaching in their wake, ready to rebuild in the ashes, this time as victors.

Around midday they came to a crossroads, where a small Catholic chapel stood riddled with bullets. There was the carcass of a burned-out bus and a broken road sign lying in the ditch. And everywhere there were bodies, most of them in uniform. They lay scattered on the ground like sacks of flour, anonymous and denied all dignity. Someone had poured quicklime over them to smother the smell. The bodies might not have smelled, but the quicklime did. It stung Adrijan's eyes.

They heard the noise of a car engine behind them. Adrijan turned to see a jeep approaching on the road. It appeared first as a tiny spot at the entrance to the valley, growing bigger and bigger the nearer it came. Adrijan knew it was him, Cvitko.

The sergeant told the men to rest. They sat down at the side of the road on a mound of dry, scorched earth. The jeep finally reached them and out stepped Major Mario Cvitković. That was his name, but it wasn't what he was called by either his superiors or his subordinates. Like the war itself, there was nothing ordinary about the military hierarchy. The men didn't call Cvitko by his name or his rank, but by the moniker he had picked up on the streets, as if they were a mob and he their boss. Cvitko, always Cvitko.

Adrijan had first met Cvitko three years earlier, when his company was transferred to the Sixth Regiment, Split, in April 1992. After seven months of war, Adrijan had found himself among strangers to whom his name meant nothing and who knew nothing of his past. For the first time in years he relished being among people who did not suspect him of anything.

It was there, in Umljanović, in the Dalmatian hinterland, that Adrijan met Cvitko. Cvitko was a stone heavier back then and still had foppish curls around his ears. Back then he was only a platoon commander. Three years later, Cvitko looked like a proper soldier. His earring had gone, his hair was cropped and he was tanned, tall and thin. He had risen to battalion commander. The soldiers loved him. People felt safe with Cvitko. He was a quick thinker who took quick decisions. And when he took a decision, he didn't change it. When the fighting was heavy, he was first in line. He was known to resist his superiors when he thought lives were being put in too much danger. The men would walk through fire for Cvitko.

And there he was, arriving in a Fiat Campagnola from the direction of Mount Malovan, like a victorious warrior directing his latest triumph. He climbed out and scanned the horizon with binoculars. They were less than four miles from Kupres. In front of them, a large, flat expanse of grass and more grass. But on the horizon they could just make out the mountain town that was their target, a church spire and ski lift. Out of use for years, the ski lift was rusted and decaying in the mountain air, merely a reminder that someone in that backwater at some point had a dream.

Dropping the binoculars, Cvitko turned his gaze on the soldiers sitting at the roadside. He began dealing out tasks. He directed one platoon to secure the devastated hotel from looters, another to scout the village along the road and demine it house by house, and a third to climb the elevation above the road and dig out a machine-gun nest. At that point, someone told him they were almost out of water. Cvitko stooped to check one of the waterskins. It was limp and empty.

Cvitko looked at Adrijan and called him by his name. Adrijan stood up and approached. Cvitko placed his arm on Adrijan's shoulder. Adrijan knew Cvitko liked him. To Cvitko, he was a kid from a small place, uncorrupted, a healthy specimen, not like the city lowlifes, wasters and junkies. Like everyone else there, Cvitko knew nothing about his past. Adrijan planned to keep it that way.

"Adrijan, Luka and you, Krešo," said Cvitko. "You'll go for water. Stick three skins on your backs and go back to those houses. There'll be a tap over there."

The three men each lifted a waterskin onto their backs. They set off down the road in the direction they had come from. Behind their backs, they could hear distant, sporadic artillery and the odd burst of gunfire. The war wasn't over yet, but it felt like it was. Both sides knew it was the final chapter. They were on the home straight, only the last few hurdles ahead of them – walking, guarding the rear, laying an ambush, more walking, fetching water. Empty, the skin wasn't heavy. But Adrijan knew it would be different on the way back.

They approached the houses. They had been gutted by fire, but not recently, meaning it might be a Catholic area. They proceeded with caution, unsure whether the approach was mined. Only bare, scorched walls remained, except for one building, the biggest, closest to the road. It was obviously the local pub. A pub isn't a church or a graveyard; it's not a mosque or a school. Everyone needs a pub. No army destroys a pub, and so this pub, still standing, welcomed a new army.

The pub would be the only place they could find water. So they moved towards it and entered to find a blonde woman in her early thirties clearing bits of glass and brick from the bar. She looked at them nervously, but the expression on her face quickly turned to relief. She was a Croat.

Adrijan slid the skin from his back and asked for water. The woman pointed to a tap and told him to help himself. "It's not poisoned," she said. "It's a bit cloudy from the earth in the pipes, but it's drinkable."

The bartender told them she owned the pub, that it had been hers before the war. Then she had spent five years as a refugee on the coast, in Trogir. She had come back and planned to reopen the pub for when traffic returned to the road. Some of the appliances were still there, others had been stolen. She had also found things that weren't hers. The coffee machine was Italian, Gaggia – new, expensive, and not hers. Whoever had been running the pub must have stolen it, like they had stolen the pub. A new coffee machine was the least she should get for all those years spent in a refugee hotel.

She held out her hand. Sanja, she said. Adrijan introduced himself and shook her hand. From her appearance, it was clear she had worked all her life, that she hadn't had it easy. But beneath all that she was a good-looking woman.

Adrijan began filling the skin with water and cast his eye over the pub. It was as if time had stopped in the 1980s. There were booths made of heavy wood, a panelled bar and red rugs on the walls. There was a battle of eras going on – in one corner, a jukebox from the 1970s and a poster of Zdravko Čolić, Yugoslavia's Tom Jones; in another, a topless Samantha Fox from the 1980s. Flags of Belgrade's Red Star, the Cyrillic on the beer glasses and the posters of Serbian turbo-folk stars were a giveaway as to where the former proprietor's sympathies lay. That would all go. Sanja would make sure not a trace remained.

As his gaze wandered, Adrijan noticed something familiar on the far wall next to the toilet door. A poster stuck to the wall with tape. It was old, yellowed and torn at the edges. But Adrijan recognized the face in the picture. And from somewhere deep in his stomach came that familiar, stifled feeling, a sharp, metallic chill.

He remembered that face well. He remembered that defiant look and pronounced nose full of stubborn irritation. He remembered that tuft of hair falling across the brow and concealing the left eye. There, in the mountains of Bosnia, on a piece of paper, Silva Vela looked exactly as he remembered her.

And as the water filled the plastic skin, Adrijan stood there looking at the wall next to the toilet door. He looked at the face that all those years had remained frozen, unchanged. He looked at the face that had turned his life upside down.

Adrijan knew that evening would follow him for the rest of his life. He would have liked to forget it, but he couldn't. He would never forget it. That evening lived on in his memory, returning persistently like an irritating chorus, like the throb of a toothache.

He remembered everything, every detail: the end-of-season fishermen's fair; the fake fishermen in striped T-shirts barbecuing mackerel of dubious freshness for tourists; Czechs and Hungarians dancing the polka to the music of a cafe terrace band. He remembered downing brandy and Coke – first one, then another, then a fifth and a sixth. He remembered DJ Robi taking to the stage with his summer hits: Bon Jovi, Madonna, Simply Red. And he remembered Silva. He remembered her arriving alone, without Brane. He remembered exactly what she had been wearing: a floral dress that was far too short, a loose bag and red All Stars.

Adrijan had always liked Silva. She was beautiful. But she had something else besides beauty. There was an air of adventure about her. In that lifeless place, only Silva looked alive, in colour, blood pumping through her veins.

He knew Silva, of course. He would say hello if he saw her out and drink coffee with her and her friends, making sure not to be caught too obviously staring at her, at her legs, her cleavage, her ankles. He wanted to make a move. But then she started going out with Brane and Adrijan decided to forget her. Until that evening, the evening Silva arrived in a floral dress and red All Stars and let him buy her a drink. Adrijan offered to request a song for her and she chose "Red Red Wine" by UB40. Adrijan bought DJ Robi a vodka and he played the song not once, but four times. As the reggae rhythm lazily unwound from the speakers, Adrijan and Silva slow-danced. He smelled her hair; he felt the soft skin of her shoulder beneath his jawline and, under his fingers, her ribs and the outline of her bra. When she rested her hand on the back of his head, Adrijan thought: this is it, this is what I was looking for.

If only it hadn't been.

After that night, Adrijan's life had turned into one long, ugly joke: detention, interrogation, needles quivering at "Yes" or "No", tracing a line on a ribbon of polygraph paper.

The skin expanded as it filled with water and Adrijan, standing there in the heart of Bosnia, recalled it all.

He recalled being plucked from his bed at dawn and taken away in a police car, his howls and screams drawing out the neighbours, who stood in silent judgement. He recalled the two nights he spent at the police station. He recalled Šain, who asked him the same questions over and over again. And the other one, in a white shirt, sleeves rolled up. Tenžer. The one who would hit him. He hit him while he was tied to a chair. He hit him in the ribs and the back, to leave no obvious trace. Then he would douse him with water and slap him with an open fist. And always the same questions: *What did you do to Silva Vela? Where did you kill her? Where did you hide the body? Explain the blood on the wood. Tell us where you buried her. Tell us where she is. Where's Silva Vela?*

And Adrijan's answers were always vague and incoherent, blurred by all the brandy and Coke. He answered, and the officers asked again, because the answers Adrijan offered were merely disjointed scraps of information soaked in alcohol. Adrijan knew this, but he didn't know the answers to their questions, so the officers asked again, and beat him again.

The water began to overflow. Adrijan turned off the tap and looked around for the woman. He approached and thanked her. And then – after a brief hesitation – he asked her a question. He couldn't help it. Curiosity was eating him up. "Tell me," he said, "that poster, by the toilet. The girl in the picture is from where I grew up, but that's a long way from here. How come it's here?"

"It's been there since before the war," Sanja replied. "Some man stuck it there, ages ago, well before all of this. He drove up one day, a bit before the war. He said he was looking for his daughter. He hoped someone might have seen her, a driver or someone passing by. God, that was ages ago... But I remember him well. He was thin, balding. He spoke the same as you, the same accent. Just the same."

Adrijan listened and pictured the scene – Jakov Vela, his skinny, stooped figure, his receding hairline and melancholy face; Jakov, far from home, telling his sad story to some bartender he didn't know, asking if she'd let him stick his missing poster somewhere on the wall. How desperate must he have been, thought Adrijan, to go all the way out there.

He looked at the piece of paper again. Back then, when everything was still fresh, the posters had been all over Misto and the surrounding area – on bus shelters, lamp posts and shop windows. Someone had stuck one of them to the bakery window. Adrijan's father didn't dare take it down, though he knew its presence was intended as a threat.

The posters were the same as the one Adrijan was looking at next to the door to the toilet: Silva's name, a description of what she had been wearing, and a contact number with the old Yugoslav dialling code. And her face – that obstinate nose, the hair falling across her brow. All the other posters were gone, taken down, ripped, washed away by rain. Only that one remained, far from home in another country, in a village on the other side of the front, next to a toilet door. Six years had passed. And two wars, in Croatia and Bosnia. Twice, the front had passed through that valley, twice armies had taken turns in conquering, razing and destroying. And as they took turns setting fire to the other's homes, the piece of paper with Silva's picture on it hung there untouched, next to the toilet door. While everyone else got older or died, only Silva stayed young, frozen on a white rectangle.

"So what happened?" Sanja blurted out. "Did they find her in the end, your neighbour?"

Adrijan heaved the skin onto his back, now heavy with water. Then he answered his new acquaintance. "No," he said. "They never found her. No one knows what happened to her."

"Her poor parents," said Sanja. "What a nightmare. There can't be anything worse."

Sanja put down the broom and they shook hands. She wished him luck in the war. Adrijan wished her success in getting her pub up and running. "When all this is over," he told her, "I'll stop by, treat myself to some pie or roast lunch. We could have a chat," he said, trying to sound courteous. The thoughts in his head were not so polite. Sanja was a good-looking woman. He'd happily have coffee with her one day, when the war was over.

As they headed back along the road towards their waiting unit, Adrijan's thoughts were not about a war that needed to end, but about Silva, about the picture on the wall, forgotten next to the toilet door.

Trucks came for them just short of Kupres.

By that time the pounding of artillery had almost petered out and the fighting front, if there even was any fighting any more, had moved somewhere north. At roughly midday, Cvitko spoke to command on the radio. He instructed the men to line up along the road and he told them their orders. "We protect the flank," he said. "Trucks will come for us."

Ten minutes later they arrived, four grey-green Deutz transport trucks. The men climbed in and the drivers pulled down the tarpaulin and drove away.

They drove for forty-five minutes, maybe an hour. For a while, they drove on asphalt and Adrijan had the feeling they were heading north-west. Then the trucks pulled off the asphalt onto compacted stone. Then they stopped. He heard Cvitko talking to someone on the radio to confirm the route. They set off again, and the road got worse and worse. Adrijan had no idea where they were. But he could feel them climbing higher and higher into the hills.

He looked at the faces of his comrades. They were understandably anxious. By that point in the war, they were unlikely to die from a bullet. But they could be killed by a leftover mine, buried long ago in the mud, half dislodged by the wheel of a truck. They could be blown sky-high by a Malyutka missile. Right then, anywhere was safer than inside that truck. The truck was a moving trap.

There were twenty of them inside, mostly from Split and a few from Omiš and Brač, mainly young. All of them had had lives before the war; they were lathe operators, traders, cement workers or milkmen. Some had wives and children at home, others had come straight out of school like innocent dimwits. Whoever they were, whatever they had done, all of them were waiting for the war to finish and to return to where they'd come from, to what they had been doing. Their lives had been put on hold, like a mid-sentence comma. They were all waiting for the torment to end, to continue the sentence. All of them except Adrijan. As the Deutz swayed around the bends in the Bosnian roads and his comrades fretted, Adrijan knew he did not want the war to end. The war had saved him. It had made him.

In war, Adrijan was good. He was sharp, fast and reliable. He coped with sleeplessness and physical strain. He was patient, he could wait, and in war you wait more than anything else. He could be quiet when it was time to be quiet. He didn't drink much, he didn't do drugs, he didn't smoke; he could be on guard at night without the embers of a cigarette giving away their position. He faithfully carried out the orders Cvitko or anyone else gave him. When it was time to shoot, he would shoot, but he never allowed himself to take pleasure in violence. Whenever anyone got hooked on violence it would usually end in trouble for him and those around him.

Adrijan was good for the war, but the war was also good for Adrijan. He revelled in the anonymity, in the implied respect that came with it. Adrijan liked the new identity he had built through four years of war. He liked it more than the old one.

The truck dragged itself along the road of broken stone through dense forest. As they climbed, the road became more and more eroded. From the cabin they heard the crackle of a two-way radio. Cvitko was communicating with someone, taking orders they knew nothing about.

And right then, as the grey-green Deutz crawled to the top of the Bosnian mountain, it became clearer to Adrijan than ever before. He did not want to pick up where he had left off; he did not want to resume where his comma was waiting.

As the truck struggled around the bends in the forest, Adrijan imagined what he would return to. He thought about Misto, about the neighbours who ignored him on the street, who passed by his house with contempt, as if passing by the house of a murderer. He thought about his father, who spent the whole day in silence, staring at the floor, and about the customers who would toss coins on the counter and walk out with a bag full of warm bread without saying a word.

He thought about the day they were drafted, when they were lined up on the basketball court, when the truck of some construction company pulled up and with it Rade, the owner of the Lantern cafe. Rade hadn't served an espresso macchiato since the war began. He was in charge of something called Crisis HQ.

There, on the court, Rade had handed them their uniforms, boots, water bottles and blankets, but not rifles or grenades. Local riff-raff didn't have the right to weapons.

Then they were ordered to fall in. There were thirty of them in formation, the cream of the 1972–3 crop – those about to leave school or starting university, deserters from the Yugoslav army, or sailors caught between voyages by the call to mobilize. The boss of the Lantern thanked them on behalf of the homeland in that awkward new Croatian he barely got his mouth around at official events. Then he saluted, called them to attention and ordered them to fall out. And the villagers stood there, in curiosity and horror.

Adrijan remembered the people who had gathered to witness the historic summons to arms, a date that would be inscribed on a memorial plaque as the village's proudest.

Adrijan saw his father among them. He saw the worry on his father's face, his understandable fear. But it was mixed with another emotion. Adrijan knew exactly what his old man was thinking. Old Lekaj saw thirty lads in the same uniform, thirty heroes going off to fight for the same native soil. And he saw Adrijan, his son, an Albanian in the same uniform, in the same formation, equal and accepted. That's what his old man saw. He saw acceptance, and the possibility of a fresh start.

But his old man was not the only one on the court that day. Adrijan saw other faces too. He saw the face of Silva's mother, the geography teacher. Silva's mother was standing right at the back, looking at other people's children standing in formation, but without a hint of compassion or sympathy. She stared at Adrijan, as if saying to him: *Aha, so that's where you're hiding.*

Adrijan remembered, and he knew he would not go back to that life, that he had no intention of returning to Misto. The old Adrijan would cease to exist.

Abruptly, the truck stopped. It stopped, then started again, then tilted to one side with a grinding of metal. The tarpaulin and the wooden frame of the truck bed began to sway. Adrijan heard a short scream of panic, then calm was restored. There was silence, and then they heard Cvitko's voice. "Everyone out," he shouted. "The front wheel's in a hole."

Cautiously, they climbed out of the truck, one by one. Adrijan looked around. They were in a dense forest of towering trees. From their silvery bark Adrijan guessed they were beeches. A few steps from the road, the forest was as dark as night, as dark as a pit. The road was hardly a road at all. It was a tank path cleared by diggers for the war. It had been made in a hurry; all around lay the rotting remains of trees toppled by the digger and tossed to the side. The earth surface was soft and moist, even then in the middle of summer.

They gathered round to check the damage. The front wheel hadn't just gone into a hole. It was suspended over an abyss, over a steep drop between the trees. As the soldiers watched, the driver tried to get the empty truck onto firm ground. He put it in reverse and accelerated, but the other wheel buried itself in the viscous ground. After several unsuccessful attempts the driver got out, shaking his head in despair. "Need to collect sticks," he said. "We'll put dry sticks under the other wheel."

Cvitko ordered the platoon to spread out in a line and move down into the forest for as many dry sticks as possible. Adrijan's boot sank into the moist black earth once, then twice, and after a few steps he was already in half-darkness. He looked around at the mildew, the moss and mushrooms, at the greenish trunks. Between those damp layers of life he looked for suitable sticks, strong enough, dry enough.

Adrijan walked and gathered sticks, descending deeper and deeper into the forest. He lost sight of the other soldiers but he could hear their voices and knew they were close. From above, light broke through the trees, a trail of light that led back to the road. Once his arms were full, Adrijan turned back.

He climbed the slope, zigzagging to avoid slippery ground and the thickest undergrowth. At one point he thought he was lost, before spotting a ray of light and the familiar stump of a felled tree. Adrijan climbed. Then his boot caught on something. Edging his foot forward, he could feel the top of his boot caught on something elastic. Three years of war told him he was already dead.

Pushing away the grass with his hand, Adrijan glimpsed exactly what he had feared: a metal wire, elastic but firm, coming out of the undergrowth and extending in the direction of the felled tree. Adrijan's standing leg was tugging on the wire, the top of his boot gently tightening it.

Adrijan knew the wire led to a PROM-1, a Yugoslav-made bounding fragmentation mine. Someone, he thought, one of ours or one of theirs, had put it there at some point to protect a position, ours or theirs. He knew that if he pulled the wire or released the tension, the mine would activate. A quiver would activate the trigger, a starlike feather. The trigger would initiate the mine buried in the ground, somewhere in the undergrowth. The mine would jump to chest height and then explode, throwing out deadly metal fragments to a range of fifty yards. After three years asleep, hidden, buried in dense, moist black earth, beneath a layer of moss, grass and fungus, the mine would fulfil its purpose.

He tossed the sticks to one side. He knew then that he couldn't save himself. The only thing he could do was to make sure only he would die. So he didn't call for help. There was no one who could be of help.

Adrijan listened to the voices of soldiers in the distance still collecting wood, soldiers more fortunate than him. They laughed and mucked about, high on the sweet taste of victory. But soon they'd hear the explosion, and the laughter would stop.

So that's it, he thought. He felt a caustic, disappointed bitterness, as if lamenting an injustice or something he had forever been denied. Then he looked around once more. He looked at the moss and the damp trees, the green canopy and wafer-thin strips of sky. He looked at the endless, shadowy green. He looked at the place where he would die and couldn't help but wonder why this place, of all the places in the world.

Adrijan took a breath, then another. Then he shifted his foot. And waited. Only briefly. Because then came the detonation and a hot whiteness. A whiteness in which everything disappeared.

8
MATE (2001)

Mate arrived in Barcelona just before dusk. He entered the city from the direction of Perpignan and Girona, through a sprawling mass of warehouses, overpasses and hangars. As soon as he got the feeling he was nearing the centre, Mate turned off the four-lane road into an outlying district and turned east towards the sea. For a few minutes he drove along streets led only by his nose. And then on a corner he spotted a vegetable store called Verduras Sant Martí and he knew he was at least in the right part of town.

He kept driving along a web of roads that intersected in a perfect grid. He drove slowly, still trying to read the names of the streets. Cars honked at him from behind and a moustachioed man in a Peugeot overtook with a juicy Castilian expletive. Mate kept driving, reading street names that meant nothing to him: Carrer de Pujades, Carrer de Llull, Carrer d'Alaba, Carrer de Ramon Turro. He was not impressed by what he saw around him. This wasn't tourist Barcelona, the Barcelona he remembered from the package vacation he'd taken with Doris years before. These streets contained no elaborate Gothic architecture, no pointy towers or charming Latin squares with

111

pergolas and bougainvillea. The streets he drove were lined with low-rise houses in urgent need of a lick of paint, cheap textile shops, cafes, electrical stores and small filling stations.

Still he kept driving and reading: Carrer de Roc Boronat, Avinguda d'Icària. Passing a familiar park and graveyard, Adrijan realized he was going round in circles.

At some point, without much thought or a plan, he turned left into a long, straight road. He drove along it, heading south. Then he spotted the name he had been looking for: Carrer del Dr Trueta. That was where his hotel was located, at number 136. Mate had no idea who Dr Trueta might have been, but, tired and sleep-deprived, he was delighted to find him.

Mate kept going south but soon realized the numbers decreased towards the city centre. Finding an intersection that was wide enough, he made a U-turn and headed north towards the outskirts. He followed the numbers as they rose and finally stopped in front of number 136. He was in the right place.

A narrow, three-storey building one storey taller than its neighbours, the hotel looked less run-down than he had expected. Outside, it was already dark and the reception desk was visible through lit windows. An old man was sitting behind the counter; he looked like he had spent his entire life there, in that very chair. Mate parked the car and went inside.

The old man looked at him with suspicion, a suspicion that only grew when Mate handed him his passport. It was hardly surprising. A man arrives in February, well outside the tourist season. He arrives alone, by car. He has a passport of some new country, a country not on the map when the old man was learning the geography of Europe. And he has no luggage, only a modest sports bag.

After briefly studying the new, exotic passport with the chessboard crest of an unfamiliar republic, he stoically gave up, wrote down Mate's details and handed back the passport.

"*Las llaves*," he muttered, and handed Mate the keys, proper old keys on a forged metal key ring, not that modern magnetic card crap. Mate was starting to like the place.

There was no elevator, so he carried his bag up the stairs to the first floor. He opened the door to room 102 and threw himself on the bed. After 600 miles from Milan to Barcelona, he needed a rest, to lie there with his arms and legs outstretched, the blood flowing once more through his numbed limbs.

It was already dark outside when he woke. He looked at the clock. Almost ten o'clock. He jumped up. He had to call Doris. She'd be out of her mind with worry.

Mate splashed water on his face and picked up the Bakelite phone. Doris answered immediately. "Hey you," she chirped. "You arrived?"

The hard part was still to come, the part where he would have to lie.

They talked briefly about the day. Mate asked after their daughter, about the pain in Doris's neck and the man who was supposed to come that morning to fix the air conditioner. He described his journey: *yeah, no surprises, a bit of rain near Montpellier, congestion on the approach to Nice.* Then they both fell silent. If he had to lie, he would wait to be prompted. Doris didn't know the real reason for his trip to Barcelona. She wouldn't like it if she did.

Fortunately, Doris didn't ask about his work. She wasn't interested in the details of the non-existent meeting the next day or the non-existent handover of goods.

Doris talked about her day, which had only just ended. No, the air conditioning man hadn't come. Yes, Tina's ear still hurt. And the weather was bad – a southerly wind, rainy but warm.

"Your mum called. Give her a ring," Doris told him. "She didn't say much, nothing important. She simply wanted to talk to you."

And as Doris talked about Vesna's call and Tina's ear, Mate got up, rifled around in his bag and pulled from the inside pocket a folded sheet of A4. He placed the paper on the bedside table, flattened it out and read his own writing, two neatly written rows of letters: *No. 38, Carrer del Comte Borell.* He already knew it by heart.

Mate told Doris to kiss their daughter and they said good-bye, sending kisses to one another down the phone. "I love you," each said to the other. Then Mate hung up, with a twinge of guilt for feeling relieved. He looked again at the paper and the address of a place he had never been to before, a place he would visit the next day and maybe, just maybe, find his sister.

Mate met Doris in 1996. The war had just finished. After five years of fighting, everything was returning to normal: the village, the people, the work. Mate was still delivering fish packed in ice. One morning, he drove to a restaurant in Tribunj, a little north of Šibenik. He remembered that morning well. The place was half-empty; tourism had barely got started. A group of Austrians had sat down after arriving by charter yacht. Mate was unloading crates of sea bream and sea bass at the side door to the restaurant. Doris was behind the bar. She was serving drinks in her aunt's restaurant over the summer, saving up to buy a second-hand car. She was twenty-three, like him. From Split. A fourth-year economics student.

He liked her immediately and asked if he could buy her a drink, which seemed ridiculous given she was standing behind a bar. In early September, when exams started, he bumped into her in Split. The next day, he asked her out, and a week later they were together. They were engaged the following spring and Tina was already on her way.

Mate loved Doris. Doris was great. But there were things

Doris didn't understand. So it was better that Doris didn't know everything.

After the call, Mate was wide awake. He got up and looked at the room: plywood furniture, an empty closet that he didn't try to fill, walls covered with deep red flocked wallpaper, bulging as if infested with maggots. Mate imagined what it must be like to sleep in the room in the heat of summer.

He lifted the receiver again, dialled a Croatian number and listened to it ring briefly before a voice answered, the voice of his mother, in their home in Misto. Mate pictured her picking up in the hall and then sitting on the sofa beneath Silva's picture. He heard his mother's voice and her first, predictable question: what have you found out?

Mate told her that he had just arrived, that everything was fine, that he'd go to the address the next day, that yes he had bought a map and checked the location. No, he wouldn't go immediately. It was too late to go knocking on doors. He tried to mollify Vesna, who was burning with impatience in faraway Misto. He knew not to stir in her too much hope. It wasn't the first time someone had got in touch saying that they had seen Silva and knew where she lived. And every time they had been wrong, so once again his mother's enthusiasm made Mate nervous.

In the autumn it would be twelve years since Silva's disappearance. In that time, Mate had finished school, started work and served in the war as a naval reservist. He had spent six years delivering fish before going into the boat engine business. He had got married and had a child, by then four years old. And all that time, Mate had never stopped looking.

The search would blow hot and cold; it would slow down and then pick up pace. But it never completely stopped. Even in periods of happy calm, Mate felt a constant, unpleasant buzzing in his head, reminding him that not everything in his

115

life was as it should be. *Where's Silva?* it would say. *Why aren't you doing anything to find her?*

But he *was* doing something. He was constantly doing something. When Mate had had the money, he had hired a detective, but the detective had quickly given up. During his work trips, he would put up missing posters, and he put ads in Croatian, German and Italian newspapers.

In March 1997, Mate began working as a rep for diesel engine producers Farymann and Perkins, driving a van to pick up boat diesels in Trieste, Milan, Graz, Düsseldorf and Genoa. He would wander red-light districts, immigrant neighbourhoods and backstreets where junkies hung out. He left Silva's picture at hotel receptions and trade fairs. He waited for the phone to ring. It rang not once but many times. Yet every call proved a red herring.

A few times, Mate believed he'd made a breakthrough, like when a bus driver claimed to have seen Silva pouring water from a bucket into a drain in front of a house in the village of Veliko Trojstvo, in central Croatia. There were two sightings in Zagreb. One claimed that Silva was running a kiosk in the Travno district of the capital, but it turned out to be a different girl who looked nothing like Mate's sister. Once, he received word that a Silva Vela was in Ludwigsburg near Stuttgart. And she was. A person by the name of Silva Vela had been living in Stuttgart for twenty-five years, running a well-established dental prosthesis surgery in Ludwigsburg. She was in the phone book. Mate met her. She was Portuguese, with a Croatian ex-husband who had family roots in Misto. She had kept the surname and had vague memories of Misto. She had stayed there a long time ago. *Damals war es noch Jugoslawien.*

This time, however, Mate and his parents had the feeling there were on to something. A sailor from Misto had docked in Barcelona with a Panamanian boat for bulk cargo. He knew

Silva from around Misto and remembered her disappearance and everything that had followed. He claimed to have seen her leaving a shop on La Rambla. The sailor had been so sure that he had followed her all afternoon, taken the same bus and trailed her to the door of what appeared to be her home. As soon as she'd entered, he had noted down the address. He had given the address to Mate. There it was, on the bedside table next to the Bakelite telephone, in a hotel room plastered with suffocating wallpaper.

When Mate met Doris, he told her about Silva, though he feared her reaction. A few girls had already fled from the burden, as if his family's misfortune was some kind of deformity, a hump you carry with you and which forever marks you out. Doris was different. She looked at his family history soberly, too soberly, it turned out. For Doris, history was history and should not come between them.

Doris tolerated the time he spent searching for his sister, but only up to a point. As soon as Tina was born, things had changed. Mate had come to realize that Doris expected him to give up. She didn't say so, but the signals she sent were clear.

When Mate talked to his parents about the search, Doris's face betrayed a suppressed reluctance to join in; when Mate would travel on Silva's trail, Doris would sink into a silent malaise a day or two before he left. Sometimes, though not often, her dissatisfaction would reveal itself in ambiguous spoken fragments: "You have to think of the living too," she would say. "Your daughter's growing. Life is passing you by."

It irritated Mate at first. Then Tina came along. She was not an easy child. She suffered from every kind of colic, rash and infection; tonsillitis and fevers would break out like wildfires in the summer. Tina would cry at night, whether from pain, nightmares or anxiety. She was late to walk and late to talk. The nursery told them she was difficult.

Work took Mate away more and more and Doris found it increasingly hard without him. She grew exhausted trying to balance her own job and parenting. Life was complicated enough without the search for Silva. Suddenly there wasn't room for Silva.

"You have a mother and father," Doris once said. "It's time they looked a bit. At this stage of your life you need to prioritize."

But no one else could take on the search. Mate's mother didn't drive, she didn't speak any foreign languages, she had barely left Yugoslavia more than once or twice. His mother was useless. As for Mate's father, he didn't want to look any more. Though he would never say it out loud, Jakov had had enough, and Mate knew it. He knew his old man had gradually given up. The realization had been painful for both Mate and his mother. Vesna had experienced it as a betrayal, while Mate saw it as selfishness. He expected help from his father, for him to roll up his sleeves when the going got tough, not to withdraw into a shell, behind four walls, like some morose, unspeaking hermit.

Mate lay on his back on the hotel bed and looked at the crimson wallpaper, at the dead flies inside the ceiling light. He knew he wouldn't get any sleep. Another ten hours, he thought. Another ten hours and he would know whether his sister was really there or if it had been another sad false alarm. He turned out the light but continued staring at the ceiling, at the dancing traces of car headlamps from Carrer del Dr Trueta.

He tried to imagine the next day's meeting. He would approach the front door, some kind of front door. He would ring, or knock. Then something would happen. Perhaps nothing. Perhaps everything.

"If she'd wanted you to find her she'd have got in touch," Doris had once said. She told him that Silva had left of her own accord and would get in touch if she wanted to. She would call, send some kind of signal. "You should be angry at her," Doris said, scathingly. "Angry that she's turned your lives upside down."

Her words had upset Mate at the time. He told Doris that she didn't know Silva, that she didn't know what she was talking about. To disappear like that and never get in touch there must have been a reason, a threat; she must have been kidnapped or have feared for her life. She wouldn't do something like that, he told her.

It was the last conversation he and Doris had had about Silva. At its core, their relationship was harmonious; they suited each other on a human, parental and political level. Mate still found her attractive as a woman and he could talk to her about anything. Just not about that. Silva became a secret.

Mate went on searching, but he hid it from Doris. He coordinated the search around his work trips, extending them by a day or two. After the trade fair in Düsseldorf, he would search for Silva in Essen and Wuppertal; before the boat show in Genoa he would scout out Turin. He invented orders and took sly days off. He didn't even tell Doris or his father when new information came to light. He told his mother, but only her. He knew it kept her alive. Vesna lived off the belief that something was happening, that something was being done, that time was not simply passing without Silva.

And that was how it happened with Barcelona. When the sailor told him he had seen Silva on the Carrer del Comte Borell, Mate kept it from Doris. He took a week off work but told his wife that he had a business trip: delivery, installation, signing of contracts.

But there would be no signing or installation. Mate had a different itinerary for the following day: to go to Carrer del Comte Borell, to number 38, press the button on the intercom,

119

ring the doorbell or knock. Then something would happen. Maybe nothing. Maybe it would be hard, horribly hard. But what if it were easy? What if Silva – a different Silva – simply opened the door, as people do when the meter reader knocks, or a neighbour or travelling salesperson? What if it were all very easy?

"If she'd wanted you to find her she'd have got in touch." That's what Doris had said. But she hadn't got in touch. She hadn't called from Carrer del Comte Borell or from anywhere else. If he found her, what would he say to her? And what would she say to him?

He looked at his watch on the pillow. It was already three o'clock. He should be sleeping, his body wanted sleep, but his mind was wide awake, alive and agitated. He closed his eyes and tried not to think. It didn't work. Around four o'clock he realized it was hopeless. He would turn up on his sister's doorstep after a sleepless night.

The next morning Mate took a diazepam and had a breakfast of yoghurt. He called a taxi. He didn't feel composed enough to drive – not there, not in a big city he didn't know.

At eight o'clock the taxi deposited him outside 38 Comte Borell. He had considered his timing carefully. It was early enough that people with jobs would still be at home, late enough that they could be ambushed as they stepped out the door.

Number 38 was a four-storey brick building from the early 1900s. It was red and decorated with stone figures that had seen better days. Mate approached the intercom and studied the names. Some were Spanish, some sounded foreign, either African or Slavic: Diouf, Djebbour, Stoianov, Popovski. None of them sounded Croatian, but somehow Mate hadn't expected to find Silva living under her real surname.

It was only then, standing at the door, that Mate realized he hadn't planned for what would come next. He waited a second, then rang the bell for one of the ground-floor apartments. Thirty seconds later, an old woman peered out from a window. Mate held out Silva's picture and said: "My sister". The woman looked confused but curious. She buzzed him in with the words "*Tercer piso*".

Though Mate didn't speak Spanish, he could understand that much. Third floor, she had told him. She recognized Silva, thought Mate. She recognized Silva's photo. He almost choked on the excitement.

He didn't wait for the elevator. He ran up the stairs, two at a time. On the third floor he found two identical doors with forged metal frames. One bore the name Vaquero, the other Djebbour. He rang on Vaquero, but there was no answer. He rang again. Same result. The apartment was as quiet as a grave.

Mate rang on the other apartment. He heard footsteps and saw a light come on in the hallway. A man in his late sixties opened the door. He looked Arab or Indian. Mate said hello in English and held out Silva's picture – that same teenage picture from so long ago. "This woman, does she live here?" he asked in the proper English he had practised at work for years. The older man looked at the picture, indifferently at first, but then, in the murky depths of his mind, Mate saw a spark of recognition.

"She lived," the man replied. "She lived. This apartment. Before. Before me. Understand?"

"She moved out? Where is she now? Did she leave an address?" Mate peppered the old Arab with questions, but the man's face was impenetrable and Mate couldn't make out whether he understood anything. He looked at Mate suspiciously and said, "*Suecia.*" He repeated it, asking if Mate understood – "*Suecia, entiendes?*" – but Mate didn't understand anything.

Finally, the man raised his hand. "Wait," he said, and disappeared back into the apartment. Mate stood in the doorway and waited for him to return. He heard quiet conversation in a language that was probably Arabic. Through the half-open door he could see part of the interior: a side table for gloves, shoes arranged beneath it, an oriental rug. On the wall he saw framed, printed words in Arabic, probably a verse from the Koran. He saw family photos of children and grandchildren. He guessed the old man had gone to get someone younger, someone with a better grasp of English.

Mate waited for what felt like an eternity, though the old man had probably only been gone a few minutes. The quiet conversation inside seemed to heat up into a hushed row.

Perhaps they're hiding her, Mate thought, and the idea cut him like a blade. Perhaps they weren't letting her go to him. Perhaps she wasn't letting *them*. Mate considered whether to step inside and end the uncertainty, but then he saw the old man's shadow in the hall. He had returned with a woman in her early thirties. She wasn't wearing a veil or Islamic clothing. With her dark curly hair, she looked Spanish. She held in her hand a piece of paper.

"*Suecia*," the old man said again. "This. They left. She and husband. For post, you understand? For post."

The woman handed him the piece of paper. Then she spoke, in much better English than the old man. "They lived here before us," she said. "They left this address for any post that arrived for them. Unfortunately it's just the name of the man, the husband or boyfriend. That's all we have."

Mate took the paper. On it was written a single name, a man's name: Javier Baumann. Below the name was an address. It was only then he realized what the old man had been trying to tell him. *Suecia* meant Sweden.

The address was so messily written he had to copy it down. He took a piece of paper and a pencil and leaned on the banister to rewrite the address letter by letter. He was careful. He knew one wrong letter could mean driving hundreds of miles for nothing. The address was a real tongue-twister: *Skogsängsvägen 10, Hisings Backa 422 47, Gothenburg, Sweden.* He handed the original paper back to the old man. Then he asked what he wanted to know most of all: "How is she?" he asked. "How does she look?"

But the old man didn't seem to understand. "*Suecia,*" he repeated. "*Suecia.*" And he lifted his arms as if to imitate a plane.

"Is she okay?" Mate asked, in the simplest English he could manage. But he wasn't going to get anything more out of the old man. "*Suecia,*" he kept repeating, like a broken record.

Mate looked pleadingly at the woman and repeated his questions.

The woman waved her hand. "We didn't know them," she said. "We are tenants, like they were. We met when they moved out. They gave us that paper. All we know is that the housekeeper called him 'Chileno'. 'Chileno', that's what she called him, always by nationality, not by name. Chilean."

"And what about her? Did you speak to her?" Mate asked, but she shook her head.

"*Lo siento,*" the woman said, speaking Spanish for the first time. "We don't know anything else. Just this. Just what's written there."

Mate stopped as if having run out of questions, despite there being hundreds more he might ask. Seizing the opportunity, the Arab woman quickly mumbled goodbye and closed the door.

He regretted not asking them to at least let him inside. He wanted to see the home where his sister had apparently lived, to smell it, to feel the walls between which her body had moved, on which her shadow had fallen. But it was too late. The door was closed, the door to an apartment he would never enter.

Carefully folding the piece of paper with the address, Mate turned to walk down the stairs. Sweden, he thought. Another journey. But this time he had something firmer to grasp hold of. For the first time in ten years, he felt like he wasn't running around in circles.

In Split, Mate found Doris in a good mood. When he walked through the door she planted a kiss on his lips and told him she had a plan. As soon as he was ready, they'd take Tina out for pizza.

He took a long shower, savouring the warmth after hours on the road. As the water ran down his body, Mate closed his eyes and played back the long journey: the bends after Nice, the climb from Liguria to Piedmont, the bridge over the Piave, the snaking road down the Velebit mountains. His body wasn't driving any more, but his head was still behind the wheel.

By the time he had finished in the bathroom, Doris and Tina were ready. Doris drove them to a pizzeria in one of the club marinas. Mate knew the marina well because he had installed motors there on countless occasions. He looked at the *pasaras*, the outboards, speedboats and sailboats dozing in the dead season, sails stowed, covered and wrapped in tarpaulin. The proximity of the boats unnerved him. It reminded him of work, and work reminded him of his lies.

They sat down and ordered three *capricciosa* pizzas. Doris was still in a good mood and talking lots. She teased Tina, commented on the menu, the guests and the waiters. Doris was happy Mate was there. Wherever he had been, whatever had happened, she was pleased to have him back.

Tina was difficult again. She ordered apple juice and then changed her mind and asked for strawberry. When the pizza arrived, she started to act up, picking at the edges but not really eating. Then she asked her mother for ice cream. When she got it, she started to sulk. Mate watched her the whole time. He looked at the coquettish bow perched in her hair, the lock of hair tucked behind her ear. He studied that sullen expression of dissatisfaction they had grown so used to. He looked at his daughter and was gripped by a feeling he feared. Can a person find their own child unappealing?

When they got home, Doris poured them each a glass of wine and went to put Tina to bed. She returned quickly, took him by the hand and led him to their bedroom. She undressed him and took his dick in her hand. She stroked it slowly until Mate grew hard. Then she straddled him, all moist, and her breaths deepened. Mate felt his indescribable fatigue give way to enjoyment. His hand passed lightly over her thighs, her ribs and hips. He looked at her. Doris was still very attractive. With age she had gained a maturity and confidence. She looked even better than when he had first seen her in Tribunj.

Mate slowly caressed her thighs as she rode him faster and faster, her breaths growing louder and deeper until she finally climaxed. Having waited for that moment, Mate came quickly afterwards.

They lay there entwined in the creased sheets, in their mixed secretions. Mate breathed peacefully, watching the reflection of the street lights on the ceiling. He could hear Doris's heart beating and her quiet, deep breaths. She was completely still, but Mate knew she was awake. He felt a strange peace, a peace he hadn't felt for a long time, a peace he did not want to disturb with unwanted news. Skogsängsvägen 10, Hisings Backa. With Doris nestled in his arms, Mate listened to her calm breaths and repeated in his head that awkward combination of sounds, over and over, as if reciting an imaginary rosary.

Sooner or later – most certainly sooner – he would have to tell her he was leaving again. But not right then. Mate didn't want to ruin the sense of perfect peacefulness washing over him like warm, cleansing water. He stroked her, let her purr, and gradually everything faded: the room, Doris, Hisings Backa, all of it gradually concealed behind a grey veil of sleep.

After work the next day, Mate visited his mother. He left Split at rush hour along the coastal road to Misto and was quickly bogged down in heavy traffic. The cars crept bumper-to-bumper along a coastline Mate knew only too well.

He passed a tangle of settlements full of vacation apartments and weekend homes, past sleeping socialist-era hotels, closed campsites, closed pizzerias, closed shops. In February, the entire coastline hibernated in anticipation of June.

Entering Misto from the Split side, by the old naval base, he drove along the rusted, barbed wire fence full of holes and ruined in parts, a fence that no longer protected anyone from anything. Before the bend at the sea, he passed the entrance to the old base, a pavilion of broken windows and empty hangars resting in the rain.

The base had once been an imposing, closed-off and secretive city. When he was a boy, Mate had been too scared to approach the fence because of legends that did the rounds in Misto about locals shot at by overzealous Albanian guards.

Few locals had ever been inside the base. Back then, children had told fantastic tales about a network of tunnels in the cliffs. It was said that beneath Cape Cross were miles of water canals the navy had drilled through bare rock. The military had built them in the 1950s to hide patrol boats in the event of an Italian invasion. Mate's father told him that back then subterranean explosions had rocked Misto for months. But Italy had never attacked Yugoslavia, and all that remained of such unhinged ambition was an empty wasteland beneath the rock.

After the Yugoslav navy left, the abandoned base was plundered. The warehouses, underground arms stores and duty offices were falling apart, their windows smashed, gates torn from their hinges. The locals took everything they could – toilets, sinks, electrical wiring and stone steps. No one went down into the tunnels any more, and in 1996, when an earthquake struck Ston, to the south, the whole coast had shaken and the portal had collapsed, closing off the underground vaults. The entire scene of devastation was surrounded by a ring of torn, rusted barbed wire that locals said had been mined by some crazy lieutenant before the evacuation. For ages, it was rumoured that some Brits wanted to buy the base, or perhaps it was Russians, maybe Hungarians, in order to build hotels on Cape Cross. But Mate couldn't believe anyone would be interested in such a rotting, ruined place. He couldn't imagine anyone being served cocktails with umbrellas there.

At the entrance to the naval base he turned sharply along the seafront and entered Misto. He passed the basketball court where the war recruits had lined up in 1991 and the school where his mother still worked. He reached the square and saw Lekaj's bakery, as ramshackle as ever.

Since Adrijan had died in the war, his father seemed to have given up. He still baked bread and stood at the counter in the mornings, but that was all he did. He didn't go out, he didn't take care of the house and garden, he didn't take care of himself. When Mate was in Misto, he would go for bread instead of his mother. He would see old Lekaj, all skin and bone, standing at the counter from six till twelve, looking at the world around him as if blaming it for something.

Mate finally reached the church and parked the car. The church was open. He pondered whether to go in, whether he should kneel at the altar of St Simeon or St Wilgefortis, the female saint with the beard of a man. Perhaps he should give thanks to someone or something for the fact that they finally knew Silva's whereabouts. But he stayed outside. He knew his mother had prayed in that church a thousand times for him and for herself.

He knocked at the door of his house and went in, not waiting for an answer. His mother was already in the hall. She gave him a hug of relief. "I knew," she said. "I knew you'd find her."

Mate told her again what he had found out in Barcelona, this time in greater detail. He recounted the conversation with the Arab man and his daughter. Then he told her about the conversation with the housekeeper. Both the housekeeper and the Arab man had recognized the picture. The housekeeper said Silva had spent four years in the building. She had lived with a man – a husband or boyfriend – who was Chilean. The housekeeper knew the man had worked in a laboratory, as some kind of doctor or scientist. She hadn't known Silva's name. But she recognized her from the picture and said that from her accent she had to be Slav.

"It's too much to be a coincidence," said Mate.

Finally, he pulled from his pocket the paper with the name and address of Javier Baumann in Sweden. Vesna snatched it out of his hands and looked at it with reverence, as if holding a monstrance. She looked at the address written in Mate's plain hand and saw tangible, irrefutable evidence that Silva was alive. She sat down, overcome with excitement.

They ate lunch together. Vesna had made chard with hard-boiled eggs and sliced pancetta that was dry and tough. When they finished, Mate drained his glass of wine and got up. He wanted to get some air before he left.

He went down to the yard as the winter dusk was setting in. He looked around at the yard and the house, trying to discern any change. But there wasn't any, not even the change there should have been.

Twelve years had passed since Silva had vanished. Mate had left home after finding a job in Split as the war was ending. A few years later, Jakov and Vesna had separated. Mate was already living in Split when his father called one day to say he had finally found work. After the factory closed, Jakov had searched for a long time for work as a bookkeeper, and he told Mate that afternoon that he had finally found it, in a warehouse in Split.

Mate's father had moved to the city. Jakov sent Mate his address and one afternoon he invited him round to see where he lived. He led Mate into an empty, practically unfurnished apartment at the top of a high-rise in the Kocunar district. He told Mate how he had settled in, where he did his shopping and parked his car, without once mentioning Vesna, their separation or the divorce. But within months the separation had become obvious. Mate never saw his mother in Jakov's apartment and Jakov no longer went to Misto. It became clear to Mate that his parents had separated for good and that neither of them considered it necessary to utter a word to him about it.

He had no idea whether his parents communicated with each other, but he guessed not. When he saw them, each would ask about the other – but in a roundabout, coded way. *Do you see her? Do you see him? What's new over there?*

When Jakov moved out, Vesna was left alone in Misto, in the family home, the last keeper of a castle abandoned by its guards. But their ghosts remained. The house was a mausoleum of their mummified shadows. Silva's room, even after twelve years, was untouched, as if she had gone away for the weekend and would be right back. The bed was made and on the walls were her teenage posters from the eighties. Like universal constants, Jesus was still pointing his finger from the kitchen wall along with the photo of Canadian woodland. When it came to the garden, Vesna still kept up appearances. She still weeded and dug over four beds of chard, kale, cabbage and onion, as if there was anyone left to eat all those vegetables.

Mate approached the door of the *konoba* and turned the handle. He opened the door to what was once his father's cave, flicked on the light and looked around. As he'd expected, the *konoba* was also frozen in time. Radio transmitters and receivers lay on shelves as the remains of Jakov's long-deceased devotion to his hobby. In the middle of the room, on a table, were a handful of LEDs, transistors and resistors, as he had left them on 23 September 1989. After that day, Jakov had never played with his radios again. Just when what he really needed was the help of strangers, he lost all desire to spend nights talking to them. He turned it all off, broke off his overseas friendships, cut all connections with his faraway brethren.

When Jakov had moved to Split, he'd left the radio receivers behind, but Mate wasn't sure whether it was because he wouldn't have room in his Kocunar apartment or because he wanted to keep one foot in his former home, his former marriage, to leave the door open a crack. Whichever it was, the *konoba* was still Jakov's. And Vesna pretended everything was all right, that it was still 22 September 1989 and the twenty-third had yet to dawn. They all lived together, all present and correct; they had simply popped out, errands to run.

Mate looked for a while at the empty, forgotten space, which smelled of glue and soldering. He looked at the resistors and transistors gathering dust that no one ever wiped away. Then he turned out the light and closed the door.

It was already dark when he got back to Split. He and Doris spent the evening in front of the TV, watching some Korean crime movie in which a sadist killed young women in red dresses. At eleven o'clock, Doris said she was tired. As they got into bed, Mate knew it was the right time to tell her. "I have to go away again," he said. "Sweden, on Monday. Volvo headquarters. There's a problem with the delivery."

Doris said nothing, but a shadow passed over her face, a shadow no one would have noticed. Only Mate.

Mate landed in Gothenburg on 1 March. To the south, in Split, spring had already arrived; the cherry trees were white with blossom and Mother Nature was in full bloom after the first March *buras.* In Sweden he was met by winter, by fat wet drops of sleet and snowploughs at work on the road from the airport.

He arrived early. Not wanting to waste time checking into his hotel, he took a taxi straight to Skogsängsvägen 10. He couldn't bear the suspense. He no longer had the strength to be patient.

They drove through the sleet, over a wide river and narrow canal. Mate looked through the window at residential districts, schools, nurseries and libraries. They looked like they had appeared all at once in the 1960s and 1970s, part of a single endeavour, the work of one hand. He looked through the window at an unfamiliar terrain. It seemed a nice place, but one that had seen better days.

The taxi driver drove him to a parking area at the centre of a residential neighbourhood of uniform, two-storey houses clad in sheet metal. There was a playground and common area between each cluster of houses. The weather was miserable, so no one was out. But there were lights on everywhere and what blinds he could see were up. As he walked, Mate saw fragments of a movie, snatches of intimacy involving people he would never meet, people reading books, drinking tea, leafing through magazines, oblivious to the foreigner peering into their bright aquarium. It was a world in which no one had secrets. Except one. One person in that neighbourhood had a secret, and that was the person Mate was looking for.

Following the house numbers, he stopped when he reached number ten. He climbed the steps to a raised ground floor and wooden veranda. On the door was an improvised paper nameplate that bore the name he was looking for: Baumann. Chileno, as the Spanish woman had called him. Mate rang the bell and waited.

He rang again, and again. Then the door opened and in front of him stood a dark-haired man with round glasses. He looked slightly startled and then said hello in a language that must have been Swedish.

"Javier Baumann?" Mate asked.

"Yes," the man replied.

"I'm looking for this woman," Mate said in English, and held out Silva's picture. The man with the glasses looked at the picture with surprise and invited him in.

There was no hallway. From the door they stepped straight into a small main room. It looked like the room of a professor – on a small table stood empty glasses, a jar of olives and an open DVD case; there were books and lecture papers on the floor. Music was playing quietly, but Mate was unsure whether it was J. J. Cale or Lou Reed. The Chilean turned the sound down and took the dirty glasses from the table. Then he called to someone in English.

A woman entered the room.

As soon as he saw her, Mate knew he had wasted his time.

There was a similarity in the head, the cheekbones, the forehead and eyebrows. The woman in front of him was in her late twenties yet wore her hair in the relaxed style of someone younger, a style strikingly similar to Silva's. But she wasn't Silva. The sailor could have been forgiven, but not in a thousand years would Mate ever believe the woman standing before him was his sister. This woman was shorter, heavier in the chest, had a different jawline and much lighter eyes. She also looked at him differently. As an old Dalmatian woman might say, she had a different *arija del vižo*. The woman was not his sister.

Mate didn't feel sadness. He felt something else, something that surprised him – shame. He felt ashamed to be there, ashamed of the enthusiasm with which he had arrived.

"You were looking for me?" the woman asked in English, though her accent really did sound Slavic. Her gaze fell on the black-and-white picture in Mate's hand. Mate saw her confusion. To her mind, she had nothing in common with the teenage girl in the picture; she bore no similarity whatsoever.

Mate explained who he was and why he had come. He told them he had been looking for his sister for twelve years, criss-crossing Europe. They listened, but Mate could see they thought he was crazy.

Then he told them about Barcelona, about picking up the scent. He described the conversation with the Djebbour family and the Spanish housekeeper. Only then did they seem to grasp the gravity of what he was telling them. "Oh my God, that's so sad," the woman said, raising her hand to her mouth.

They introduced themselves. He was a postdoc molecular biologist. Her name was Rumena, and she was from Bulgaria. She had worked as a doctor in a clinic in Vienna when Javier was a postgraduate student there, then they had lived in Spain while Javier was doing his doctorate. They had moved to Sweden in January and both found work – she as a dermatologist, he at the university. They had only met the Djebbour family once. "But how could the housekeeper have made such a mistake?" asked Javier.

"Oh my God," Rumena said again. "What a story, what a terrible story."

They offered him a glass of red wine. Mate hesitated but then realized he was already too tired to move. He sat down and took the glass offered to him by the Chilean. He sipped the Chilean Cabernet and liked it. As the wine ran down from his palate into his body, Mate felt the life returning to his limbs. When the Bulgarian woman had stepped into the room, all his strength had left him; momentarily, his body had felt like a deflated bag of skin. With the wine, he felt his strength return. He realized how tired he was and that he hadn't eaten since the day before.

Rumena came out from the kitchen with a tray of Bulgarian and Spanish tapas: tapenade, *ajvar*, cheese, chorizo, mixed salad sprinkled with cheese, cucumber in yogurt, and bread. Mate was famished. He grabbed the chorizo with both hands and dunked the bread in the yogurt; the cheese crumbled over the table. Then the woman brought a bottle of rakija. It smelled intensely of fennel. She poured each of them a glass. "For your sister," she said, and raised her drink. "For your search. For you. You are a brave man, very brave."

They got drunk that evening. They sat there in that Swedish home, home to two people Mate would never see again, opening bottle after bottle, wine then rakija, rakija then wine. Javier told him his family history, a complex thriller of politics, military coups and executed dissidents. The drunker they got, the more Dr Baumann would hug him as Rumena repeated over and over again what a good brother he was, how brave he was. These are good people, Mate thought in a drunken haze. The kind of people I'd like to have back home. To get to know them and spend time with them.

It was gone three in the morning when he left Skogsängsvägen. He took a taxi back to the hotel, where he would sleep for half an hour in his clothes, his bags still packed. At 6.15, he caught a flight via Frankfurt and Zagreb to Split.

His head was killing him, the hangover only beginning to lift as he flew over Austria, the Alps poking up from the ground below. He asked the flight attendant for a tomato juice to fill his stomach and stave off any urge to vomit. Looking down at the sharp peaks that stretched endlessly into the distance, he prayed for his headache to pass. Never had he wanted to get home so much.

He arrived late. Tina was already asleep. On her pillow he placed a cuddly toy he had picked up in the airport shop. He lay down on the sofa and looked at Doris. I must look a wreck, he thought.

After a shower, Mate went to bed. He felt the ache from the alcohol still throbbing in his temples. Doris approached and put her hand on his forehead. "You look terrible," she said.

"I'm tired," he replied.

"It shows," she said.

"I'll be all right. I just need some sleep."

Doris didn't reply. Her gaze was calm and penetrating, her eyes as dark and intelligent as that day in Tribunj. She lifted her hand from his head but kept looking at him. Then she spoke. "I'm sorry," she said. "I'm sorry it didn't work out."

"What didn't work out?" asked Mate.

"You know what," Doris said. "That you didn't find her. That you went in vain."

Then she rolled over to her side of the bed, wrapped herself in the covers and turned out the light.

9

GORKI

Gorki stopped his car at a viewpoint on the coastal road shortly before Misto. He scaled the bank to a position that he remembered offered the best view of the village and looked down on a landscape he had once known like the back of his hand.

Misto had changed in fifteen years. The basic contours were the same. Cape Cross still stood over it, the stone cross now decorated with lights. Gorki could still make out the old part of the village, a cluster of houses on an elevation around the church. He recognized the old harbour and the small fishing boats clustered in the shallow marina. And the oldest row of vacation homes, built under communism, also looked the same.

But the changes were obvious. There were new roofs and plastic windows on many of the old houses, loud, shiny colours among the facades of the oldest stone homes. The row of beachfront properties didn't stretch just to the breakwater any more but almost as far as the Stella Maris chapel. The houses furthest from the centre were the newest and, as could be expected, the biggest and ugliest. The north side of Misto had at least doubled in size. The south side remained the same.

Behind the bend and the basketball court still stretched the rusted wire of the naval base, and behind the wire a no-man's land of weeds, empty hangars and pillaged pavilions.

Gorki stood at the viewpoint and was surprised to feel so ill at ease. The view of Misto left him feeling morose, as if all those years had not passed. As if it had all happened yesterday.

He spat over the cliff and watched the gob of phlegm fall. Then he turned around and got back in his car. The autumn days were short, and he wanted to get as much done as possible.

For Gorki, Misto was never more than a point on a map, a sign at the side of a road he had taken a hundred times. Then overnight that sign had become part of his life. He remembered perfectly the day it had happened. It was September, the last autumn of communism. September 1989. Sunday the twenty-fourth.

He drove past the entrance to the former naval base, stripped bare, rusting and overgrown. He passed the basketball court and arrived in the centre. He looked at the familiar church, the familiar cafes, the familiar houses. If he tried hard enough, he could recall every single inhabitant of those houses, by name, by family. He had a memory like an elephant, which helped in his work, as it had helped in his previous job. He remembered everything, even what he shouldn't. And he remembered Misto – the names, the faces, the locations, the distances. He knew everything about that place, more than he cared to.

On that day, 24 September 1989, Gorki had entered Misto for the first time in his life, along the same road, past the base which at that time still housed the Yugoslav military. He arrived in the early afternoon, responding to a phone call that had sounded innocuous: a teenage girl, seventeen years old, had disappeared after a drunken party and not returned home. He remembered the family who had called him. The parents – a thin, unforthcoming father with a guilty face and a slightly overweight, agitated mother – told him that their daughter had gone missing and showed him a picture. It was the first time he saw Silva Vela, her dark eyes and truculent face.

That Sunday, he had believed the girl's disappearance was a classic case of childishness that would resolve itself by the morning. When it didn't, Gorki thought they would find the girl – dead or alive – within a matter of days. But weeks passed, then months, and still he couldn't find Silva Vela. Nor could anyone else.

Gorki parked outside the church and took a good look at the familiar scene. The church looked the same. The parish house had been renovated and its approach smartly paved. The Partisan memorial still stood in the same place, but the words had been chipped off its stone plinth so the dedication couldn't be read. The holes left behind in the limestone walls had turned black and looked like scars or marks made by small beaks. Gorki stood in the middle of the square and looked at the houses, one by one: the Lekaj house, the Šustić house, the Bakić house, the Končurat house, the Skaramuča house. He wondered whether the same people still lived there.

Leaving his car on the square, he entered one of the side streets. He passed the hair salon that had since closed. Ten yards further on, he spotted the door he was looking for. He checked the name by the bell. CAPTAIN FILIP PADOVAN, it said. He was in the right place.

He rang the bell. A woman in her late sixties opened the door. Margita, the captain's widow. Gorki remembered her from before. He prayed that she didn't remember him.

"Hello," he said. "I'm Šain. We spoke on the phone."

"You're from the agency?" she asked.

"That's me," he said.

"Come in," said Margita, and showed him inside. She motioned for him to sit at the kitchen table and offered him coffee, which he declined. She told him she had elderflower juice, which Gorki accepted. As Margita poured him his drink, he looked around at where he found himself, at the heavy cabinet, the lace doilies, the souvenirs from the captain's voyages, a crucifix above the kitchen door and, next to the window, a framed picture of St Anthony of Padua holding a lily, his finger pointing to the sky.

Gorki recalled that Margita had been religious. Such things don't change, and so too the house remained the same. But Gorki did see something that hadn't been there before. On the table was a folder full of A4 papers: contracts, powers of attorney, cadastral records. And poking out from the pile were freshly stamped deeds. She's ready, he thought. Ready to do business.

The captain's widow placed the juice on the table in front of him and slid a mat under the glass. Her manner was pleasant, but reserved and slightly cautious. She behaved towards him the way you might towards someone you don't particularly like but who you believe you might get some money out of.

Margita sat down opposite him and took the file in her hands, signalling that she was ready to talk. She looked at Gorki, and in an instant her expression changed.

She recognizes me, Gorki thought. She remembers me.

The widow did remember him, and Gorki wished she didn't.

If it hadn't been for Misto, everything would have been different. Misto and Silva Vela had turned his life upside down. He had known it then just as he knew it now.

In September 1989, Gorki had arrived in Misto with his whole life ahead of him. He was twenty-six years old, a police officer and a member of the Party who had passed his law degree with flying colours. In January that year he had been hired by the Split Secretariat of the Interior Ministry of the Republic of Croatia as an inspector in the violent crime department. In January he got his badge, in March he got married, and in April he bought a high-rise apartment through the housing cooperative. In 1989, Gorki was a man without worries. He should have had a long, comfortable life ahead of him, a career full of success and culminating in a job with the public prosecution or the higher court, perhaps in politics.

Gorki knew he was good at his job. He knew the trade and had a good memory and a fast mind. But Gorki wasn't naïve. He also knew his surname opened doors for him at work and in his private life. He was the grandson of Albino Šain, a Hero of the People immortalized in Partisan monuments, who had gone through the battles of the Neretva and Sutjeska with Tito, the Albino Šain who in September 1943, when Italy capitulated, had led a column of Partisans along Solinska into liberated Split. Books had been written about his grandfather's heroism, his exploits depicted in stirring films that Gorki had never liked.

For a long time, a memorial to the Unknown Soldier stood on the seafront in Bisak, cast in the likeness of Albino Šain. As a boy, Gorki would accompany his grandfather to Bisak for revolutionary commemorations. He would stare in wonder at his grandfather, alive and well, and at his bronze, dead copy. The two Šains would stand side by side, the same slight build, the same sharp cheekbones and high forehead. His grandfather, by then quite old, would usually give a long, rambling speech while Gorki gazed at his bronze twin. He hadn't been back to Bisak for some time but was told that the statue had been blown to pieces. Someone had placed a stick of dynamite under it in the first weeks of the war; the municipal cleaners had swept up the bronze remnants and taken them to the dump.

Gorki had suffered a similar fate in 1990; a stick of dynamite was placed under him and his life was blown to bits.

In a matter of months, the world that Gorki had come to depend on, that he believed eternal, crumbled before his eyes. New faces turned up, people who spoke in a different tongue and told different stories, whether true or made up. Suddenly, the Šain name didn't open any doors. It wasn't enough that he bore the surname of his heroic grandfather; at his grandfather's urging, his father had named him Gorki after the Russian writer and socialist Maxim Gorky. When the war came, that name followed him like a dirty word. Gorki had woken up in a new world in which he was perceived as toxic.

He tried. He tried to demonstrate his professionalism, that he knew how to do his job. He believed that thieves would always be thieves and that the country would always need police officers to catch them. Just as society always needed surgeons, pilots and spies, so it would need him. He believed that.

Then Misto happened. Silva Vela happened.

Had he found the missing girl, things might have been different. He would have had a trophy to show off, a reason to trumpet his expertise or at least be able to pour out his heart to the newspapers, playing the martyr. But Silva Vela had buried him. She was a blank page in his dossier, an unsolved case that had first seemed so banal, so simple to crack. Those who didn't like his grandfather, his Partisan heritage and the fact he was named after Maxim Gorky had an undeniable argument. They could point a finger at his obvious failure.

That's why he had tried. He had tried more than ever, more than for anything else. He had questioned dealers and informers in Split, studied hours of VHS security videos from the bus station and customs and walked the length and breadth of Misto. He had sent police patrols criss-crossing the dark rock at the water's edge, the hollows, the craggy, exposed limestone and sinkholes of the karst; he had deployed divers to search the seabed in the cove. And then one day he found a bank clerk who testified that Silva Vela had left the country. From then on, the case became an unsolvable nightmare. The investigation mutated into a bureaucratic back and forth with the Italians and Austrians, with Belgrade and Interpol. Memo after memo after memo, until at some point Gorki realized no one was looking for the girl, not even him. The system was going through the motions, to no effect. Finally, in mid 1990, Gorki had also given up. The humiliation came a few months later: reassignment to a desk job in the passport department. The bosses were waiting for him to lose patience and quit before he could be fired. And a few months later, he did. Gorki hadn't been back to Misto since.

During the investigation, he had questioned almost everyone in Misto. He remembered them all: the Bakićs, the Rokovs, the Šustićs, the Končurats. He remembered Mrs Padovan too. He had questioned the captain's widow in that very room, in the very same chairs. St Anthony with the lily had been in the same place, and the crucifix above the door. But the old captain was alive back then. He had sat in the corner, wheezing from the tobacco that would kill him thirteen years later. Gorki remembered both of them well. The widow remembered him too. But she didn't say a word, not wanting to spoil the deal they were about to seal.

"Right," said Gorki, sipping his elderflower juice. "You know everything. You know the terms, you know the price. Have we agreed everything, or is there something else?"

"Perhaps we can go over everything once more," said Margita, opening the file. Gorki had been a police officer for a long time; he knew how to read people's reactions. The old woman was hesitating. She was buying time, procrastinating, as if she hadn't made up her mind.

Gorki took his briefcase and pulled out a bundle of papers, among them a contract. At the top of the contract was the logo of the Irish property fund he represented. He read her the terms once more; they were more than generous. Margita would sell 9,000 square metres of Rokov's Land behind the Stella Maris chapel to Smart Solutions Estate. Immediately, she would receive a deposit of thirty euros per square metre, and the contract would have an annex: Smart Solutions Estate would pay fifty euros per square metre for the land and another fifty if and when the local assembly reclassified it as construction land. The contract would be valid if all co-owners – the Padovans, the Bakićs and the Rokovs – sold up to the Irish fund. If the reclassification failed, Margita would keep the deposit, 27,000 euros, as soon as she signed, no strings attached, no ifs, no buts.

The widow listened, composed and nodding. Before, she had been the owner of a barren wasteland worth nothing, a steep, rocky slope on which nothing but weeds had grown for a hundred years. And suddenly that collection of rocks, Spanish broom and juniper had turned to gold as if by magic. She would get a million euros for what had until the day before been nothing but a parched mass of thicket. And Margita, Gorki knew, needed a million euros. She needed it because her husband had recently died, because her pension was 280 euros a month, because her son had got himself into financial difficulties and had offered the bank the house his mother lived in as collateral. Gorki knew that at that moment he was Margita's only way out.

"You must understand…" the old woman muttered. "I never thought…"

"People don't usually think," Gorki replied. "It just happens."

"If my son didn't need help…"

"I know. You'd never sell. But that's life, and these are the crosses we bear."

"My husband would turn in his grave," she said. "He wanted to save it for the grandchildren."

"We can't turn back the clock," Gorki replied, the comforting adages tripping off his tongue. "He would have done the same. We have to think about the future. About the children."

It wasn't the first time Gorki had been in such a situation. He knew what had to be done. A door stood before them, and that door needed to be opened. He had to tell Margita what she wanted to hear. That it was for the good of everyone – for her and her son. That there was nothing to be in two minds about because there was no choice. Land is just land, not a kingdom, not a crown, not a noble title or pledge of honour. Just land. A strip of coastal rock that she would sell for her own good and for the good of everyone.

Then he took the contract and a pen in his hand and placed them on the table in front of the widow. He waited. He was in no hurry. These things take time. He had learned that they cannot be rushed.

The old woman looked lost in thought. Then, as if pushing aside any doubt, she put on her glasses and picked up the pen. Her signature was unpretentious, conventional, like that of a schoolgirl.

Margita set down the pen and took a deep breath. Then all of a sudden she leaned over and her jaw began to tremble uncontrollably. She started to cry, quietly at first, then harder, sobbing. Finally, she rubbed her eyes and said, "I'm sorry."

Gorki continued to wait patiently.

"I'm sorry," Margita repeated, still sobbing. "It's not you. It's just hard. It's hard without him. It's hard being alone after all these years."

And while the captain's widow cried, Gorki tried with all his might to suppress the feeling sweeping over him like a wave: shame. He put the contracts in his briefcase, shut it and looked at the glass of elderflower juice in front of him, at St Anthony with the lily, at the floor. Right then, he had only one, irresistible urge – to run from that house.

"The money will be in your account tomorrow, by three, by close of business," he said.

He stood and held out his hand. The old woman squeezed it weakly and followed him to the door. On the doorstep, Margita told him: "I remember you. I remember you from back then, when you were what you were before."

Gorki stopped and replied: "And I remember you from then. When I was what I was before."

"Who would have thought," said the old woman.

"Thought what?"

"This," she replied. "That you'd be what you are now, and I'd be what I am."

She didn't wait for a reply. Nodding at him kindly, she closed the door, and the porch and street sank back into darkness. Gorki looked briefly at the door that had closed, and descended the steps of the captain's house.

Gorki had begun working for the property fund shortly after the war. He got the job after replying to an ad looking for someone with a law degree. At first, he had concealed the fact he had been in the police. It quickly became clear, however, that his former trade was invaluable. Gorki's job was to investigate. Not crime this time, but misfortune.

What Smart Solutions Estate did was simple. It bought and sold land. It bought cheap and sold expensive. It bought remote coves, run-down vineyards, hillsides covered in tangles of rosemary and juniper. Then it sold it on as building land: consolidated, listed in the land register and included in the urban plan as a tourism or residential zone.

Gorki knew his employer bribed politicians. Company lawyers visited mayors and councillors on Croatian islands, showed them stunning PowerPoint simulations made with AutoCAD and Corel and took them out for dinner and boat trips. And when the partying ended, the company gave them some pocket money, usually with lots of zeros. Gorki didn't have any moral issue with such practices. Not any more. From the start, he had told the Irish it was not something he wished to do. He imagined walking into the office of some municipal mayor, some dark-haired young man in a white shirt, the ideal conservative son-in-law. He imagined surreptitiously passing an envelope containing 1,000 euros to a man with a crucifix on his desk and the embroidered words of the national anthem on the wall. Gorki had stooped to many things before, but not to that. He didn't have the stomach for it.

His job was different. He did what the company called "prep". They identified a promising location, usually a cove near a settlement. Then they made contact with the local authorities and tested the water, saw whether they might play ball. That's when Gorki would step in. He would trawl through the cadastre and try to discern from the thicket of outdated records who actually owned the land. He would root out long-lost nephews in Australia and Argentina, disentangle family trees and hunt down distant descendants who would find out from him about the carob and fig trees in their name. A spider's web of land plots, ownership structures and names from Split, Zagreb, Auckland and Perth would form before his eyes.

Nephews and nieces, grandchildren and great-grandchildren of ancient brotherhoods, shipowners, landowners and holders of farming rights would stand before him in a maze of graph paper.

Then, when that was done, he would start on the more important part of the job: the investigation.

It was Gorki's job to find the soft underbelly, the weak spot. There are any number of reasons why someone might sell a birthright by the sea: urgent surgery, a bank debt, a workplace accident, a settling of accounts with relatives in Serbia, an alcoholic son, a child getting divorced or struggling with a gambling habit. Over time, Gorki had learned that none of the reasons were ever pleasant.

Having left the Padovan house, he headed uphill, through the web of streets behind the church. He passed behind the Lekaj bakery, the bakery he remembered well and which, he was surprised to see, looked just the same, working just as it always had. He passed the old rusty van, which, if he remembered correctly, sat in the same place as fifteen years before. He reached the top end of Misto, where the houses thinned out, each one set on a large plot. He walked until he reached a door to a garden. He banged the knocker and entered.

The garden was nothing special – beds with concrete borders planted with artichoke, tomato and kale. The entrance to the house was from a raised ground floor; a wind chime made of metal hung above the door, rattling in the breeze. He climbed the steps and rang the doorbell. He had dealt with the Padovans. The Bakićs were next.

A fairly attractive, dark-eyed woman in her early forties opened the door. She wasn't among the owners Gorki had identified in the papers, so he guessed she might be the daughter-in-law. She said hello and invited him in. The man he had been negotiating with met him in the hallway. Tomo

Bakić was the owner's son, a balding, portly man in his fifties with a mild Zagreb accent. They shook hands and he showed Gorki into the living room. He introduced his sister and his wife, invited him to sit down and said they would call his mother. "It was a bit difficult, you know," he told Gorki. "She wasn't easily persuaded."

Nothing new, thought Gorki. He sensed he was about to witness a dose of family discord.

"Jola, the man's here about the land," the wife called out. For a while, there was silence. Then came a clatter of metal and a woman entered the living room in a wheelchair. Gorki knew her, and everything about her. He had a copy of her ID card, proof of ownership and baptism certificate. But this was the first time he had laid eyes on Jolanda Bakić.

The old woman in the chair wheeled herself to the centre of the room and stopped directly in front of Gorki. She was in her eighties, grey-haired, thin, but still with an air of authority about her. Gorki knew she was in the advanced stages of stomach cancer. The disease had already taken a toll. Everything about her looked pale, wrinkled, waxen and dead. Everything, that was, except her eyes. Her eyes could not have been more alive, and she fixed him with a look of such defiance that it was obvious she already despised him.

"Mum, this is the man. The one we talked about. He and I have already discussed everything. Just hear him out, Mum, all right? Just listen to him."

Gorki explained the offer. It was more or less the same as for Margita Padovan: a generous deposit, the price for the agricultural land, and the bonus after reclassification. They would get 35,000 euros right away, the rest as soon as the urban plan changed.

As he talked, Gorki observed the people in the room. The daughter leafed through a newspaper, stealing a look at him every now and then as if trying to discern where the catch lay. The son smiled ingratiatingly. Gorki knew the son had spoken with a rival agency. He also knew they had offered him more. But the Irish were offering money up front, and Gorki knew that he and his sister needed the money right away. Jolanda's son's tiling business had gone bust and the bank had seized his warehouses on the eastern outskirts of Zagreb. Jolanda's granddaughter, her daughter's daughter, was about to start specialist training at the Royal Ottawa hospital in Ontario. Everyone needs money, but the people sitting before Gorki needed it urgently. And they knew, as he knew, that the old woman had only three months left to live, maybe six, maybe nine. If she should die before the deal was done, sorting out the inheritance could take even longer. The three people on the sofa wanted it finished before the old woman kicked the bucket.

Having laid out the terms, Gorki handed them the contracts. As the daughter and the wife studied the small print, Gorki cast his gaze around the room, taking in the details. On the walls, there were letters of thanks from socialist sport associations and failed factories; over the door hung an old, rusted British Sten sub-machine gun, obviously a trophy from the Second World War; on the shelves were the complete works of Tito and a black-and-white photograph of a good-looking man with fair hair smiling at the camera. The picture had been taken somewhere in the mountains and the man had a red star on his cap.

"Could you give us a moment?" the daughter finally asked, and Gorki nodded. He stepped out onto the veranda.

Looking down on Misto, Gorki eavesdropped on the goings-on inside: a family discussion, a few raised voices. Gorki couldn't make out exactly what was being said, but he knew the essence. The old woman didn't want to sell. She was chiding them. It's a birthright, she was telling them. It must be preserved for their descendants. Once it was sold, there would be no going back. Don't be selfish, the son and daughter were telling her. Think of those younger than yourself. The daughter-in-law wasn't saying anything but fixed the old woman with a scowl full of hatred. The son and daughter asked their mother to think of her grandchildren, to think about the future. What they didn't say was *You're going to die soon anyway.* They didn't say it, but they all knew it was true.

The conversation died down and the son called Gorki back in. He found them in the same positions, lined up on the sofa. But they didn't look like they had before. The wife stared angrily to one side and the daughter was on the verge of tears. A rift had opened and Gorki knew it would never close. From then on, nothing in the family would ever be the same.

"We've decided," said the son. "We accept the terms. We'll sign immediately."

Gorki handed the children the contracts and the son passed his to his mother. The old woman in the wheelchair looked at it as one might a repulsive, dead insect. Then she put on her glasses and read the signature that was already on it. "Gorki Šain?" she said.

"That's right," replied Gorki.

"Any relation to Albino Šain?"

"Granddad."

"My husband fought in the war with your granddad. Second Dalmatian Brigade. They fought together at Dinara, Livno, the Neretva, Sutjeska. They entered Split together in 1943."

"What was his name?"

"Mirko Barić. Grenadier, Second Dalmatian. They called him Bjondo."

"I know that name. My granddad mentioned him."

"And my husband mentioned your granddad. He often talked about him."

"That's nice to hear."

For a millisecond, the old woman's face seemed to soften, as if she had been moved by the words they had exchanged. But then her expression hardened again, as before, to one of merciless contempt. "Gorki Šain?" she said again.

"Tell me."

"You know something?"

"What?"

"Your granddad would have shot the likes of you."

She looked at him once more, like she wanted to cut him in two. Then she dropped her gaze, took the contract and signed it in one long, agitated motion. She handed it back without looking up.

Gorki headed down to the sea and along the coastal path. He walked past rows of empty apartment buildings, through an ugly landscape of wrought-iron fences and plastic window shutters, closed until the arrival of the first tourists in June. After a few minutes the asphalt ran out and Gorki entered Rokov's Land.

He kept walking, along a well-trodden stone path that divided the cliffs from abandoned olive groves. He soon reached the chapel on the headland. He went around the headland and the view opened up onto the neighbouring cove.

The Rokov house stood alone, looking exactly as it had when he last saw it, the grounds circled by a wall with an arched doorway. The dry dock was still there, a sloping concrete slipway that descended from the bank into the pebbly shallows.

Fifteen years earlier, when he was investigating the disappearance of Silva Vela, Gorki had gone to every house in Misto, searched every closet, larder and woodshed. He had gone to the Rokov house too. He remembered how bizarre it had been, like a manor house from the outside and a stable inside. He remembered the dry dock full of old junk and waste, the complete chaos in the courtyard. But he also remembered the grand stone portal and the well with the arched roof. He remembered the residents too: the head of the family, a strange, bearded man who spent all day planing and touching up boats; the son, Brane, a timid, skinny teenager who had found himself at the centre of the drama given that he was – or at least believed he was – Silva's boyfriend; and the mother, Uršula Rokov, whom he remembered best of all. She must have been a little over forty back then. Tall, with grey-blue eyes, diva-like in her striking appearance, Uršula was not easily forgotten. She looked like she didn't belong there. Not in that house, not in that village, not in that universe.

In a few minutes he would see them again, and find out what they looked like now and how they lived.

He had investigated the Rokovs, of course, as he had investigated all the other owners of Rokov's Land. As far as he had found out, Tonko Rokov still owned the boatyard and fixed up boats, but his business, apparently, was not going well. Uršula was still a housewife, while Brane, whom he remembered as a young, fragile lad, had finished in the maritime faculty and the cadets. He had become a sailor and, as far as Gorki knew, was a crew member on a boat owned by a Norwegian company and which sailed under the Panama flag. Gorki had found one property in Brane's name, an apartment on the third floor of a Split high-rise. Brane had obviously managed to strike out alone.

Gorki had known the Padovans would be a pushover and the Bakićs would be a bit more difficult, but he had no idea how it would go with the Rokovs. There were no older people with carcinomas, no sons with gambling debts or warehouses put up as collateral. He had nothing to offer the Rokovs by way of salvation. The only thing he could give them was lots and lots of money. But he didn't know what kind of people the Rokovs were or whether money meant much to them.

He approached the house, surprised at how quiet it was. There wasn't the usual sound of banging from the slipway or any voices from the house. He reached the portal. On the arch above the doors he noticed the inscription ROCCO ROCCOV AND HIS CHILDREN, and the year 1812. Whoever built the house had had pretensions to be more than they were.

Unable to see anyone at home, Gorki climbed to the dry-stone terrace alongside the house, crossed the garden and came out on a slope at the back. He walked a hundred yards through untended olive groves and terraces overgrown with carob, fennel and thistle. He reached some kind of shed he hadn't noticed before. It had a flimsy wooden door without a lock. He opened it.

If the shed had once served some kind of agricultural purpose, that was no longer the case. Inside were old, barely used cement bags stiff from damp, and an abandoned pile of construction sand. An old oar leaned against one wall, and a roll of some kind of white, webbed material against another. Gorki touched it and flinched. Sharp, glassy edges pricked his fingers. He realized what the material might be: fibreglass woven roving, used for patching up and reinforcing plastic boats. It looked like it had been lying in the damp shed for some time. Old Tonko Rokov had obviously given up on the roving or – more likely – on his job in general.

Gorki left the shed and continued his climb. The olive trees quickly began to thin out, and he came out on a mound that afforded a view of Rokov's Land, a slope of ten acres that swept down at a gentle angle towards the cove.

On one side of the cove was the Rokov house, on the other the Stella Maris chapel. In between rested a virgin nothing, a wasteland of long-forgotten olive groves waiting to be consolidated, bought up and cultivated. Gorki looked out at grey-green terraces full of dense, unfettered flora. But in his mind he saw something else: a web of land parcels coloured yellow and red. He saw their owners, the Bakićs, the Padovans and the Končurats. He had bought up every plot on behalf of Smart Solutions Estate bar one, the biggest. Without the Rokovs' four and a half acres, nothing would come of the Sunset Residence project.

Gorki stood on the rise above the cove until the sky began to redden to the west with the early autumn sunset. Then a light came on in the Rokov house. Someone was at home.

When Gorki entered other houses in Misto in 1989, he had been there to talk to witnesses, searching for any useful detail that might complete the picture of Silva's disappearance. That was not why he went to the Rokov house. Theirs was the home of a possible suspect.

In the first days of the investigation, he had been sure Brane Rokov had harmed the missing girl. He had been certain of it, a certainty based on what he arrogantly believed back then was "intuition".

Brane Rokov had been going out with a girl who was immeasurably better-looking than him, and he obviously wasn't happy. The girl had twisted him around her little finger and broken his heart. The night she disappeared she had cheated on him with another local lad. Brane was a sensitive, brittle teenager, but Gorki had believed him capable of rage. He entered the Rokov house led by intuition, by the kind of hunch he later learned only existed in novels.

He hadn't got far. Brane had a rock-solid alibi. He had

arrived in Misto the morning after having spent the entire night on a bus, which the driver and the other passengers confirmed. As the investigation progressed, it became clear the girl had been up to her eyes in drug dealing. Then the bank clerk appeared and sent things back to square one. It turned out that Silva had run away. She hadn't been killed. Gorki's intuition was worthless.

Gorki reached the slipway. Once, Tonko would have ten boats at a time in his dry dock. That day there were only two, and they looked to have been sitting there for some time. There was no sound of work.

He passed beneath the stone arch erected long ago by Rocco Roccov and his children. He entered the courtyard. It looked abandoned, though tidier than the last time he had been there: no more pickled vegetables or jams on the terrace or the porch.

He knocked on the door. "Anyone home?"

Uršula Rokov opened the door and Gorki froze. She hadn't changed a bit. She must have been almost sixty, but she remained attractive, her long, dark hair falling to her waist and her eyes still a penetrating ice blue. She looked at the intruder on her doorstep and straight away it was clear that Uršula Rokov recognized him.

She said hello, courteously but questioningly. "Yes?" she added. "What do you want?"

"I'm here about the land," Gorki replied. "We spoke last week."

"That was you?" Uršula asked.

"Yes."

She laughed. "Small world. I see you've changed profession."

Uršula showed him into the living room.

"Wait here. I'll get my husband," she said, and disappeared into the house.

The room she left him in was a strange mix of grandeur and misery. Against one wall stood a baroque dresser that would not have looked out of place in a Split antique shop. There was a large table made of solid oak, and heavy, dark curtains hung from brass rails over the windows, thick, tasselled pull cords touching the floor. On the walls were portraits of ancestors in the traditional costume and red hats worn by common folk on special occasions.

But behind all the contrived grandiosity were signs of obvious poverty. The house was long overdue a new coat of paint; from the kitchen came the sound of a tap dripping into a cheap tin sink; a cord was missing from one of the curtains so it couldn't be drawn; the tables wobbled; and an archipelago of marks on the walls suggested the roof was leaking. The Rokov house looked like something out of a novel tracing the fate of a nineteenth-century family from petty thieves and cocky upstarts to powerful and dignified gentlemen, ending in misery and damp with the crazy, decadent descendants. Gorki had the feeling that he had burst in right at the end of the novel, in the final chapter.

Uršula Rokov returned after a few minutes. Dragging himself slowly behind her was the hulking, bearlike figure of Tonko Rokov. If she hadn't aged a day, the same couldn't be said for the old master of the house. Grey and stooping, he looked dishevelled and dirty. He didn't say a word, not to his wife nor to Gorki. Instead he looked at the floor as if he found it all so hopelessly tiresome.

It was time for Gorki's spiel. He showed them the Corel rendering of Sunset Residence, laid out the financial terms and calculated the deposit and final price after reclassification. The Rokovs were last and they knew it, so he dispensed with the haggling and offered them ten per cent more than the others. He set out the offer and delivered all the lines designed to open doors already ajar: *You can't take land with you to the grave; It's just sitting there anyway; Think of the nest egg you'll have for old age; You can't always count on your health; You can invest the money in the house, renovate it, attract some tourists.*

Not once did Gorki call the land in question by its name. Not once did he mention "Rokov's Land". It wouldn't have been advisable to remind them of the fact they were selling a birthright that carried their own name.

They'd be crazy not to accept, thought Gorki. For a wild, barren heath that served no purpose they'd get as much money as their son would for eight years at sea. But Gorki didn't tell them that. He was too experienced. He knew he would only hurt the sale were he to insult the sellers' precious birthright.

When he had finished talking, Gorki looked at the husband and wife to see their reaction. Uršula had listened carefully, interested in what he had to say. Tonko Rokov showed no reaction. He stood there, vacant, dark, unspeaking, like an impenetrable black wall. Gorki wasn't sure he had even listened. But he had. Because Tonko opened his mouth and uttered one short, simple sentence: "Rokov's Land is not for sale." Then he left the room.

Uršula remained at the table, seemingly stunned into silence. Gorki expected her to follow her husband, but she didn't. Instead, she looked imploringly at Gorki, a look that said *Please, you talk to him.*

Gorki stood up and went after the old man. He found him on the slipway rummaging around among old wooden blocks, logs and battens. Gorki approached and Tonko turned around. "So, you never found her?" he asked, completely calm.

"Who?"

"You know who."

"Silva Vela?"

"Her."

"No. I didn't. Nor did anyone else."

The old man nodded as if to digest what he had heard. Then he asked another question: "So you're not with the police any more?"

"For some time now. Fifteen years."

"Anyone in the police looking for her?"

"I don't know. I don't think so."

"And her family? Are they looking?"

"I don't know. I haven't seen them since then."

"So you're not interested? You don't ever wonder what happened?"

"You have to understand something," Gorki replied. "That was a long time ago. A long and painful time. Things have changed. The country has changed. We've changed."

"We're the same as we always were," the old man responded. "We just like to pretend we're different because it suits us."

"Mr Rokov," Gorki retorted impatiently, "I'm not here about that —"

"I know you're not," the old man said. "You're here to make money off my birthright."

Gorki realized his mistake. He had shown impatience, and impatience means you care. You care because you stand to make a lot of money on something. At the first sign of impatience, a landowner usually withdraws, distrustful, into a shell. But Tonko did not look distrustful. He looked angry. The old man's face darkened like the sky before a sudden storm, and right then Gorki knew there would be no Sunset Residence on Rokov's Land.

"You're wasting your time here," the old man said. "You won't get Rokov's Land from us."

Gorki looked at the old man standing in front of him blinded by some uncontrollable pain. He knew he was wasting his time. He knew he couldn't change the outcome, but he nevertheless had the need to make one last, desperate attempt. "All right. But why?" he asked. "Why, for God's sake? You're hurting everyone. Yourself… your wife… your son. The neighbours, the other owners. You're hurting me and the people I work for. You're hurting Misto by holding it back. You're hurting the Končurats, the Bakićs, the Padovans. Why? Because it's your birthright? Because of your pride?"

The old man's face became twisted with rage. "Because I don't want us to have the money," he said. "I don't want anyone to get the money, so none of us can spend what we haven't earned. Because we're the dirtiest generation. Because we think we can live without working, because we think we can spend what we haven't earned, because we think we deserve to live well. But we don't deserve to. That's why I won't sell. So that everyone will be worse off. Because they all deserve to be worse off."

The old man gasped for breath and Gorki thought he was about to collapse. Recovering, he spoke again.

"Go on," he said. "Go on or I'll call the police, if you're not still the police. Wouldn't surprise me in this country if the police were buying and selling land on the black market. Things have got that bad."

Tonko turned his back on Gorki, went into the ground-floor workshop next to the dry dock, and closed the door.

Gorki looked towards the house. Uršula Rokov stood in the doorway, rooted to the spot, having watched the scene unfold in front of her. She looked disappointed but not surprised.

She approached Gorki and held out a piece of paper. It was the rendering of Sunset Residence. "Don't forget this. You left it behind," Uršula said. Then, as if it was pointless saying anything else, she turned back round and walked away.

*

Gorki returned along the shore to the village. The sun was setting behind the headland, casting a warm, red light on the rock at the water's edge, on the bramble and bushes of Rokov's Land. Bathed in the evening twilight, the maquis of the never-to-be Sunset Residence looked almost beautiful. Under this red light, the heath and thicket briefly looked like something worth getting worked up over.

Rokov's Land, Gorki knew, would remain exactly as he saw it then. Nothing would be built there, at least not until that generation died out.

Gorki knew what would come next. The son of the Padovan widow would sell his apartment to stop the bank from taking his mother's house. Because of that house, he'd put his own family in a rented apartment, probably prompting his wife to leave him. He'd see his children every other Saturday and Thursday and for years to come he'd visit his mother in Misto with a bitter taste in his mouth, thinking: this is all because of you and that land of yours.

Old Jolanda Bakić would die three months later, or six, or nine. She would die in the midst of a family quarrel, her daughter and daughter-in-law at her side, looking at each other askance. With the old woman dead, the Bakićs would sell her house to pay off their debts. But it would be too late for some: the son would lose his storehouse on the outskirts of Zagreb and the granddaughter would miss out on the hospital in Ontario.

But that wouldn't be all. Gorki would call the Padovans and the Bakićs the next morning and inform them that the deal was off because not everyone had agreed to sell. By the afternoon, they would know it was old Rokov. They'd try to persuade him, but Tonko wouldn't give in. Then they'd try threats and insults. Old Tonko would stand firm. There would be harsh words, shouting, perhaps some pushing and shoving, dissolving over time into a whispered small-town quarrel. For decades to come, they would pass on the street, in the shop, in the church without acknowledging one another, turning their heads the other way. They would file pointless lawsuits and turn neighbours, relatives and friends against their enemy, until the quarrel began to resemble a chronic illness no one knew the cause of, let alone how to treat. For decades they would live in muted hostility, passing the animosity down to their children and grandchildren, until at some point they would forget how the quarrel had even begun. But that would not lessen the hatred. Void of content, it would simply become the norm, like a chronic cough or rheumatism. The hatred would settle, quietly festering like an infection, a dry, muffled curse echoing in an empty room.

Nothing would be the same, Gorki thought. Except for Rokov's Land. That would remain an empty, useless maquis, lashed by rain in the autumn and dry as gunpowder in summer, ripe for irrepressible wildfire. Then, in five or fifteen years, someone else would come along, like him, and snap up the land as if plucking a ripe, low-hanging pear, perhaps even cheaper if the misery had grown any greater. Apartments, villas, condominiums or timeshares would sprout on Tonko's birthright, only the buyer wouldn't be Smart Solutions and the development wouldn't be called Sunset Residence but something equally ridiculous. Gorki knew it. There were no victories in that war, only delayed defeats.

He reached the church and got in his car. He drove away, but he didn't feel like leaving yet. There was something else he wanted to see.

Gorki drove along the fence of the naval base until he reached a damaged section. He stopped the car at the side of the road and turned off the headlights. He got out of the car and clambered through the hole in the fence.

Walking through the base, he was surprised at how much bigger it was than it looked from outside. Behind the first row of pavilions was another, and behind that one was the magazine – a storehouse with a curved roof between the gorge and the stone parapet. In the centre of the base was the command building, the biggest and most ambitious. In front of it was a concrete parade ground, where the sailors must once have lined up under the flag.

He walked past the barracks, broken glass grinding beneath his shoes. The ground was covered with bits of rusty metal, shattered glass and hypodermic needles. All the windows were broken, the wooden frames pulled out, doorsteps carried away.

Gorki entered one of the buildings. It was even worse inside. The terrazzo floor tiles and the parquet had been pulled up and the sinks wrenched from the washrooms, leaving only rusted pipes poking out from the walls. It was a picture of complete and utter ruin. But someone who knew what they were looking at might spy in all that decay a hidden essence, at least seven acres of prime seafront location, an asphalt access road and a network of paths within it. It was also surely connected to the electricity, water and sewage systems. It had a breakwater and an operational shore. It had tunnels that were blocked and inaccessible but which could be used for marine tourism. It was a wasteland and at once a winning lottery ticket, one that needed no reclassification, was of no particular interest to the eco-warriors and involved no negotiations with crotchety old grandmas. Instead of a dozen owners, the base on Cape Cross had only one: the state.

Turning back towards the road, Gorki couldn't make out the hole in the fence, so he wandered around briefly on the wrong side of the barbed wire. Finally, he spotted the contours of his Volkswagen Touareg. He pressed the button for the central locking and the car greeted him with a yellow blink in the darkness.

He knew the Irish had contacts in the defence ministry. He knew they were paying one of the undersecretaries, who had arranged some military land for them in Istria. He would suggest they pull some strings, because the base represented everything they needed, all in one place and without any mad Tonkos, any haggling with descendants or legal back and forth with distant relatives.

Having made it through the fence, Gorki got into his car and headed out of Misto. As he drove, he looked at the sleepy village below him, at the pale lights on the promenade, the beacon blinking on the jetty. Above Misto, only one bright light shone in the wintry darkness. It was the newly illuminated stone cross above Cape Cross, the cross beneath which Silva Vela had spent her last night in Misto.

Gorki stopped the car. He sat there for a long time on the climb leading to the viewpoint, his foot on the brake.

The urge was too much for him. He turned the car on the narrow road and headed back down towards the village. He drove once more past the basketball court, the church, the post office and the bakery. Finally, he stopped at the top end in front of an unlit house, the home of Jakov and Vesna Vela.

He turned off the engine and looked at the house, silent and enveloped in darkness. Gorki sat there in the chilly car and his mind returned to a place he had seen so many times. He recalled the narrow hallway with the metal coat stand. Left of the door was the son's room. He recalled the terrazzo tiles, the wooden table against the long wall, the pile of washing waiting to be ironed, the small table with the television and the picture of Jesus above the kitchen door. He recalled the door to Silva's room, a white door with a paper heart stuck to it and the words *Keep out*. He recalled the child's bed, the teenage posters on the walls, the desk and the pens standing in a beer can. He recalled the closet of clothes and the hidden drawer full of secrets.

Gorki sat there in the dark car, as still as a statue but moving in his mind through a space frozen in his memory. Then he gave a start. A light had come on in the house and through the curtains he could see the faint outline of a figure.

He felt cold. He turned on the engine and drove away.

10

BRANE (2005)

As he did every night, Brane set his alarm for 3.40, for the third shift on watch. As he did every night, he woke prematurely in his dark cabin, opened his eyes and knew immediately that he wouldn't get any more sleep. He looked at the clock. It was 2.50. Another sleep-deprived day awaited him.

Brane turned on the light and got out of bed. In the bathroom, he washed his face and looked at himself in the mirror. He didn't like what he saw.

He had long stopped taking care of his body, and the scars of neglect showed in his puffy face and the sickly hue of his skin. Unruly grey hair stuck out over his ears. Layers of flesh sagged beneath his shoulders and around his waist, while his belly and hips had dissolved and mutated into a roll of white, sagging flesh. Brane hadn't weighed himself in years. But every day he felt more and more sluggish. He felt his body giving up on him, breathless when exerted, and when he climbed steps he felt an intermittent pain in his knee. He knew he should stop eating bread, potatoes and rice. It was simple, but still he couldn't summon the willpower to do it.

Brane washed his neck and armpits with his hands and

dried himself with a towel. He wondered whether to put on his uniform but then realized there was still a while until his shift began. Wearing a vest, he lay down on the bed, though he knew sleep would evade him. After a while, he got up and sat at the table to check his emails.

As usual, his inbox was empty except for spam: housing offers, university courses, penis enlargement surgery. He moved the cursor from one to the next, deleting them all. Then right at the bottom he saw a message from the day before, early afternoon local time on the South China Sea. It was from Uršula. His mother must have sent it as soon as she got up. The subject line began with a threatening question mark: *? GET IN TOUCH?*

Brane moved the cursor and hit delete. Uršula's email disappeared.

He got up. Suddenly he was wide awake and in a bad mood. He put on his uniform, buttoned up the white shirt of chief mate and straightened the epaulettes with their three yellow stripes. He checked the time. There was still half an hour until he started his shift on watch, but he decided to go up to the bridge anyway. Whoever was there would be glad of the company.

Brane walked down the corridor past the captain's cabin and climbed the metal stairs. He turned next to the saloon and climbed again to the deck above. As he walked, he noticed the boat rocking and how the metal side panels creaked. When he opened the door of the navigation bridge, he saw why. The South China Sea was heaving.

Two days before, as soon as they had passed the Strait of Malacca, a warm wind had begun blowing from the east, bringing rain. The forecast had said it would pick up by the afternoon, but it was obviously early. The waves had grown during the night, hitting the boat on the flanks at the widest point, the worst possible place. The *Mary Laetitia* was a big, robust ship, but in such conditions even she pitched and creaked, her metal sides screaming under the power of the water. They had another three days and two nights to the port in Shenzhen. Three long, uncomfortable days, thought Brane.

He went onto the bridge and said hello. Serhij, an old Ukrainian able seaman, stood at the helm. Juoni, the Finnish second mate, stood in the officer's position in front of the engine control panel. He was staring through the bridge windows at the raging sea. He looked at the new arrival. "Rough night," said the Finn. "I'll get you a coffee before I go."

At exactly four o'clock, Juoni brought them coffee in plastic cups and they performed the handover. Brane read the radar and GPS and checked the course on the compass. From the Navtex printer he read the latest, fairly ominous weather forecast. He checked the chart on the screen of the ECDIS to see if any other boats were nearby. There were a few, most of them plying the same route as the *Mary Laetitia*. On the tracking display were small red dots with boat numbers. The AIS showed them all edging along the same imaginary line – from the Strait of Malacca and Singapore to port in the Pearl River Delta. The bloodstream of the global economy, Brane knew, coursed along that imaginary line. Shoes, bags, toys, phones and balls went in one direction, to the West. German cars, printing machines, machine pumps and colour Doppler scanners went the other, to Chinese ports. The *Mary Laetitia* was taking the latter route, east.

Juoni put the hot coffee on the shelf of the control panel. Serhij took a sip of his, still staring into the angry, watery void. Then Juoni said goodbye and went to his cabin to get some sleep. Brane and the Ukrainian were left alone, another shift ahead of them on third watch from four till eight in the morning. Just the two of them on the bridge, chief mate and able seaman. And the *Mary Laetitia*, big and plump. And all around them water, endless water.

The wind had changed direction and was blowing a little more from the east. Brane instructed the helmsman to turn six degrees to the east so the waves would hit them in the bow, not at the widest point. He pulled on the control panel potentiometer to alter the angle of the rudder. The boat slowed. The needle showed a speed of eleven knots. "I'll check the engine and lower deck," said Brane, and the Ukrainian acknowledged him with a nod.

Brane descended the metal stairs one floor, then another, then another. He took a look at the fire station, entered the corridor, went down another floor and lifted the latch on a metal barrier. He opened a door and entered the cargo space. He flicked the light switch. The lights blinked and came on, illuminating deck minus four.

He stood in the cargo control cabin, rows of cars stretched out in front of him for as far as he could see. Thousands of Audis, SEATs and Volkswagens, hatchbacks, minivans and SUVs with blue and grey paintwork dozed in the hold, metallic body panels shimmering in the miserly light. Minus four was only one deck. The *Mary Laetitia* had six of them, holding a total of 6,137 cars. Those 6,137 cars had been loaded up in Rotterdam under the personal supervision of Brane, who as chief mate followed each one into the hold before signing the manifest. Those 6,137 cars were heading to Shenzhen to meet their new owners – Chinese architects and accountants, lawyers and executives, engineers and Party secretaries. Six thousand-odd people soon to sit in their fragrant interiors, on new upholstery, proud and satisfied that every day, in every way, they were moving up in the world. Brane envied them. It must be nice, he thought, to want what money can buy.

The cargo was in place, secure and dry. Satisfied, Brane turned out the light and closed the barrier. He went down more steps, two decks lower, until he reached a large metal door. He turned the handle and opened it. A torrent of sound almost pinned him to the wall. The engine room roared as engine rooms always roar.

He put on ear defenders and went in. By the door, he pressed the button to activate the dead man alarm system: if something was to happen to him and he was unable to reset it within fifteen minutes, an alarm would go off on the navigation bridge and in the room of the duty engine officer. Brane descended to the next deck down, onto the engine floor. He stopped at the foot of the engine, taking in a sight he had seen so many times but which never ceased to amaze him – the roaring, unremitting motion of a Wärtsilä-Sulzer RTA96-C. As big as a three-storey building, it stretched as high as the metal vault of the engine room, thundering in the bowels of the ship with its fourteen cylinders generating 107,000 horsepower, guzzling 110 litres of fuel a minute. While those on the bridge patiently observed the raging sea and the rest of the crew was asleep, there, in the unmanned machinery space, that Finnish wonder was working and working, unmonitored, unflagging and unbreakable, driving that torpid metal hulk, the *Mary Laetitia*, ever onward through angry waters. Brane looked at the steel beast in silent wonder, as if gazing at a majestic cathedral.

After approaching the control panel and checking that everything was in order, he climbed back up to the exit, deactivated the dead man alarm and closed the engine room door. He took the metal staircase back to the bridge but had to pause halfway, gasping for breath. He felt a burning sensation in his chest that he didn't like.

He reached the bridge and Serhij, standing at the helm, looked at him worriedly. The helmsman looked tired. Brane could see he needed a break. "It's all fine down there," he said. "Go take a break. I'll watch from now on."

Serhij looked grateful. He nodded and went down the stairs. Brane was left alone on the bridge, 150 feet above a wild ocean. He looked at the shelf in front of him, where his untouched and now cold coffee still sat. The sight of it suddenly made him feel sick. He took the cup and poured the coffee into the bin.

His fingers touched the potentiometer and straightened the rudder. The *Mary Laetitia* accelerated to eighteen knots, ploughing through waves that were growing stronger.

Brane must have fallen asleep. He didn't know when or for how long, but he must have fallen asleep, and it was only a sound that woke him.

It wasn't a loud sound. More a muffled clang, just once, like the sound of metal snapping. The sound – imperceptible, quiet even – nevertheless reached the navigation bridge over the din of the engine and the raging sea. Brane heard it and was shaken from his slumber.

He looked around but couldn't see anything wrong on the bridge. The engine was still spinning monotonously, the *Mary Laetitia* driving on doggedly through the waves at the same speed and on the same course Brane had set. Serhij wasn't on the bridge; he must still have been downstairs in the saloon, drinking coffee. Brane checked the time. Ten to five. If he had dozed off, it couldn't have been for more than a minute or two. Nothing looked or sounded untoward, as if nothing had even happened. Except for the sound he had heard – *if* he had heard it. A sound that was gone, that had disappeared as if he had dreamed it.

Brane pulled on his coat and went out onto the deck. The wind was raging, pouring fat drops of rain onto his eyelids and cheeks. He looked around but could see nothing but the dark sea and the shimmering white crests of its waves.

He returned to the bridge and saw Serhij, who looked harried, agitated. "What happened?" the Ukrainian asked.

"Nothing happened," Brane replied.

"Are you sure?" asked the old helmsman.

"Nothing. Nothing happened," Brane repeated, and the helmsman asked if he had heard a sound.

Brane didn't reply, but his silence didn't satisfy Serhij. The able seaman went out onto the deck. He turned on the reflectors. Beams of light illuminated the water at the ship's stern. The *Mary Laetitia* was still pitching on the waves. Creaking and howling, it scaled walls of water, forging on. There was nothing visible behind the stern except wave after wave.

The helmsman returned to the bridge. He looked at Brane. "Should we slow down and see?" he asked.

Brane hesitated and then said: "No need."

"Sure?"

"Sure. No need."

The Ukrainian didn't look reassured. He took his place in front of the ECDIS screen and gave Brane a suspicious, searching look. "You heard it," he said. "You heard it too."

"I didn't hear anything," Brane replied.

"Sure?"

"Sure. I heard nothing. Just the normal noise. Just the hum. The sea."

The helmsman kept looking at him and Brane realized he had to put an end to the conversation. He pressed the potentiometer and accelerated. The engine soughed deeply, intensely, and the *Mary Laetitia* gave a start, sped up and drove her bow into the waves. The frothy sea reared up and poured over the prow, a gush of salt water soaking the glass in front of them. Serhij was still looking at him dubiously, but Brane didn't flinch. He overrode the main engine protection and increased rpm to full ahead. The noise intensified, a rumbling was heard and the metal flanks of the *Mary Laetitia* seemed to shudder briefly. Then the ship picked up speed, eating up the sea at a sharp angle to the waves. It was now going at twenty-one knots.

"It was just a noise," Brane mumbled. "Just the humming of the sea. Nothing more."

But he didn't look the helmsman in the eye. He looked straight ahead, at the open ocean and the sky above it, reddening with the early summer sunrise at 5.15.

In the morning, they spotted scratches on the side of the ship, low down, practically at the waterline. They ran along the starboard side from the bow to a third of the way down the cargo hold. It was as if giant fingernails had scratched lines along the side of the ship. At the bow end, they were deeper and whiter, as if drawn with chalk. Towards the middle of the ship they became barely visible, parallel lines.

After watch duty, Brane came across the captain, the second mate and some seamen inspecting the scratches. He went out onto the deck and the captain, Broos, looked at him quizzically. He called Brane aside and led him to his cabin, closing the door behind them. Brane was on his third voyage with Broos, making a total of eleven months together on the ship. Not once in those eleven months had he set foot in the captain's cabin.

Broos was Dutch, a thin, reserved, sixty-year-old man with a pointed jaw. He didn't talk much and kept himself to himself. Come early evening, he would shut himself away in his cabin, slowly draining a bottle of barrel-aged gin one drop at a time. He drank constantly but was never drunk, and he would turn up for watch clean-shaven and as sharp as a razor. He was sharp and sober then, even though a half-empty bottle of gin lay on his cabin pillow as a reminder of the sailor's nocturnal pastime.

The captain asked him what had happened.

"Nothing," Brane replied irritably, though he realized his irritation might give the game away.

"Something happened," said the Dutchman. "Those scratches didn't appear by themselves."

Brane considered what to reply, whether to suggest the ship had been scratched by some drifting cargo container or runaway platform. He knew that whatever he said would only insult the captain's intelligence.

"If something did happen, I don't know about it," Brane told him. "I didn't hear anything. Nothing."

"You sure?"

"Sure. It was a rough night. Rain and force seven sea. You know what it's like."

For a second the Dutchman seemed to hesitate, as if Brane had convinced him. It had been a rough night, that was true. With the rain and a force seven sea, Brane wouldn't necessarily have heard. Not necessarily. But he had heard.

"All right," Broos said following a brief silence. "Let's hope it wasn't anything serious. Let's hope no one reports a shipwreck or a disappearance."

But they did. Two days later, a warning arrived on the Navtex. A Chinese fishing boat had disappeared 390 miles south of Macau, on the same route as the *Mary Laetitia*. A red fishing vessel, sixty feet long, with nine crew members on board. The scratches below the bow had since been washed by the sea. Initially white, they now showed traces of red paint.

Broos summoned Brane that afternoon. He told him he had no choice but to contact the DPA, the designated person ashore. The DPA was their link with the world, their foreign minister, their saviour in such situations. The DPA was Norwegian and the business rep. His name and contact number were all over the ship: on the bridge, in the washrooms, in the engine room and the cargo control cabin.

"The DPA has to decide," said Broos. "Sorry, it's not my call any more."

Brane left the captain's cabin dejected. He only had a vague idea of what might follow. He went out onto the deck and saw a group of Filipino sailors in orange company overalls. They were having a heated discussion about something in their own tongue, a tongue Brane didn't understand but which he could distinguish from hundreds of others. Explosive, full of crackling consonants, it sounded like a fistful of marbles tossed down a metal staircase.

As he approached, the Filipinos fell silent. They greeted him and moved to let him pass. He was the chief mate and they mere sailors, sailors who didn't see home for fifteen months at a time. An invisible wall stood between them, even then. Brane walked through the group. He lifted his head and his eyes met Nazario's.

Brane hadn't sailed with him for long. But he knew him. Nazario had been sailing for decades, for various firms, on all sorts of boats – tankers, roll-on-roll-offs, cruisers. He was said to have seven children back home. Under his overalls, a large silver cross hung from his neck.

Nazario looked at him, but there was no longer any fear in his eyes, any humility, any respect for the white man, for the three yellow stripes on Brane's epaulettes. It was a look of defiance, a look that said: *murderer.*

Brane passed through the group without a word and slipped into his cabin. He wanted to sleep, at least a little, an hour or two, before the night watch. But already he knew it was pointless even trying.

They entered port in Shenzhen two days later, at dawn. That night, like every other night, Brane had been on watch from four till eight.

Shortly before dawn, they saw a faint ribbon of light on the horizon, becoming clearer and brighter the closer they drew to port. Entering the bay, the thin band of light grew into an immense, trembling, pulsating wasps' nest. To the left was Macau; to the right, Hong Kong and Kowloon. Ahead and to the right was Shenzhen, and beyond, on the Pearl River estuary, the shimmering lights of Guangzhou. Seventy million people lived within a sixty-mile radius of the city, a fact Brane found hard to comprehend.

The docking manoeuvre awaited them. At 5.30 Brane woke the captain and the chief engineer. At around six, they were joined on the bridge by a Chinese port pilot. Brane looked at him. He was short and quiet and held himself like a military man. He looked at them grumpily and it occurred to Brane that he perhaps knew about their collision with the fishing boat. He dismissed the thought as irrational.

As they pulled into port the sun was just coming up. Bathed in a reddish light, the port sprawled before them like Tolkien's Mordor. Hundreds of cranes, metallic praying mantises, poked out through the reddish haze, row upon row stretching as far as the eye could see, reflected, upturned, on the calm surface of the water. The oil and grease that polluted the water only made it more beautiful. In the morning calm, its oily surface shimmered with the colours of the rainbow.

The docking manoeuvre took four hours. By around midday they were moored to the ferry dock and operatives of the concessionary company began unloading the cars. A short time later, Broos called him. "The DPA is here," he said. "You need to talk to him."

They sat in the captain's cabin. The Norwegian DPA was a young bureaucrat with steel-rimmed glasses. He looked like he'd never set foot on a boat, let alone sailed one. But he also had the air of someone who solved problems quickly and efficiently.

It didn't look good, he said. Neither for the firm nor for Brane.

"There's no sign of the fishermen, and there are firm indications that you hit them," the DPA said, choosing his words carefully. "It's simply a question of when the port authority will spot the scratches on the side. For now, our best bet is to play dead. If they launch any kind of investigation it'll be bad for the firm and for you."

Brane knew what was coming, so the DPA's plan didn't surprise him. A new chief mate was already on his way. He would land at six from Sydney, in time to finish the cargo transfer and for the *Mary Laetitia* to set sail again. As for Brane, it would be best for him and for them if he was to distance himself from the ship, to leave as quickly and as quietly as possible.

The DPA pulled a wad of papers from his pocket: a termination agreement, a Chinese transit visa and a one-way ticket from Guangzhou Baiyun to Split via Frankfurt and Zagreb. The flight was at 8.25 that evening.

"I'm afraid you have to hurry," said the Norwegian. "The airport is far away and you don't have much time."

Brane went to his cabin and quickly got ready. He stuffed his clothes into a bag and packed his laptop and toiletries. Then he said goodbye to the rest of the crew. When he offered his hand to Serhij, the Ukrainian took it reluctantly. He shook hands last with Broos. The captain forced a smile, but there was nothing friendly in it. "It's better for everyone this way," he said, and Brane thought he'd rather punch Broos in the face.

At 8.30, Brane was on the Lufthansa flight as it climbed steadily over the Pearl River Delta. Dusk was falling on the megalopolis of Guangzhou after another working day, and on the edge of the horizon he saw the port of Shenzhen. He looked at the clusters of cranes. From the plane they resembled tiny giraffes. By that point, the *Mary Laetitia* was already unloaded and empty. In thirty minutes, maybe an hour, it would leave its berth to make way for the next ship, heading south. And in Brane's cabin, on his still-warm bed, would be the new chief mate. At four in the morning, the new boy would wake in Brane's cabin, climb the metal stairs to the bridge and take Brane's place at the radar and control panel. Brane knew that even when he got home, he would wake at three in the morning, in time to take watch.

The plane made a semicircle and Shenzhen's port disappeared from view. As they climbed to cruising altitude, Brane could see only the ocean through the window – water and yet more water, stretching as far as the eye could see. Those men were somewhere in that blue abyss. Somewhere in that azure, on the surface of the sea or under it, was the wreckage of a red metal boat, sixty feet long. And on it, or in it, were nine people, by then certainly dead.

It struck Brane how strange it was that he didn't know their names. He hadn't found them out, and even if he had, he would never have remembered them.

He thought about that as the plane entered a cloud and the view through the window disappeared behind a white veil.

After an interminable flight to Frankfurt, ninety minutes to Zagreb, an hour to Split and much waiting around between flights, Brane landed on the Croatian coast late in the evening.

His was the last flight that day and was stuffed to the gills with people from all over the world trying to reach Dalmatia before nightfall. Returning sailors, businesspeople, students from Zagreb and a few pre-season tourists dozed, exhausted, in their seats. At the back of the plane was an entire sports team, in matching blue and white tracksuits. They were lean and muscly like soccer players and, to Brane at least, looked unbelievably young. He didn't recognize any of them, though he would have struggled to recognize even a soccer star. Of all the passengers, only the players weren't tired. They clowned around and made a noise as the rest of the plane sank into slumber.

When the plane had taken off in Zagreb, everyone around him had fallen asleep. Not Brane. After travelling so far he was unbelievably, unspeakably tired but tormented by jet lag and the usual insomnia. At that moment it was four in the morning on the South China Sea. He thought of the *Mary Laetitia* sailing south-west towards Singapore. Were he on the boat, Brane would be on watch, from four till eight. Were he on the boat, he would be awake and chipper, looking at the ocean. Instead, he was looking at the backs of heads in the seats in front of him.

He observed the rows of women's hairdos and men's necks, the unfamiliar, anonymous physiognomies, realizing all of a sudden how estranged he had become from this country and these people after fifteen years at sea. For a brief instant, one of the men in front of him turned his head, looking over his shoulder, probably for a flight attendant. His face was familiar. Brane didn't know from where or when, but it was familiar.

The man was sitting three rows in front of him, on the other side of the aisle. His eyes were closed, like he was meditating. Then he pulled some papers from his briefcase and began looking at them. Brane's eyesight was still sharp. He couldn't make out the first word of the heading, but he could read clearly the next two: PROPERTY HOLDINGS. He looked at the man, at his strong neck, round cheeks and high forehead, and he knew he had seen him before.

At eleven o'clock the plane landed in Split. It had recently stopped raining, and they stepped out onto a runway still wet from the light spring shower. Brane pulled on his jacket. His nostrils were besieged by the intoxicating, wild scent of the south. The rain had stirred up the flora and there was a purity to the air. He felt a gentle breeze from the surrounding fields, carrying with it the scent of immortelle, mimosa, oregano and fennel. Brane breathed it in and realized that, out of everything, it was the only thing he had missed. Nothing else. Just that smell.

He stood at the baggage belt. The man with the property papers stood next to him. Brane observed the other man, trying to make out the familiar details of his face, the characteristics that were least likely to change over time: the shape of the nose, the eyebrows, the eyes.

The baggage started arriving. The man's bag was among the first. It was a small one, the kind people take on a business trip of one or two days. Brane caught a glimpse of the name tag. On it was written a name and a Split address. The name was printed in large letters: GORKI ŠAIN.

He read the name and a face surfaced from his memory, the same face, the same eyebrows, the same nasal contours, but sixteen years younger, with more hair and fewer pounds. With the face came a picture, a picture of a room, a room within the Secretariat of Interior Affairs of the Socialist Republic of Croatia, Sukoišanska, Split. An average room, nothing special, with a suspended ceiling, built-in air conditioning and files stacked high against one wall. A framed portrait of Tito hung on the wall, and beneath Tito, that man, Gorki Šain, sixteen years younger and thirty pounds lighter, asking him where he had been and what he had been doing on Saturday, 23 September. Gorki Šain thought Brane had killed Silva Vela. He didn't know how or where, but he believed Brane was the killer. Brane knew that was what he thought, and Šain knew that Brane knew.

Brane's luggage arrived. He took the straps of the large cloth bag, the kind sailors usually use because hard, angular suitcases take up too much room in the cabin of a ship. He followed the man along the corridor, the man who once, a long time ago, had him in his cross hairs.

A watertight alibi had saved him. He knew that. He was saved by the fact that on the Friday, 22 September, he'd gone to the student admin office of the maritime faculty in Rijeka only to find it shut for afternoon break. He was saved by the fact he'd spent a good part of that afternoon filling in forms, that he'd had to wait until five o'clock for the notary office to open and to stamp the copies he had made of his documents, and that it had been six o'clock before he'd managed to pay the tax to transfer to the higher diploma in maritime studies. The next available bus back to Misto was on the Saturday, at nine in the evening; he'd arrived home on the Sunday, at six in the morning, before sunrise, when the Autotrans bus had stopped on the coastal road above the town. He had intended to spend the night at home on Rokov's Land, but instead spent it sprawled across two seats on the night bus wending its way for hours along the old, winding road from Rijeka towards Zadar, through Karlobag, Jurjevo and Ažić Lokva. He remembered that night clearly, the night he'd spent squashed in an uncomfortable seat, crumpled and sleep-deprived as the bus swayed from one bend to the next. It had been awful at the time, but afterwards he was eternally grateful: his alibi was as watertight as alibis get. There was the bus driver, the co-driver and four or five other passengers tortured by every bend in the road. They all remembered him, and they were all able to describe him precisely. There could be no doubt whatsoever about Brane's whereabouts the night Silva vanished. Had there been, he would have faced a very different fate.

Brane headed for the airport exit, Šain still ahead of him. He looked smart, dressed like a businessperson, not a police officer. They reached the revolving doors at the same time. Šain's bag got stuck and he stepped back, turned around and apologized politely. He looked Brane in the eyes but gave no sign of recognition.

They emerged into the parking area and Brane paused to see where Šain was heading, what car he drove. Šain pressed the button for his central locking and four indicator lights flashed. The ex-copper must have come into money: he drove a big, dark four-by-four, a Touareg. He tossed his bag onto the back seat, opened the driver's door and then looked back at the building of the airport as if looking for someone, or something.

Gorki Šain cast his gaze around the car park until he spotted him, Brane, at the terminal exit. He spotted him and quickly looked away, as if Brane's face was unfamiliar, insignificant. Although he'd averted his gaze, Brane knew Šain had recognized him.

Brane flagged down a taxi. "Split," he told the driver, and got into the back seat. The driver turned on the radio. The news was on. The prime minister, Ivo Sanader, had visited eastern Croatia, and Hajduk Split had lost at home to Rijeka. The European Union had opened and closed chapter twenty-five of accession negotiations with Croatia. Brane had no idea what chapter twenty-five was.

After the news came the election campaign coverage. The presenter introduced one of the candidates for the Split municipal council. The candidate spoke with a rich, manly baritone in the crisp Štokavian usually employed by priests and soldiers. The journalist introduced him as "former Croatian army fighter and war hero Mario Cvitković". The name meant nothing to Brane.

Cvitković spoke briefly about rebuilding society and national values. But the taxi driver clearly wasn't interested and soon changed the station to one playing Croatian pop.

They headed in the direction of Split and it began raining again. The car was pleasantly warm, and as they passed Kaštel Lukšić, Brane grew drowsy listening to the raindrops tapping on the windows. After Kaštel Gomilica, after a day and a night without sleep, his body finally succumbed.

Entering his apartment, Brane caught that smell that apartments have when they haven't been lived in for some time – stale, musty air and dust.

He turned on the light in the hallway, followed by all the other lights. He opened the windows to let in some fresh air, turned on the boiler and plugged in the fridge. Then he opened his bag and unpacked. It took him all of twenty minutes – twenty minutes to move back in after five months away.

When he'd finished, Brane went out and rang the doorbell of the neighbouring apartment. Mrs Majda Luketin was a widow in her early seventies and the only neighbour Brane communicated with. He had left a key with her while he was away. She collected his post, paid the utility bills and opened the door when the man came to read the meter. Brane checked the time. It was late, almost midnight. But he could hear the television on in the Luketin apartment. He knew Majda was late to bed, late to rise.

Majda was surprised to see him, having expected him to return in June. "You're early," she said, and Brane saw how pleased she was. At one moment it seemed like she wanted to hug him, but Brane was relieved when she reconsidered.

The widow invited him in, but Brane declined. She went inside and came back a minute later with a bundle of papers. Paid bills, she said. For the cable TV, rubbish collection, internet and electricity, as well as Brane's contribution to the upkeep of the apartment block.

"We split the cost of fixing the elevator, and this is everything together," she said, and handed him a piece of paper on which she had written the total. Before departing, Brane had left Majda a lump sum. It turned out he had given her 122 euros too much; Majda offered to return the difference, but Brane told her to keep it.

"I'll be back at sea soon, better you hold onto it," he said.

"I'm happy you're finally back," Majda said, and looked like she meant it. Brane forced a smile, but it came out more like a grimace.

He returned to his apartment, which had grown cold because of the open windows. He closed them and went to take a shower. He stood under the water for a long time, taking care not to look in the bathroom mirror, not wishing to see his flabby, white flesh.

After leaving the bathroom he put on a dressing gown, and for the first time he felt good, like he was home. For the first time he felt ready, ready to do what he had been putting off.

He went into the room at the back of the apartment, the one room he hadn't entered yet. He turned on the light, pulled up a chair and sat on it. He looked at the wall where her picture hung.

Silva Vela looked exactly how Brane had imagined her for the past seventeen years. Wherever she was, however she might have changed, for seventeen years she had remained the same in Brane's mind. From the wall of Brane's room, Silva looked impudently into the camera, a dark lock of hair falling across her left eye. Brane remembered exactly where he had taken the photo: on Cape Cross, on the plateau beneath the cross, the evening they had first made love.

It had been a warm summer's evening. He took the photo up close with his father's old Olympus, the sun setting behind Silva. Then they kissed and she slipped her hand under his T-shirt. When the sun had disappeared, Brane pulled down her jeans and entered her, slowly and gently. He listened as her breaths grew deeper, finally becoming moans of pleasure. He had never been so happy, neither before nor since. Recalling that night, Brane felt his dick grow hard. He stroked it, slowly at first and then harder and faster until finally he came. He let out a long, loud breath of release that resounded awkwardly off the walls of the empty room. Everything that happened, happened fast. He wiped himself off, turned out the light and closed the door.

Still he didn't feel like sleeping. He was wide awake like it was morning, and on the South China Sea it really was morning. He sat at his computer, deleted all the spam from his inbox, all the ads and petitions, until he spied another email from his mother. It had arrived the day before, in the morning, while he was flying over Asia. It screamed of desperation: *Please call. So I know you're all right.*

He looked at it for some time and wondered whether to hit delete, but he knew that Uršula would write again, and again. In the end he wrote back.

Crossed South China Sea today. Another twenty days in the Indian Ocean. Everything's fine. I'm fine and well. Satellite signal is weak. Will call when I can, if anything changes.

He read what he'd written and thought it over once more. Then he clicked send.

11
JAKOV

Jakov didn't go home after work that afternoon. He went to the shops to buy Tina a birthday present.

It was the end of December and the days were short. At seven o'clock, the DIY warehouse emptied of customers. The sales staff left one by one, saying goodbye to him at the door. At 7.15, Jakov locked the till and signed out of the computer. He turned off the background music and the decorative lighting on the facade. Lastly, he went to the central control and turned off all the lights, row by row. The warehouse fell into darkness.

Jakov took off his store coat and put on his jacket. He pulled on his gloves and turned to the exit. At the door, he turned around once more to look at the 43,000 square feet of warehouse space – tidily stacked planks, panels, metal construction materials and styrofoam boards. He looked at the shelves upon shelves full of tiles, pipes, teak and hardwood flooring, bathroom and electrical supplies. Shiny and new a moment before, stainless steel bathroom taps now glinted dully in the half-dark. He punched in the code for the night alarm and carefully locked the door, turning the key four times.

It was a rainy evening, plus it was Friday, plus it was Christmas, so the roads were packed. Jakov sat in his Opel Ascona and headed in the direction of the new shopping centre on the east side of Split. At about 7.30, an indescribable bottleneck formed at the city's main junction to the east. Roadworks had narrowed Solinska down to one lane and nerves were fraying. The rain started coming down harder. Jakov turned on his wipers and looked through the wet sfumato of the windows at the traffic jam ahead of him. Heavy, fat drops slapped against the glass and the surrounding gloom was sprinkled with warm, red spots – the brake lights of cars like his, queuing hopelessly.

Finally, the bottleneck cleared and the line of traffic moved forward. He turned off and took the bypass heading north, towards the cargo port. It was a smart move. In ten minutes he was at the shopping centre.

Jakov didn't go to the shops much, hardly ever at that time of year, and when he did go shopping, he went into the city. So when he walked into the shopping centre, he was completely overwhelmed, suffocated by the audiovisual aggression of it all, by the ceaseless thrum of shoppers. From all sides came the whining of festive songs, "Jingle Bells" and "We Wish You a Merry Christmas". The whining was replicated by dozens of battery-powered devices, dolls, sleighs, reindeer, robots and fire engines. The entire place was choked in Christmas lights, falling like waterfalls from balconies, ceilings and display windows, blinking monotonously. Jakov felt like the world was twinkling before his eyes; his temples began to throb with the dull pain of a migraine.

The shopping centre was packed with people. They stalked around like ravenous animals, as if the shops were to close the next day and never open again. Families moved in packs, lugging behind them bags brimming with shoes, clothes, toys and food. Some bags contained strange combinations:

a shoebox and slender candlesticks; a jar of mayonnaise and salted cod tails. He observed the faces of people in a hurry, merciless, sullen, focused on that final, fateful plunder. He looked around, genuinely taken aback, and thought that never before, not even in war, had he seen the human race fall so low.

He knew he wouldn't hold out in such a place for long, so he concentrated on finding a toy shop, buying a present and fleeing as soon as possible. At one end he spotted a big Lego store. He went in and raced for the shelves of bricks. He spotted one stacked with Harry Potter-themed boxes. He knew Tina liked Harry Potter.

Jakov stood before the shelf full of big, brightly coloured boxes. He studied the illustrations, the magical cars, the steam locomotive and the tiny figures that meant nothing to him. In the end he chose the biggest and most expensive box, the one with Hogwarts on the front. He grabbed the box, paid at the checkout and hurried to the car as fast as he could. It was only when he sat in the driver's seat that he realized he had forgotten to ask them to wrap it. He remembered he had an old roll of wrapping paper at home. He indicated left, pulled out and headed back to his apartment before the birthday party.

Jakov had lived in the Hercegovačka apartment since he and Vesna divorced. Almost a decade had passed since then, but he still had the feeling he was there only temporarily.

He had left Misto when life with Vesna became intolerable, for both of them. It was a decision he had arrived at over time, but when he finally took it he had no doubts whatsoever. He woke one morning and realized it was time. Over breakfast, he announced to Vesna that he would move out, and for a brief instant he had the sense that she was relieved. He certainly was. Overnight, a suffocating burden had been lifted from his shoulders.

The house they lived in had belonged to Vesna's mother, so it was natural that he would be the one to move out. There was no longer anything keeping him in Misto. He didn't own any property, the factory had gone bust, and Jakov had grown to realize that the ties he had with people in his home town were weak and superficial. For too long he had lived in a happy marriage, and a happy marriage will empty a person of any need they might have for other people. He had nobody left in Misto. Nobody and nothing.

After the war, the economy picked up, slowly but surely. There were jobs again, for bookkeepers too. Jakov took an IT course, applied for a few jobs and in September 1998 he was offered work in Split with a building materials wholesaler called Drvograđa. The boss was a former shop manager who had got rich during the war. He was loud and liked to show off. Jakov assumed he was in the habit of paying bribes, but there were worse employers. He told Jakov he had hired him because he liked employing older, more experienced people.

It wasn't the best job in the world or the best paid. But it was unexciting and stable, and it paid the bills. It also meant Jakov suddenly had to find a place to live in Split. He had opened the classifieds and found an ad for an apartment on Hercegovačka. It was on the ninth floor of a socialist-era high-rise with a view of the cargo port, the shipbuilders' and the rail yard. He took it, believing he wouldn't stay long, simply until he got his affairs in order and bought a place of his own. In the end, he never left.

The Hogwarts box under his arm, Jakov called the elevator and pressed the button for the ninth floor. He had a feeling of ease as he unlocked his front door.

It was a feeling that had not come along immediately, nor was it something Jakov had expected. But when it had come, it stayed, and it grew with each passing year. The apartment had become home.

He unlocked the door and entered. He hadn't been there since the morning, so the apartment was cold. He turned on the oil heater and turned off the boiler. He had a roast chicken in the oven but he decided not to eat it. He was going to a birthday party, and at birthday parties there was always food. He took the wrapping paper, glue and scissors out of the kitchen cupboard and began wrapping the present.

Since he hadn't planned to stay in the Hercegovačka apartment for long, he hadn't brought many things with him, just some clothes, a shaver and his documents. Everything else in his life up till then remained in Misto – his radio receivers, books, tools, family heirlooms. He was surprised to realize after a few months that he didn't need or miss any of it. He hadn't left behind anything he needed, anything he was attached to or that was important to him. It was an unexpected discovery but one he found liberating.

Jakov continued to live that way. He only bought new clothes when he threw out old, and he abhorred flowers, vases, photos and decorations. He realized he felt good if he could pack all his belongings into two suitcases. That's why the apartment on Hercegovačka looked like a student rental vacated for the summer: clean and empty, full of flat surfaces without tablecloths, rugs, carpets, ashtrays, vases or pedestal fruit bowls on the table.

He finished off the wrapping with orange crêpe paper and put the scissors and glue back in the drawer. He put the present under his arm, turned out the light and looked around once more at the dark room. He knew he would much rather stay home with a bottle of beer in front of the TV, but he didn't have a choice. He had to get through it – a loud, chaotic children's birthday party that he would much rather avoid.

But being his granddaughter's birthday, he couldn't avoid this one.

Mate opened the door. They hadn't seen each other for a few weeks and Mate had three days' worth of bristly stubble on his face, which suited him. Mate hugged him in the doorway. "And here's Granddad, at last," he said. Jakov knew that Mate was genuinely pleased to see him.

He stepped inside. Tina's friends were sitting or lying on the rug in the living room. There were about ten of them, more boys than girls. They were rolling around in a pile of Lego bricks, dolls and playhouses, each doing their own thing, it seemed, more than playing together. Tina was among them. Seeing Jakov, she ran into his arms. "Granddad!" she screamed, grabbed the present and started greedily tearing off the paper. Her face turned sour. "I've already got this," she said. Quickly losing interest, she returned to the rug.

The grown-ups were sitting at a large, oval table. Jakov could see Doris, Doris's parents and some unfamiliar older relatives, all from Doris's side. Right at the end of the table was Vesna.

A year had passed since Jakov had last seen her, on Tina's previous birthday. Vesna had changed. Even before, the years had taken their toll, but now Vesna had embraced the change more elegantly. She had cut her hair short, allowed her grey to show and changed her glasses. She had been thin for some time already, much thinner than him. Now, with short grey hair, she looked like an old but stylish professor from some refined northern European school. She held out her hand to him like a courteous stranger. He took it and asked how she was. Fine, she said. And he was fine. Everyone was fine. Everything was all right.

Doris offered him a rakija, which he downed in one. He was hungry, so he wolfed down two sandwiches of French bread filled with salami, mayonnaise and boiled egg. Then he drank a glass of wine and felt a pleasant warmth seep through him. He'd had a long day at work and was tired.

The adults at the table were locked in conversation. Jakov half listened, pretending to be interested. Vesna was also quiet. The two of them sat there, at opposite ends of the table, like jurors, unmoved by the conversation that in the meantime had turned to politics and become rancorous. Then at some point a quarrel broke out among the children on the rug. Jakov didn't even try to understand what it was all about. He just observed Tina. She was the loudest, lecturing each of her friends like a strict headteacher with an affected falsetto full of theatrical authority. Jakov watched her and listened, struck by the uneasy feeling that he had seen it all before.

He listened to the voice of his granddaughter, observed her pompous manner and studied the contours of her face, her fine yet sharp nose, her thin eyebrows and long jaw. And he realized for the first time that what he was looking at was a copy of Silva, Silva who had also once been eleven years old, who like Tina had taken charge, judged and meted out justice. She'd always had the last word.

It hadn't got her far, Jakov thought. Or perhaps it had – farther than anyone had wanted.

Jakov watched and listened as his granddaughter adjudicated the quarrel, and his eyes met Doris's. They looked at each other briefly, quizzically. Doris couldn't know what he was thinking. Doris had never met Silva. She couldn't know how alike her daughter was to her aunt, to the aunt Tina had never met and perhaps never would.

"You all right, Granddad?" asked Doris.

Jakov nodded. "Don't worry, sweetheart," he said. "Everything's fine."

The argument gradually died down. The grown-ups called the children to the table, and when they had all gathered Doris brought out a cake in the shape of the number eleven, with candles on it. Tina blew the candles, once, then once more. Mate preserved the moment with his camera and Doris shared out the cake. It was heavy and tasteless, full of margarine and cream.

Jakov took a forkful of cake and washed it down with a glass of fizzy wine, which tasted horribly sour after the sweet cream. He began to feel a headache coming on from the wine. He took the rest of his slice to the balcony to get some air. He stood outside in the pleasant, cold air and through the illuminated balcony window he watched the silent movie playing out in the room. Sparklers. Children munching cake. Tina holding forth, loud and authoritative. And Vesna, sitting silently in the corner, a shadow of mild boredom covering her face like a silk veil. Vesna isn't moved by any of this, he thought. Just like me. And he felt a sharp pang of guilt in his stomach.

He kept watching the silent movie. He watched Doris, brisk, busy, directing the show, lighting candles, dishing out cake, pouring smoothies for the children. And the whole time a trace of underlying, deep-rooted anxiety on her face.

Something's not right, thought Jakov.

He sensed Mate looking for him. He opened the balcony door and went back inside, into the throng.

When the relatives began leaving, Mate took Jakov to one side and told him he had a favour to ask. He had to help Doris clear up, so it would be a big help if Jakov would run Vesna back to Misto.

It wasn't completely clear whether Mate genuinely needed help or if it was simply another desperate attempt to reconcile the two of them. But Jakov didn't care, and he knew Vesna didn't either.

Mate walked them to where the car was parked and kissed them both. They got into Jakov's car for the first time since 1998 and their breakup.

They turned onto the bypass at the filling station and every now and then Jakov would glance at that new, remodelled, elegantly ageing woman sitting in the front passenger seat. He studied her like a stranger, and in some ways she was.

For a long time they drove in silence. There was no small talk, no *How are you?*, *Everything all right?* or *How's work?* That suited Jakov. It suited him that they were past that phase.

Somewhere near Misto, Vesna spoke. She spoke as if she was unsure whether she should but couldn't hold back any longer. "Something's not right there," she said, not as a question but as a statement.

"No," Jakov replied.

"It's worse than it looks," Vesna added.

"Did he tell you something?" Jakov asked, but he already knew the answer. Of course he had. Mate always confided in his mother.

"A few days ago," she replied. "They've drifted apart. They constantly fight. They had a fight today, a bad one."

"Today? This afternoon?"

"Yes. It's not all right. It's really not."

And you know why, thought Jakov. He knew Vesna was somehow involved, but he didn't say anything, because if he had it would have only ended in a row, which would be of no use to Mate nor to them.

They turned off the coastal road towards Misto, passing along the fence of the old naval base. A sign hung from the fence with the name of the new Irish owners and a picture of the tourist development they planned to build. They passed the old basketball court, by then a beach adventure park, crossed the square in front of the church and passed the Partisan monument, still vandalized, its letters still missing.

When they reached the house, Vesna asked if he'd like to come in, and he accepted.

They sat down in the kitchen. Vesna cleared a pile of school tests from the table to make room and offered him a cup of heather tea. The tea warmed him up and broke through the alcoholic haze in his head.

He looked around the kitchen. Vesna still kept the house in perfect order. Everything was spotlessly clean, polished and in its place. But Jakov couldn't shake the feeling that he was looking not at a real, living home but a mummified body. Everything was the same. The same table, same chairs, same metal coat stand. The same framed Canadian landscape, the same Jesus in the oleograph with the dried olive branch in one corner. Starched and lifeless like flowers in a herbarium.

Jakov took care not to let his gaze wander too far. He knew it was not just the pictures and the furniture that were the same. Behind his back was something else that hadn't changed. A white door. A door with a paper sign that read *Keep out*. A door to a room and in that room the same bed, the same posters, the same closet containing the same clothes, the same calipers and protractor exactly where they had been the last time he opened that door. A chill ran through him and he wanted to leave as soon as possible.

He finished his tea and told Vesna he was leaving. She walked him out and stood at the top of the steps, smiling kindly. It was then that Jakov remembered how much he had loved her.

At the top of the steps, he looked at Vesna. He looked at this slim, elegant fifty-six-year-old woman, at her charcoal jumper, her narrow hips and fashionable bevelled glasses. And he remembered. He remembered how, when they were together, they would imagine their lives in old age, their retirement, a joint future of peaceful leisure. And Jakov had always imagined Vesna exactly as she was now.

He waved and got in his car. He turned onto the coastal road and after the second bend, before the tunnel through Cape Cross, he was hit by a cold and unexpected sense of regret.

Look what you did to us, he thought. Look what you did to our lives. How could you be so selfish?

The thought passed in a flash, brief and wicked. Jakov kept driving, into the night on the road to Split, to an apartment on the ninth floor, to what was home.

12
ELDA

(2008)

At four in the morning, Toronto still buzzed with the night-time sounds of a metropolis – distant sirens, the thump of music and, from Nassau Street, the intermittent rumble of the subway. The sound of the traffic on Spadina Avenue did not relent for even a second, and even though the jazz concert at Grossman's Tavern had finished hours ago, Elda could still hear the voices and footsteps of the last guests leaving.

Standing in front of the bathroom mirror, applying make-up with short, sharp movements, she finished off her well-rehearsed morning ritual. When she decided it was enough, Elda looked at herself in the mirror and was pleased with what she saw.

She had never been particularly beautiful and never would be. Elda had realized as a teenager that she had the kind of wide face and small eyes that were unlikely to win many admirers. But Elda had learned early how to hide her faults, to enhance her prettier side and make the most of what she had. It was a skill she had perfected over twenty-odd years of practice.

That morning was no different. With gentle strokes of an eye pencil, she widened the contours of her eyes and gave them an alluring, eastern Slavic look. She brushed her peroxide blonde hair sharp against her cheeks to elongate her face and accentuated her thin lips with a dark pink lipstick the colour of wine. Then she slipped on a dark sweater with a discreet V-neck that showed off her long, elegant neck. Elda was still slim in her forties, and her face and hands bore only a few, well-concealed wrinkles. Her small breasts, which she had once resented, had become an advantage as she grew older, and her torso remained thin and firm. Elda was forty-four years old. But she knew she looked better now than when she was thirty.

Satisfied with her efforts, Elda left the bathroom. She packed her toiletries bag and finally, for the last time, zipped shut her big Samsonite travel case. She checked once more whether her passport, ticket and hotel confirmation were in the right place and looked one last time at whether the apartment she was leaving was in a reasonable state. The boiler was turned off, as was the water at the mains. Everything was in place, everything was in order, just as it always was when she left.

At 4.15 she peered through the window. Toronto by night was gleaming with artificial light. Further down the avenue she could see the skyscrapers in the port district, the contours of the Molson Amphitheatre and the ice hockey arena. Two dark vertical structures stood out against the blazing light – the towers of two neo-Gothic cathedrals. And behind and above everything, the CN Tower soared into the black sky, a red light blinking on its peak.

Over the road, Kensington Market was still bustling, the music of the street buskers, reggae clubs and late-night bars blending into one. From the intersection of Cecil and Huron she heard shouts and cries for help. She spotted an argument playing out on the street. A bearded taxi driver with a turban – probably Sikh – was angrily confronting a driver who had cut in front and scraped his bumper. Car hazard lights pulsated in the half-dark as the drivers became locked in an ever fiercer shouting match. Elda hoped it wasn't the taxi she had called.

It wasn't. Soon, from the direction of Dundas Street, another taxi appeared and stopped right in front of the entrance to her building. She pulled on her coat, grabbed the suitcase and her laptop and cast her eye once more around the apartment. She turned out the lights and carefully locked both door locks.

"The airport," she told the driver, who nodded and set off west in the direction of Mississauga. The driver didn't speak a word, but Elda noticed the name on the ID on the dashboard: Dalibor Jukić. He had to be Croat, but at four in the morning Elda wasn't up to compatriot conversation. She pretended not to have noticed and sat in silence for the rest of the journey. When they pulled up at Pearson Airport, she gave the driver a generous tip and thanked him in English. Dalibor Jukić thanked her back. His English wasn't so good, and by his accent he sounded like he was from Dalmatia. Elda thought how strange it was that two compatriots should meet on the other side of the world, part ways and disappear into the infinity of a major metropolis, never to meet again.

Although it was early, Pearson was already packed. She checked into her flight to Frankfurt, handed over her luggage and found gate twenty-eight. It was only then, sitting on a metal airport bench, that she realized how tired she was. A long day at work and an almost sleepless night were behind her. Ahead of her were an eight-hour flight, a transfer, jet lag and a two-day conference she already saw little sense in.

She realized she needed coffee. She went to the nearest open counter and ordered a coffee in a paper cup. It was filter coffee, bitter and insipid, and she regretted not having an espresso. She set down the cup and opened her laptop to check the news.

First she browsed the Canadian newspapers she usually followed – the *Toronto Star* and *Toronto Sun*. They were full of pensive articles about the stock market crisis, serious texts full of gloomy humility alongside jagged trading graphs. She ran through the main Canadian headlines before moving onto the Croatian portals and, as always, she was struck by the same insipid feeling.

Elda Zuvan had lived in Toronto for ten years. For seven years she had been in charge of the local branch of an agency specializing in Adriatic tourism. For seven years she had sold Croatia, mainly to Canadians. But as time passed, she had the impression she understood Croatia less and less.

And that was the feeling that grabbed her then. She looked at the screaming, bombastic headlines full of tabloid rage and vitriol. The texts she read dealt with things she didn't understand and had little to do with the world outside Croatia: war crimes, bodies found in caves, angry veterans, soccer refereeing mistakes, business scandals, corruption trials and bags full of cash exchanging hands outside filling stations. It was not just the content but the tone that was strange. It was full of angry irritation, the indignation of a child unjustly deprived of something by its parents. Elda was always struck by the same feeling, a feeling she recognized and for which she felt guilty. Every day, she felt less and less connection with the country spewing from those headlines. She made a living from selling it, but she understood it less and less. She loved it less and less.

She closed the laptop and pushed it to one side. She picked up an agency brochure she had been given to take with her, headed CROATIA SUMMER 2009. The illustration on the cover showed a cove with blue sea, a stone church and a pebble beach. That was the picture she sold to her clients: a picture of Polynesia, a remote Arcadia where time stood still and life was slow, peaceful and full of kindnesses. Sometimes, caught up in work, Elda would, for a moment, believe the picture. Then she would open the Croatian newspapers and the make-believe would end, as it had ended then.

Suddenly Elda was wide awake. She paid for the coffee and stood to stretch her legs. As she did so, a ground flight attendant announced that Flight LH471 to Frankfurt was ready for boarding. Elda picked up her laptop, her bag and coat, showed her passport and ticket to the flight attendant and entered the tunnel to the plane.

Somewhere around mid-afternoon, Elda felt her body begin to rebel. Her calves and neck hurt from so long sitting down, and there was a twinkling in front of her eyes from the white artificial light. Sentences, pictures and information penetrated the grey veil of exhaustion to reach her mind, but nothing stuck, nothing could get through to her consciousness. Jet-lagged and drained after eight hours stuck in a conference, Elda wanted just one thing – for it all to end as soon as possible.

Since nine in the morning, she had been sitting in an uncomfortable office chair in the Messe Frankfurt congress centre, with a laminated badge pinned to her chest and ear-phones for simultaneous translation of an investment panel called *Business Opportunities – Investment Roadshow Croatia Autumn 2008*. Since nine o'clock, hoteliers, property developers and reps from charter agencies and tour operators had lined up to present their magnificent plans, plans for which they needed someone else's money. From morning till late afternoon, Corel pictures of apartment developments, yacht clubs and harbours, financial projections and simulations flicked across the screen in front of Elda. Everyone taking the stage had offered something, and for what they were offering they needed capital. But they knew, as the people in the audience knew, that it wasn't going to happen. Fannie Mae and Freddie Mac had collapsed, Wall Street was in free fall, and the world of property sales had evaporated like soap bubbles in a matter of weeks. The wheels were still spinning, but nothing was moving. Those gathered at the Messe Frankfurt had come to reassure themselves and everyone else that everything was all right, that the world was still rotating on its axis. But nothing was all right, and everyone in that room knew it.

So since nine o'clock Elda had listened to presentations of projects that would not happen and looked at simulations of buildings that would not be built, Corel fantasy drawings replete with palm trees and promenades, yachts and pergolas. And occasionally a picture of the country in question would flash up on the screen. Between the slides and columns of numbers would appear a photograph of some wretched, wild cove, a sleepy and forgotten village so far removed from the people watching, from that hotel and congress centre.

Elda's eyes were beginning to sting after hours beneath neon lights. She closed them and savoured a few seconds of dark relaxation. Then the presenter introduced the next speaker, an Irishman who represented an investment fund called Smart Solutions Estate. He started to speak and showed them pictures of two new investments, a marina and a tourist development on former military property, one somewhere in Istria and the other in Misto. Elda opened her eyes. What she saw on the screen looked little different to the dozens of other pictures they had been shown since the morning: a row of apartment blocks, a marina hotel and a dog-leg marina. And inside the marina were simulations of magnificent yachts. The project's "selling point", as the Irishman called it, was the network of old naval tunnels that offered the potential of adventure tourism. The Irishman pressed the remote and the picture of the marina was replaced by a column of numbers.

He began to present the "timeshare" options and Elda realized she wasn't interested in the slightest.

Her eyes started to wander around the room. She looked at the backs of the businesspeople's heads and played at spotting the Croatians among them. Her gaze passed from one weary person to the next, each fighting to keep their eyes open, until she reached someone at the end of the room who looked wide awake. He was a moderately handsome man in his mid thirties, and he was looking straight at her.

The young man's gaze was intense. When he realized she had noticed, he turned away and looked back at the podium. Elda turned her head but kept him in her peripheral vision. As soon as he saw Elda look away, the stranger began observing her again.

Elda wasn't used to this. She knew she didn't often turn heads and wasn't used to being stared at by someone younger than her, being singled out from dozens of other women in the room. She felt a strange, uneasy lust.

When the Irishman had finished, the presenter brought the first day to a close and invited them all into the lobby for cocktails. The throng began to withdraw to the exit. Elda tried to spot the man who had been watching her. She found him, and the man averted his gaze once more.

In the lobby, Elda took a glass of champagne and knocked it back thirstily. After so many hours, her throat was dry and the alcohol helped get her blood circulating again. She quickly took a second glass, took a sip, but then forced herself to pause. She knew that downing two glasses would knock her out.

She stood by the wall and scanned the crowd, looking again for her mysterious suitor. He was still watching her, but this time he didn't look away. They looked at each other for a while, interestedly, and finally the stranger deigned to approach. "I know you," he said.

He couldn't have come up with a more clichéd chat-up line, Elda thought.

"Split, 1989," the stranger added. "You were working at Yugobank. Your hair was similar, only lighter. You went Interrailing around Spain that summer – Toledo, Barcelona, Segovia… You took a picture of yourself in Madrid, on Plaza Mayor."

Elda looked at him, stunned. A man she had never seen before had approached her on the other side of the world and told her things about her past that only those closest to her knew. She felt uncomfortable.

"How in God's name do you know all that?"

"Because we met then. You were the last person to see my sister before she went missing."

Elda realized her mistake. She had seen that face once before. She recognized the same serious eyes, the brow, the same long jawline. But back then it had still been the face of a child, not a grown man. A picture formed: a cafe in a street that back then was called Workers' Promenade, Elda on one side of the table, dressed in the dark suit of a bank clerk, and two men on the other. One of the men was middle-aged, but his face escaped her. The other man was young, more like a big kid. The kid sat in the cubicle listening, nervously attentive, to what Elda had to say. Surfacing from the past, the same face was in front of her.

Mate Vela reintroduced himself as the brother of Silva Vela, the Silva who had disappeared in 1989 and had the whole country looking for her. He worked for a ship management company, he said, which dealt in boats, motors and parts and which was looking for contracts in new marinas where it could offer servicing and spare parts.

It was Elda's turn. Her company was looking for new tourist capacity to complete its catalogue, but it wasn't working out.

The crisis, she said. The crisis, agreed Mate. The world had changed overnight. None of their previous calculations stood up any more. All financing sources had dried up. They had all pulled back, licking their wounds and waiting.

They talked for a while about work, and finally he spoke the words she had been waiting for: would she like a drink at the hotel bar? They went down to the bar and sat in a cubicle with leather seats. Elda ordered a glass of dry white wine and he did the same. The server opened a bottle of Rainer Wess Riesling and poured. Elda took her glass and asked Mate the question she had been too afraid to ask before.

"So, where was your sister in the end? Where did you find her?"

"We haven't found her," he replied. "Not a trace."

"You don't even know if she's alive?"

"No. But I think she is. If she wasn't alive I guess we'd have somehow found out."

Up until then, Mate had been mysteriously unforthcoming. Then the floodgates opened. He had been looking for his sister since 1989, he told her. He was the only one who hadn't given up. He had received countless tip-offs over the years, but none had worked out. He had been everywhere: Trieste, Graz, Barcelona, Genoa, Ljubljana and Gothenburg. A few years ago he'd made a website; people still contacted him through it, sent messages, left information, even so many years on. He had recently taken the search onto social media. People had recommended Facebook, saying it was growing fast. He was satisfied with the results. Lots of people were getting in touch and you never knew when something useful might turn up.

They ordered another bottle. While the server opened it, Mate continued. "What happened destroyed us," he said.

His parents had split up and hardly spoke. He had spent a lot of money and time searching for his sister, but he had no choice. Every morning, he was tortured by the same thought – that Silva was somewhere out there, that she might need help, that she hoped he was looking for her, that he had given up.

"A day I don't look for her is a day I hate myself," he said. "That's what my wife doesn't understand. She thinks that at some point I should have drawn a line. That I should have stopped and said *That's enough.*" The words tumbled out as if they'd been queuing up. Then Mate said: "I'm so happy I can even talk to someone about it, because I haven't been able to, and I miss that."

Elda looked at him, and right then she knew she'd ask him to her room.

Later, upstairs, Mate was gentle, almost fragile He lay beneath her and let Elda lead, his hands running lightly over her back and buttocks as Elda's body bent and ground rhythmically on top of him. Elda felt beneath her a sharp, skinny body. She had never slept with anyone almost ten years younger. She was used to middle-aged lovers with spare flesh and the beginnings of a paunch. What she felt beneath her now was dry bone, fibrous tissue, thin limbs. Her breathing deepened and she came with a loud moan. She rolled onto her side and looked at him. Mate gave her a meek look of gratitude. He stroked her side and she placed her hand on his.

For a long time, she couldn't fall asleep. She felt the warm body of a man next to her and listened to his quiet, steady breathing. She listened to the gentle hum of the hotel ventilation and looked through the window at the bright night sky and the blinking of planes moving across it. She felt good for the first time in ages. She tried to hold onto the feeling, to keep her mind there in that room, there and then. But she couldn't. Her thoughts fled to another place, to another time.

The central bus station in Split: she stands at the international counter, young, twenty-five years old and spending the salary she has earned working in a bank. She is tanned from the summer sun and afternoons on the beach. She has bought an Interrail card with which she plans to travel around Provence, Castile and Andalusia, and now she is queuing for a bus ticket to Trieste. She has to wait a long time; in front of her is a group of backpackers with blonde hair and the Danish flag on their backpacks. The backpackers are having some kind of disagreement with the woman behind the glass, who is gesticulating and trying to tell them something in broken English.

Elda waits. She waits, but it doesn't bother her because she's young, because for the first time she has earned her own money, and because she is about to have the best six months of her life. She starts talking to the girl behind her, who is younger than Elda. They chat and laugh. They bad-mouth the witless Danes and the awful English of the woman behind the counter. They talk like old friends, although they have never met. Then Elda buys her ticket to Trieste, shakes the girl's hand and wishes her a good trip.

She remembered that face and that meeting for a long time afterwards. And then she completely forgot both, until that night when they surfaced from some nook of her cortex where she had mislaid them long ago. The man breathing beside her – Mate Vela – looked like his sister. Not completely, not like twins. But there was a resemblance nevertheless, in the delicacy of his bones, in the length of his jaw, in the curve of his brow and his eyes. It was strange how that girl had brought them together, Elda thought. Decades on, she had inadvertently led her brother to Elda's hotel bed.

That morning in Split, Elda had wished the stranger at the bus station a good trip. Precisely that. She remembered it well.

Whatever happened next, her wish had apparently gone unfulfilled.

Elda thought about it briefly, then embraced the sleeping stranger. Without waking, the man pulled her to him.

She woke early, well before Mate. She slipped out of bed quietly so as not to wake him and went to the bathroom. She took a long shower, rinsing from herself the new, unreal male scent. Then she took up her tools – lipstick, eyeshadow and mascara – and readied her morning facade. She knew that mornings rarely flatter women of her age, women like her. She wanted to look respectable for when Mate woke.

Elda was already dressed and ready to go out when Mate opened his eyes. She wished him good morning and watched as he washed and dressed. She looked at him for any sign of discomfort, guilt or a desire for whatever was going on between them to end as soon as possible. Miraculously, she found none. She had expected to, but there wasn't a trace.

They went to the hotel restaurant and sat down for breakfast as if they were a couple. Elda was surprised at how much that small rite pleased her.

They sat in the corner, away from the rest of the guests. She passed him the sugar and a spoon, and he passed her the warm butter. His head down, Mate placed a slice of *Leberkäse* on warm bread, then he lifted his head and looked at her. For a while, they looked at each other in silence.

"It's all right," Elda said. "I know everything. And it's all right."

He smiled. "It's not that," he said. "It's not what you think it is." He hesitated, as if searching for the words, then said: "I'm pleased. About all this. I liked it. I can't remember the last time I was able to talk like this. I really missed it." Then he added, meekly: "I'd like us to stay in touch. I'd really like that."

They fell silent again. But neither of them looked away. They looked each other straight in the eyes, and in Mate's penetrating gaze there was not a trace of unease or guilt. He looked at her like someone who was happy.

After breakfast they both checked out and emptied their rooms. When Elda came down to the lobby, Mate was waiting for her at reception. "I didn't want to leave without saying goodbye," he said.

They went outside. It was January. From the other side of the Main, a harsh, cold wind blew across the plain from the direction of the forest. Elda wrapped her face in her scarf and turned to her freshly minted lover. She approached and pressed her lips to his. He returned the kiss. For half a minute, maybe more, they stood there, lips locked, as if neither of them wanted to break the embrace. Then Elda pulled back and whispered: "You'll be late."

She watched him get into a taxi. The taxi pulled away and turned the corner, and Elda suddenly felt the cold. Her flight wasn't until late afternoon, but there was nothing keeping her in that bleak, foreign city. She regretted not getting in Mate's taxi, not driving with him to the airport and spending another half hour or so together until his flight. But it was too late. It was just her and Frankfurt.

The rest of the morning she spent wandering around the city, between office blocks and old half-timbered breweries. Bored of tottering around, she eventually hailed a taxi and went to the airport four hours early. She checked in, handed over her luggage and went to her gate.

It was still early in the day and the terminal was depressingly empty. She sat down at the far end, in the corner, and connected to the internet. She searched for a name: Silva Vela.

The website popped up immediately, with a heading that read LOOKING FOR SILVA VELA. The text described the circumstances of her disappearance, the colour of her hair, her height and age. The site offered a reward to anyone who might help find Silva. Everything was in Croatian and English. Only one message wasn't translated. It was written in big letters, in a different colour and different font. It was only for her: *Silva, call us. We're looking for you. Your family.*

At the centre of the page was a photograph of Silva. It was the same photograph Elda remembered pinned up in doorways, hair salons and bus stops in Split. In the picture, Silva was seventeen years old and looking at the camera with an air of defiant optimism.

Elda returned to the top of the page and looked for a contact. All the contacts listed were Mate's: landline number, home address, mobile phone and email. It was the same email address Mate had given her a few hours earlier.

Opening a new mail, she typed in his address. She thought for a second, unsure whether what she was about to do was wise, then she wrote six words: *Glad we met. Stay in touch.* She wondered whether to add a smiley or a heart at the end. Better not, she decided. She didn't want to force Mate into a promise he didn't want to make.

She pressed "send". She hovered over her open laptop, like a child wincing at the mess they have made. Then she heard the ping of an incoming message. *I'm glad too,* Mate wrote. *Write when you get to T.*

Elda sat there in the chair of a half-empty international airport. A jet-lagged Indian family dozed on the seats opposite her.

The gate for Toronto slowly filled with tired, disinterested travellers, numb from hours of waiting and the changes in time zone. They sat there, heads in newspapers or books, eyes open or closed, waiting for the empty, dull, in-between time to pass. Elda sat among them. But for Elda it wasn't empty or dull. Elda felt swept up in a storm.

She looked at her laptop, at the words on the white screen. She clicked "reply", then a heart, and pressed "send". No way back now, she thought. Whatever came of it, something had started.

The reply came quickly: another heart, but this one split in two by a jagged line.

Take care, will write from T, she wrote, and sent it on its way to Split. Still overwhelmed with excitement, Elda closed the laptop. The gate was filling up with people of all different colours, ages and races.

Elda observed heads, hair, brows and the backs of necks. And then she realized: among that mass of foreigners, she was looking for a familiar face, a tuft of hair or a neck. That she was looking for someone who might be missing, who might in any way resemble Silva Vela.

13
MATE (2012)

Shortly before eight o'clock, Mate was first at the office.

It was cold. After the long weekend, the stale air smelled of glue, thinner and paint. He hung up his coat, pulled up the blinds, turned on the electric radiator and opened the window to let in some fresh air.

It was January, the day before Epiphany. The lowering sky above the Kozjak and Mosor mountains promised unrelenting rain, and soon. The marina was usually dead at that time of the year anyway, but that morning the southerly wind and rain-heavy sky had driven away any remaining workers or boat owners.

Through the window he saw a row of identical, padlocked concrete jetties, each lined with dozens of small boats slumbering peacefully, waiting for the marina to come alive in spring. Wherever he looked, Mate saw yachts, cutters, outboards, lobster boats, *pasaras*, double-ender *gucs* and dinghies, wrapped in tarpaulin and protective foil. Mate had sold spare parts for many of them – anchors, motors, fenders and winches. The boats rocked languidly on the swell, their lines creaking as they pulled tight. From time to time, a gust of wind would shake the lateen yards, the stays and shrouds, transforming the wintertime marina into a chorus of wind chimes.

Mate closed the window as soon as the first raindrops began to fall. The office still smelled stale. It was a mix of office, shop and warehouse, and in the thousand square feet Mate rented were piled all sorts of chemicals – cans of primer and antifouling paint, jars of marine putty, bottles of thinner and kegs of epoxy resin. One spark and his entire business would go up in a cloud of stinking chemical smoke.

He checked the time: 8.20. The secretary would arrive in ten minutes, followed by Srećko, who worked behind the counter, just before nine. He had ten minutes for his morning ritual.

Turning on the computer, he waited for it to boot up. He checked the business email for any messages that might have arrived over the weekend: spam, requests for quotes, messages from suppliers; a notice from the customs authority that Srećko would have to sort out during the day; and a long-overdue delivery notice for a fifty-seven horsepower YANMAR inboard motor ordered before Christmas which had finally reached customs.

He deleted the spam, confirmed receipt with customs, checked the mail once more and closed the inbox. He slid the mouse to the edge of the screen and clicked on an icon tucked away in the corner. It opened a web page, one Mate opened every morning.

For nine years, Mate's day had begun with the same ritual. He would open the page he had created, look at the picture of his disappeared sister and check whether anyone – his sister, or someone who might have seen her – had got in contact.

In the beginning, people got in touch. Not often, but every month or two some well-meaning member of the public, some poor wretch or sadist, would write or call to say they had seen the girl in the picture, or that they knew of someone who knew where she was. For nine years Mate had checked every single tip-off, even those he knew were wrong or were spiteful pranks.

While he and Doris had been married, he'd got into the habit of checking Silva's page at work, out of sight. They had been divorced two years, but still Mate would open the site in his office, always in the morning, always early, before anyone else arrived. Over time, fewer and fewer people made contact. There had been a brief spike in interest when he'd opened a Facebook page dedicated to the search. There were messages of support, sympathy, suggestions and proposals. But it had all died down again, the wave receding just as it had arrived.

"Good morning."

A voice came from the door and Mate looked up. It was Srećko. He shook the water from his umbrella and deposited it in the stand before sliding off his raincoat. He wore a wide smile, full of goodwill as always.

"Anything new?" Srećko asked.

"Yep," Mate replied. "That YANMAR arrived at last."

"Thank God," said Srećko, pulling off his wet socks.

Mate stood up and approached the counter. He showed Srećko the mail, told him what to do and returned to his computer to finish his morning task. He opened Silva's page and looked at the header, the contact box and Silva's photo. Silva looked back as if trying to provoke him.

He opened the new messages folder. Like every morning, he expected to find it empty, a gaping nothingness. But it wasn't. There was a message in the inbox, pixels flickering, alone against a bare white background.

As soon as he opened it, Mate noticed something strange about the message: there was no text, no sign-off, and it was sent from an address that contained no discernible name or surname. It had been sent by a stranger, a phantom, by someone who wished to conceal their identity. It contained only a link, a link to a Facebook profile. Mate clicked on it.

He stopped briefly, quiet, paralysed. He looked at the screen in front of him and tried to fight back a wave of excitement.

Mate waited for Srećko to get off his call with the customs authority. Then he told him he had to go, urgently, and that he wouldn't be back for the rest of the day. He told Srećko to deal with the customs issue himself because it looked like he would have to take a short trip.

Then he shut down his computer, pulled on his coat and hurried out.

That day, it was Mate's turn to spend the afternoon with Tina. He went to Doris's after lunch, at about three. Tina was already dressed and ready to go, but it was clear from her face that spending the afternoon with her father wasn't top of her teenage wish list.

When Tina had been small, Mate was able to play with her, entertain her. But now she was fifteen. She had purple streaks in her hair, drew superheroes at the edges of her notebooks and listened to Beyoncé and Shakira. Tina was way past sweet shops, indoor playgrounds and the zoo.

They spent the whole afternoon wandering around in the rain, Mate sneaking a glance at his daughter from time to time. The bigger she got, the more she looked like the aunt she'd never met. She had the same eyes, the same contour of the nose. Even the black hair that fell over her eyes reminded him of Silva.

Mate remembered his sister when she was Tina's age. They would spend the whole day roaming Misto, as thick as thieves. They would go swimming, wander to the Stella Maris chapel and climb Cape Cross in hopes of catching sight of some secret tryst. They would hang around outside the store in the marina collecting discarded bottle tops to take to the shop-keeper, Agata, in exchange for Coca-Cola. They were rarely home, rarely indoors. Looking back, it seemed like one long, uninterrupted summer, a summer that had lasted for years.

Tina resembled her aunt. But there was one big difference. Silva had been full of life and elan. With Silva, the glass was always half-full. With Tina it was always half-empty, something Mate had reluctantly come to realize. She got it from her mother, he thought bitterly. Doris was like that. She would rather see a problem, rather find fault. She was always half-satisfied, half-happy.

The afternoon dragged on. They watched a movie on DVD, went for an ice cream, then another. At about seven o'clock, Mate realized that both he and Tina were surreptitiously checking the time.

"I'll go home a bit earlier," said Tina. "I'm chatting with the girls at eight."

He took her home before the agreed time, at 7.40. Doris didn't say a word and simply gave him a look of disapproval. She offered him coffee, but her manner suggested she would rather he decline. He did. He said goodbye at the door and returned to the car. He got in and opened his laptop. He clicked on the link again. For a long time he looked at the unmoving page and the face that looked back at him.

Mate didn't dare say anything to his mother, not yet. He wasn't sure about his father.

There was only one person he wanted to talk to, could talk to, and that was Elda.

Their relationship had unravelled over several years, slowly, thread by thread, like a brittle piece of paper that crumbles to powder. It started with small secrets, small lies, petty moods and grudges. Over time, the moods and grudges grew worse, as did the distrust. Things that had once seemed like charming human imperfections grew with time into irritating character flaws, and he and Doris grew apart, slowly, steadily and coldly, like two bodies passing each other in space and moving on, each taking its own path into the cold void. Through ten years of marriage, he and Doris had developed the ability to politely, detachedly tolerate one another. It was a skill that could have saved them in the long run, had Doris not discovered Elda's existence.

At first, Mate and Elda had only written to one another. They had kept up a relationship that in every message became more serious but existed only in inboxes, folders and files. In the first year, they met only twice, when Elda came to Croatia on business trips. The second of these occasions, they met in a hotel that Elda had booked on the outskirts of Split. It wasn't Frankfurt or Genoa. The hotel was a few miles from Doris and their home, and the waiters spoke Croatian and looked at Mate as if they wanted to wink at him conspiratorially. Mate had felt an unspeakable shame.

Had the distance remained, the relationship would have probably fizzled out or been reduced to a long-distance correspondence between friends. But in September 2009, Elda took a job in the office of the Chamber of Tourism in Vienna. She moved close by. Too close. That was the instant Mate's marriage was condemned to failure.

They met in Vienna, Split or – most often – Zagreb, in business hotels, in anonymous rooms of cherrywood and brass, rooms where dressing gowns hung on the back of the bathroom door and the minibar always held gin and vodka. When they met, they would grab at one another like they couldn't get enough. Then, after, when calm had been restored, they would talk. Mate had never found it so easy to talk to someone as he talked to Elda.

It took just a few months for Doris to find out. It was no surprise; the signs were everywhere. Mate was always travelling, often at weekends, and at work they never knew where he was. He didn't even make an effort to delete Elda's emails from his inbox. Later, Mate would read in some newspaper about Freudian slips, about mistakes that aren't mistakes but are in fact your subconscious desire to knock over the vase with your elbow or to utter something completely inappropriate. Mate realized his incaution was exactly that – a Freudian slip. Somewhere beneath a membrane of common sense, a little dwarf in him wanted the vase to fall and shatter, wanted Doris to find out, for their marriage to come to an end. And that's what happened.

At the beginning of 2010, Doris sat down at his computer one day while he was shaving in the bathroom. She found a message from Elda – the first, the second, the seventh and fiftieth. After a scene that was unpleasant and brief, Mate left the family home for the last time. He spent that night in a hotel – the same hotel where he'd first gone astray with Elda. The next morning he logged into Skype and told Elda he and his wife had broken up. She hurried to Split the next weekend. After spending the afternoon in the hotel room, they went out into the city. They sat down in a cafe on the shore and ordered two glasses of wine.

Mate was pleased to find that his feeling of shame had melted away, as if it had never been. All he felt was serenity.

In early autumn that year, Elda found a job in Split and returned home for good. She rented an apartment in the Meja district, but Mate didn't move in. They were together constantly, but they each had their own place and they lived apart. Elda said it would be better like that, at least in the beginning. That beginning had lasted nineteen months already.

Mate drove through the Marjan tunnel connecting Meja with the rest of Split and turned right at the archaeological museum. He continued straight along the coastal road, beaches on one side and the dense, black Marjan pine forest on the other. Between the sea and the forest was a narrow row of houses inhabited in the main by the families of the pre-Second World War nobility, the Communist elite or transition-era profiteers. The houses were lavish affairs, equipped with status symbols such as security cameras and automatic gates. But wealth in Meja stopped on the doorstep. Between the houses, the neighbourhood was rough-hewn and untidy. The approach roads were worn away, there were no walkways or paths, and to reach the houses higher up you had to climb primitive, roughly cemented steps.

It never ceased to surprise him that Elda had rented an apartment in such an area. After years spent in Toronto, it was as if she wanted to be close to the sea and the pine trees. As if, after so many years working in tourism, she had fallen for the same fairy tales she sold clients.

Mate turned into one of the narrow roads between the houses, drove a short way uphill and parked by an improvised concrete staircase. He climbed the stairs and rang the bell at the gate. Fortunately, Elda was home. She came out into the yard and let him in. When he stepped inside the apartment, she threw her arms around his neck and nipped at his ear. "I was just about to call you," she said. "I was missing you."

He kissed her and she led him into the bedroom, but Mate asked her to wait. "I have to show you something," he said. "Something important." He opened his laptop and showed her the picture.

It was the Facebook profile. The person it belonged to was called Silvija, and her surname – according to the profile – was

Aleksić. But there was no doubt. Silvija Aleksić was Silva, Mate's sister. The similarity was undeniable: the same shape of the face, the same nose, the same smile lines. The hair was different. The photograph was slightly blurred, not new, it seemed. But it was Silva.

By the looks of things, Silva wasn't particularly active on Facebook. There were no comments, no posts or photographs. It didn't even say when or where she was born. But there was the name of her husband – Miomir Aleksić – and an address: Yuri Gagarin 138, New Belgrade, Serbia. And there was the name of a child: Jovan. That morning, Mate found out he had a nephew in Serbia.

Elda bombarded him with questions he couldn't answer. No, he didn't know who had sent the link or why. No, he hadn't rummaged around in the IP address. He had sent a reply but got nothing back. He didn't know how Silva had come to be in Belgrade or why she hadn't got in touch. But from the crumbs of information he had, he could cobble together some kind of reasonable explanation: she had obviously been in a relationship with someone from Belgrade; she had obviously kept it secret; she had been underage, so she couldn't simply leave with him, she'd had to run away. Perhaps they had been in hiding. Perhaps she'd had to avoid getting in touch. Then the war had started, the Iron Curtain had come down between Serbia and Croatia. And then what had happened after the war ended? He didn't know; he couldn't even guess. But there was something secretive about the Facebook profile – no mention of where she'd been born, her nationality or her family. That secrecy spoke volumes. She didn't want her identity or her whereabouts shouted from the rooftops.

It was all guesswork. He knew nothing for sure, except that his sister lived at Yuri Gagarin 138. Her face, which he remembered so well, looked out at him from the Facebook page. The face was the same, but not the expression. The expression was meek, resigned, not in any way rebellious. In the years that had passed, Silva, it seemed, had changed.

He closed the laptop and Elda looked at him. "When are you going?" she asked.

"Tomorrow morning," he replied, and curled up on the bed.

Mate arrived in Belgrade at around four in the afternoon. It stopped raining as he neared the city on the main road from the Croatian border. But Belgrade was still wet. He looked at the soaked cars, the soaked trams and the endless mass of people jostling on the walkways, umbrellas in hand. The Sava was swollen and turbid. At the confluence where it flowed into the Danube, the waters gushed together in a confused, muddy-brown vortex.

He had reserved a room online in a part of the city called Savamala. For a long time, he wound his way through a complex of steep roads that ran down the hillside to the river. He drove between soot-stained interwar buildings of two or three floors, old toolmakers, tinsmiths and restaurants serving traditional Serbian fare until he spotted a steep, narrow street and a parking place. He parked his car and checked in. He tossed his bag on the bed and immediately ordered a taxi from reception. He had no intention of wandering around. He wanted someone to take him straight to the address, and fast.

The taxi drove for a while along the river. Mate wasn't sure which one, but he suspected it was the Sava. They passed a decrepit interwar hotel and the bus station, where he saw homeless people sleeping on the street. They passed rail lines, parked cars and building sites, then they crossed the bridge. From the passenger seat, he turned to take in the panorama of the city – a row of buildings along the riverbank, the fortress at the confluence of the rivers and the pointed baroque tower of the Cathedral Church of St Michael the Archangel.

Crossing the river was like entering another city. The roads were wide and on the left and right were gigantic rows of socialist high-rises, broken up now and then by skyscrapers. At one point, between those residential blocks, he spotted the construction site of an unfinished church. The workers were building it as if in the Middle Ages, brick by brick, and Mate could already discern the roof of a Byzantine dome. They had built the dome carefully and slowly, as if the concrete towers and everything else around them did not exist. Mate was struck by the poignancy of the scene.

An Orthodox cross hung from the rear-view mirror and an icon of a bearded saint sat on the dashboard. Mate looked at them and the driver noticed. "Dalmatian, right?" he said to Mate. "We're compatriots. I'm from Obrovac," he explained, referring to a town in the Zrmanja river canyon near Zadar. "I *was* from Obrovac," he said.

The taxi driver turned towards a row of residential buildings along a riverside promenade. Finally he stopped at the entrance to one of them. "It's here," he said.

Mate waited a long time for the elevator. When it arrived, he pressed the button for the top floor. Getting out, he began walking back down the stairs, looking at each door on the way down for the surname Aleksić. He hoped there wasn't more than one Aleksić family in the building, a possibility given its size.

He found a nameplate that read ALEKSIĆ on the eighth floor. He stopped and looked at the ordinary, anonymous door of yellowy plywood. He tried to summon the courage to knock, imagining the scene about to unfold. Then he knocked.

For a long time he heard nothing. Then came a patter of small feet and the door opened. Standing there was a boy of five or six, surely Jovan, his nephew.

"Is your mother home?" Mate asked, and the boy disappeared into the apartment. It smelled of goulash or stewed meat with paprika.

For a while, Mate didn't hear anything. Then a woman stepped into the corridor in an apron and approached the door. She looked at Mate, confused, and asked what he wanted.

He was startled by the similarity. She had the same eyebrows as Silva, the same face shape, the forehead and lips. She even wore her hair in the same style as Silva had done, long ago, before everything. Standing before Mate was a woman whom even he might have mistaken for Silva. Only she wasn't Silva. She wasn't, because his sister would have been forty by then. But the woman looking at Mate from the door was barely more than twenty. The woman standing before him was the young mother of a small child.

The woman looked at him mutely, without a hint of recognition, then spoke with an accent from the Dalmatian hinterland or Bosnia. "Yes?" she said. "What do you want?"

"Nothing," said Mate. "I made a mistake. Wrong door."

He hurried to the elevator, trying to escape the woman's gaze. He didn't want anyone, not even a stranger, to witness his moment of weakness. He called the elevator, and as it descended he began wrestling inside with the torrent of shame sweeping through him.

Mate didn't stay the night. He left for home that afternoon having paid the hotel for only a few hours' stay. He headed west out of the city as darkness was falling, passing once more through New Belgrade, past the rows of immense residential buildings, shopping centres and office high-rises. As he looked at the thousands of illuminated rooms, he thought of the sender of the mysterious mail. It must have been one of the Aleksićs' neighbours or an acquaintance, someone who saw her every day in the elevator or the parking area, who sold her newspapers or bread or caught the same tram. It must have been someone who knew her name, who somehow stumbled upon the website Mate had made and believed they had uncovered their neighbour's secret. From the shadows, they had intervened in her life and in Mate's too. That person was in one of those illuminated honeycomb cells, imagining what they had set in motion. In silence and anonymity, they would continue their secret life, thinking they had uncovered the hidden truth about their neighbour. About Silvija Aleksić, the Croat.

He kept driving, out of the centre and towards the periphery. The high-rises began to thin out, replaced by settlements of low, unfinished houses separated by sparse patches of trees. All the settlements looked similar: in the centre, a shiny new church, and around it rows of houses lined up along village streets, each made of red brick, no plaster in sight, and most of them unfinished. In each settlement he saw a boules court. And where there were boules, there were Serb refugees from Dalmatia. On warm days they would crowd around those courts, waving their arms and talking loudly, giving full voice to the Ikavian dialect and southern gesticulations they had brought with them. But right then, on a rainy evening, the courts were empty, strips of trimmed, fine earth abandoned on the Pannonian plain, plucked from their own world and tossed into another where they did not belong.

Mate paid the toll and crossed the border, where the road improved as it crossed the Croatian section of Pannonia. He drove through forests of oak, followed by vineyards, cornfields and plum orchards.

And as he drove, the feeling grew inside him, so strong, so firm that he knew it would never leave him – the feeling that it was time to stop. He recalled all his journeys around Europe, wanderings around Trieste, Barcelona, Sweden, Austria and the fuel pumps of Hercegovina. He remembered all the doors he had knocked on, all the airports, police stations and Red Cross offices he had visited. And it all felt so pointless.

He tried again, as he did every time, to recall scenes from the distant past: Silva as a child, hanging around in Misto; the games they played together; the laughs they had. He recalled collecting bottle tops outside Agata's shop, swimming beneath the Stella Maris chapel, playing leapfrog, hopscotch and What's the Time, Mr Wolf? He pictured limpets in a bucket of sea water, hunting for mussels in Travna cove. He remembered when Aunt Zlata was still alive, when he and Silva still shared a bedroom, when Silva would read girls' magazines with a light under her covers at bedtime.

Sometimes the trick worked. But not now. He felt dry and empty. He no longer knew why he was doing this. Instead of Silva, he saw a ghost without shape or features, a spectre he had been grasping at for more than twenty years.

He drove without stopping until he reached the Lika region of central Croatia, where he was overcome by an indescribable tiredness. He turned off into a rest stop and fell asleep on the back seat. When he woke, it was already morning. It was cold, and a fine sleet had started to fall on the plains around Gacka.

By nine he was in Split, but he didn't head home or to Elda's since he knew Elda would be at work. He headed for the eastern junction and turned at the bus depot onto Hercegovačka. He called the elevator and pressed the button for the ninth floor. He knew Jakov would be home. His old man was working afternoons that week.

Mate rang the doorbell and Jakov let him in without a word. He must have looked terrible. His father didn't ask him anything. He just frowned and poured him a Turkish coffee.

"You were right," Mate said. "You were right the whole time."

"About what?"

"About her. About Silva. It's pointless. All of this is pointless."

Jakov's face darkened. He said nothing.

"You were right," Mate said again. "If she wanted to, she'd call. And if she didn't, fuck her. She can go to hell."

His father stood up in silence, buttered a slice of bread and handed it to him. Mate wolfed it down and Jakov placed his hand on his son's head, on his hair. Mate had no memory of his father ever stroking his head, ever comforting him, even as a child. Jakov placed his hand on Mate's head, as if blessing him. "Eat that and get on home. Get some sleep," he said. "Leave her. Just like she left us."

Jakov topped up Mate's coffee. On a grey morning, the coffee smelled invigorating and life-restoring.

PART THREE

SILVA RETURNS

14
JAKOV (2015)

Silva's remains were found on 16 May 2015, in an abandoned naval tunnel below Cape Cross. Workers found them a little after ten in the morning as they laid dynamite to blow up rock that had come away from the walls. They went behind the rock and there, in a dark cavity, they found a small, curled-up human skeleton.

She was found by workers of the Split construction company Lukaprojekt. At the beginning of December, Lukaprojekt had begun clearing the area of the former naval base for an Irish investor's hotel and marina development. By the beginning of January they had demolished all the pavilions, the magazine and the central washrooms, and in February they began building a new tourist complex according to the plans of Smart Solutions Estate. By April, on the grounds of the former barracks, they had already laid the foundations of the hotel, timeshare apartments and marina reception. In May, the workers entered the abandoned naval tunnels that had once served to hide patrol boats. They were in a bad state. The earthquake in Ston in 1996 had shaken the entrance to the tunnels and undermined the structural integrity of the ceilings, causing some parts to collapse. The tunnels were full of huge lumps of concrete.

In May, explosive technicians from Lukaprojekt dynamited the interior of the tunnels to clear a path to the end. Then that May morning, at the end of the tunnel, they came to a massive section of the ceiling that had come away. At 10.15, they went behind the rock to drill holes for the sticks of explosives. It was there that they found the bones, white and blanched by time, salt and damp. The skeleton lay there peacefully, curled up. As if a child had died while asleep. With the bare bones could just be made out the remains of clothing and traces of a red raincoat.

Jakov was informed the same day, at around two in the afternoon. He worked the morning that day and was finishing his shift at the warehouse till when a voice on the PA system called him to the entrance. Two police officers were waiting for him. It didn't even occur to Jakov that they might be there to talk about Silva. When they told him, he practically waved them away. "It can't be her," he said. "Must be someone else." Nevertheless, he changed out of his work jacket and got into the police car.

When they arrived in Misto, they didn't turn into the town but stopped at the roundabout, at what was once the entrance to the naval base. They got out and told him to follow them. It was the first time Jakov had ever set foot inside the old barracks.

They walked between the stumps that remained of the old pavilions, where the contours of new, two-storey villas were emerging, with large spaces that looked onto the sea. Passing a big sign bearing the name Smart Solutions Estate, they walked downhill in the direction of the sea, to the old military jetty, then along the shore to the cliffs beneath Cape Cross. They came to the entrance to one of the naval tunnels. Jakov knew the tunnels existed; he had seen them from the sea when he and Vesna had gone fishing in their small boat. But this was the first time he had been so close.

The entrance was crowded. Jakov could see workers, obviously distressed. There was an ambulance, a coroner, photographer and several police officers. And in the middle was a man who appeared to be giving out orders. Jakov didn't recognize him at first. Only when the man addressed him directly did Jakov recognize him as Tomislav Čović.

Jakov had met Inspector Čović only once, in September 1991. Back then, Čović had been young and arrogant. He had changed in the intervening twenty-four years into a middle-aged man of unhealthy complexion, slightly overweight and greying at the temples. He noticed Jakov and shook his hand, the expression on his face one of obvious unease. "Come with me," said Čović, and he turned towards the tunnel entrance. He led Jakov to a cast-metal coffin set on the pebble shore.

Up until then, Jakov had believed it was all a mistake. He had been sure the remains were not those of Silva. They couldn't be. Approaching the coffin, he realized he'd been wrong.

He stood over the metal box and looked inside. He saw the preserved remains of a skull, ribs, and long bones that may have been from the upper arms or lower legs. Inside the coffin, next to the skeleton, lay the rotten, dishevelled remains of a bag and clothes. It was Silva's shoulder bag. The clothes in it were those Silva had been wearing that day.

The jeans and T-shirt had been so eaten away by mould and damp that they were almost unrecognizable. But he could still make out Silva's shoes, the white rubber trim of the sole and the round symbol bearing the words *All Star*. He recognized Silva's bag and her hairband, and there were visible remains of a red plastic raincoat. For the first time in decades it had been exposed to the sun, and it was still red and shiny. The remains of the red raincoat fluttered like tiny flags on the morning's southerly wind, fluttering in celebration that their subterranean captivity was at an end.

When the workers from Smart Solution Estate found bones in the tunnel on 16 May, they halted work, emptied the tunnel and informed the police. The police arrived from Split at around midday, cordoned off the site and began the investigation. Then one of the locals told them that a long time ago a girl had disappeared. The police headquarters in Split rummaged through the archive and found that the last person in charge of the case had been senior inspector Tomislav Čović. It was Čović who informed Jakov of the discovery. Jakov passed on the information to Vesna and his son.

Mate responded in the same way Jakov had done an hour earlier: with disbelief. "It can't be," he said, and listed all the reasons they had repeated for years: that she had been alive the next day; that she had left; that she hadn't returned to Misto on the Sunday. He echoed exactly what Jakov had said that morning before he saw the bones, the hairband and the remains of the raincoat.

Vesna reacted to the news differently. Jakov didn't call her. He went to her house, to his former home in the narrow road behind the church. He entered the kitchen, sat down at the table and told her what had happened. Strangely, Vesna did not seem surprised. She just nodded, as if finding out about the death of an old acquaintance, someone who had been ill for a long time anyway. "We have to get everything ready for the funeral," she said, and lit a candle beneath the picture on the wall. For a short time they sat there at the kitchen table in silence, as if unsure what to say to one another. Then Jakov stood up. At the door they expressed their condolences to one another and kissed on the cheek.

*

They went to the morgue the next morning to identify Silva's remains.

Mate picked them both up and drove them to the hospital. They got stuck in traffic at the eastern entrance, where over the years a labyrinth of warehouses, shacks and pavilions had sprouted up, a Wild West of funeral homes and snack bars for hospital staff. Mate nudged his car through the chaotic tangle until he found a parking place on an abandoned patch of gravel near the oncology department, next to an orchard of fig trees where a dog barked angrily.

They entered the pathology building, where Čović was waiting for them. He held out his hand and Jakov shook it, but Vesna didn't. Vesna hadn't forgotten.

Čović knew where they needed to go. He led them through a maze of corridors choked with filing cabinets. They went down one floor, then left, then right, then another floor down, until Jakov had completely lost his bearings. Finally they entered the basement, which unlike the corridors was brightly lit. For a warm May morning, the room was cool. Inside was a man in a lab coat and surgical cap. He removed his gloves, shook their hands and pulled out a metal drawer. Inside was all that was left of Silva.

Jakov had already seen. Mate and Vesna had not. When he saw the bones, Mate did not collapse, he didn't cry. But it was clear he was horrified. Mate had never believed it was possible. Like Jakov, Mate had thought Silva was somewhere far away but alive.

Vesna was calmer. She took a long look at the handful of white bones then bowed her head over the frigid drawer. She picked up Silva's hairband and lifted it to her lips. She kissed the multicoloured plastic band and put it back in its place, next to the empty, lifeless skull. "It's her," she said, and

Jakov looked first at her then at Mate. Mate merely nodded in agreement and the pathologist closed the drawer and led them to the door.

The three of them went out into the corridor with the inspector. Jakov knew there was no escaping the scene that was about to unfold. And Vesna staged it. She approached Čović, right up to his face, and fixed him with a look of contempt. As Mate tried to calm her, Vesna hissed with unrestrained disdain: "So much for your search. You didn't lift a finger. Not a finger."

Čović stood there in the corridor, silent and contrite. When Vesna had calmed down, Mate took her by the shoulder and led her to the elevator.

They left the building and went to the car. The dog in the fig orchard was still barking, as if consumed with rage at everyone and everything. They stood there on the gravel, searching for something to say to one another, after everything.

"The funeral needs to be arranged," Mate said to his father. "You start on that and I'll take *mama* to Misto."

"Look after her," Jakov replied. "Give her a couple of Xanax and tuck her in."

"Don't worry. It'll be all right," said Mate, with that same protective tone he'd had when he was seventeen.

Mate helped Vesna into the car and drove away. Jakov watched his son weave his way through the funeral homes and snack bars and out onto the main road in the direction of Misto.

Jakov set off on foot. He walked for a long time through the new part of Split, along wide avenues, between rows of socialist high-rises, improvised markets and parking areas. Then at some point he realized he didn't want to go home, that he felt better walking.

He continued on foot towards the city's northern shore. He walked in the direction of the industrial zone, turning west at the rail yard and continuing along the fence of the shipyard. After half an hour he came to the Olympic swimming pool and soccer stadium. He headed down to the sea.

Passing the wholesale fish market, he came out on the shore. Before him lay an improvised marina that the shipyard had built for its workers in the 1960s. He looked at the dilapidated concrete jetties where the former members of the shipyard management, former pipe fitters, former electricians and welders kept their boats. Those that had seen better days rested in the dry dock, propped up on wooden blocks, stumps and logs. It was May, so the repair work was in full swing, everywhere the sound of sawing and planing. The air was heavy with the smell of paint.

Jakov approached the water, which, as always in the marina, was cloudy and red from spilled antifouling paint and sandpaper shavings. In that blood-coloured soup he spotted a school of mullet searching for something to eat within the poisonous waters.

He sat down on a bench. He looked at the bay, at the dark, still Marjan forest, at the chimneys of the cement factory, the jetty of the naval port and – far in the distance – the outline of Trogir. The day was clear and beautiful. It was warm and crisp, sunny but fresh from the pleasant breeze off the sea. Perfect. Just like that day, he thought. The day Silva disappeared.

Jakov tried to visualize what he had seen: a hollow skull, bare joints, long tibias and femurs; traces of a disintegrated raincoat and a multicoloured plastic hairband. Suddenly, it felt painfully real. *It was real.* It was really her. There, in that drawer, was his daughter, the daughter he had taken swimming in the summer, from whose feet he had plucked the spines of sea urchins beneath the Stella Maris chapel, whom he had listened to practising on the school melodica. And whom he had come to hate over all those years. He had blamed her for leaving, cowardly and selfishly, without a trace, without a message, without any compassion for those she left behind.

But Silva hadn't left. She hadn't got in touch, because she was dead. And her bones had lain underground, in the dark and the damp, a matter of miles from their house. Had they known, everything would have been different. His life would have been different. Vesna's life would have been different, Mate's too.

Nearby, a man began using an orbital sander on his boat. Jakov first heard a loud buzzing before he was hit with the sharp smell of heated plastic; the air filled with a fine red dust, microscopic particles that coated the bench, his clothes, the leaves on the trees and the surface of the water.

He stood up and checked his watch. It was eleven o'clock. Mate and Vesna would already be in Misto. They would have already entered the house, hung a black sheet from the window, lit a candle and covered the mirror. They would have already gone to church, to Father Dražen, to agree on the burial.

Jakov tried to visualize the scene, a scene he knew so well: the old part of the town, houses clustered around the church, houses that by then had ugly plastic windows and simple terrace extensions; the post office below the old town; next to the post office the bakery and municipality building; in front of the municipality a Partisan statue, still scarred by vandals the last time he had seen it; the marina, and in the marina, small boats; the boules court; the basketball court; and by the sea, clusters of ugly, brightly coloured houses with apartments bought by Slovenians, Austrians and Hungarians, and a row of houses stretching all the way to the headland, to the Stella Maris chapel, bigger and uglier the further away they got. All of it could be seen in one glance from the viewpoint on the road above the town.

Right then, Jakov thought, Misto already knew. The news would have spread like wildfire, from the beach to the streets, from Rokov's Land to Cape Cross, from the bench in the marina to the apartments below the coastal road. The news was already being passed around in church, on the bench in front of the post office, in Vesna's staffroom and Agata's store. By then everyone in Misto would have known that Silva had been found dead in the tunnel.

One lie had been put to bed, he thought. And from that point onwards, there would be no more peace in Misto.

15

GORKI

Gorki heard the news in Zagreb, in the congress centre of the Westin hotel, late in the afternoon of the same day.

That 16 May 2015, he was sitting in the congress hall of the hotel at the *Adriatic Business Days* conference organized by a media house. In the basement hall, lit with white neon, he listened to speeches about hotel advertising and investment in tourism portfolios. The hall was packed with bankers, hoteliers, media and PR people, spin doctors and dealmakers. Since the morning, Gorki had watched their PowerPoint presentations and listened to speeches that, though mainly in Croatian, were peppered with English jargon such as "best-case scenario", "target group" and "SWOT analysis". Around four o'clock, shortly after refreshments, Gorki felt his mood begin to sour.

He surveyed the room as if seeing it for the first time. What he saw was one set of people lying to another set of people, who knew they were being lied to just as the liars knew they knew. And as they lied to one another, they patted each other on the back, laughed politely and congratulated themselves on another successful day. Gorki watched them, struck by the sudden realization that should an asteroid hit the hotel and reduce everyone in that hall to ash, no one would notice. The tourists would still turn up, houses would still be built, banks would still open their doors and newspapers would hit the stands. The world would keep turning.

Gorki wondered whether to leave, to go to the bar and order a double whisky. But he didn't want to get a reputation within business circles for being drunk, so he stayed put. On the stage, a representative of the media house was presenting the advantages of a certain advertising package. Gorki took his phone from his pocket and decided to kill time by surfing the news sites. He opened one portal, then another. On the third he came across a headline that grabbed his attention: HOR-RIFYING DISCOVERY: CORPSE FOUND IN NAVAL TUNNEL IN MISTO, SPLIT.

There was no photo of the tunnel or the crime scene. All the journalists had by early afternoon was the news of the discovery, which they had published online as soon as possible. Alongside the text was a photograph of Misto, probably taken from a tourism site. Gorki looked at the familiar scene, frozen, hazy on the blurry phone screen: the old town; the church; the marina; the houses stretching out towards the Stella Maris chapel. And on the other side of the cove, sharp cliffs and the round hill with the stone cross on the top. Cape Cross.

He read the article, trying to piece together the crumbs of information: the body of an unidentified person; the aban-doned tunnel of a former military base; advanced state of decay; police have yet to identify the body; as yet no sign of foul play. Stating the obvious, it said that an investigation was under way.

The text was formulated in the same stuffy language used in police statements, a language that hadn't changed since his time in the force. A hot wave of horror swept through his body. Staring at his phone, at the picture and headline, he sat there in a hall full of unfamiliar people as a single thought passed through his mind.

Please, not her, he thought. Please don't let it be her.

But he knew already that the body in the tunnel was that of Silva Vela.

It was the next day when Gorki found out that the remains had been identified as Silva's. He received a call early in the morning from a landline in the Split area. On the other end was a man trying hard to speak "proper" Croatian but unable to suppress his Ikavian dialect and Dalmatian accent.

He said he was calling from Split central police station regarding the case of Silva Vela. He introduced himself as Tomislav Čović. Gorki remembered him immediately. A quarter of a century before, Čović had been a young rising star, dark-haired, good-looking, politically correct. Gorki recalled the morning he had handed over the case files. Čović had leafed through the papers and talked to Gorki in a reserved, polite manner, but not once had he looked at him. His eyes were fixed somewhere above Gorki, on the window or the ceiling. Čović tried to fight back his contempt, but that contempt would not be denied. He despised Gorki. He despised his heroic surname, his granddad immortalized in bronze, and the forename he had taken from a Russian intellectual.

And now Čović needed him.

The next day, Gorki got in his car and set off for Dalmatia. He drove along the main road, came off at the exit, paid the toll and by about eleven he was on the coastal road above Misto. He turned onto the approach road and drove past the former naval base.

As he drove, he observed the development that he himself had lobbied for. There was little left of the former base: a few concrete quads, an asphalt path and fence posts. Apartments stood where the sleeping quarters had once been. Cement grey and unfinished, the apartment blocks clustered tightly around the marina and a small patch of beach. Gorki noticed they had more floors than the plan back then had permitted.

He arrived at what was once the entrance to the barracks and drove inside. Čović was waiting for him on the former parade ground. He was standing next to a police car and nervously checking his phone. After a quarter of a century, Čović had changed: he was fatter, slower and more tired. Gorki recognized in him that same ashen complexion, the same aura of Sisyphean exhaustion that he'd felt during his days in the police. Čović stood by the car, tired and flustered, and he looked at Gorki.

Gorki knew exactly what Čović saw: the grandchild of a war hero, child of the Communist elite, stepping out of a metallic grey Volkswagen Touareg and checking his Rolex to make sure he was on time. Čović saw the man who had landed him in the shit.

They shook hands, cold but courteous. Then Čović led him to the spot where they had found the body. They walked along the beach then took the concrete path that ran along the shore until they came to the tunnel entrance. Čović turned on a flashlight and entered first.

The tunnel was longer than Gorki had imagined. It stretched deep into bare rock, bending slightly to the right, probably so the interior could not be attacked by torpedo. It was just wide enough to conceal a light patrol boat. One side was cut from bare rock, on the other was a walkway with bollards. They took the walkway, stepping over stones, lumps of concrete and exploded rock. The deeper they went, the darker the tunnel became and the more debris littered their path, the fragments ever bigger. The damp ceiling neverthe-less still sparkled and shimmered, reflecting the restlessness of the dark, rippling water. Gorki felt like they were entering some kind of eerie, mystical church full of flickering candles.

Right at the end of the tunnel they came to a tilting concrete block. It was the size of a large car, collapsed on its side, with a sharp tip pointing at the ceiling. Right there was a cavern in the ceiling, a huge gash in the bare rock. Gorki observed where the rock had fallen from and Čović noticed his gaze. "It didn't look like this in your day," he said. "It seems the earthquake brought down the ceiling, the one in Ston in 1996."

They went behind the rock. The skeleton had gone, but a white chalk outline remained. Gorki observed the outline, bent over as if in prayer. He felt a burning sensation in his chest. He had spent months looking for Silva. Years later, instead of Silva, he had found a pattern on the floor.

Čović looked at him, a look loaded with judgement. The officer's disposition was starting to unnerve him.

"We searched the tunnels," said Gorki, as if in self-defence. "We searched them straight away, the first day. We sent in patrols who combed them with lights and dogs. Back then it was still an active military installation. We couldn't just wander around wherever we wanted. We looked at them immediately, the first day, and then we didn't come back again."

"Were you here then?" Čović asked him.

"No, I wasn't," Gorki replied. "We were looking everywhere: in the hollows, in the olive groves, up in the gorge on Prosika. We had divers in the sea for five days, and they also checked the tunnels on the first day. We had eighty people on the search for the first five days. I couldn't be everywhere."

Čović crouched by the white outline, as if the skeleton was still there and he was inspecting it. "There was no problem identifying her," he said. "Whoever did it made no effort to hide the victim's identity. We found a bag next to the body.

All her documents were inside – her ID, even her passport. Who takes their passport to a village fair?"

Someone who plans to leave, Gorki thought. "Did you find any travel tickets?" he asked.

"We found something that could be a ticket, but the paper had disintegrated from the damp, even in a plastic sleeve."

"You can't make out where she planned to go?"

"No, unfortunately not."

Gorki stood there, still looking at the unusual outline in the shape of someone praying. "Was she killed here?" he asked.

"Not likely," Čović replied. "The body was in the foetal position, almost perfect, arms crossed at the chest. There were no traces of blood or signs of a struggle."

Gorki nodded. He understood what Čović was saying. Someone had brought the body there, probably when the rigor mortis had subsided. She had been killed somewhere else and the body hidden temporarily. A day or two later, she was brought from there to the tunnel. And then the killer had walked away.

He looked at the white outline on the ground and thought. He thought about how the ill-fated case had toyed with Silva Vela. Had they searched the tunnel on the third day, or the fifth, and not the first, they would have found the body. Had the body not been in a prohibited military zone, someone would have come across it. Had Yugoslavia not fallen apart, had the base not been abandoned, the army itself would have found the body. Had rumours not spread that the army had mined the base, locals or looters would have found her, or walkers, or kids out playing. Had the earthquake in 1996 not brought down parts of the ceiling, adventurers exploring the tunnel would have come across the body. Had he not bought the base on behalf of Smart Solutions Estate, someone else would have restored the tunnel and found the body. Had the Irish not had trouble with the spatial plan, work on the development would have started sooner and the body would have been found earlier.

As it was, they had searched the tunnel on the first day, not the third. The tunnel had been in a military zone. Yugoslavia had fallen apart. The army that built the tunnel had left the base, despised and with its tail between its legs. No one stepped inside the base for years, and no one believed it wasn't mined. And when they did begin to enter, the collapsed ceiling had already hidden Silva's body. Silva's body had been covered with a cloak of bare rock. It had lain there undisturbed, behind a massive lump of concrete, and waited.

It had waited for Gorki to buy out the former owner, to negotiate a deal with the defence ministry, to bribe the state secretary, for the project to become part of the local tourism strategy, for the county to adopt the spatial plan, for the municipality to adopt the details of the organizational plan. Dozens of meetings had gone by, in government ministries, command centres and the offices of the state administration, the spatial planning department and tourism associations. Dozens of documents had to be signed, stamped and notarized with appeal deadlines and directions for legal remedy. And all that time, Silva Vela had been waiting for the saga to end, for the outside world to enter her dark, damp cathedral and finally discover her.

"There's one thing I don't understand," said Gorki, looking around once more at the inside of the tunnel.

"What?"

"How could anyone have got the body in here? Whoever it was would have had to pass the guard at the entrance to the barracks, then the parade ground, the duty officer's hut and the guard at the jetty."

"I don't know," Čović replied.

They stood there for a short time, until Čović's light began to wane. "Nothing else for us to do here," he said, and turned to leave.

The two men set off in the direction of daylight. Before they reached the bend, Gorki turned back once more. The rock lay there on its side, pointed and threatening like a meteor.

Soon afterwards, they came out onto the shore. While they were in the bowels of the hill, a southerly wind had started to blow off the sea. Waves were striking the limestone beneath Cape Cross and a fine salty spray fell on the path along the seafront.

They reached the place they were parked. Čović looked once more at Gorki's car with an expression of righteous disapproval. Gorki noticed, and thought how much he despised that man right then, just as he had hated him the first time they met.

"You didn't exactly distinguish yourself," Čović said. "But you probably already knew that." He began to list Gorki's sins: the body was right under your nose and you didn't find it; you let the chief suspect walk free; you disregarded an anonymous tip-off and the only physical evidence. All because of the statement of one witness who obviously got confused. You based everything on that one woman, what was her name, Zuvan? On a woman who claimed she had seen Silva Vela the following day but who turned out to be mistaken. "That's a lot of errors on your side," Čović said, his tone one of exasperated righteousness. "A lot of errors."

Go fuck yourself, Gorki thought, but he simply gave a nod and walked to his car. Turning the ignition key, he muttered to himself: "Go fuck yourself, fuckwit." He drove past the former duty hut and the entrance gate, the duty hut where the staff sergeant had been on duty that night, the gate where a guard had stood. Another had been posted on the jetty.

If someone had brought the body over land, a dozen people would have seen. If it had been brought over land. Because the tunnel could also be reached from the sea. By sea, a boat could arrive unnoticed and sail inside the tunnel. Gorki thought about that as he turned onto the coastal road in the direction of Split.

The funeral looked like a typical village funeral.

That morning, someone, probably members of the local church brotherhood, had lifted the stone cover from the grave and set it to one side on wooden planks. That morning, someone, probably the sister, had swept and aired the mortuary in the cemetery grounds, collected the dead flowers and thrown them away. At around midday, someone, probably Father Dražen, had unlocked the cemetery chapel and lit a candle at the altar, and at the same time the locals had begun to gather on the seafront.

By two o'clock, the whole village was at the marina: relatives, friends, neighbours, the brothers and parishioners, the Končurats, the Rokovs, the Skaramučas, the Padovans and the Šustićs. At exactly two, Father Dražen came down with two altar boys, and at 2.10 a brass band arrived, ordered from Split. The musicians climbed off the bus, carrying trombones, horns and tubas.

It began at quarter to three. The band began to blow, the brothers lifted the coffin and the head of the brotherhood took position at the front of the cortège, holding a silver-plated cross on a staff. The cross set off first, followed by the band, then Father Dražen and the altar boys. The coffin followed, then the family, and behind the family a procession of neighbours, friends and acquaintances. The cortège headed to the old part of the town, past the municipality, the church and Lekaj's bakery. It arrived at the cemetery a little after three o'clock. The coffin was placed on a catafalque in front of the mortuary and the garlands set next to it. The brothers wiped the dust from their hands, the music fell silent and Father Dražen began to pray over the coffin.

Like any ordinary village funeral, thought Gorki. Only this funeral was far from ordinary.

Next to the open grave, on the stone cover, lay the coffin, in front of the coffin the cross, and in front of the cross a photograph of the deceased, Silva Vela, as they all remembered her, Gorki included: a teenage girl looking defiantly into the lens, her straight, dark hair falling over her eyes. She was seventeen years old, and around her bier stood her friends and classmates. But her friends and classmates weren't seventeen any more. They were forty-three. Silva's schoolmates were middle-aged women with big hips, stomachs and stretch marks. Her adolescent friends had grey hair and beer bellies. The deceased's generation had married, had children, fought a war and won, sailed the world or grabbed public sector jobs. They had their own craft and tourism businesses; some were already ill and popping pills, had high blood pressure and dragged their feet because of shooting pains in the knee. They were all well into middle age and now they were burying the first of their dead, their classmate. That classmate was not forty-three years old but seventeen, frozen in time like a fossil broken off from the polar ice.

Gorki stood discreetly to one side and observed the burial that had just begun. He observed Father Dražen, who had also changed since 1989, putting on weight and assuming the expression of disinterested cruelty common to priests stuck in a small place for too long. He observed the deceased's father, just as thin, timid and inconspicuous as he remembered him. He observed Silva's twin brother, who still looked youthful and lean. He observed Vesna, the mother, who had changed the most out of the three of them. Thin, her hair cut short, she looked like Joan of Arc from that old French silent movie they used to show in school, like an austere saint about to be tortured on the coals and tossed into the same pit where her daughter had been interred.

Father Dražen rang the bell and began to pray.

"Father, into your hands we commit the spirit of our sister Silva, firm in the hope that she, like all who die in the Lord, will be resurrected on the last day. Dear Lord, mercifully hear our prayers: open to your servant the gates of Heaven."

The priest continued with the only words that Gorki knew and remembered: "In the name of our Lord Jesus Christ, Amen," to which those present replied with a quiet, choral "Amen".

As Father Dražen spoke, Gorki continued to observe the crowd, studying the faces he remembered, trying to figure out what had happened to them in the intervening years. He noticed Mrs Padovan, Margita, the captain's widow, remarkably still alive. He spotted the old baker Lekaj, standing discreetly apart from the mass. He noticed too the cafe owner who had gone into politics. And Uršula Rokov. But old Tonko was not with her, nor Brane. As they buried the girl he loved, Brane must have been sailing some faraway sea.

"Till we all go to meet our Lord and so forever be with You," said the priest, and Gorki looked on, this time at the unfamiliar faces, trying to figure out their connection to the familiar, how and when they had entered their lives. Near Mate he noticed a woman in her early forties, of slight build and short hair. And next to her stood a girl in her twenties who so obviously resembled Silva Vela that she must have been Mate's daughter. Behind Mate and the girl was another face Gorki felt he knew, a woman, dressed up but not particularly pretty, who glanced at Mate from time to time. Gorki knew the face, but couldn't place it. Then he remembered. It was Elda Zuvan, the woman who thought she had seen Silva the day after her disappearance. Gorki was surprised to see her attending the funeral at which the evidence of her error was being buried. Zuvan had changed, taking on an air of elegance she had lacked as a young woman. She stood there in the crowd, contrite, regarding Mate with a caring tenderness that Gorki could not fathom.

"In the name of the Lord, Amen. Eternal rest grant unto her, O Lord, and let perpetual light shine upon her," said Father Dražen, before finishing with "Rest in peace", to which the congregation once more mumbled in unison, "Amen". The brothers wound a thick, knotty rope around the coffin and lifted it into the air. But they failed to lift at the same time and the coffin tilted to one side with an unfortunate scraping sound. Finally, they managed to manoeuvre the coffin into the grave and the family members and neighbours began throwing flowers into the hole. Jakov moaned in pain and Mate began to weep. Only Vesna did not cry. It was as if she was all dried up, as if, after all those years, there were no more tears left to shed.

With the rope, the brothers lifted the stone cover and closed the grave, tossing the garlands of flowers on top. The brass band broke out the funeral march for the last time and a few cries could be heard from among the mourners. Misto had said goodbye to its greatest, unhealed wound.

Gorki looked at them all together: the shopkeepers and fishermen, the office workers and apartment lessors, the waiters and olive growers, the teachers, pensioners and sailors. For twenty-six years they had lived together in peace, lulled into the belief that Silva had run away somewhere, a falsehood that he himself had served up to them. And now they knew it was untrue. Now they knew Silva had been killed. By an outsider, perhaps, or – worse still – one of their own, someone they passed every day.

And that evening, after the emotion of the day, when the streets fell silent and the lights were turned out, the locals would talk only of that. In their homes, in front of the flickering TV, they would start to surmise, to guess, to whisper their suspicions.

I wouldn't wish that upon anyone, thought Gorki, and slowly set off along the path through the cemetery to his car.

16
ELDA

Elda had always known it was a Saturday. She had known that all along. But the first time she said it was the first time they corrected her.

"Saturday? You mean Sunday?" the inspector had said to her.

"Not Saturday. Sunday," Mate's father had said to her, that first time they met, all that time ago in the cafe near the bank.

They corrected her once, then twice, then a third time. Then, at some point, she simply came to believe that they were right.

Saturday or Sunday. Both were the weekend. Besides, six months later, after wandering around France and Spain, how could she even be sure? And if she wasn't sure, it meant her memory was playing tricks on her. Because memory could not compete with fact. And the facts showed that at around eleven o'clock that Saturday Silva had been in Misto, not Split, and that she had disappeared from Misto the following morning, after she had told some local lad about her trip.

On Sunday, not Saturday, she must have sneaked out of Misto and arrived in Split early in the morning. On Sunday, not Saturday, she was at the bus station counter buying a ticket to run off. That's what the facts said. The story made sense, the pieces fitted. There were no holes. And so Elda had come to believe it. She began to speak of it as a reliable and verified truth.

But now she knew. Now it was crystal clear that they had been at the bus station not on Sunday but Saturday. On Friday morning, at the end of the working week, she had picked up her pay from the salary department, bought traveller's cheques and spent all afternoon getting what she needed for her trip. Walking around the city centre, she bought a sleeping bag, camping mat, backpack and travel pillow. Shortly before closing time, she exchanged her Yugoslav dinars for Deutschmarks in a bureau de change. Then on Saturday morning – Saturday, not Sunday – she went to the train station, where she bought and stamped her Interrail pass. At the bus station opposite, she bought a ticket to Trieste. She didn't do that on the second day, but the first. That day in between, that empty Saturday, that day of nothingness that she had convinced herself existed, had in fact never happened. She had seen Silva in Split that Saturday morning. Silva hadn't travelled back to Misto by the slow bus; someone had driven her. Perhaps she had thumbed a lift. Silva had bought her bus ticket the day before her death. Whatever the destination, she had never used it. She never left.

For more than twenty years, Elda had lived with the version that the police, Jakov and Mate had convinced her of. And now, before her, stood the bare, dry, brittle evidence that it was a lie, evidence being buried before her eyes in a village cemetery to the mournful sound of a brass band and the smell of incense bringing the ceremony to a close.

With ropes, the brothers lifted the casket carrying the bones of Silva Vela and carefully, trying not to scratch the ash wood, lowered it into the hole. As they did so, Elda watched the frozen faces and listened to the disturbed cries that broke the silence. Elda did not cry or mourn; she could not mourn someone she had never known. Elda looked at the faces of the people around her and tried to imagine, from those faces, what their world would look like tomorrow.

She looked at the grieving family. Of all of them she best knew Tina, who sometimes visited at the weekends, who was half-heartedly studying economics while not telling her father anything about her grades or her sex life. Tina stood over the bier, hand in hand with her father, observing the funeral with a kind of startled indifference. Elda wondered: did Tina have any idea how much she resembled the woman being buried, how much, in face and body, she was a copy of her aunt?

Just behind Tina and Mate stood Doris. It was not the first time Elda had seen her. She had found out early what Doris looked like. Over the years they would run into each other in Split, when Doris would fix her with the kind of look abandoned wives use to flog the women who have stolen their husbands. But the funeral was the first opportunity Elda had to take a longer look at Doris, without being noticed. She observed her elegantly thin neck, her finely elongated earlobes, her harmonious profile with the slight Greek nose and almost perfect brow. Doris was not dressed in black. She wore a formal suit with a short dark skirt that showed off her elegant waist and stunningly beautiful legs. For the first time, Elda realized that the ex-wife of her beloved was a beautiful woman.

Finally, Elda looked at Mate. She devoted the most attention to him, trying to discern on his face even the slightest trace of emotion. She found none. Mate was paralysed with the impenetrable face of a samurai. He stared at the ash casket as it was lowered on ropes into the grave, as it hit the concrete floor, as the brothers pulled out the ropes, as the family members and neighbours tossed in flowers. Only when the brothers lifted the stone cover to finally, for the last time, close Silva's grave did Mate's face break briefly, like a calm sea at night disturbed by a gentle breeze, and he shed a tear. When the grave was covered, when the stone slab sat in the groove with a hollow sound, Mate's samurai-like composure was restored.

The funeral was over. As the brothers placed the flowers on the grave, the priest shook hands with the family one last time and the mourners began to disperse. Mate approached her. Without looking her in the eye, he touched her wrist protectively and said, "Let's go."

Were it a normal funeral, after the service the mourners would gather in the family home of the deceased, drink wine and eat cheese and pancetta at the kitchen table. They would sit there, mournful at first, until the wine diluted the stress and everyone descended together into drunken, melancholic laughter. But this was not that kind of funeral. They had not buried a body but an old, dry skeleton. Everyone who should have done had already knocked on their door and expressed their condolences. So that evening, at the Vela home, there were no condolences, no wine, no talking over the kitchen table. Instead, there were embraces and departures. Mate said goodbye to his mother and father and left for Split with Elda.

Evening was falling. It had been a lovely spring day, but the swimming season was still some way off, most of the vacation homes were dozing in the half-dark, and the only lights on the road were from the odd lamp post or the neon signs of restaurants. As Mate drove, Elda watched him, curious. She tried to start a conversation, but Mate wasn't up for talking.

They arrived in Split at around 10.30, driving through the Marjan tunnel to Elda's rented apartment. Mate parked the car on the gravel at the foot of the stairs.

"Sleep here," Elda told him. "Don't be alone tonight."

Mate nodded and locked the car. They climbed the steps together and entered the house. Sitting on the sofa, Mate undid his black tie, got rid of his stiff dark jacket and took off his shoes. Elda went to the kitchen and made them chamomile tea. That night called for chamomile and diazepam.

Mate curled up on the edge of the bed in the foetal position. He was still and his eyes were closed, but Elda knew he was not sleeping. She knew that pictures were passing through his head, pictures of the funeral, pictures of the past, of his dead sister and the years of searching, pictures from Belgrade, Trieste and Gothenburg, pictures of dry bones, an ash casket and filling stations in the middle of nowhere where he had pinned up posters.

She lay down next to him, slipped her arm under his and pressed her body into his. Mate didn't return the touch. He just lay there, like a small child seeking protection.

Elda watched the city lights moving across the walls of the dark room. She looked at the back of Mate's head, at his short bristly hair and his back, still firm and muscular. She listened as the city surrendered to the spring night and thought about how happy she was, how she had all she wanted, how she loved what she had, and how she owed everything to a lie.

She hadn't lied intentionally. She hadn't knowingly not told the truth. It had been inadvertent, spoken with the best of intentions. But that untruth had had consequences, which had other consequences, and the final consequence was her happiness. The happiness she was enjoying right then.

Beneath her hand she could still feel the rising of ribs, Mate's breathing, his quiet heartbeats. Mate had grown calm and begun to breathe more regularly. He had finally fallen asleep. But Elda knew that sleep wouldn't come for her that night.

17
GORKI

(2015)

He saw Čović again three days after the funeral. They met at the entrance to the public prosecution office on Gundulićeva.

Following that cold, awkward conversation in front of the tunnel in Misto, Gorki had thought Čović would not need him any more. So he had been surprised when the police officer called the day after the funeral and asked if he could go over some details with him once more. Čović had proposed that they meet outside the public prosecution office. Gorki knew why. The basement of the building held the evidence from all unresolved cases in which charges had never been filed. Somewhere in the bowels of that building must have been the evidence in the case of Silva Vela. Evidence that he had gathered in 1989, as well as what Čović had found with the body in the tunnel.

They met, as agreed, at ten o'clock. This time they didn't feign politeness. They greeted each other coldly, curtly, not even shaking hands. Then they entered the building.

A long time ago, the municipal court had been in the building of the public prosecution, and so Gorki had often been inside. But not for more than two decades. Surprisingly,

256

little had changed. On the walls, he saw framed Croatian coats of arms, crucifixes and liturgical calendars. But beneath that thin veil, the building was the same as he remembered, one of sturdy, modernist staircases and big windows with opaque glass and frames of dark wood. However much they tried to hide it, the building still screamed socialism.

They went down one flight and turned right. Gorki knew where they were going. Evidence had been stored in the basement in his day too.

After walking along the basement corridor, they came to a dark wooden door. Čović knocked and went in. With a strange feeling of satisfaction, Gorki saw that the evidence storage room had not changed a bit: by the door, a counter, behind the counter a clerk, and behind the clerk a packed room with shelves from floor to ceiling. Gorki looked at the sea of shelves full of boxes and files and imagined what they must all contain: guns, nooses and gloves, knives flecked with blood, tapes of secret recordings, documents, contracts, confidential annexes, papers containing all manner of financial acrobatics. The entire privatization process of the 1990s was in that room, all the political affairs and corruption scandals, the mafia ambushes, all the war crimes, the prisoner torture and burning of older villagers. Everything that the police and the courts had not cleaned up, rinsed off and tidied away ended up in that room, and there was a lot of it. All the chaos and injustice of this country had been compressed and squeezed into one small, stuffy room.

Čović approached the counter and handed over his ID. The clerk nodded and disappeared somewhere among the shelves. He returned a few minutes later with a cardboard box. He handed it to Čović, who took it from him carefully as if handling a monstrance. He placed the box on a nearby table and opened it.

257

"Here you go," Čović said, and gestured to the items.

Gorki looked at the table. He saw the piece of wood he had found in Lekaj's *konoba* in 1989, Silva's bag, Silva's clothes or what was left of them, a transparent plastic case and inside it the things Silva had readied for her trip – ID, money, passport, bus ticket.

"May I?" Gorki asked, and Čović nodded.

First he looked through the bundle of money – two currencies that no longer existed: Yugoslav dinars and Deutschmarks. He looked at the forgotten Yugoslav notes with lots of zeros, their value eroded by inflation. The biggest was of 5,000 dinars, "dinars" written in Slovene, Macedonian, Croatian and Serbian. Tito's portrait looked artificial, fake, like a cyborg. He had already died when the note was printed. The zeros spoke to the fact that his life's work had fallen apart.

Unlike the dinars, the Deutschmarks were all of the same denomination – 100 – and relatively well preserved. He flicked through the bundle of notes, each bearing an eagle with its wings spread wide. Gorki was surprised. There were several thousand marks in the bundle. It was a lot of money, certainly more than a schoolgirl should have been carrying.

He picked up the old red Yugoslav passport. On the front were six flaming torches and the name of the state in the Latin and Cyrillic scripts. He opened the passport and was taken aback by what he saw.

Although he had seen Silva's picture many times, it had always been the same picture, *that* picture. In the passport was a different picture, one he had never seen before, obviously taken when the passport was issued. Silva must have been fourteen or fifteen years old, a young girl. And in the picture she looked like a young girl – innocent, startled and inquisitive. He had spent so much time thinking about that girl, but never had it occurred to him that she must have once been an innocent child. The picture in the passport had been taken two or three years before Silva's death, but it was as if decades had passed between this picture and the other.

Gorki put down the passport and picked up the last item preserved in the plastic case. It was the remains of a bus ticket, faded and eaten away by damp. The paper ticket had fallen to pieces, and on one of the pieces could be seen the words *Bus Station Split*. The destination couldn't be made out. It was impossible to discern where Silva had been heading. Wherever it was, she never made it.

He looked at the remains of Silva's clothes: strips of red raincoat, the remains of her shoes and preserved scraps of skirt.

The last item on the table was the piece of wood found in Lekaj's *konoba*. It was the first time Gorki had seen it since 1989. He felt a surreal sense of déjà vu. Plucked from obscurity, before him lay a piece of treated, indented wood that looked like it had been pulled from a fence or a floor. Even then, decades later, traces of blood were still visible.

"Did you check for prints?" Gorki asked.

Čović nodded. They hadn't found any. Not on the clothes, nor on the wood. If there had been any on the clothes, they had been washed away by time and the damp in the tunnel. And as Gorki knew, there had been no prints on the wood back then either.

"Anything else?"

"On the clothes there are traces of sea salt," replied Čović. "And gasoline, which we can't explain. And on the raincoat and the bag there's a lot of glass."

"Glass?"

"Yes. Very fine particles of glass. We can't explain those either."

"And the blood on the wood? Today you have DNA."

"The blood on the wood is the victim's," replied Čović.

"You're sure?"

"We're sure. The lab in Zagreb confirmed it today."

Ah, thought Gorki. That's why you called me.

Čović closed the box and returned it to the clerk. He thanked him and left down the corridor towards the stairs and the exit. He said nothing. He looked worried. And Gorki knew why.

Given that the blood on the wood was the victim's, Čović believed Adrijan Lekaj was the guilty party. He believed that, and he hoped that was the case, because that would be easiest. Čović would lay the blame at the feet of a dead man and close the case as solved.

And that's what Čović would do, were Adrijan Lekaj simply a dead man. But he's not, thought Gorki. Adrijan Lekaj was a fallen soldier, a hero of the Homeland War. His name was inscribed on the memorial plaque to Misto's dead soldiers, at the site of the first falling-in, next to the basketball court. Misto didn't have many fallen heroes. Three, to be precise. Čović didn't want to be the man to blacken the name of one of them by declaring him a murderer.

What he would like, if at all possible, would be for someone else to give voice to such a scandalous thought. Gorki, for example. Gorki the Commie, who didn't care anyway.

As they headed towards the exit, Gorki thought of Adrijan. He remembered the morning they had taken him into custody, when they had plucked him from his bed in a vest and manhandled him into a police car. He recalled old Tenžer, beating him about the ribs and back with heavy forearms. He remembered the baker's son sobbing, cuffed to the table and then curled up on the floor of his cell, his body throbbing, black and blue, from Tenžer's fists. He remembered too the lie-detector test, which Adrijan passed without a hitch.

They left the public prosecution and Čović held out his hand, conciliatory this time. He hesitated, then asked: "So, what do you think?"

"I don't think it was Adrijan," Gorki replied.

"Why?"

"Because it wouldn't explain the phone call," Gorki said. "That's why."

Čović shook his head in obvious disapproval. "It must have been him," he said stiffly. "If not him, who?"

Do your fucking job, thought Gorki, but all he said was "Goodbye", quickly, coldly, without a handshake, and walked off down the street.

Gorki didn't go to his car. He realized he needed a walk. He took a narrow pedestrian street towards the centre, past the theatre and the Venetian rampart. The bell of the Franciscan monastery signalled midday as he came out on the seafront.

He walked the length of the old fishing marina in Matejuška, watching the boats rocking on the southerly wind. On one of the boats, a fisherman was folding a longline into a plastic basin. On the promenade stood a rangy, bearded man selling maggots for bait from a plastic bowl of water at his feet. The maggots were wriggling around in their tiny, plastic sea, full of verve and life, blissfully unaware of the fate that awaited them.

Gorki sat down on a bench by the breakwater. He watched the ferries coming and going, and the yachts from the nearby sailing club. He watched a workman patching up a boat in the dry dock – first a layer of fibreglass meticulously applied by hand, then a layer of resin, and on top of the resin gelcoat. He worked with dedication and composure, taking care that the surface of the boat was straight and smooth. He paused from time to time to take a drag on a cigarette.

At the workman's feet lay a roll of fibreglass, sparkling in the sun.

Gorki looked at the roll and thought about Čović. He had been a police officer for so many years yet was still incapable of putting two and two together.

He sat there for a long time. Clouds gathered above the islands, growing dark. Rain was coming.

The workman also saw that the weather was changing. Before the first drop fell, he closed the tin of resin and stowed away the fibreglass. He took another drag on his cigarette and downed tools.

Then the rain started. The first drops were big and warm. Quickly, the rain grew heavier, into a proper spring shower. But Gorki stayed put, on the bench in the marina, next to where the workman had been patching up the boat until a few minutes before. As the rain fell, he sat there and thought. He felt good. He finally understood.

If Brane Rokov earned a good salary at sea, he tried hard not to show it. The apartment he had bought wasn't in any of Split's more prestigious neighbourhoods, by the southern shore, by the beaches, the tamarisk and palm trees. Instead, Brane had bought an apartment in a faceless socialist block, neither luxurious nor dilapidated, a building that did not stand out in any way from the hundreds of others in the city.

At quarter to six, Gorki was sitting in his car, which was parked at the kerb in a quiet residential street. Around him was Skalica, a district where, in the 1960s, employees of since collapsed socialist enterprises had been given apartments. On the other side of the road from his car, hidden by a row of pine trees, was the entrance to a building, an unremarkable entrance no different from the dozens of other entrances in that same street along that same row of trees. The address was Put Skalica 15, the last registered address of Brane Rokov.

The building was long; it had four floors, with five entrances from the street and a row of shallow balconies. It was a dirty yellow colour with sun baffles that had seen better days. The edges of the balconies were trimmed with red-painted verticals that created a cheerful, symmetrical grid. The building had a basement and windows at street level, and the entrances were at the top of elegant, covered staircases of terrazzo.

At 6.15, Gorki spied what he had been waiting for – Brane Rokov walking down the steps to the street.

With the help of a former colleague, Gorki had got hold of Brane's address from police files. The address where Brane was registered corresponded with the cadastre ownership records. But it was only then, when he saw Brane, that Gorki knew for sure that he lived at that address. Brane was there, in Croatia, not on a boat far away.

Gorki hardly recognized Silva's former boyfriend. Back then, Brane had been a slight, delicate boy who Gorki felt almost sorry for even as he was being interrogated as a suspect. Physically, he was unrecognizable. He had the same dark hair and pale complexion but was now extremely overweight, with rolls of fat around his waist and thighs; when he walked he dragged his legs as if struggling to shift his own body. But it was definitely him. There was something about that face, those moist, vulnerable eyes, that hadn't changed and which Gorki could not forget.

He waited for Brane to move down the street. When he was sure he was far enough away, Gorki got out of his car and entered the building. On the mailbox he read ROKOV, FLOOR III. There was no elevator, so he took the stairs to the third floor, where there were two identical doors of grey-blue hardboard, each with a peephole at eye height. On the first door was the surname Luketin. There was no name on the second door. It must be Brane's.

Gorki rang anyway, just to be safe. Twice, three times. Not a sound came from behind the unnamed door, but the other door opened. An old woman in a housecoat and slippers poked her head out from the Luketin apartment and looked at him suspiciously. "Looking for Brane?" she asked.

Uncertain whether to lie, Gorki didn't answer.

"He's not home," the old woman continued. "Want to leave a message?"

"No, it's all right," Gorki replied.

"You a friend of his?"

"I think I made a mistake," Gorki told her. "Wrong entrance." He didn't move, but neither did the old woman, who was obviously waiting for him to leave. Gorki turned and began walking down the stairs; the old woman watched him for a while from the door and when she was satisfied he was indeed leaving she closed her door.

Gorki returned. Carefully, he approached the Luketin apartment, listened at the door and peered through the peephole. Then he went back to the other door. He took out a small knife and a credit card, pressed the knife into the lock and pushed back the latch with the card. The lock was cheap and loose. After a few seconds, the door clicked and opened. He had left the police a long time ago, but the tricks that the thieves had taught him still served him well.

He entered the apartment and quietly closed the door.

A short hallway led to a living room connected to the kitchen. The apartment was small, modestly equipped and practically empty. He entered the living room. It was surprisingly bright, with a view through the window to the soccer stadium and the cranes of the shipyard.

The apartment looked unoccupied. The kitchen was clean, so clean it looked as if no one ever cooked in it. The table was bare, a smooth surface of grey laminate, no tablecloth or ashtray, plates or glasses. If the occupant had clothes, they were all stored away in the closet. The brightly coloured squares and circles of a screen saver provided the only sign of life, rotating across the screen of a computer that had been left on.

He opened the kitchen cupboards and drawers but found nothing of interest. He went into the bathroom, but even there he found nothing but toothpaste and a large, spotlessly clean towel.

Next he opened the closet in the living room. There were some clothes, but not many, and covers, pillows and pillowcases. It looked like the closet of a short-stay tourist apartment.

Gorki closed the closet and cast his eye around the living room, until his gaze fell on the computer. He sat down at the desk and touched the mouse. The rotating squares and circles disappeared from the screen and were replaced by the Google home page.

He hesitated. Then he clicked on the Gmail icon. Rokov's inbox appeared.

It was depressing. Besides spam and ads, Brane communicated only with his crew agent. They regularly exchanged emails to discuss dates, visas, hotel bookings and plane tickets. According to an e-ticket in his mail, it seemed that Brane had arrived in Split at the end of February. In early April, his agent had sent him an Ecuadorian visa, hotel confirmation and ticket for his next voyage. On 13 July, Brane was due in the port of Guayaquil.

Brane had been in Croatia since the winter. He had been in Croatia on the day of Silva's funeral. Yet he hadn't gone to the funeral of his former girlfriend.

Gorki trawled through Brane's inbox, trying to find anything of significance among the rent-a-car ads. Then he spotted an address that Brane kept receiving mail from. It began "urokov@". It must have been Brane's mother.

She had written to him in February, again in March and twice in May. She had written to him the previous week. She was sending emails to her son even when he was in Croatia.

Brane hadn't replied to most of them. To a few he had, and Gorki began to read the replies, one by one.

In March he replied that he had just set sail from Cape Town, when in fact he had arrived in Split six days before.

The day after Silva's body was found, his mother wrote him a short, alarming message: *DO YOU KNOW WHAT'S HAPPENED?*

Brane didn't reply for three days. When he did, he wrote from Split, from his apartment, the day after the funeral.

Left Anchorage, Alaska. Problems with communication. Won't be in touch for a while.

Twenty minutes later, he wrote again. Just one sentence: *I don't walk to talk about it.*

The same day, Uršula wrote to him twice. Brane didn't reply. She wrote to him on the day of the funeral as well, in the afternoon. He didn't reply to that message either.

Brane was hiding. He was hiding from his own mother, in Split, half an hour by car from his family home. And all that time Uršula was writing to him, over and over and over again.

Gorki moved the cursor around Brane's Gmail account, trying to discover whatever he could. Then a noise came from outside. He thought he heard the sound of whispering and metal hitting metal on the staircase. He stopped and listened. Nothing. The entrance was deadly still. From the bowels of the building he could hear the usual noises: a shower running, a television turned up too loud, the spin cycle of a washing machine.

He turned back to Brane's inbox, before realizing he wasn't going to find anything else of interest.

As he stood up to leave, he noticed another door off the corridor, to a room he hadn't yet checked. He turned the handle, but the door was locked.

He returned to the kitchen. He opened one of the drawers, where he recalled seeing a bunch of keys. At the bottom of the drawer he spotted a flat key without a ring.

Gorki approached the door, pushed the key into the lock and turned it carefully. The door opened easily, without a sound.

The darkness surprised him. The window slats were closed as far as they went, but light broke through the gaps to make a pattern of lines on the opposite wall. Gorki touched the wall by the door with his hand, looking for a switch. He flicked it and the room was filled with bright light.

He cast his eyes around the room. It was then that he saw it.

Three walls of the room were perfectly ordinary. To the left was a double closet with suitcases stacked on top of it; to the right was a narrow single bed; and on the street-side wall was a window, blinds down. The fourth wall was the one facing Gorki. That was where he saw the shrine to Silva Vela.

In the centre of the wall was a copy of Silva's photograph, enlarged many times over. It was the same photograph as the one in the case file. Staring at him from Brane's wall was a disproportionately large Silva, blown up to display all the blemishes and acne scars on her skin, hair falling haphazardly over forehead and eyebrows.

Brane had stuck smaller photographs around it, dozens of them, maybe hundreds. Some showed Silva as a child or a teenager. In some, Silva was alone, in others she was with other girls, friends, classmates, room-mates. But most were of her and Brane, photographs taken in Misto and Split, on the beach or on a boat, on Cape Cross, on the terrace of the

Lantern cafe, on the bench by the marina and on the exposed rock at the sea's edge beneath the Stella Maris chapel. They posed, for each other or together, smiling and carefree, against a backdrop of one long endless summer.

Gorki looked at the bizarre shrine, and the more he looked, the more he came to understand its founding principle. There was something that had been erased from that altar, removed as if by tweezers. It was Silva's death. There was nothing in that shrine to suggest that Silva had disappeared or died, not a single newspaper clipping or missing poster. On that wall, the story of Silva ended on 23 September 1989. Nothing existed beyond that Saturday in September. Nothing was important. Nothing happened.

Brane had made a temple to the living Silva.

Gorki felt a deep sense of unease take hold of him. He turned out the light and closed the door.

He peered out onto the landing. There was no one there. Cautiously, he stepped out of Brane's apartment. Again, as before, he thought he heard a noise on the same floor. He looked at the door to the Luketin apartment. He saw nothing through the peephole, yet he couldn't shake the feeling of a human presence behind the door.

Halfway down the stairs, he realized he had forgotten to lock the room. He had forgotten to put the key back in the drawer. He had left it in the lock.

He was about to go back when he heard a door opening on the ground floor. He couldn't go back, not any more.

Descending a little further, he spotted someone coming the other way. It was Brane Rokov.

Brane was climbing the stairs, slowly, his body straining with the effort. Gorki continued downstairs, recalling his surveillance training – don't turn away and don't drop your head. Walk calmly and disinterestedly. Never make eye contact.

And that's what he did. They crossed on the stairs, without reaction, greeting or glance. He had no idea whether Brane recognized him. But he knew he would notice the key. He would know someone had been in that room.

Gorki reached the ground floor just as he heard a door opening on the third. Then a woman's voice. He couldn't make out what she was saying, but he knew. Mrs Luketin was telling her neighbour about his secret intruder.

Leaving the building, he walked briskly down the street. He decided to keep walking and to return for the car later as he didn't want someone to notice and take down his licence plate number. A few seconds later, from behind his back, he heard a dull thud followed by silence. He kept walking. It was only when he heard the scream that Gorki turned back.

A woman was screaming in panic outside number fifteen and a group of people had begun to gather, staring at something on the kerb. One of them looked up in horror. The woman was still screaming, louder and louder.

Gorki approached. On the ground, directly below his balcony, lay Brane Rokov. His lifeless body lay on the concrete, still enormous but at the same time somehow brittle, like a broken wooden doll. His limbs were unnaturally twisted and his eyes stared at the edge of the kerb and the drain cover. A pool of dark, greasy blood was spreading from his head. A thin line trickled towards the drain and started to drip down into it.

He looked up, towards the balcony Brane had thrown himself from. The balcony was empty, ordinary, like all the others, the only difference being the door left casually open.

On the adjacent balcony stood Mrs Luketin, silent, her hands over her face.

The crowd was growing bigger. Gorki knew the police would arrive soon.

He headed for his car, turning around once more before he got in. Then he sat in the driver's seat and turned the key. The engine purred. He put it into first gear and slowly pulled away.

18

VESNA

Trouble was brewing in school.

The week before, Vesna had given one of her classes a test on climate zones. Out of twenty-six, sixteen had failed. On Monday, she gave back the test marks, and on Tuesday the problems began.

After lunch break, Vesna returned to the geography class to find the words *VELA THE WITCH* written on the board in large, spiky letters. She made the class monitor wipe it off with a sponge and sent the whole class to the head. The head asked to see her at the end of the day.

The conversation didn't go the way Vesna had expected. The head had nothing disapproving to say about the children. Instead, he told her he had again received a petition from the parents, the third in the past five years. It wasn't normal, he said, that in his school the biggest problem was geography.

Vesna wanted to say something in self-defence but the head cut her off. He told her that at the end of the school year she would be eligible for retirement, and that, for the sake of everyone, he expected her to take it. If not, he would ask for a commission to assess her fitness for work.

She left school feeling betrayed. She went home, got changed and went down to Agata's store to buy a can of tomato purée and some salt. It was there, in Agata's store, at around one o'clock in the afternoon, that Vesna heard the news that Brane Rokov had jumped from his balcony.

"Brane Rokov gone kill 'imself," said old Agata, pulling grapefruit from a crate and stacking them on a shelf. She showed little sign of alarm. A few neighbours were waiting at the counter, among them old Mrs Padovan and the Bakić daughter-in-law. Neither of them said a word. The sale of their plots on Rokov's Land had fallen through because of old Tonko Rokov. They had little sympathy for him or his family.

Vesna bought what she needed and headed for home. She thought about the skinny, mild young man who used to come to their house. She remembered how much he had looked out for Silva, how much he had suffered. He had been a fragile, sensitive child, obviously too sensitive. Things would have turned out different had Silva spent more time with him and less with random louts.

When she got home, she watered the garden, trimmed the kiwi and made herself a simple lunch of chickpeas in olive oil. As she was eating, the phone rang. It was Jakov. He was coming from Split in the afternoon with Čović, the police officer.

"He has news," Jakov said, but he didn't know what kind.

Jakov and Mate arrived first, followed by Čović. The officer declined coffee but accepted a glass of water. He sat down at the table and told them what they already knew: that Brane Rokov was dead. He hesitated, as if reluctant to go on. Then he spoke the following sentence, cautiously, fearfully: "We believe Rokov did it," he said. "That he killed your daughter. And he killed himself because he suspected we were on to him."

Vesna looked at the other faces around the table. Jakov didn't bat an eyelid. Mate's brow furrowed in pain.

Čović laid out the evidence: on Silva's clothes they had found traces of what looked like fibreglass; in Misto, only Brane's father fixed up boats with fibreglass; and on the bloodied wood there were traces of boat paint. "That's the material evidence," he said, "some of which we found recently, some of which was overlooked by the investigation in 1989."

The officer went on.

"But that's not everything. Rokov's behaviour had been strange. Everyone says that since then, since 1989, he hardly ever came to Misto. He didn't even come when he was in Croatia, not even to visit his parents, not even for the funeral."

"But you knew all that before," said Mate. "What's new?"

"What's new is what we found yesterday," Čović replied, "when we searched his apartment after the suicide."

The officer tossed a bundle of photographs onto the table. They showed a wall in a small, ordinary room. The wall was covered with photographs of Silva, clustered around a large photograph in the centre. It looked like the kind of place where someone might cast a spell.

"That's what we found when we entered the apartment," said Čović. "That's what it looked like."

Vesna watched Mate's reaction. He clenched his fists angrily, trying to hold back the rage sweeping through him. Were Brane not dead, she thought, Mate would have killed him.

"We believe Rokov killed himself because he thought we were investigating him," Čović continued. "His neighbour says that an unidentified man came looking for him the same day, that he wanted to enter the apartment. There were indications of an attempted break-in. It seems Rokov believed we – the police – were on to him."

"But you weren't," Vesna interrupted him. "You weren't on to him, were you?"

Čović's cheeks turned red. "No, it was a coincidence," he said. "And we don't know who the man was. Whoever he was, he wasn't one of ours."

"Didn't Brane have an alibi?" asked Vesna. "Wasn't he on a bus that night?"

"That's what it says in the records," the officer replied. "But you have to understand that everything done back then was done wrong. That was the Communist police. All they were interested in was spying on people. There was the driver and four passengers on that night bus. The driver died in 1993, and two of the passengers moved to Serbia and another to Sydney. We found the fourth. He's seventy-nine years old and has early-stage dementia. We don't have anything to confirm that Brane was really on that bus. No one in Misto saw Brane get off the bus. And besides…" Čović stopped, as if deliberating whether to go on. "Rokov was a sailor," he said. "We can't be sure the police didn't offer him a pass. You understand? In exchange for his cooperation —"

"Cooperation? What do you mean?" asked Mate.

"You know. Cooperation abroad. I'm not saying that's what happened. But it's possible. No one in the police at that time would ever admit it."

Mate looked at Čović darkly. Čović glanced at Vesna, sensing her scepticism. He went on, as if trying to convince her.

"Rokov had a motive," the officer said. "Jealousy. He probably caught her with another guy. Or he found out what happened. Or he suspected. He had a reason. He obviously had an unhealthy fixation, as you can see from the photos. We have those photos. We have the material evidence, which means, for us, that the case is closed."

"So you'll take it to the prosecution and the court?" asked Jakov.

Čović had to stop himself from laughing at Jakov. "Of course not. How can we take him to court? He's already dead."

"Then what?" Jakov asked.

"Don't you see?" Vesna jumped in. "Nothing. That's what. Nothing."

Even as she said it, she could see the anxious look on Jakov's face, as if he had feared such an outburst.

"How convenient," she went on. "You don't have to prove anything, no lawyers, no evidentiary hearing, no witnesses to contradict your story. No one will ever be convicted and no one will ever know it was him. You'll have one less unresolved case, one less problem. And everything will stay between us, at this table."

As soon as she said it, she sensed the nervousness in the room. Mate was still trying to stifle his rage and Vesna suddenly had the feeling it was being redirected at her. Jakov was giving Čović a guilty look, as if apologizing in her name. It was that same Jakov who had once so disgusted her: accommodating, obliging, conciliatory towards any kind of authority, accepting of all the shit served up to them. Vesna watched his subservient attempt to smooth over the incident and found herself hating him all over again after so many years.

She needed to get out. She needed air. She stood up and went out onto the balcony. She looked through the window into the lit room, where Čović was talking and Mate and Jakov were nodding in a manner that appeared conciliatory. Then the officer began to say goodbye. He shook their hands and looked timidly towards the balcony door, as if uncertain whether to say goodbye to Vesna too. He decided against it and went out into the yard. Vesna watched from the balcony as he passed between her beds of kale and onion, opened and closed the gate and moved off down the street.

Vesna turned and looked at the room. Jakov and Mate were sitting at the table. Mate still looked good for his age, but the older he got the more he resembled his father. His temples and brow were taking on the same shape as Jakov's and his hairline was receding the way his father's had. Father and son sat there talking, like twins separated by some journey into space that had left one older than the other. They spoke quietly and seriously, probably about her, probably in a tone of fatherly concern that, if she could hear it, would drive her mad.

Turning again, she looked out over Misto. Evening was falling and the street lights had come on in the marina. The boules court shone like a metropolis and she could hear the baritone of the players yelling over each other. Behind all the illuminated windows, people were watching TV, washing their hands, dining on chard, chicory and dandelion greens, arguing and having sex. It was already June. Too early for tourists, but Misto had shrugged off the winter slumber and was swimming in the glow of what already felt like summer. It looked for a moment like a warm and peaceful place where life was good. But it was an illusion, an illusion that Vesna knew was about to end. Misto would find out: Tonko's boy had killed Silva. He had killed Vesna's daughter.

Brane. She tried to picture his face: large, timid eyes, nose and brow. It was a face that gave no sign he was capable of aggression. But it might have been deceptive. People could be deceptive. People are masters of illusion.

Inside, she heard Mate and Jakov standing up and looked around. Jakov waved, disappointment in his eyes, while Mate came over and gave her a hug and a kiss on the cheek. Both of them looked at her with a caution that seemed insincere, as if looking at a psychiatric patient who should not be riled.

Vesna waited for them to get in the car and drive away. When the rear lights of the car reached the coastal road, she went back into the house. Only then did she see that Mate and Jakov had left the photographs on the table.

Picking up the photographs, she looked at her daughter, hanging on the wall of a narrow and depressing room in a cramped city apartment. Silva looked at her from the wall, as if asking *Do you get it now?*

She laid the photographs on the table. Then she remembered. She remembered Brane sitting at that table, that very summer, on the same chair where she now sat. It could have been June or July. She remembered that morning. She remembered serving him bread with mortadella and a glass of milk. He had been polite, almost amiable. She remembered thinking she wouldn't mind him for a son-in-law.

He sat here, she thought. He ate a sandwich with butter and mortadella, and he laughed, and Silva laughed too and seemed perfectly happy.

Was it true? Was it really him?

She sat there in the kitchen, asking herself that question over and over again. But no answer came.

PART FOUR

RED WATER

19
GORKI (2016)

He had to admit, the Irish had pulled out all the stops for the opening of Misto Sunset Residence.

The previous day, the landscaping firm had planted oleander, olive, lavender and rosemary. The steps and paths of polished stone glinted in the sun and the handrails and benches shone with fresh paint. For the event, Smart Solutions Estate had hired ten charter catamarans, tied to a jetty that had once belonged to the Yugoslav Communist army. The masts of the catamarans and the first row of apartments were decorated with flags of various colours that fluttered in the afternoon breeze coming off the sea.

Provocatively dressed hostesses with little to do stood around, smiling at the guests. On the restaurant terrace, a band played congenial swing and old hits by Oliver Dragojević, Split's favourite son, Tom Jobim, the father of bossa nova, and Frank Sinatra. Men in pirate costume and striped sailor T-shirts crowded around the stage by way of dour tribute to local tradition.

Gorki could just about picture what the event manager had been thinking: a fishermen's fair for VIP guests with fish served from mock crates before pirates pretended to do battle in celebration of the town's history as a place of warriors and brigands. Everything was in place and the only thing spoiling the perfect summer party was the wind. The sea breeze was too strong for that time of year; it blew from the west in gusts that made the flags flutter and lifted dresses and tablecloths.

He stood to one side with a glass of white wine and observed the people slowly gathering. It was the usual crowd: the county prefect, the mayor, the minister of tourism, the Irish ambassador, tour operator reps, journalists, councillors, the parish priest and a few locals. He spotted the owner of the Lantern cafe, who had since become county head. There was a well-known retired soccer player, at least one former beauty queen and two female television presenters.

Finally, one of the television presenters walked onto the stage and coughed into the microphone. The band fell silent. She invited the minister of tourism and then the director of Smart Solutions Estate to join her, and the pair briefly greeted the guests and wished them a good time. The presenter then called on the new mayor. Out walked Mario Cvitković, as tall and imposing as ever.

Newly elected mayor Cvitković took the microphone and began his speech. He greeted the guests from the world of politics, business and the church. He stressed the importance of investment as the driver of tourism development and employment and called on all those present to encourage further investment to lure "high-quality guests". Gorki had worked in tourism for long enough to know that the industry, like the Nazis, divided people into "high-quality" and "low-quality".

He stood to one side, listening to Cvitković's address, and watched with wonder something he had noticed before: Cvitković worked a seductive magic on his listeners. Tall and striking, he held himself like a natural leader, with a rich baritone and a placating, harmonious air. Gorki knew exactly what the people saw in him: a war hero, a colonel in the Croatian army, twice wounded and now an advocate for "conservative renewal", for national values and a better investment climate. But Gorki recalled the Mario Cvitković of before, before he became a political star, before he was a colonel, before the first shots of the war were fired. He remembered him from when he had just been a bum, a mid-level drug dealer, when Gorki had interrogated him at the police station, convinced he was the reason Silva Vela had run away.

Gorki wondered whether Cvitković would recognize him after so many years. And, if he did, what he would do. Would he claim he was the victim of a political vendetta? Would he pretend not to remember him? Or would he simply pat him on the shoulder and lavish him with one of his infectious, charismatic smiles.

Cvitković finished his speech to enthusiastic applause. Gorki looked at the people in the crowd and pondered all the things he could tell them about Cvitko. But even if he wanted to, no one would care. Between truth and legend, everyone prefers legend.

The mayor left the stage and the band started up again. The wind picked up, lifting the tablecloths, as hostesses carried around drinks and waiters rolled out trolleys laden with food – shrimp cardinal, tuna with capers, octopus salad, beef carpaccio and lobster mayonnaise.

Elbows at the ready, the high society guests set about the food as if threatened with starvation. Gorki took another glass of wine, uncomfortably aware that it was his third already, and began to walk around, observing in peace the creation he had been part of.

Leaving the party behind, he climbed the stairs to the upper terrace, taking in the rows of new, spotless apartment buildings, their blinds all neatly lowered.

Gorki climbed through the empty development, to the third and then the fourth row of villas. He turned right, skirting a green island of tamarisk, and skipped up three steps to a raised ground floor and terrace. He took out a key and unlocked the green PVC door of number sixty-four.

Turning on the lights, he looked at his new property, an apartment of 300 square feet with a terrace. It was a timeshare, and the Irish had given Gorki week forty-one in lieu of the second tranche of his commission.

When he was negotiating, Gorki had checked the calendar to see when week forty-one fell. It was mid October. He figured it was better than nothing. The Irish owed everyone – contractors, subcontractors, the state, the banks. Someone owed someone else who owed someone else and so on. The small sum owed to Gorki was somewhere in that circle of debt. He had to settle for what he could get: one rainy week on the terrace.

Gorki looked at the apartment and was surprised to find it was actually quite nice, white and still sterile from having not yet been used.

He looked at the small, functional kitchen, at the unplugged fridge, the bar and bar stools for partying and the terrace furniture that someone had brought inside to protect from the rain. He took one of the chairs out onto the terrace, sat down and took in the view, imagining what it would look like in the middle of October, when the days were getting shorter, the beach bars and pizzerias were closing and the rain clouds gathering over the mountains.

What a sight, the autumn *jugo* driving lead-grey waves through the channel, a sight Gorki would watch from his own theatre box in apartment sixty-four.

He could still hear the music and the voices of the guests from the shore. The yachts in the marina were decorated with bunting that flapped in the wind. The apartment settlement glinted, shivered and vibrated. And on the other side of the cove was the other settlement, the real, ordinary settlement where the hoops had been torn from the basketball court and letters gouged from the Partisan monument, where the tamarisk by the harbour was shrivelled from drought and the public phone bashed up. It looked dilapidated, abandoned compared to the new, phoney newcomer. Gorki looked at the silhouette of a place he knew so well, at the old part of the town on the rise, at the church tower, at the pebble beach, the outline of the headland and the Stella Maris chapel.

And behind the chapel, where the houses ended, was no-man's land – ten acres of maquis, thicket and brambles, without a single house or cultivated field. That was Rokov's Land. Gorki felt a burning and stabbing in his stomach. He had unfinished business.

He knocked back the wine from the glass he had borrowed from the party without permission. It was his fourth, and after four glasses of wine Gorki realized he could not leave Misto without finishing what he had started. He had to dispel the last remaining doubt and then never return, not on week forty-one or any other week, not next year or any other year.

Gorki put the chair back inside, walked out and locked the door. He would finish the investigation he had started so long ago.

He headed along the shore, past the small boats in the marina, the boules court and the former fishing cooperative. The asphalt quickly gave way to stone and in a few minutes he reached the Stella Maris chapel. He looked at it. It seemed pitifully small, dwarfed by the enormous apartment blocks.

After passing the chapel, he came out on the headland. He saw the Rokov house. There was no sign of life, no boats in the dry dock or any evidence of work going on.

He walked along the path and approached the house, but instead of going to the door he turned along the wall of the garden and came out behind the house. He walked through the olive terrace and reached the shed.

It had the same rotten door. He pushed it open with his hand and went inside. This time, the shed was empty, no more webbing, resin or fibreglass, only the remains of torn and long-ago hardened cement bags on the earthen floor, scraps of paper and grey, dusty stains.

Standing there, he looked around. He looked at the place where Silva Vela had lain for twenty-four hours, her body concealed, tucked away under rolls of fibreglass.

He remembered clearly that they had searched Rokov's Land on the third day, only when it was clear that Silva had not simply drowned or fallen drunk onto the limestone rock. Only then had they searched Brane's house. And if the police officers had come across the shed then, Silva's body wouldn't necessarily have been inside.

Gorki stepped outside and pulled the door shut. He turned around to face Rokov's Land. Decades on, Tonko had still not sold. Overgrown with brambles, it sat there as a monument to his stubbornness. Rokov's Land, Silva's first, short-lived grave, lay untouched, as if the carob and bramble were a mausoleum, the only mausoleum Silva would ever have.

He went down to the house and looked to see if anyone was home. Finally, at the door to the workshop, he spotted old Tonko. He looked the same as ever, only greyer in his otherwise dark, bristly beard.

Tonko looked at him. He looked at him with hatred, though Tonko seemed to look at everyone that way. He stared at him, briefly, in contemptuous disbelief, then nodded towards the door of the house. "If it's her you're looking for, she's inside," he said.

Gorki approached the arched doors with the dedication to ROCCO ROCCOV AND HIS CHILDREN. He went through and up the stairs to the house. He knocked, but there was no answer. He knocked again. When there was still no answer, he went inside.

He found Uršula Rokov sitting at the table in the main room. It was the first time he had seen her in twelve years. This time, however, the years had taken a toll.

Uršula's face and posture still hinted at the beautiful woman she had once been. But she was as thin and dry as a charred twig, her hands and face furrowed with lines and creases. She was shelling broad beans from long, plump pods at the table. She heard the door and looked up at him. There was disappointment in her eyes. But not surprise. It was as if Uršula had been expecting him.

Gorki said hello. No sooner had he spoken than there came the sound of coughing and heavy footsteps on the stairs. Tonko walked in. "So, you again," he said.

"Afraid so."

"If you've come about the land, you can leave now. I didn't sell it then and I'm not going to sell it now."

Uršula set aside the bowl of beans and gave Gorki a look of resignation. "Let him be, Tonko," she said. "The man hasn't come to buy the land."

"Then why?" asked the old man.

"He's come because he knows. Isn't that right?" she said, looking at Gorki. "You've come because you know."

Gorki didn't say a word. Uršula stood up and took the beans to the sink to wash them. "I always knew you'd come, sooner or later," she said, and turned on the cold water tap.

20

URŠULA (1989)

The hardest part had been getting it from the shed to the boat. Of everything, Uršula remembered that was the hardest.

She did it in the middle of the night. She pulled away the fibreglass wrapped around the body, leaving thousands of tiny glass strands on Silva's body, in her hair and on her clothes. As she dragged the body to the sea, those strands pricked her hands and tore at her skin.

She dragged her across the scree for a long time, fifteen minutes, maybe more. She dragged her to the house, then to the shore and the slipway. At the slipway, she placed Silva's body on its back, tugged the rope to pull in the boat and manoeuvred the dead body, limp and heavy like a sack of potatoes, into the boat. Silva lay curled up, lifeless, on the wooden frames and planks of the hull.

The motor didn't start first time. She remembered that too. She yanked the pull cord as hard as she could but the white Johnson motor, six horsepower, only coughed and spluttered. She pulled the cord again and again, the quiet of the night broken by the rattling of the white engine cover decorated with a picture of a horse. Five times she tried. Six times. Finally, the sound of salvation. The Johnson revved into life.

She headed for the channel in front of Misto. When the boat came round the headland at the Stella Maris chapel, Uršula realized she had underestimated the weather conditions. Earlier in the evening, a stiff breeze had begun to blow off the mountains, growing stronger. By then, the icy wind was coming from the direction of the Prosika canyon, stirring up the sea and tossing sharp, salty spray into her face.

Uršula sailed deeper and deeper towards the centre of the channel, but at some point she realized it wouldn't be wise to go any further. She was too far out, the wind and waves were strengthening, and in such conditions the body would wash up on the shore within a few hours. She let the motor idle while she thought. Then she remembered the tunnel.

She headed east, towards Cape Cross. The waves were hitting her in the bow, so the boat was more stable and the motor calmer. She steered a wide arc around the town and the harbour and then, as she approached the base, she turned off her light. She knew that the sound of an outboard would not disturb the soldiers. It was autumn, when the locals chug slowly up and down the shore trawling for squid. She knew no one would be in the tunnel. The military had abandoned it to ruin long ago.

The sea grew more restless the closer she got, as the waves crashed against the rocks and bounced back. Uršula was fortunate that the moon hadn't come out, so the night was still completely dark. In that darkness she soon spotted a whitish horseshoe shape – the tunnel entrance.

She eased off the motor and the boat slowly approached the entrance. Nearing the cliffs, she became sheltered from the wind and the sea calmed. She corrected direction and carefully entered the tunnel. Once inside, she turned off the motor to avoid making too much noise. She rowed into the tunnel. She rowed, and the tunnel was as quiet as a church.

At the end of the tunnel she spotted a concrete platform. She knew immediately that that was the place. That was where she would leave her.

No one had ever had a son like Brane. Devoted, hard-working, intelligent and gentle, he was the kind of son a mother dreams of.

Life with Tonko on Rokov's Land wasn't always easy. It meant living in want, in dirt, in an old house that was falling apart, where there was never enough money for a lick of paint, to fix it up, to replace the roof tiles or treat the damp. It was a life far from the town, far from people, with Tonko, who – God forgive him – was not the easiest man in the world. When she was young, there were other paths Uršula could have chosen. She could have imagined for herself a better life than the one she ended up with.

But she didn't regret it. Because along with Tonko, with Rokov's Land, with the paint flaking from the damp kitchen walls, came Brane, who grew into the kind of child she had always wanted, who in fact surpassed everything she had ever wanted in a child.

Everything was supposed to work out. Brane was supposed to finish school and start university. Brane was supposed to start a family. They were supposed to leave him Rokov's Land for him to cultivate, build a house and bring in tourists, or to sell and invest in his own family. Then Brane was supposed to take care of them in their old age, because Brane was a caring and devoted son.

That's what was supposed to happen.

Then *she* happened. Miss Vela.

Uršula had liked her at first. She was likeable, that's what anyone would have said about her. She was good company and knew how to talk maturely and sensibly with adults.

When she entered the house, she would be sure to say hello, to sit at the table and chat, to ask if she could help with anything. She was that type, the type that knows the way to anyone's heart, Uršula's too. That summer, Brane glowed with happiness like never before, a happiness that left Uršula feeling ever so slightly jealous.

Brane started coming home later and later, with his shirts and breath smelling of beer and cigarettes. Sometimes his room smelled of straw, a smell Uršula didn't recognize at first but which she came to learn was the smell of ganja. That's what they called it – ganja.

Then came the signs, the small pieces that over time would form a picture.

One morning, while tidying the courtyard, she found a used needle in a pile of leaves. She thought it was odd but at first it didn't mean anything to her.

In late August, she found a small spoon from the kitchen in the courtyard, at the foot of the wall by the cactus. The underside was dark and strangely scorched.

Then, on the last day of August, she found a package. She found it in the shed in the olive grove, in the old wood-burning stove. She was worried wasps had made a nest inside the stove, but when she opened the little door that morning she found a bundle the size of a small book, wrapped in brown tape. Uršula was no expert, but it was the 1980s and Dalmatia was in the grips of a heroin epidemic; the newspapers and television news were full of alarming stories of addiction. She knew enough to recognize what she had found.

She didn't call the police. Later she came to realize her mistake, but at the time she believed the package was Brane's.

She placed it back, withdrew and watched. Three days passed when, in the middle of the night, Uršula heard the sound of movement in the yard and saw a shadow. She watched as Silva walked along the path towards the olive grove. The next day, she got up early and checked the stove. It was empty.

At first, when Uršula checked the stove, she would sometimes find smaller packages, maybe two. Other times, there would be nothing. Silva was constantly bringing or taking something away. Then, a week before *that night*, Uršula heard footsteps and whispering in the courtyard. She saw two silhouettes and heard Silva's muffled voice. In the morning, when she checked the stove, she found a package like the first one, wrapped in brown tape.

After that, Uršula no longer cared if she was caught snooping. Whenever she could – and that wasn't very often – she would follow Brane and Silva around the town. One day, she came up with an excuse to go to Split. She found the student dorm where Silva was staying and, when Silva came out, Uršula followed her all day. Silva went to school at eight and initially Uršula saw nothing untoward. But after two lessons, Silva was gone, heading into town. On the way, she stopped briefly in a doorway before continuing to the city centre, to the square inside Diocletian's Palace. There, Silva leaned against a wall and waited.

Every now and again, someone would approach and exchange a few words with Silva. Silva would nod and say something and the stranger would hold out a banknote. Taking the money, Silva would motion with her head for the stranger to enter a doorway. Uršula had heard a lot about drug dealing, but now she was seeing it with her own eyes.

She planned to tell Tonko that evening. She went to the dry dock and found him lying on the ground under the keel of a half-decker, immersed in work, grimy and dirty. He hardly looked at her. Uršula realized that even if she told him, he wouldn't believe her, that he'd just find it bothersome. Tonko was like that: all mouth and no trousers. To Tonko, the most important thing in life was that nothing should change and he should not be forced into doing anything. Tonko was capable of leaving everything as it was, even as it crumbled around his ears.

That was not what she wanted to happen to Brane, so she resolved to stay quiet and this time to do it herself.

She spied on Brane and Silva. She followed them. She eavesdropped on them when they withdrew to his room. That's how she overheard the conversation, when Silva urged Brane to give up the maritime faculty and run away with her. They would take what she called "Cvitko's stuff", get on a bus and flee to Germany. They would sell the stuff there and start something new. "We'll finally get out of this shithole," she said.

Brane resisted. He rejected the idea, refused to go along with it. But Uršula knew her son, and she knew Silva well enough too. She knew exactly how such conversations ended. They ended with Silva slipping off her bra strap and showing him her tits. She had the pussy. She was the ruler and he her subject.

They had obviously had the same conversation several times. Uršula overheard it only twice, Brane's arguments growing weaker, his resistance softening and less convincing.

That Thursday, Brane travelled to Rijeka. Before leaving he spoke to Silva on the landline. Uršula listened in from the phone on the landing. Silva told him she planned to leave on the Sunday, with or without him, and that she would buy her ticket on the Saturday. Uršula had two days to save her son's life.

Once Brane left, she made her preparations. In the dry dock, among Tonko's things, she found a piece of wood that seemed strong and jagged enough. The wood had been sharpened at one end, and had rusted, dangerous-looking nails sticking out of its sides. Tonko used it to buttress supporting blocks and as a lever to open paint tins.

When Tonko wasn't looking, Uršula slipped into the shed in the olive grove, cleared it of junk and prepared the ground. She found a pile of old tarps; she thought she'd be able to keep the body there longer.

That night was the fishermen's fair. Making sure she wasn't spotted, Uršula observed the daughter-in-law who wouldn't be, slow-dancing with the baker's son and slowly, coyly surrendering to his embrace. She followed them to the cross on the mound at Cape Cross and listened to them panting in the darkness. She longed for Brane to know what was happening, but she knew he would never believe her.

She took the long route home, through the olive grove. She knew it was only a matter of time before Silva turned up to take the stash before her trip.

Silva arrived at four in the morning. She crept to the shed and slipped inside, unaware that Uršula had already hidden the package somewhere else, at Silva's home. Silva would never find out. As soon as the girl stepped inside, Uršula struck her.

She struck her once, twice, three times, ten times, twenty. All the hatred went into the first blow. Uršula thought of Silva's feigned sweetness, of the scorched spoon and the needle, of the strawlike smell of ganja, of the shirt that stank of beer, of Silva saying *this shithole*, of her heavy breaths with the baker's son between her legs. Uršula thought of it all and hit and hit and hit, until she realized she was no longer hitting a living body but a lifeless rag, a piece of meat that did not struggle or resist.

She stopped and stepped back. She looked at the limp body beneath her. Silva lay on the ground, face up. Her eyes were open, but they were absent of life.

Uršula put down the wood and wiped her hands.

21
GORKI

She turned off the tap and put the bowl of just-washed beans on the table. She looked at Gorki and asked him: "Isn't that why you've come? Because you know."

"Yes," he replied. "I know."

"When did you figure it out?"

"Too late," said Gorki. "Only when they found the body. That's when I saw the obvious, that it was someone from this house. And that someone couldn't have been Brane."

"So you didn't think it was him?"

"No," said Gorki. "Never. Not at any moment. Brane was on the bus that night."

For a flash, he thought he saw relief on Uršula's wrinkled face.

"So it was you who put the package in the Velas' drain?"

"Yes. That's where it belonged. Not here, not in my garden."

"And the wood in Lekaj's bakery? You put that there too?"

Uršula winced. "Yes, I did. And I called the police from the public phone, if that's what you want to know."

Her cheeks flushed red. Of everything, thought Gorki, she's only ashamed of that. Ashamed, because she knew the consequences of putting the wood in Lekaj's *konoba*, of making that call. The police had tortured Adrijan for days. The whole town had despised him. Had she not done what she did, his life might have turned out differently. Perhaps he wouldn't have ended up going to war. Perhaps he'd still be alive.

"That was the moment he turned against me," said Uršula, pointing her finger at Tonko. "He already knew what I'd done. He heard the noise in the courtyard. He saw me moving the body. He heard me trying to start the motor. He didn't help me because he's a coward, like all men. But he stood with me. Up till that moment. When he found out about the wood in Lekaj's *konoba*, and that I'd made the call. That was it. In the end, I only asked for one last thing – that he not tell Brane. And he didn't."

"But Brane did know, didn't he?" asked Gorki.

Uršula didn't reply. She turned to face the sink and tossed the empty bean shells into the bin. She washed her hands in cold water and then turned back to him. For the first time since he had arrived, she appeared to break. Her face crumpled and her eyes looked on the verge of tears. "You think I got away unpunished, that I should be punished?" she asked.

A sound came from outside. On the other side of the cove, in Sunset Residence, there was music, spotlights moving across the sky, and something happening on the stage, perhaps a fashion show or a mock pirate battle. Bass rhythms and pulsating coloured lights carried across the water.

"That's what you think, that I haven't been punished?" Uršula continued. "I know that's what you think. But believe me, I have been punished. I've been punished like no one else."

She paused before continuing.

"Twenty-seven years have gone by. For twenty-seven years my husband has slept in his workshop. For twenty-seven years he hasn't spoken a word to me. The day we buried our son he didn't want to hold my hand. For the past twenty-seven years we have eaten apart, and every day I see him judging me. But I couldn't leave, because if we had separated, Brane would have found out why. For twenty-seven years I've been condemned to live in this worm-eaten house like a dungeon. My own son despised me, he never visited me, never answered my letters. Then he killed himself because of me. And what's worse, the whole town says he killed himself because he had a guilty conscience, because he committed a crime – a crime that I committed. I didn't just kill him. I dragged his dead body through the mud."

And that's why you need me, thought Gorki. She needed him so she could be found out. So that the world would know it was she who did it, and not her son.

"If only they'd accused him," Uršula said, "then I could have come out publicly and taken responsibility. But what can I do now? I can fight the rumours, tug people by the sleeve. I can beg the police to charge me, but no one would care, no one would even listen to me."

She poured the beans into a pan and covered them with cold water. She placed the pan on the stove and lit the gas. Then she rubbed her eyes, which had grown wet.

"You think I've gone unpunished? Oh, I've been punished. We've all been punished. For a long time I didn't realize that, but now I understand. I understand that everything that followed was punishment. First the factory went under. Then the cooperative. Then everyone became consumed with hate. Then the war. And those young men started to die. Then Adrijan Lekaj died. And then came those bloodsuckers, those parasites, buying up land and building wherever they wanted. And then, finally, you came along…"

From the other side of the cove came the sound of a

commotion, a series of explosions, and the evening sky was lit up in red and yellow.

"But you, you were the worst," said Uršula. "That was the biggest punishment, the final blow. *You* came. *This* came. And you all started grabbing what you could get, pulling each other by the neck, fighting for an extra 200 euros, for another hundred square feet of thicket. The beast took hold of you, the plague… And I watched it all these years, and I was the only one who understood, the only one who knew what no one else knew – that I was the cause of it all. That all of it was punishment for what I did."

All of a sudden, unexpectedly, a tear ran down her cheek. Gorki looked at her and was sure: it was the first time Uršula had cried in twenty-seven years.

But her weakness was short-lived. Uršula wiped her eyes, her sullen composure restored. From the stove came the sound of water boiling and the room filled with the bitter smell of cooked beans. Looking at her, Gorki wondered whether to take the opportunity to admit to her that he was the one who had broken into Brane's home. But he didn't. He knew that even then, even in that state, she was capable of killing him.

"So now you know," she said. "You can go."

Gorki understood that the conversation was over. He stood up and walked out. Tonko followed him, since Tonko – as Gorki now knew – didn't sleep in the house. The evening visit over, Tonko would return to his cave and spend the night there.

He reached the courtyard and headed for the doors. He briefly stopped beneath the arch carved with the words ROCCO ROCCOV AND HIS CHILDREN, then turned one last time to look at the house of the killer, and the house of the victim. Uršula stood at the top of the stairs; in the backlight of the bulb behind her, she looked even thinner.

She stood there, watching the stranger leaving her home. All those years, she perhaps hoped that the burden would be lifted, that it would finally ease when someone found out. Someone had found out, but Uršula showed no sign of relief.

As they stood there, from the sky came the soft bang of fireworks, rockets exploding high above the cove, a waterfall of white flares descending like a shimmering curtain across the sky. And from the other side, from Sunset Residence, there was applause and cheering.

Gorki left the Rokov courtyard and headed back towards Misto.

Gorki walked along the shore, around the headland and past the apartment development that was now dark and empty. He turned along the path towards the old part of the town, behind the former bakery and past the old cooperative van, reduced over time to a pile of rusty junk. He climbed past the last houses until he reached his destination – the viewpoint on the coastal road.

He stopped to catch his breath. He took his blood pressure tablets out of his pocket and swallowed one without water. He knew he had overdone it with the wine.

After waiting for the tablet to kick in, he turned around. He looked out at Misto from exactly the same spot where he had first seen it in 1989.

It was past ten o'clock and the town was in darkness. The only sign of life was in Sunset Residence. The new settlement shone with street lights, spotlights and neon, and from the terrace came the sound of live music, drunken screams and laughter. The fireworks were just ending. After a series of small, multicoloured explosions, a big rocket lit up the sky, exploding into hundreds of yellowy lights that trickled back down to earth. They fell on the boats, on rooftops and gardens, like biblical flares sent by an exasperated God.

"All of it was punishment for what I did," Uršula had said. And her face right then had looked like the face of a mad person.

Gorki stood at the viewpoint and looked down on the same familiar cluster of houses, a cluster of houses he had first entered as a young man and which he was now leaving tired and old. And suddenly he knew. Uršula wasn't mad. What she had said was true.

He thought back to school and reading the Greek play *Antigone* in which the king won't let his niece bury her dead brother. He remembered too the story of Moses, a story he had seen told in Hollywood Technicolor. When the Pharaoh sins, God punishes the Egyptians by sending plagues of frogs and locusts, poisoning their livestock and turning water to blood. Finally, as cruel retribution, he condemns all their firstborn sons to death.

Misto had left Silva Vela unburied for twenty-seven years. For twenty-seven years she had lain under the curved roof of a tunnel, like a dead rat or stray dog. And in those twenty-seven years, God punished us all, Gorki thought. All of it was punishment: the failed factory, the failed cooperative, the war and Colonel Cvitković, Rokov's Land and its rampant thorn bushes, and Sunset Residence. And that, on the other side of the cove, that was punishment too: the fake pirates, the week forty-one timeshare, the hostesses letting drunk marketing executives grope their tits.

A picture appeared in Gorki's head, a picture he saw so clearly it seemed not to be the result of drunken delirium: dark water shifting inside the tunnel at the naval base. The night was calm and without wind yet the water was restless, rocking and striking the walls in waves that bounced back and crossed one another. It was evening, and the water was a deep blue. Then suddenly blue changed to red. The water took on the colour of blood and started to rise like some biblical flood. The red water rose and rose, submerging the rock that had broken away, submerging Silva's bones, then the tunnel and the barracks and Cape Cross. It rose and reared up, swallowing all before it, inch by inch: the marina and the basketball court, the boules court and bell tower of St Spyridon, the top end of the village and the bottom, the Stella Maris chapel and Sunset Residence with its eight rows of timeshare apartments. The red water rose and rose, steadily, relentlessly, until everything was submerged: Misto, the mountain, and this land that deserved no better than to be flooded.

Gorki gave a start. Dizzy, he grabbed tightly at the rail so as not to fall into the abyss. He was drunk, drunker than he had realized. He wouldn't drive home to Split that night. He would spend it in apartment sixty-four, on a bare mattress, robbing his new property of its virginity.

He walked, swaying, down to the houses and headed for the shore. As he walked, Gorki considered the last decision he had left to make.

In the morning, he could go to the police and seek an audience with Inspector Čović. He could lay out his conclusions, tell him what he had found out and reveal that Uršula had confessed.

The day after that, Čović would arrest her. He would appear triumphantly before the microphones and declare the twenty-seven-year-old mystery solved, that he had solved the case that the old police, the police from before, could not – or did not want to – solve, that he had done what Gorki Šain had not. He had found the killer. Uršula would exchange one jail cell for another, a better one. For Uršula, the punishment would come to an end.

"I've been punished." That's what she had said. And Misto had been punished. And he himself had been punished. Gorki knew that.

He reached the shore and walked along the row of tamarisk towards Sunset Residence. He passed the old entrance to the naval base, by then unrecognizable, and continued towards the terrace, the epicentre of the lights, the voices and the music.

Then he knew.

In the morning, he would wake up sober. He would drive to Split and straight to the office. He would make a few urgent phone calls and answer one email that couldn't wait.

And he knew something else. He wouldn't call Čović, and he would never tell anyone what he had found out. Not then. Not ever. He wouldn't tell anyone who had killed Silva Vela. He had no reason to.

Arriving back at the party, Gorki waded into the crowd and spotted a server carrying a tray of drinks. Gorki helped himself to a glass of wine. He took it, and he knocked it back.

22

URŠULA

(2016)

That morning, Uršula realized she would have to go into town. She had opened the larder and found it empty. No sugar, no pasta, no oil. The only thing in there was an open bag of flour. For a long time, Uršula had baked bread rather than buying it. But that morning she couldn't bake bread because she didn't have any yeast. She had no other option but to go to Agata's store.

Uršula preferred to avoid the store. She preferred not to go into town at all if she could help it.

Nevertheless, she got ready, got dressed and left the house at around ten o'clock. The door to Tonko's workshop was open, but he was nowhere to be seen.

She took the coastal path to the shrine on the headland. There, at the Stella Maris chapel, she rounded the headland and Misto came into view. She stopped, unable to go on, struck by a wave of unbearable aversion.

Sitting down briefly on the low wall in front of the chapel, she looked at the small statue of Our Lady behind bars and the damp trinkets eaten away by salt. Then she stood up and went on, to do what she had to.

It was December. The days were short. The sun came up a bit before eight and went down in the early afternoon. Daylight hours were few and the sun a pale, weak imitation of that old, warm sun of August and September. Since All Souls', southerly winds had brought heavy rain to Dalmatia, soaking the rocks, the maquis, leaves and bones. The tourist season was long since over. In Misto there remained only the last few inhabitants, tottering like little rodents around a town four sizes too big for them. In the centre, the last remaining cluster of occupied indigenous homes huddled around the church. Beyond lay the other, far bigger Misto, the one of dead and empty vacation homes. And beyond them, like the last concentric circle, stretched the new Irish tourist development, by then completely lifeless. The settlement still had that shiny newness to it, but it too was being eaten away by damp, beginning to erode under the unrelenting rain. Time is incorruptible, and it would take its toll.

Uršula passed where the cooperative used to be, where the oil mill once stood, passed the old basketball court and the former Partisan monument. She took the street up past the council building to the square, without bumping into anyone.

Reaching Agata's store, she hoped there wouldn't be any customers inside. And there weren't. Old Agata was sitting on an upturned beer crate and reading the newspaper. When Uršula walked in, Agata said hello. She only did that when it was just the two of them. When the Bakićs or the Padovans were in the store she made sure to skip the greeting and act cold towards Uršula.

Uršula bought what she needed: eggs, oil, pasta, yeast and tinned tomatoes. Agata totted up her bill on a piece of paper torn from a notebook. She didn't use the till outside of the tourist season. She knew that when the tourists left the coast, the tax inspectors left too.

She stuffed the groceries into a woven bag and slowly walked home. She walked along the cooperative pier, past the line of tamarisk planted along the harbour, and in a few minutes she was at the chapel on the headland. She stopped and performed her ritual of leaving five Croatian kuna for Our Lady behind the bars. She knew there could be no forgiveness for her sin. Nevertheless, every time she passed the headland, she would leave a coin – for something or for someone.

When she reached home, she found Tonko working in the dry dock. For a long time, nothing Tonko had done had any purpose, brought in any kind of income. When the Skipper's Club in the town centre bought a boat lift, Tonko lost the last of his regular clients. Yet he was constantly in the dry dock, constantly doing something that made sense only to him – picking up and moving blocks and logs, pouring paint from one worn-out bucket to another, sanding the same wooden boats whose owners had no intention of returning. Tonko at least knew how to keep himself busy. She didn't. She had never been able to.

She went up to the kitchen and put the shopping away. She kneaded the bread and put it in the oven, chopped a piece of lamb into cubes, sliced an onion and sautéed it in oil. Soon the kitchen was filled with the sweet smell of fried onion. When the onion was brown and sweet, she tossed in the cubes of meat, then the tinned tomatoes, celery, carrots and bay leaf. She lowered the heat and poured in some wine.

Then, like every morning, she set to work on the house. She opened the windows in one bedroom, then the other, then her dead son's room. As she did every Friday, she boiled the bedclothes in a washtub. She did the dishes and left them to dry. Then she hung the clean bedding on the line on the south side of the house. The big white sheets waved towards the channel and the islands, as if futilely signalling surrender.

The meat sauce was ready around midday. She took it off the heat and replaced it with a pan of water. When the water boiled she threw in a handful of pasta. It was cooked in no time.

She mixed the pasta and the sauce in the pan and put the warm pan on the table. She sat down at the table and waited. She knew there was nothing else to do but wait.

Five minutes later, she heard the dull thud of Tonko's footsteps. She had never understood exactly how he always knew when food was on the table. But he did. She never had to call him.

Tonko washed his hands and sat at the table. He took the lid off the pan and, without a word, without waiting, grabbed the spoon. He served himself half a bowl and began to eat, quickly and mechanically.

Uršula watched him eating. She watched how food simply disappeared in front of Tonko. That brief moment was all that was left of her marriage.

With the last mouthful, Tonko stood up in silence, wiped his hands and went down the steps.

As soon as he had left, Uršula began to eat. Not before. She knew that Tonko didn't want to eat with her, the same as he didn't want to sleep with her. So she let Tonko eat first, so that, when he was gone, she could eat in peace.

For a long time, Uršula had had no desire for food, and so this time too she ate just a few forkfuls and tossed what was left of the meat to the cats in the courtyard. Outside, she saw Tonko sitting beside a boat and slowly painting the wooden hull. She looked at him, even though she knew he would not look back.

Going back inside, she did the lunch dishes and finished cleaning the kitchen. She scrubbed the stone floor with a wet cloth and hung the cloth on the line to dry. It felt like rain, so she took the bedding off the line and carried it inside. After a few hours the sheets already smelled of sea air.

She looked at the time. It was 2.30. There were a few hours of daylight left and then the long, debilitating, endless evening.

In the bedroom, the bed smelled of fresh sheets. Lunch had left her feeling sleepy. She lay down and closed her eyes. Pictures passed through her mind, always the same pictures.

The scene is always the same, the same picture and place.

She sees herself lying down, on the same bed, Tonko beside her, facing the wall. He gives no sign of life. She doesn't know if he is sleeping or feigning sleep; she will never ask, and he will never tell.

Uršula lies there, and as she lies there, her heart races with excitement.

She has just dragged the body of Silva Vela to the shed in the olive grove. She tosses the body in the corner and covers it, at least until the morning, with Tonko's rolls of fibreglass. She hides the bloody piece of wood in the old stove, the stove which up until then had held drugs. Then she returns to the house. She puts her bloodstained clothes in the washing machine, disinfects her bramble cuts and gives her hands a good scrub to wash away the strands of fibreglass. Then she showers to wash away everything else: dust, blood, excitement.

Then she lies down. She lies next to Tonko, who is breathing deeply, sleepily, and she listens to the cove, still quiet before dawn. From the centre of Misto come the last sounds of the fishermen's fair – workers dismantling the stage, musicians packing away their instruments, technicians taking apart the lighting and sound systems.

And then, shortly before sunrise, Uršula hears the sounds of the harbour. She hears the loud coughs of the fishermen, their hushed conversations, the clattering of engine starters, the intermittent popping of diesel motors. Even though she cannot see the outside light through the heavy shutters, Uršula knows. By the sounds of the harbour, she knows it is dawn and that the fishermen are going out to sea, to pull on their reels and lift their pots while the sea is still calm and the southerly wind hasn't picked up.

Soon the harbour grows quiet, but the town wakes up with the sound of the trumpet from the base and the bell of St Spyridon. Eventually, she hears the sound she's been expecting. Up on the coastal road she hears the bus stopping, then pulling away again. She knows it's the night bus arriving from Rijeka.

Then silence. For a long time, she doesn't hear anything, then comes the sound she has been waiting for impatiently. She hears steps in the courtyard, Brane climbing the stairs, opening the door and entering the house. She hears him kick off his shoes and take off his coat. She hears him enter the kitchen and find the cheese sandwich she left for him on the table. Hungry from his journey, she hears him eat it.

Uršula hears her son undress in his room. She hears him brush his teeth. She hears him shower, and she hears the water trickle down his tired, warm skin. Brane changes into the clean clothes she left for him on his bed. She hears him briefly shuffling around his room before he lies down to catch some more sleep before the morning begins.

She hears Brane breathing, first loud, then quiet and steady. When it is completely calm, she knows her son is asleep.

Uršula gets up. Quietly, she opens the door to his room and looks at him. She looks at Brane sleeping, sleeping the sleep of the righteous. She hesitates, not wishing to wake him. But then she can't help herself and she enters. She approaches his bed, leans over him and strokes his face. Her lips touch his cheek, still cold from the water. She kisses him.

"Everything will be fine," she whispers. "Everything will be fine."

She kisses him once more and slips out of the room.

23

MATE

On 23 September, the anniversary of Silva's death, Mate went to Misto to put flowers on his sister's grave.

That year, the twenty-third fell on a Saturday. Mate went to the florist early in the morning to buy a bouquet of chrysanthemums. When he returned home, Elda was already up and ready. Mate asked Elda if she would drive instead of him. It was still warm, an Indian summer, as it had been in 1989, and the coastal road was busy with tourists. They found Misto still thronged with people for the last few days of heat. The seafront cafes were still working, the beach was covered with towels and a rhythmic bass thumped from the direction of the apartments. At the hotel pool, a DJ was playing electronic music that echoed off the cliffs and reverberated around the cove.

Elda turned off the coastal road towards the centre and was about to turn for the cemetery when Mate told her he wanted to see the house once more, to see how it had changed. She didn't say anything but turned towards the centre, past the council, the old bakery and the parish church. A few minutes later, they were outside the house where Mate had grown up.

The changes were obvious. The house was freshly plastered, the windows to the south had new awnings to keep the sun out and Vesna's rows of artichoke, kale and tomato had gone from the yard. Instead, in front of the house was a perfectly mowed lawn of English grass. Reluctantly, Mate had to admit that the Dutch owners had put in a lot of effort.

Vesna had sold the house early in the summer of 2016. Mate remembered well the moment she had informed him. She called on the last day of school before summer break. She told him that, from that day, she was finished with school. She had decided to retire as of the first day of September. "I can't look at them any more," she told him. The children, she said, were inconsiderate, disagreeable and wicked.

The same afternoon, Vesna had told him she didn't intend to live in Misto when she retired. She couldn't take the locals any more, nor the former pupils, her former colleagues or the old women in Agata's store. So she planned to sell the house, give half the money to Tina as down payment on an apartment and buy a studio in the city with the rest. She'd be closer to him, Elda and Tina. She didn't mention Jakov.

Early summer was the best time to sell property on the coast. Within two weeks, Vesna had sold the house to a Dutch couple, both professors. When Mate heard how much she had got for it, he could hardly hide his disappointment. He thought Vesna could have got a better deal had she waited. But Vesna had obviously been in a hurry, and Mate suspected why. He knew Vesna never believed Brane had killed Silva. That meant she lived every day with the thought that she might pass her daughter's real killer on the street, in school, in the store, on any given day, and not know it.

She moved to Split a month after selling, buying a gloomy basement apartment near the rugby field, not far from the city centre. Mate would sometimes see her in the company of an older doctor, a widower. Vesna didn't introduce them, but when the doctor ran into Mate in town he would greet him lovingly, as if greeting a stepson.

And so Vesna severed that last, tenuous link that connected them all to Misto. Those links had frayed over decades, severed one by one by each family member, Mate included. Vesna just cut the last. And when she did, Mate was surprised to find it hit him hard. If he was ever to spend time in Misto again, it would be as a tourist, sleeping in a hotel. The thought left him with a feeling of unease.

Now he sat there in his car in front of the house where he grew up. The summer was drawing to a close and the house was lifeless, the shutters closed. Nevertheless, the lawn was impeccably maintained; a sprinkler was on and it was clear the Dutch couple were paying someone in the town to take care of the garden.

It felt surreal, sitting there, observing the house. It was the same house, the house he remembered. But still, it was different. Mate felt like he was looking at a twin of his childhood home, a twin somehow separated at birth and which Mate was seeing for the first time; he recognized the similarities, but it was abundantly clear that this was not the house he knew.

He looked at the house – old but new, ancient but refreshed – and tried to imagine what it looked like inside. In his mind, he imagined climbing the steps, unlocking and opening the door. He imagined the hallway with the metal coat stand and the shoe cupboard, and the kitchen with Jesus above the door and the small glass table set against the long wall. He imagined the door off the hallway, the door to Silva's room. What had the Dutch couple done with Silva's room? Who had they put in there? Did that person know they were sleeping in the room of a dead girl? Did they know that one night a girl had gone from that room to a violent death?

The more he thought about it, the more Mate realized how pointless such questions were. The house had been in his mother's family for five generations. His great-great-grandfather had built it 180 years ago. Grandma Franka and Grandpa Mate must have died in that house. In 1978, when Mate was five years old, Aunt Zlata had been found dead on the kitchen's square floor tiles. Before Zlata, Grandpa Mate's mother and father must have died in that house, and his father's father, perhaps his brothers too. Five generations had died in that house, in the attic, in the bedrooms, in the *konoba* and on the kitchen tiles. The Dutch couple had bought an old house, a house with a past. It had said so in the ad: VINTAGE HOUSE IN SCENIC HISTORIC COVE. They had bought it with all its deaths, because of its deaths, each death settling like a layer of sediment, a welcome and precious patina. Silva was just another layer of death. Thirty years had passed. As long as they were alive – he, Vesna and Jakov – the embers of memory would continue to smoulder. When the three of them died, Silva would become an urban legend, a family tale to be told over a glass of Prosecco, rice balls and fried dough. Soon she wouldn't even be that. She would sink into nothingness, another nameless shadow on the walls of a house owned by two Dutch professors.

Mate was struck by the horror of it. But however horrific, it was undeniably, unavoidably so.

He was jolted from his thoughts by a human figure. A man Mate did not recognize approached the sprinkler and turned off the water. He looked towards Mate and Elda, surprised to find two strangers peering into the garden. It was time to go.

"Come on, I've seen enough," Mate said. Without a word, Elda turned the key and pulled away in the direction of the cemetery.

*

Elda got out first. She walked along the gravel path then stopped, swaying, searching for Mate's arm to steady herself. "It's the heat," she said.

Elda was eight years older than him. The difference could be felt the last few years. Elda was past fifty and feeling the effects of her age. Her periods were irregular, long and painful and she would experience cold flushes and tingling. She stuffed herself with hormones, which messed with her digestion, gave her headaches and left her feeling drowsy. She went to her gynaecologist, who performed a dilation and curettage procedure. A week later, she told Mate she couldn't fight the grey any more; she cut her hair short and dyed it silver.

Overnight, the new Elda appeared, the Elda with a dodgy knee, grey roots and hot and cold flushes. With her short silver hair, Elda sometimes reminded Mate of Vesna. He noticed her discomfort when they were out together with other people. "Soon they'll think I'm your mother," she said once, to which Mate didn't reply. At forty-five, Mate still had his sporty physique, still watched what he ate and looked pretty much the same. Even if he'd wanted to, he couldn't change anything. And he didn't want to. It didn't bother him. Nothing about Elda bothered him, never had, never would.

They entered the cemetery arm in arm. The whiteness was blinding, the limestone graves reflecting back the burning heat of the sun that had shone on them since the morning. Holding Elda by the arm, Mate walked between familiar graves – the pre-war chapels of Italian families, graves of shipowners and priests with pretentious statues of the Madonna and tiny angels, a few graves of boat captains marked with anchors in relief. There were barely a dozen different surnames, from Skaramuča to Bakić, Končurat, Vela and Padovan. Some graves were neglected, but most were polished and heavily decorated. There were a few Mate didn't recognize, but he was already advanced enough in age to know most, among them his school-teacher, his first doctor and the former parish priest with the strange surname Fulgencio, whom he vaguely remembered. Right by the gate was the grave of a school friend who had died while diving. Next to the mortuary was the grave of Captain Padovan, who used to scare Mate and his mates away with an air rifle when they stole cherries from his garden. Old Mrs Padovan had died a month earlier and so the family tomb was piled high with dead flowers.

Next to the Padovan tomb was that of the Lekaj family. While the others were inscribed with names going generations back, there was only one Lekaj. In the centre of the white gravestone was written ADRIJAN LEKAJ, FALLEN CROATIAN SOLDIER, 1971–1995. The coat of arms of Croatia was engraved next to the name.

Every time he saw Adrijan's grave, Mate would feel a twinge of guilt, as he did then.

He recalled, as he did every time, how he had hidden on his knees behind the cooperative van. He remembered the noise of crickets all night from the cypress trees, Adrijan emerging from his house late at night to get some fresh air. He remembered pouncing on him, hitting and kicking his back, his jaw, his legs and ribs. How he had laid into him furiously, vengefully, until he heard voices at the top end of the street.

They walked past the mortuary to the new part of the cemetery behind the church where there was a row of identical concrete graves, some of them closed and decorated, others empty, staring up at the sky in expectation of their first residents. At the start of the row, right by the apse of the church, was the Vela family plot, a cement box. The names of all those buried there were written on the headstone. Mate looked at the vertical list of names and next to each name the dates of birth and death: Great-Grandfather Špiro; Grandpa Mate; his *nona*; and last of all, Silva.

There were no pictures next to the names, only the years the people had been alive. Anonymous, faceless numbers. Silva was the exception. Next to Silva's name was an oval picture framed in ceramic. The picture was not the one Mate remembered, the one everyone remembered – the picture of an impudent seventeen-year-old who believed the world was hers. Vesna had given the ceramicist a passport picture of Silva taken by a photographer when Silva was fifteen. Her hair was still cut in a straight bob. It was the year Silva had begun high school. She had just moved into the student dorm in Split.

It was that summer, the summer they had gone with friends to Travna cove to harvest mussels, when they had baked potatoes on a fire, when Brane had devoured Silva with his eyes. Even then, before anything had even happened, Mate remembered noticing the way Brane looked at his sister.

Then Silva had begun kissing and cuddling with the lad from Zagreb. That was the night they started going out. They were together for three weeks that summer; Mate never found out whether they ever saw each other again. He was Silva's first boyfriend.

Silva had seemed so much older than him that summer.

He and Elda stood at the grave. Silently, as if by unwritten agreement, Elda took the dead flowers to dispose of and filled the vase with water from the cemetery tap. Mate trimmed the stems of the chrysanthemums and screwed up the paper they were wrapped in. They placed the flowers in the vase full of fresh water. Then they lit a candle, the flame almost invisible under the glare of the midday sun.

When they had finished, Mate stepped back and crossed himself, quickly, awkwardly, as if it didn't agree with him. He looked at the grave, at Silva's picture, then at Elda. Elda stood next to him, over the grave of a stranger, the grave of a woman she had seen only once in her life, briefly, a long time ago. But it was an encounter that had changed her life, and Mate's.

Mate and Elda stood at the grave at exactly midday, the hottest part of the day. The shadows of the cypress trees had disappeared and the gravestones radiated heat. Mate could feel the beads of sweat running down his forehead. He looked at the grave of his sister, then at the curious, new, silver-haired woman standing next to him. And right then Mate knew. He knew that Silva had brought them together.

The feeling passed through Mate like a cold breeze. In death, his dead sister had sent him a final gift. Though she hadn't managed to look after herself, she had taken care of her twin brother. She had sent him the woman standing next to him.

Elda was her gift. And Mate was grateful to her.

He leaned over the headstone and ran his fingers over the oval picture of his dead sister. He kissed his forefinger and pressed it to her face, in gratitude. Then he straightened up and looked at Elda. He smiled at her and held out his hand. She took his hand in hers and gently squeezed it.

Split, January 2016–July 2017